"The perfect combination of science fiction, noir, and detective drama, Chemical Burn *drips with snark and action. Fans of Larry Correia's Monster Hunters or Jonathan Maberry's Joe Ledger will love this."*

— Bryan Thomas Schmidt,
Hugo nominated editor, *Shattered Shields*

CHEMICAL BURN

Alyshia,
It's all about
the smiles!!

CHEMICAL BURN

Quincy J. Allen

WordFire Press
Colorado Springs, Colorado

CHEMICAL BURN

ISBN: 978-1-61475-305-6

Cover Designed by Duong Covers

Art Director Kevin J. Anderson

Book Design by RuneWright, LLC
www.RuneWright.com

Published by
WordFire Press, an imprint of
WordFire, Inc.
PO Box 1840
Monument CO 80132

Kevin J. Anderson & Rebecca Moesta, Publishers

WordFire Press Trade Paperback Edition March 2015
Printed in the USA
wordfirepress.com

DEDICATION

To Kathryn, my greatest supporter. To Mardee, the first reader. To Guy, the only guy who has every edition. To Lou and Peter and David and Travis and Aaron and Bill and Mark and Jim, my comrades in arms. To Vivian for some fantastic input. And finally, to Kevin J. Anderson and Rebecca Moesta who continue to teach, illuminating paths for the rest of us to travel.

PART ONE

REAGENTS

Irony on Ice

Irony stings when I'm on the receiving end and about to die. Until now, it's always been some other dumb slob who got in over his head. Then I'd come along and cash in his chips. In those days I had eyes as cold and merciless as a shark's—like the eyes I'm staring into now. It's simply my turn, I suppose, but for the first time in my life, I'm scared for … well … me.

I never thought I'd go out like this—fires burning everywhere, wrecked tanks and planes tossed around like the broken toys of an angry child. I can hear screams through the assault unit's canopy—dying soldiers who had no idea who or even what was killing them, let alone why. Circles of glistening pavement surround each fire, pools of dark tarmac against sparkling, white snow.

I glance at the lifeless console of my assault unit and wonder how they … he … found me. He's shut me down completely. There's no way to power up or pop the canopy, which means I can't even face him down and see who's better.

Irony.

There's this superior little smile on his face, and he's wearing a long black coat that brushes the snow—like the coat I sometimes wear. He has a black ghost-suit beneath, like the one I'm wearing. He's pulled the hood back, exposing a thick shock of black hair slicked back above thin, angular features reminiscent of my own.

How many times had I been in his position? Too many, I think with a good bit of shame.

A weak smile bends my lips. At least they didn't copy my mohawk.

A smooth white control appears in his hand. They're used to shut down the machine that is about to become my coffin. Twenty-five years, and I never got around to changing the access codes to my equipment. What can I say? I didn't think I'd need to. Countless light-years from home, there was no way they'd ever find me … at least I thought. I guess I got rusty. Careless. Now I just want a way out of this goddamn cockpit.

He disappears from view, and I can hear him climbing up the hull … slowly, patiently … savoring the kill, like I would. His face appears before me, and his smile grows. It's almost like looking into a mirror, but there are subtle differences. He sets the remote on top of the canopy, reaches into his long coat, and pulls out a massive burner from one of the deep pockets within. Burner's that size are designed to torch their way through heavy armor … armor from home.

"How did you find me?" I ask.

He cocks his head to the side, looking at me like a piece of meat.

Without a word, he pulls his eyes away from mine and keys in the detonation sequence.

"Come on," I say, "I gotta know."

His finger hovers above the actuator, and he looks at me with an almost pitying look. "The portals," he says.

As his hand descends, I can only think of how this all started with my fucking dry cleaning.

Dinus Interruptus

Rain fell all day and into the evening, and with the sun on the other side of the planet, yes, it actually was dark. Some clichés simply can't be avoided. My assistant Rachel and I were celebrating the closing of what I had dubbed The Three Monkeys and a Football case. The Comparsi twins, who weren't really twins at all, were also in attendance. It was their case, after all. We—me and my friends, not the monkeys—were sitting around a table at the Sunset Grill. I'd invited my buddy Xen too, but I hadn't heard from him in a few days. *Probably working on the data I'd sent him*, I thought.

The twins wore matching, blue, high-sheen suits. Their short, blond hair and close-cropped beards made them look like the Hollywood trash they were. Rachel looked immaculate in a slinky, black satin dress that drew the eyes of every straight man and at least bi-curious woman who walked by. Long, auburn hair done as usual in a simple ponytail draped down between her exquisite shoulders, and her hazel eyes were easy for people to get lost in. She used her looks to get information, and she was damn good at it, dodging would-be suitors like a matador. Under that flawless surface lay one of the most dedicated, trustworthy, and decent humans I'd ever met, and I'd met quite a few over the years. She was absolutely, unequivocally my best friend on Earth.

Normally, service at the Grill was outstanding, but tonight was a little different. We'd been seated, provided water, and given menus quickly, but we spent the next forty-five minutes making small talk, mostly about the three monkeys and the amusing irregularities of simian mating habits. Unusually packed for a Wednesday night, the Grill sported a crowd thick with Hollywood *wannabes*, a couple of *has-beens*, and the odd *is* scattered throughout.

Must be a premiere or something, I thought.

I had gone to the bar a couple of times for drinks and managed to get mai-tai shooting out of the noses of both twins not once, but twice, so I already considered the evening a victory. As we continued chatting, I habitually scanned the crowd, and from the corner of my eye caught sight of a waiter approaching from behind me.

I didn't recognize the guy, but it should have struck me as odd that he held the serving tray with a fresh, white towel draped over his hand behind it. The staff didn't use towels like that.

In retrospect, the guy didn't feel like a waiter. As he approached, I reached into an inner pocket of my coat, pulled out four straws and laid them on the salad plate in front of me—one of them noticeably shorter than the others.

"Isn't it just hysterical?" Stevie Comparsi asked with a distinctly effeminate lisp.

"I really don't understand why they kept doing it," his un-twin Riki said, smiling broadly. "I mean, honestly, after two days straight, breaking only to eat bananas and throw crap at each other, you'd think they would have gotten bored with—"

I pulled a twelve-inch meat cleaver out of another, pulled a whetstone out of a different pocket, and prepared to sharpen the blade. The coat, like me, isn't from around here. It's got damn near everything in it but the kitchen sink.

My friends looked at me with shock pasted to their faces.

"What?" I asked innocently, grinning at the circle of wide eyes as I casually held the lethal kitchen implement. I made rhythmic whisking noises as I ran the blade across the stone. No one at the table said a word.

"I'm sorry for the delay, folks," the waiter said as he came up behind me. "We had a change of staff at the last minute…" The waiter's voice trailed off as he looked over my shoulder and spotted the heavy meat cleaver.

I stopped sharpening and turned to him with a genuine smile. "Oh … no worries," I said. "In fact, you just saved somebody's life." I waved the cleaver in the general direction of my companions. "We were getting ready to eat one of our own, but we hadn't gotten down to drawing straws to see who ended up on the rotisserie. You do have a rotisserie back there, don't you?" I asked.

The twins giggled while Rachel doled out a faint smile in my direction, shaking her head lightly. She'd been inoculated against my antics three years prior during the Green Orca Case—Orca, in this case, referring to a man, not a whale. That was when we'd first met, I'd saved her life and, as a result, she worked first for and then with me. It was an important distinction … for both of us.

The waiter didn't look amused. He leaned in close enough to whisper and not be heard by anyone else. "Put the fucking cleaver down on the table and rest your hands on either side of the plate," he hissed.

I felt something hard pressed into that classic spot between shoulder blades—the one where guns always get jammed when assholes make unreasonable requests. I heard the all-too-familiar "snick" of a hammer being pulled back. Through a mai-tai haze I began to suspect this guy might not be the waiter, or if he was, he was having a really bad night.

My eyes got wide, and I stopped smiling.

"And don't move or yell," he added, "or you get it … then the lady." Although the twins didn't notice the change in my expression, Rachel did.

"Jesus, man, it was a joke," I said quietly, laying the cleaver down. "I'm a very big tipper, I swear! Twenty … sometimes even thirty percent!"

"Shut your fucking mouth, would you, Case?" the waiter-turned-gunslinger growled, just loud enough for everyone at the table to hear over the crowd.

"How rude!" the twins said in unison. They had finally figured out something was very wrong.

"We'd never let our staff speak to customers that way," Stevie blurted.

"I never did understand that fad about the New Cruelty," Riki added in his partner's ear.

The twins ran an up-scale Italian restaurant on the other side of town. They had exceptional food, but to celebrate I'd had my heart set on burgers and fries, so I'd suggested the Grill.

"Okay folks," the gunslinger grumbled, clearly running out of patience, "here's how this is going to work. Case is going to reach into that coat of his, drop a hundred bucks on the table, and then he and I are walking out the front door. The three of you are going to the bathroom. You can all use the ladies' room, right boys?" He tossed a sneer at the Comparsi twins. They both glared at him. "If any of you stops on the way there, he gets it. If anyone reaches for a cell phone, he gets it. If anything else goes wrong … a cop walks through the door, lightning strikes, a plague of locusts … if I get a hangnail or stub a toe on the way out … he gets it. Get me?"

They all nodded.

Rachel looked at me, asking with her eyes what she should do. A pang of worry shot through me at the thought of her getting hurt. She could take the guy apart in close quarters—I'd trained her myself—but I didn't want to see her take a bullet. Besides, I really wanted to know what this asshole was after. Someone had gone to considerable trouble to interrupt my dinner plans, and I rarely kill the messenger. I prefer to kill the sender.

"It's okay Rachel," I offered quietly. "Do as the man says."

"That's right, Rachel," the gunslinger agreed. "Do as the man says. Now, Case, grab your wallet real slow and put the money on the table. I don't get paid by the hour, and I have some other work tonight that's more pleasure than business."

I slowly lifted my hand and slid it into another inside coat pocket. I felt my way past a few miscellaneous items I'd been saving for a different rainy day and wrapped my hand around my billfold. I pulled it out, opened it, and separated a hundred-dollar-bill from the thick stack within. I dropped the C-note on the table and started to put my wallet away.

"Hold up," the gunslinger said abruptly. "Gimme the stack," he ordered. "And hand it over below your elbow. We don't want the customers to get suspicious, do we? That would be bad for everybody." I could actually feel the man grinning.

"Son-of-a—" I grumbled, but he jabbed the gun hard into my back.

I pulled out the stack of hundreds and moved my hand below and behind me. The gunman leaned the serving tray up against the leg of my chair, the towel still hiding the gun. I felt the money pulled away and heard him slide it into a pocket.

"Okay. Now, everybody play their parts so we can all get on with our evenings."

Everyone stood. Rachel and the twins put their napkins on the table and walked towards the restroom. I turned towards the front door, my escort close behind. We picked our way through the crowd, walked through the front doors, and stepped into a hard-hitting downpour that quickly soaked us both and, regrettably, flattened my mohawk.

"To your right," the man behind me said. "The limo."

A few car-lengths up sat a black, über-stretched limo, double-parked with the motor running. I headed towards it and scanned the street. There were no pedestrians, and it occurred to me that I could spin and clobber the guy, taking my chances with the pistol. However, I really hate getting shot, and I wanted to know who was in the car.

It turns out that was a miscalculation I later blamed it on the mai-tais. I should have taken my chances with maybe getting a bullet there on the sidewalk as opposed to the near-certainty of getting one later on. Getting shot has invariably been what happened to me in situations where I got abducted and driven someplace in a limousine. It had happened before … more than once. Granted, I didn't know I'd get shot for sure, but statistically speaking, the probability of a bullet wound was pretty high. Had I simply stopped, turned around, and taken the guy's head off, I probably would have avoided the twenty-four hours of chaos I endured before a particularly unpleasant plane ride … but I'm getting ahead of myself. Whoever sat in the limousine clearly needed me a hell of a lot more than I did them. A door in the middle of the limo opened as we approached, and I stared into darkness.

"Please get in," a woman said, her silky, central-European accent floating up out from the abyss.

Bad News

I stepped into the limo and settled into plush, black leather. All I had seen in the streetlight as I got in were the long, athletic legs of a tanned woman wearing a gray business skirt and expensive, medium-heeled shoes. I thought it odd there were no lights inside, but I should be the very last person to criticize someone's eccentricities. Besides, I can see better in the dark than any human. The gunslinger closed the door behind me, and as I leaned back I heard the locks engage. I sat with my back to the front of the car, and an opaque glass partition behind the woman hid the rear area of the limo.

She pressed a button on the panel next to her, and dim internal lights came on, bathing us in soft light. I found myself faced with a raven-haired beauty attached to the business end of the legs.

Stunning, I thought as I soaked in her features.

She wore a gray, European business jacket and skirt with a low-collared, white blouse underneath. She ignited a high pressure lighter and lit the end of a slim cigarillo, drawing in several puffs till it glowed brightly. Billows of smoke curled around her shapely face. There were subtle, Eastern Bloc angles and curves to her features cast harshly in the bright flame. With a click she closed the lighter and slid it into the inside pocket of her jacket. Silent internal fans pulled the smoke up to the ceiling where it disappeared.

"I guess you won't mind if I smoke, will you?" I asked and reached into a pocket.

"Please be careful, Mister Case. Sudden moves could be … misinterpreted." I picked up the trace of a central European accent in her sultry voice, a trace most people would have missed. I tried to figure out if I'd pissed off any Europeans recently, hoping to get a clue as to why someone would go to the trouble of asking me so *nicely* if I'd go for a ride. There were those two thugs I'd killed down at the docks a few weeks back, but I was fairly certain no one had seen me. It had been nothing more than taking care of a couple of assholes who tried to mug the wrong asshole. I tallied the list of likely Europeans and came up with a big, fat zilch.

"Don't worry," I reassured her. "If I had wanted to cause violence, I would have done it before I got into the car. I'm curious at this point." I smiled.

From an inner pocket I pulled out an oiled leather tobacco pouch and a drop-away pipe. I quickly packed it, pulled out a lighter of my own, and lit up.

"How quaint," she said.

"Quite," I said with a faux English accent as I put the pouch and lighter back in my coat. "A friend of mine turned me on to the pipe instead of cigarettes. I still grab for a cigarette when I'm stressed, though." I smiled, leaned back comfortably, and drew long puffs as I waited for her to tell me why she—or they—had gone to such lengths to get me into a limousine on a stormy Wednesday night.

Looking down, I noticed there were temperature controls on the panel of the door near my hand. I placed my hand on it and crossed my legs to try and obscure her vision. Without looking, I bumped the temperature up a couple of degrees. The woman didn't seem to notice, or if she did, didn't say anything.

"Go ahead, Victor," she said to the driver. The limousine pulled away from the curb and headed off into the rain, aiming for the freeway.

"It's a lovely suit," I purred, looking her up and down.

"Thank you, Mister Case. Valentino." She didn't seem to mind me eyeballing her. "You're a lot younger than I thought, and I had heard you were young. Are you twenty-five? Six?" It was her turn to look me up and down carefully.

So this is a referral, I thought. *She doesn't know me directly but needs me for something.* I smiled. "I'm a *bit* older," I said evasively. "Healthy living. Your waiter owes me four … err … *eight* grand, by the way." I bumped the temperature up a couple more degrees. "By the lack of any accent, I'm assuming he was a local contractor."

A slight look of embarrassment crossed her face. "My apologies, Mister Case. We were somewhat pressed for time and had to make do. Victor, would you please compensate Mister Case from the slush fund? With interest," she added, raising her voice so the driver could hear her.

"Interest?" I asked. "In that case, it actually was only four grand, not eight." I smiled, not at all embarrassed.

She smiled back like a mother catching her kid with a hand in the cookie jar. She nodded her head once knowingly. "Your reputation precedes you, Mister Case, and business is business after all."

After about thirty seconds, the partition window behind me opened. A black leather glove poked through, holding a folded stack of crisp, hundred-dollar bills roughly double the thickness of what I'd given the waiter. I spotted a black tattoo on his wrist. It looked like foreign letters, but I couldn't make them out.

"I love working with professionals," I said mostly to myself, smiling as I took the cash. I kissed it and nodded to the woman. Pulling out my wallet, I separated half of the stack and stuck it into the billfold. I folded the rest and slipped both into my coat. The temperature was starting to come up closer to my comfort level, and I noticed a slight sheen on the woman's exposed skin.

"You don't seem to mind the heat, Miss …" I hesitated. "I'm sorry, but I didn't catch your name."

"Natalia. And I had some idea you preferred warmer climes. I want you to be comfortable, Mister Case."

That made me even more curious. Whomever she had spoken with knew quite a bit about me. I used the heat gag when I could to distract people and give me an edge. It was subtle, and I couldn't use it often. Only a short list of people knew about my preference for heat.

"Natalia," I repeated. "It's a pleasure to meet you. And as Marilyn Monroe would have said, 'I *do* like it hot.' It reminds me of home."

"And where is home?" she asked.

I paused the way I always do when people asked me that particular question. I gave the standard answer. "Let's just say I'm not from around here." I gave her a warm, secretive smile and relaxed my shoulders.

"Do you know anything about dry cleaning, Mister Case?"

"Hunh?" Although my face and posture only showed it a little, the question took me off-guard—not because I was unaccustomed to strange questions, but because, as a matter of fact, I know a great deal about dry cleaning. I regained my composure and relaxed back in my seat, pulling on the pipe and watching the billows shift and twist their way up into the ceiling vents like fat, wispy serpents. Gears rolled in my head, and I had a good idea why I was in the car.

"That is a very strange place to lead a conversation, isn't it?" I looked past the woman to the opaque glass behind her. I very much wanted to know who was back there. I grinned broadly, waving at whoever observed us and, no doubt, listened in. The woman looked calmly back to the glass and then returned her gaze to me, a faint smile crimping the corners of her lovely lips.

"Privacy is of some import to my employer, Mister Case. Please forgive the impropriety."

"No trouble at all," I said cheerfully. "I'm a bit of a recluse myself. And it is *your* ride. I'm just a passenger." I drew on my pipe. "So what's this about dry cleaning?"

I bumped the temperature up a couple more degrees, prompting a polite sigh from Natalia. She opened the top button of her blouse, and treated me to a grander view of what could only be described as magnificently tanned cleavage. My smile stretched my cheeks to their limits.

Natalia sat up and put out the cigarillo in the ashtray built into the door and stared into my eyes, painful loss filling her eyes. "Xen Li is dead, Mister Case," she said slowly.

My heart dropped. Genuine sadness filled her voice, almost despair, but she also watched my reaction closely, as if this involved something both professional and personal. My expression went from openly cheery to a very deadly calm. I felt the old me take hold—the killer. That part of me is a predator. Heartless. Vicious. A half-dozen heartbeats passed before I spoke.

Natalia suddenly looked uncomfortable. The young cheery fellow before her had been replaced by something very different. Few people ever see this part of me, and when they do, they usually end up dead. Natalia found herself faced with a cold-blooded killer, and she knew it. I watched her fight the urge to shy away.

I spoke slowly. "I want you to tell me *how*." She slowly took my hand in hers to try and ease the rage she could see burning behind my eyes.

"I'm sorry." She took a deep breath. "We found him in a sealed vat of a concentrated tetrachloroethylene-variant at our facility. All that remained were his clothes, glasses, some hair, his fillings, and a volume of his DNA mixed in with the solution." I saw Natalia holding back tears. She was good, and there was only a glimmer, a slight sheen, but they were there. She took a deep breath. "Someone threw him in, sealed the door, and opened the valves. It's an industrial-grade variant of a special compound we are researching. We're hoping to market it to abatement companies that clean up crime scenes and suicides. It's designed to quickly and thoroughly break down biological material. In this case it did its job all too well." Her voice wavered as she spoke.

She had known Xen and liked him, I thought … or more, I realized.

"When?" I was all business now. I simply don't permit people to hurt my friends without settling the score on my terms. And when my friends have been killed … those responsible meet violent, bloody ends. *Always.*

"Three days ago."

"Who?" I asked, the rage building up.

"We don't know, but we're looking into it. Xen was working on something very important for SolCon. Something new. Something … revolutionary." She peered at me closely. "But I think you already knew that, didn't you Mister Case."

I paused. There were implications that could jeopardize the identity I'd maintained for twenty years, but Xen was more important than that. "No one was supposed to know about that. And yes, I did." I felt sick to my stomach. "It seems I may have gotten Xen killed," I added.

"After we discovered his … well …" I saw that she couldn't speak of it. "We were forced to do a deep search of all his materiel, both in his office and home. In his home we found some interesting chemical data. You sent that data, Mister Case."

"Whoever did this is dead," I said, "and you better keep your people out of my way, or they'll end up the same way." It was the old me talking, and part of me was ashamed of it, but the sorry truth is that I sometimes don't have any control over him … and don't want to. What can I say? I'm a work in progress.

"I'm very sorry about your friend, Mister Case," Natalia said as rain droned against the roof. She still held my hand. "But if we're going to find out who killed him and why, we need to get down to business." I thought I saw moisture welling up in her eyes again, but she fought it. The predator in me didn't care about her feelings … only about the inevitable bloodletting that lay ahead.

"Yeah," I said distantly. "Let's do that." I focused on Natalia, all business.

"The chemical data you sent him," she started, "how did you come by it? You're not a chemist, are you?" she asked.

"Me? No."

"Then how? Who gave it to you?"

I scratched the back of my neck and thought back to my youth. "My father, actually. He knew a thing or two about chemistry … and dry-cleaning," I said a bit elusively. I felt the limousine exit the highway.

"Can we talk to him?" she asked. "Xen hadn't completed his work."

"I'm afraid he's not available. Not on …" I paused, "… *in* the country … and I haven't seen him in a long time."

"Pity," she said sadly. "A silicon-based molecule in this application is a revolutionary idea."

"Old hat for him, I would think," I added, reminiscing about my father.

"Do you have any way to reach him?"

I looked at her and shook my head. "No. I wish I did," I added sincerely. I took a few puffs on my pipe and thought about a far off place for a few moments, about something unreachable.

"Could *you* finish the work?" she asked. I picked up an eagerness that seemed out of place. Corporations always want new products, sure, but her tone, the way she pressed the issue, it gave me the sense that they, or *she* wanted something else.

"Me?" I smiled at the impossibility of the notion. "Like I said, I'm the furthest thing from a chemist. It broke my father's heart, too," I sighed deeply. That last bit wasn't entirely accurate, but I liked to think it was true, especially near the end of things. "I'm more of a hands-on kind of guy," I continued, "but such is life." I stared out the deeply tinted window and, based on the neighborhood sliding by, realized where we were headed. "Xen's place?"

"Correct."

"Won't the cops have it locked down?" I asked. "Or do they even know he's dead?" I realized that my buddy Captain O'Neil certainly would have mentioned it if he knew Xen had been murdered. The two had met a number of times, and O'Neil knew that Xen was one of my closest friends.

"Of course they know he is dead, Mister Case," she said a bit defensively. "This is a murder after all, of a SolCon contractor. We're very interested in finding those responsible. I'm *very* interested … for both the company and for personal reasons, if you catch my meaning. We're working with the Oakland police department, and they've already granted us access."

That explained why O'Neil didn't know. O'Neil and the Oakland homicide chief had actually come to blows a few years back. They didn't speak to each other unless they absolutely had to, and then only through clenched teeth. I also couldn't help believing that Natalia and Xen were involved—romantically, it seemed. *Good for Xen*, I thought. I always considered him a bit introverted, but to hook up with a woman like Natalia … well … I hoped Xen had been able to enjoy everything Natalia clearly had to offer.

"I think I understand," I said. "It also means we have something in common. We both cared about Xen a great deal."

She smiled lightly.

I saw two black SUVs pull up in perfect unison on either side of the limo. The rear windows of both vehicles rolled down. Gun barrels slid out into the night, pointing at the forward section of the limo.

I leapt forward, grabbed Natalia, and pulled her down onto the floor. We landed with a thud, and I rolled on top of her, my hips pressed between her legs.

"What the!—" Natalia shouted.

"Hang on!" I whispered into her ear, covering her with my body as much as I could. I couldn't let her get killed if I wanted to find Xen's killer.

Machine gun fire shattered the night, and even through the heavily tinted windows and the downpour outside, it bathed the interior in bright, flickering-orange light. Bullets bounced off armored steel, glass, and pavement, filling the interior with thunder.

We heard the limousine's engine roar as Victor hammered the gas, and the rear tires screamed, breaking loose from the wet pavement for thirty yards as they fought the mass of the heavily armored sedan. The headlights of the two SUVs drifted back to the rear-quarter of the limousine, and the gunfire stopped briefly.

"Friends of yours?" I asked.

"What do you think?" she replied, a bit perturbed but remarkably calm for a business executive—man or woman—exposed to gunfire. Most suits would have shit themselves after the first shot.

Engines roared as our pursuers pulled forward again, drawing even with the limo. Gun barrels slid out to fire another volley when the limousine swerved violently to the left. Metal screeched on metal as the two vehicles smashed together. Tires squealed on the left as the driver slammed on his brakes. A second later, a deafening crash filled our ears when the SUV smashed head-on with a garbage truck going the other direction. The SUV's horn stuck with the impact and faded quickly behind us.

Then a machine gun from the other SUV cooked off. The thunder of ricochets again filled the compartment, and as I looked up, I saw the barrel drift down towards the front tire of the limo.

"This thing have solid tires, by chance?" I asked, yelling over the sound of the gunfire.

"Of course," she hollered back matter-of-factly.

"We're gonna need 'em!" I yelled as the sound changed from bullets hitting steel and glass to hitting pavement and solid rubber. I could feel the front tire start to bounce and bump unevenly as chunks of it were chewed away by the barrage.

The limousine lurched again, to the right this time, and we careened off the SUV. Both vehicles swerved back and forth several times, crashing solidly against each other, but the greater mass of the limo began to win out. Each crash pushed the SUV closer to the curb.

I heard a squeal of rubber as the SUV's tires locked up. The limousine passed a light-post that the SUV must have barely avoided hitting. The window between the driver and us slid open.

"Where to, madam?" Victor shouted over the roar of the engine. His voice was pained but calm, thick with Russian origins. By the sound of it, he had taken a slug.

"Are we near Xen's house?" I yelled.

"Yes!" he replied.

"Drive this thing through the front doors!" I ordered.

"Are you out of your mind?" Victor hollered back.

"Just DO IT!" I screamed. I turned to face Natalia, and our noses nearly touched. "We can't out run them, and if they catch us in the open, the five or six guys in that SUV will tear us to pieces. In cover we have a chance. *Trust me.*"

"Do it, Victor," Natalia yelled.

"*Da!*" Victor obeyed.

The limousine swerved around several more corners with the sound of multiple machine guns bouncing bullets off the back of the limo and into the rear tires.

"Hang on!" Victor yelled.

I grabbed Natalia tightly and rolled on my side with my back facing the front. The front of the car bounced off the curb, absorbing our momentum as the front end tore up a big chunk of Xen's lawn. With the impact Natalia and I slid neatly up against the base of the front seats. The limo ran over several bushes and small trees in Xen's yard and passed through the yellow police-line tape barring the front doors. The tape made a lot less noise than the doors as we passed through. With a deafening sound of crunching metal and splintering wood, we came to an abrupt stop.

Tires squealed behind us as the second SUV came in for the kill.

A Minor Secret

The old me took over, and my conscience dissolved into fiery ash. I smiled, savoring the feel of the predator I was designed to be. Nothing remained but the hard-wired desire to eradicate the target. It was time to play.

The instant the car came to a stop, I rolled over Natalia, grabbed the door handle, and opened it a crack. I heard Victor's door open. A second later, the bark of a Kalashnikov filled the night as Victor fired at the SUV. I peered through the crack of the door and saw several rain-hazed shadows dive for cover. Sparks from Victor's gunfire spattered across the side of the SUV, and I turned to Natalia as she got to her knees.

"You okay?"

"Yes," she replied calmly.

"When I say go, follow me out the door straight ahead, through the doorway, and into the kitchen."

"Wait," she urged.

"What?" I was impatient, hungry for the kill.

She shifted her body around me to the back seat and hit a panel underneath the back seat. It flopped open revealing several weapons.

"Here, take this," she said, offering me a Glock .40.

"I don't like guns."

"What?" she said shocked.

"I don't like guns. They're not any fun."

She stared at me in disbelief, blinking slowly.

"Suit yourself," she said finally, shaking her head as she reached in again. "I do," she added as she slipped the Glock onto the back of her belt and grabbed a Kalashnikov. She removed her suit-jacket and shoes. "Is there any broken glass out there?"

I quickly lifted my head over the window frame and looked at the ground between the car and the kitchen.

"No. A few boards, some splinters of wood. I don't see any nails sticking up either."

"Good."

Machine gun fire rattled off of the back of the car. Victor's Kalashnikov erupted again, pinning down our assailants.

"GO!" I hissed as I opened the door. Placing my foot on the doorframe, I leapt like a cat, spanning the eight feet to the kitchen doorway without touching the ground. Natalia peeked out the door, saw it was clear, and rolled out. She came up in a crouch, laying down a burst of suppressing fire with the Kalashnikov as she ran. Victor saw her make the dash and opened up with two fast bursts. Bullets sprayed out into the night, bouncing off the SUV and forcing several of our assailants back into cover. I turned in the doorway and watched Natalia cross the short distance like a commando, obviously combat-trained.

"Victor! *MOVE IT!*" I yelled.

Natalia spun around in the doorway, kneeling below me. She flipped the selector of the rifle to single-shot and aimed out the shattered front doorway.

Victor rolled over the hood of the car, using it for cover, and dropped behind the door I'd left open. I could see him favoring his left leg. Wedging the barrel in the crease between the door and body of the car, Victor aimed another burst of suppressing fire into the street and then bolted towards us.

Just as he started to move, I saw three shadows pop up from their cover and take aim.

Crack! Crack! Natalia's rifle barked. One shadow dropped where he stood, and the other spun off behind a tree. The third opened fire on full auto and sent a hailstorm of bullets into Victor's path. He spun around like a top. The Kalashnikov flew from his hands and sailed off deeper into the house with a loud clatter. He dropped limply, face down at Natalia's feet, his head and arms flung through the doorway. There was blood everywhere. Natalia looked down at the prone body but said nothing. She fired three more rounds into the street to keep the gunmen pinned down.

I bent down, grabbed one of Victor's arms, and dragged him quickly inside. As I pulled, Victor's coat and shirtsleeves slid back, and I noticed a black tattoo on his wrist:

Церковь дом бога.

I rolled Victor's body over onto his back, revealing a hopeless reality. With rounds through his neck and head, he was dead before he hit the ground.

"Leave him," Natalia said when she turned and saw her driver. I picked up no emotion at all: not sadness, regret, shock … *nothing*. Victor was just a body to her. I filed that little fact away along with the others.

"Where to now?" she asked as she flipped the double banana clip around in her rifle. She switched the selector back to full auto as gunfire came through the front doorway again, sending chunks of plaster flying from the thick, adobe-spackled walls.

"Downstairs," I whispered, nodding my head towards a door at the back of the kitchen.

Natalia stuck the barrel of the rifle around the corner and, taking one quick peek, unloaded a long burst outside without looking. She heard the satisfying yelp of a man catching a piece of the burst, and we both enjoyed the sound of his screaming.

"Nice shot," I said, grinning.

"Thank you, but won't we be cornered down there?" she whispered.

"No," I said confidently.

Making sure we were behind the counter, I reached into an inner pocket and pulled out a baseball-sized sphere. Translucent, like smoky glass, it had a seam down the middle and two small black rectangles embedded in the center. With a twist, the two halves came apart and, holding up the first, I pressed a few times on the small, black control. I caught Natalia looking at it, but she couldn't possibly recognize the characters. I set the device to double-trigger, quarter-second and placed it at knee-level on the kitchen-island facing the doorway. Clicking on the readout of the second half, I set it to quad-trigger, four-second and placed it directly below the first one.

Natalia got a confused look on her face when I grabbed a bag of potato chips off the counter, tore it open, and emptied the bag on the floor just inside the doorway. Chips scattered across the tiles and over Victor's body. I wish I could have captured the baffled look on her face as I tossed the empty bag on the counter.

Through the downpour, I heard someone run across the yard and take cover behind the limousine.

"Move. Through and down," I said quickly, pointing towards the door at the back of the kitchen with my thumb.

Natalia ran without hesitating, crouching as she skirted around the island and scuttled to the back door leading downstairs. She reached the door, silently opened it, and bolted down the stairs, her bare feet making almost no sound at all.

She's good, I thought. *Definitely combat trained.*

I straightened up, turned, and walked casually back towards the door to the basement. As I rounded the corner of the kitchen island, I heard a man rush up against the wall outside and then a rustle as he quickly peeked around the corner and drew back.

"One ..." I said, counting the motions in front of the burner as I closed my eyes and walked towards the basement door.

The gunman, seeing my exposed back, took the bait hook, line, and sinker. I could almost see it in my head. He came around the corner, the second motion in the doorway triggering the first of my devices. In the quarter-second it took for the barrel to traverse from straight up to just shy of drawing a bead on me, the device I'd placed—called a *burner*—cooked off. An intense, metallic hissing sound filled the room, like magnesium burning. The kitchen burned with an impossibly bright light and intense heat, and the blast-wave hit the poor bastard square in the face. It cooked his skin, fused his eyelids open, and burned out his eyes. His clothes ignited as well. I knew because I'd seen it before. *Many* times.

"Two." I smiled wickedly. The gun clattered to the floor, and the man screamed in agony.

"Mamma mia!" another gunman yelled from out near the limousine. I paused in the doorway as the burning man rolled around in the foyer, his cries pitiful. But I have no pity for men like him. Neither did his friends apparently, since they didn't seem interested in putting him out. Instead they choose to watch his polyester clothing burn and melt into his skin. I stood in the doorway, waiting for them.

Natalia stood at the bottom of the stairs, her body hidden behind a wall as she aimed the Glock up the stairwell. "What are you doing?" she hissed.

I looked at her calmly, pressed a finger to my lips to quiet her, and gave a reassuring *I-have-everything-under-control* look … which I did.

I turned back to the kitchen to see another man peek around the corner and disappear. The heat of the first burner had charred a wide, black circle around the doorway, and the paper of a hanging notepad still burned.

"Three," I said to myself and headed down the stairs calmly whistling a few bars of "Singing in the Rain." I pictured the next few seconds in my head. The gunman waited a few seconds to make sure there wasn't another bomb. He'd certainly been horrified by what happened to his partner, and the timing between the glance and the first cook-off had been almost instant. When nothing happened, he moved through the doorway.

I heard potato chips crunching under his feet.

"Shit!" he blurted.

I knew exactly where he was, the timing working out perfectly.

He moved over Victor's lifeless body, chips crunching with each step, and slipped into the corner of the kitchen. He probably had is back against the charred wall and his gun barrel held steady at waist level, pointed at the stairwell. If he had any brains, he'd be crouching to keep as much of the island between him and the door as possible, for all the good it was about to do him.

"Four," I said for the last motion trigger. Then I started counting seconds. "One …"

"It's clear," he hissed. I heard a second pair of footsteps hit the potato chips. The second guy probably didn't even register the sound his feet made as he moved. With that much adrenaline, focus can be both a friend and an enemy. Gunfights are like that.

"Two …" I continued, looking down at Rachel and smiling.

"They're downstairs," the first gunmen whispered. I heard their feet still shuffling across the chips.

"Three ..." My smile turned to vicious delight. I strolled to the bottom of the stairs, cool as a cucumber. "Four," I said and looked up at the ceiling above me, waiting for the inevitable.

A second metallic hiss erupted from the kitchen, and the stairwell was bathed with the acidic glow of bright light. Natalia and I heard the two men erupt into screams.

She looked at me with a half-impressed, half-horrified look on her face. "What the hell are those things?" she asked, incredulous.

"Oh ... nothing," I said and shrugged innocently. "I think those boys have probably had enough, but we should get going just the same. The cops have got to be on the way, although the rain and traffic will slow them down. I hope they bring a fire engine or two," I said, a bit embarrassed. I felt kind of bad about what I'd done to Xen's kitchen.

I pulled off my shoes and left them at the base of the stairs. I looked up and saw both of our footprints coming down, outlined in Victor's blood.

"Wipe your feet," I said.

Natalia looked down and realized that the bottoms of her feet were covered. She wiped them back and forth on the carpet, stretching her toes to clean them.

I walked across the main area of the basement—a nicely appointed home-theater—and stopped at a door in the corner. Natalia backed away from the base of the stairs, her Glock raised in one hand and the Kalashnikov held over her shoulder with the other. She kept looking down occasionally to make sure she wasn't leaving a trail. We could both hear all three burning men still screaming.

"Where are we going?" she asked over her shoulder.

"This way," I said with a friendly smile on my face. I opened the door and motioned for her to go in.

"That's a closet, Mister Case," she said dryly as she stepped in. I found it interesting that she already knew that, and I stacked the fact on top of the others in my head. She pressed back some dusty ski-jackets and pants, crouching slightly to get under the shelf and clothes-bar inside.

"Of course it is," I replied calmly as I stepped in and closed the door behind me. The small closet was pitch-black. I could feel her leaning up against me, bent at an awkward angle. Even sweaty as she was, she smelled fantastic. I raised my hand, accidentally brushing up against her breast as I did.

"Hey …" she said.

"Sorry," I half-apologized as I slid my hand along the top of the doorjamb. I pressed a recessed button hidden there. We heard a loud click, and a seam of pale light appeared at the back of the closet. I shifted around her and pushed open a door.

"After you," I said gallantly.

"How did you know…?" she started.

"I built it," I said before she could finish the question. I could feel my conscience slipping back into place as the predator faded back into the depths where I keep him.

Natalia slid between the jackets and stepped into a passage that looked to be made of smooth, gray plastic. Four florescent lamps were spaced evenly down its hundred-foot length. My foot bumped into something as I stepped through the back door of the closet. I looked down and saw a pair of small running shoes. It occurred to me that Xen and Natalia were about the same size.

"Hey," I said, reaching down to pick up the shoes. "These may fit."

I held the shoes out to her and pushed the door closed behind me with a click. She leaned the rifle against the wall. "It's empty," she said as she stuck the Glock in her belt, dropped the shoes on the floor, and quickly put them on.

"Leave the rifle. I'll come back for it later."

Natalia finished lacing up the shoes. "A bit loose, but passable," she said. "Thank you, Mister Case."

"After what we just went through … call me Justin."

"Justin," she started, "how could you possibly build this?"

"I have a lot of tools," I answered evasively. I strolled down the passage, and Natalia followed close behind, the Glock back in her hand. Another doorway stood at the far end of the hallway. Beyond the door lay a tight, spiral staircase going up. I flipped a light switch on the wall, but nothing happened that Natalia could see.

We walked up the stairs, and I pushed open a trapdoor in the ceiling. We stepped up into a well-lit laundry room with a wide sink, a washer-dryer set, and a row of paneled closets. I'd bolted a tall laundry basket to the top of the trap door. As I closed the door, the seams of it were partly covered by the edges of the basket.

"Clever," Natalia said. "Whose house is this?"

"It's one of mine," I said simply.

From the laundry room we stepped out into a stone-tiled living room with floor-to-ceiling glass along one wall facing out onto a swimming pool. Widely spaced leather furniture made a wide conversation pit on one side, and a dining area lay beyond. Natalia yawned and stretched her arms out.

"Adrenaline wearing off?" I asked her.

"I believe it is," she said a little tiredly.

"Do you need to be anywhere tonight? This place is about as safe as it gets. You can stay till morning."

"How many bedrooms," she asked suspiciously.

"Four," I said grinning. I knew a closed door when I heard one, although I wasn't interested in trying to open it. Rachel's face leapt into my mind, which caught me by surprise. I also had too much respect for Xen to try something like that. Although she didn't show it, I suspected she was truly grieving over his death.

"You need anything to eat or drink?" I asked.

"No thank you. Where am I going?"

"Down that hall," I indicated the one on the far side of the main room past the dining area. "Do you prefer regular, foam, or waterbed?" I asked.

"Foam. Why?"

"Last door on the right. All the doors have locks on them," I said and smiled.

"Good night, Justin."

"Good night."

She walked towards the bedroom, and I headed down an opposite hallway that bordered the open-air kitchen. I entered my bedroom and locked the door behind me, reveling in the blast of 100-degree air that washed over me. Reaching into my pocket, I pulled out my cell phone and typed in "safe—don't worry—everything under control." I hit SEND, and the cryptic message shot off to

Rachel's phone. I was too tired to give her the whole story, and besides, the story wasn't over yet. I lay down flat on my back on top of the covers, closed my eyes and didn't move for six hours.

o o o

I woke up at three-thirty a.m., totally alert. There were no more sirens at Xen's house, but I could see the red and white flicker of emergency vehicle lights reflecting off the houses. The helicopters were gone as well, the neighborhood finally quiet. I rolled out of bed and went over to the large, sliding glass doors that opened onto my patio and pool. Flipping the latch, I slid them open and stood naked in the moonlight, letting the cool air slide over my body. The sound of the fountain outside the door soothed me.

"Terminal," I said over my shoulder. A panel folded out of the wall opposite my bed, revealing a pair of large computer screens and a small keyboard that I almost never used. I turned back into the room, leaving the doors open, and walked over to the panel. It sat at a perfect height to allow me to stand and work. I reached into a slim, tall nook between the two screens and pulled out a thin, silver circlet of metal. It slipped on easily, resting gently around my forehead.

"Power." Both screens came to life, revealing images of a green logo surrounded by symbols in my own language. As it was a client terminal, the system automatically connected to my mainframe. "Search: keyword SolCon," I said.

Boxes of data appeared, instantly filling the screens. On the left SolCon's corporate Internet website appeared: on the right, a listing of connect points that included usernames, IP addresses and the geographic areas where they were registered. The perimeter of each box had strings of characters in the same language as the logo.

"Scroll right, use left," I said, and the listing on the right began scrolling upwards quickly, faster than a human eye could follow. My eyes flickered back and forth between the two screens. When I blinked on a word or symbol on either screen, it would flash red and transition to the data behind the link.

Images, articles, reports, user data, and financials flashed across both screens as I absorbed data at an inhuman rate. My eyes bounced back and forth, digging into various facets of SolCon's business, employees, and corporate partners. If the data was out there and connected to a system, I could get at it, and my mainframe could hack through most of the puny human security protocols it encountered.

The system did run into several more resilient security barriers, but it's smart enough to stop at government networks locked down with newer encryption protocols. The system would also stop at networks capable of identifying the subtle intrusions and violations it could inflict upon digital victims. There are ways to hack through those without raising alarms, but it wasn't necessary to get what I was after. The biggest challenge I usually faced was when the data wasn't on a machine connected to a network. Most people don't know this, but the only really safe computer is the one that's powered down. There are ways around that, too, but it's a lot more complicated. As I dug into SolCon, I found links back to DiMarco, so I dug into those, too.

I kept digging for three hours, and as I did, several pictures took shape about SolCon, Natalia, and DiMarco. DiMarco's accessible network was pretty straightforward, and I got most of what I wanted. I was surprised, however, to run into not one but two inner networks at SolCon that my system shied away from. The first was heavy-duty encryption, and the second involved security protocols much beefier than any run-of-the-mill chemical company required. My digging still unearthed a great deal of data, but the pictures were not complete. I also added a new name to add to the list of players—Pyotr Nikolov, head of SolCon's U.S. operations. As I read, a dangerous picture of the Russian formed—more sketch than picture, but he was clearly into a lot of shit. I wasn't after him, though. I wanted DiMarco. Finally, with every reasonable search-point for DiMarco accessed, the screens stopped flashing.

"End left and right," I said as I breathed deeply, trying to make sense of all the data. I'd culled a lot of data, even for me. The boxes disappeared, leaving the original logos. I removed the circlet and returned it to its cubbyhole. "Close panel."

The monitors went black as the panel silently folded back into place. I turned, walked out onto the patio, and stood next to the fountain. I stared fondly at the sky for several long minutes, wishing

I could see the stars beyond the glow of Los Angeles. I sat down, crossed my legs and positioned myself comfortably, palms resting on my knees. I closed my eyes and began processing the data roiling through my skull.

For two hours, I sat motionless. Eventually, my internal clock told me it was eight-thirty. I went back into my room, got dressed in the clothes from the night before, and walked out into the kitchen.

Draping my coat over a tall chair in front of the breakfast counter, I pulled out the makings for omelets. I chopped up everything I needed and set some orange juice on the counter just in time to see Natalia walking down the hall in the clothes she'd worn the night before. She carried Xen's sneakers.

"Good morning!" I said cheerily. "Sleep well?"

"Like the dead," she replied. "And good morning to you, too. Breakfast?" She sat in the chair next to my coat and dropped the sneakers on the floor.

"If you like omelets, it is." I turned around and ignited two burners of the gas stove. I pulled down two small skillets from the hanging rack and placed them on the blue flame. A splash of oil went into each, and then I turned to face Natalia. I poured juice into both glasses, handed one to her and added three teaspoons of sugar to my own, mixing it up with a spoon. "SolCon is a front," I said bluntly.

She looked at me, mouth agape, but she quickly regained her composure. Wary, her eyes narrowed a fraction of an inch and shoulder muscles tightened. I watched gears start to turn behind her eyes.

"What makes you say that?" she said as she picked up her glass.

"Let's just say I did more than sleep last night."

"A front for what … or who?"

I smiled at her, enjoying the façade. "Four layers back sits Solntsevskaya," I explained. "In Russia they're the biggest boys on the block, aren't they? I mean, they go *way* beyond 'mob,' right?"

I could see that she knew I was dead on. A barely perceptible look of impressed fear fluttered across her face as she sized me up.

"Yes," she said quietly, exploring my face over the lip of the glass. She set the glass down and placed her hands under the counter.

"What I can't figure out is why SolCon would be paying Xen to research a new dry cleaning fluid that has no other application,"

I said, giving her my best confused look.

"Diversification."

Plausible, I thought. I knew SolCon had already developed the advanced tetrachloroethylene product for abatement—and body disposal, if the truth be told.

"Really?" I said a bit suspiciously. "SolCon is into explosives—nice irony there, considering their owners—military-grade fuels, a bevy of industrial adhesives and acids, space-age polymers and a whole slew of other high-tech molecular applications. But there isn't a single product in their repertoire that even closely resembles something as insignificant …" I changed my voice to that of a commercial, "… as commercial applications for making evening gowns last longer and look brighter after you take them to the dry cleaners.…" I spoke normally again. "The silicon molecule won't, for example, dissolve bodies. It has no other application," I emphasized.

I took a long swig of my orange juice—perfectly sweetened—and set it on the counter. I wanted to let her mull on all of that, so I turned around and grabbed the two containers of chopped vegetables, quickly tossing each into the pans with a satisfying hiss. I went about sautéing them, glancing back to see her face. I caught her hands sliding nervously underneath the countertop as she eyed me with a calculating gaze.

While the vegetables cooked down, I grabbed three eggs, wacked each with the edge of a knife, and poured the contents into a mixing bowl. I whisked them to a froth, threw in some spices, and with a final whisk, poured half of the beaten eggs into each pan. I waited silently while the bottoms cooked.

"Perhaps they're trying to increase the perception that they're widely diversified," she offered.

"Perhaps," I nodded, smiling broadly with my back to her. After a minute, the tops of the omelets began to solidify. I grabbed a pan in each hand, lifted them up, expertly flipped both omelets simultaneously, and caught them as they landed neatly into their respective pans. I set them down, threw on some grated pepper-jack cheese and folded them over into perfect half-moon shapes. A few quick flops melted the cheese inside. Turning off the burners, I lifted the pans once again and, spinning around with a dramatic flourish, dumped a perfect omelet onto each of the waiting plates.

"Voilà!" I said triumphantly. "Breakfast is served!" The pans went into the sink next to me. I placed a fork on each plate, slid one in front of Natalia, grabbed my own, and leaned up against the stove, waiting to see if she would add anything. Seconds ticked by as I took a couple of bites, grinning widely despite mouthfuls of egg.

"Delicious," I said mostly to myself. The smile on my face was openly victorious, expectant, and accusatory all at once. I didn't take my eyes off her.

"As I said, diversification," Natalia said evenly, not touching her plate.

"Would it surprise you that Xen was being paid as a consultant for research and development into *jet fuel*? On the books, at least." I took another bite, chewed it and swallowed, smiling the whole time. "As far as SolCon is concerned, they'll be getting more efficient planes, assuming the fuel ever works. And if it doesn't, the cost of the project gets written off. Xen pretty much had carte-blanche and reported to only the project stake-holder."

"Interesting." she said slowly. I could see her wondering how I could have learned all of this … and learned it overnight. We both knew I was spot on, and I could see it scared the hell out of her.

"It *is* interesting," I said cheerily. "And do you know who the stake-holder of the project was?"

"Who might that be?" she said, smiling uncomfortably but knowing what I was going to say next.

"Why, *you*." I took another bite of the omelet and chewed thoughtfully. "The back of the car was empty last night. I didn't think of it in the heat of the moment, but if someone had been back there, I'd like to think you would have mentioned it. People don't just forget that their bosses are still in the car being shot at. They forget purses, not people. There was no mysterious employer in the car, because there's no mysterious employer *at all. You* initiated the project and never told SolCon what you were doing." She looked nauseous. "You haven't touched your omelet," I said with a cheery smile. "Are you okay?"

"I've lost my appetite," she grumbled, staring down at the plate in front of her. She looked up into my face, searching for something—anything—that would get her out of the conversation, but I could tell she came up short. "How could you possibly know all of this?" She finally asked incredulously. "About the project."

My face finally turned serious. "Like I said, I have a lot of tools." I smiled brightly again and took another bite of my omelet. "But don't worry. I think we're on the same side … well … sort of. You have nothing to worry about from me. Now eat up."

"I'm not sure I understand," she said quietly. Clearly defeated, she picked up the fork and took a small bite. I let her pick at her omelet for a few more minutes while I finished mine, chasing it with the sweetened orange juice.

"You know," I started, "I took a pretty thorough look into your background as well."

"Did you?" she said, her disappointment only lightly veiled.

"Yeah. Born Natalia Ludmila Voinovich in Tbilisi, Georgia, schooled at the University of Warsaw with a Bachelors and Masters in finance, both cum laude, and on to the Bank of Switzerland for three years. Then you had a two-year stint at Proviron as a Product Manager, four years at Fidea as a Senior Product Manager and now VP at SolCon. That's an impressive career."

"Thank you."

"You know," I continued, "it's interesting…."

"What is?" she asked, clearly not wanting to hear the answer.

"Every phone number listed in your resume … I was able to dig that up, too, by the way … they all seem to go to the same central office in Lyon, France. I think INTERPOL is based out of there, isn't it?" I asked suggestively.

"That is interesting," she said in a flat tone. She looked ill.

"Isn't it? It's a funny thing, too," I continued mercilessly.

"What?" She didn't look like she could take much more.

"There's no mention of combat training," I said in an overly confused tone. Then I looked her square in the eyes and was very serious. "You handled that Kalashnikov last night like the Spetsnaz … those are Russian special forces, but I'm pretty sure you already knew that." She gave me a blank stare. The seconds ticked by.

"What size are you?" I asked out of left field, a smile lighting up my face.

"I beg your pardon?" She blinked in confusion. I could see her mind racing, trying to figure out what my game was.

"What size are you?" I repeated. "Say, for example, in a swimsuit."

"What has that got to do anything?" she replied in a classic *are-you-a-pervert* tone.

"We have to attend a brunch," I said as if it was the most reasonable answer in the world.

Baffled and frustrated, she blurted, "We just ate!"

"You hardly ate anything." I pointed to her plate.

"You ruined my appetite!"

"Not my fault. Besides, we're not eating brunch, we're watching it."

Her face went blank in utter confusion, and she blinked her eyes a few times. "We're *watching* brunch?" She was clearly getting tired of feeling confused.

"Well, watching someone else eat it."

"We're watching someone else eat brunch," she repeated, all hope for reason abandoned.

"Some*ones*, actually."

"Who?" She gave me an *if-you-don't-tell-me-right-now-I'm-going-to-shoot-you-with-my-Glock* look.

"Does the name Gino DiMarco mean anything to you?"

"Of course it does. Everyone knows about Gino DiMarco."

"How about … Pyotr Nikolov?" and I got the accent right. "Does everyone know about him?"

Natalia's eyes got wide, and I might as well have coughed up a rat and spat it on the counter top. "No," she said quietly with a trace of fear.

"Well, it seems as if there's a brunch meeting … today … between the SolCon folks, specifically one Pyotr Nikolov and the head of VeniCorp, namely …"

"Gino DiMarco," we said together.

"How do you know all this?" she asked. "It's ridiculous. You couldn't possibly."

"It's not ridiculous. Like I keep telling you, I have a lot of tools. You'll have to get used to that … and this is just hacking mail servers, mostly. Well … maybe a bit more than that … But still … easy peasy."

"For you, maybe," she accused, sounding almost jealous.

"Well, I do have a little help."

"Such as?"

I paused, smiling that knowing little smile I have when people ask about my personal life. "That's a long story … and we have to get going."

"Where?"

"My boat. That's why I asked you what size you were."

"We're going to watch other people eat brunch … from your boat?" she asked, sounding as if I was making less and less sense with each passing moment.

"Precisely!" I grinned like a madman, which I think she suspected was the case. "It's perfectly simple."

"I hate you Case," she said. "I guess I'll have to accept that I'm stuck with a lunatic, at least in the short term. I might as well make the best of it."

Sighing, "I get that a lot." I gave her a coy look. "And I liked it better when you called me Justin." Coyness turned into a provocative grin, and I flexed my eyebrows at her like Groucho Marx.

"Case it is then," she said.

"Eight," I blurted, pointing at her.

"What?" She simply couldn't keep up with my style of conversation, although, thinking about it, I hadn't met anyone besides Rachel who could.

"I bet you're a size eight," I clarified.

"Yes. Good guess."

"Educated one. You're a little taller and somewhat better endowed than my assistant. Back there," I pointed down the hallway leading to where she had slept. "Last bedroom on the left this time, with the waterbed in it … There's a shower and some women's things. Get cleaned up and check the closet for a swimsuit that will work. You'll find some wigs in the walk-in as well. See if there's one you like."

"You're out of your mind, Case. You know that?"

"You won't be the last to say so," I said grinning as she walked off. "Oh, and quickly. Brunch is at ten-thirty, so we have to be out of here by nine-thirty."

"Whatever you say," she said, standing up and grabbing the sneakers.

"You don't mean that," I said and winked. "Wear regular clothes. Take anything from the closet you like. You can change into the suit on the boat." I smiled at her retreating legs and swinging butt. "I promise I won't look."

"You're right on all counts," she said flatly, and kept heading down the hall.

While she got ready, I went back to my bedroom and took a fast shower. When I finished, I pressed a door-sized wall panel just inside the bedroom door. The panel moved in slightly and swung out revealing a walk-in closet. I grabbed a black, skin-tight t-shirt from the closet and a baggy pair of blue jeans, putting them both on.

I walked to the bedroom door, but paused with my hand an inch from the handle. I returned to the closet and opened it again. A black touch pad decorated the back wall. I placed my palm on it and lifted my fingers and thumb in a sequence to unlock the safe. A small, hidden door set at face level swung outwards. Among an assortment of gizmos and data drives lay a sheathed, edged weapon—a combination of combat-knuckles and two blades. Closing the safe, I pulled the weapon out of the sheath and slid my fingers through the holes in the combat knuckles.

The dull, black hilt felt smooth and natural in my hand. As my fingers wrapped around it, the weapon made a high-pitched humming sound that increased, quickly going beyond the audible range.

It was called a *vlain*, a combat vibrablade common in the military where I come from. Made from a single piece of ceramic polymer, it's harder and lighter than titanium and impervious to metal detection. A six-inch, stiletto blade with a serrated edge along the back protruded from the end of the hilt closest to my thumb, a blood-runnel etched down both sides. Another six-inch blade curved out from the end closest to my pinky and extended forward in line with the knuckle spikes, which were each about an inch long.

I slid the blade back in its sheath, the whine spinning down when I released it. I hooked the sheath over my belt, securing it tightly. I walked back to the kitchen, collected everything from breakfast, and dropped it casually into the sink. Then I went to the living room and waited for Natalia to finish getting ready.

Natalia finally walked out. She had selected black, loose-fitting gaucho pants with a black belt and a light, baggy green blouse. She'd slung a small red purse over her shoulder—one of Rachel's favorites, I recalled, which made me feel a little guilty. Xen's sneakers were back on her feet, and a short, red wig topped off the ensemble.

"You look great," I said. "C'mon, we'll take my truck." I stood up and put on my coat, making sure she didn't see the vlain. "Do you still have the Glock?" She pulled it out from the back of her belt and held it up. "Good. The truck is through there," I indicated a door to the left of the foyer. With Natalia in the lead, we walked into the garage. Natalia headed towards my beat up, blue '03 Ford F-250 4x4. It was raised about six inches, had oversized, off-road tires, a roll-bar, and bumper guards. Grabbing a beat-up, straw cowboy hat and pair of Ray Bans off the shelf just inside the door, I got into the truck. Natalia clicked in her seatbelt as I sat down.

"Careful, that thing sticks sometimes," I said as I pushed a pair of swim fins and diving mask off the seat and onto the floor at her feet. "Don't mind the dive gear. I don't normally have passengers."

She unbuckled the belt easily and clicked it back in. "Seems fine to me," she replied. I shrugged.

The rest of the garage was empty, save for a motorcycle along the far wall of a type I'm sure Natalia had never seen. Her eyes lingered on it, but I said nothing. It didn't have a motor at all, just a solid block of silvery metal and black bodywork all around. I put on the hat and sunglasses, adjusted the weapon hooked into my belt, and started up the truck.

"Nice hat," she said grinning.

"Yee haw," I said calmly.

Pulling down the sunshade, I pressed the door remote, and the garage door slid quickly open. I pulled the truck out, and closed the door behind me. We travelled in silence. I had no more questions for the time being. I think she wanted to avoid getting that confused look she got every time I spoke. Fortunately, traffic was light, so we passed through downtown quickly and headed towards Marina Del Rey. At the marina I pulled into a large parking lot, found a spot close to the docks, and turned off the truck.

"Did you remember the swimsuit?" I asked.

"In the purse I took."

"Good." We got out and walked to the third pier, stopping at the last boat on the end. On the left stood a muscular, ebony-skinned man of middle age, bare-chested and not a trace of fat on his frame. The sun shone off his bald head as he untied the ropes of a large, cabin-cruiser fishing boat moored to the dock. We could see a small group of mostly overweight men drinking beer and laughing with each other. On the right was a thirty-foot, black, Velocity VR1 powerboat.

"Hey, Boom-Boom!" I called. "How's my boat?"

Boom Boom Llanos had been a friend since the Green Orca case. He'd taken me out in his boat for a sneak-and-peak, and we'd been buddies ever since. He turned, his face lighting up when he saw me, and he waved at us vigorously. He spoke with a light Caribbean accent. "Justin! Good to see you man. And the boat's fine. They were here yesterday scrubbing hulls. They got yours and mine at the same time."

"Taking another charter out?" I asked.

He nodded. "Studio execs. 'Gone fishin,'" Boom-Boom said imitating them. "I heard one of them tell his wife that he would be working late."

"Typical," I said smiling. "We're only going to be gone an hour or so. By the way, this is Carla," I added motioning to Natalia. "Carla, Boom-Boom Llanos."

"Pleased to meet you," Boom-Boom said, nodding his head in her direction.

"Hi, Boom-Boom. Nice to meet you, too."

"Don't have too much fun while you're out there," I called from the side of my powerboat.

"Yeah, right," Boom-Boom said sarcastically. "You either," he added, raising an eyebrow in Natalia's direction ever so slightly. "Catch ya later, man."

"See ya," I replied, waving. I helped Natalia into the boat. "Go change downstairs. I'll pull us out."

She wordlessly went down into the cabin and closed the door.

I untied the mooring lines, hopped back in the boat and took off my coat, throwing it on the bench behind me. I plopped down into the driver's seat and pulled out the key from under the dash where I kept it. The boat fired up on the first turn, and the powerful engines grumbled to life. I easily backed it out and pulled into the bay. The email from Pyotr's assistant to DiMarco had included directions to where Nikolov kept his yacht. It was about a half-mile across the bay on the south side, near the Mason Yachts International facility. I idled out of the inlet and slowly pulled into the bay on relatively calm waters, so I pushed the throttle up to run at about ten miles an hour. Leaning back in my chair, I took a moment to simply enjoy the sunshine.

"Natalia?" I called below deck after a few minutes.

"Yes?"

"Before you come up, can you open that hatch to the right of the door and bring up the black nylon bag that's on the top shelf? And bring a towel with you, same compartment."

"Of course!" she yelled. "I'm almost done."

After a couple of minutes, Natalia opened the door and stepped out into the sunshine. It took everything I had not to whistle.

"Excellent choice," I said, grinning like a teenager as I took in Natalia's bikini. I knew perfectly well that Rachel kept one-piece suits in the closet, but Natalia had gone for a fairly revealing selection in crimson that highlighted both her full tan and red wig—among other things.

She glared at me. "Don't say a word, Case. This is business."

"Of course," I said still grinning like an idiot. "Mum's the word." Then something strange happened—in my head. I saw Natalia, and there was no doubt she was a sight to be seen, but I could only think about Rachel. And as I thought about her, I got this funny feeling in the middle of my chest, like a spark or an ache. I'd never felt it before, and I really had no idea what it was.

Natalia handed me the nylon bag, breaking me out of my reverie, and stood next to me. She looked where we were headed. "Got any sunglasses?" she asked, holding her hand over her eyes.

Without looking I opened a small compartment next to the steering wheel and handed a pair of Oakley's over my shoulder. Natalia grabbed them and put them on.

"Hop up onto the bow, will you?" I asked. "Just lay on the towel, facing me," I added, reaching into the bag.

She climbed up, threw down the towel and lay on it, leaning up on her elbows with her ankles crossed. From the bag I pulled out a device that looked like a small white funnel with a gray pencil stuck through the middle. The whole thing was attached to a gray pistol grip with a single button for the trigger. I slid open a small panel on the side of the grip and adjusted the range to one-hundred yards. Closing the panel, I held it out to Natalia.

"Here, take this."

"What is it?"

"Shotgun mic … sort of."

"I've never seen one this small before." Natalia gave me a sarcastic look. "I bet you get that a lot, don't you," she added.

Smiling, I reached into the bag, pulled out two small ear-buds, and put one in my ear. "Use this," I said, handing the other one to her. She did so, and it was small enough to disappear almost completely. I increased the throttle a bit and turned the boat into the bay, away from where I knew Nikolov's boat was moored. I traveled up about a quarter of a mile then turned back down towards the ocean at a diagonal towards the Mason shipyards. As we approached I toggled the ignition and revved the throttle, making it appear as if I was having engine trouble. I stalled it out a few times and, as we approached the pier, turned the boat around, backing it smoothly into the last empty slot furthest from the shore.

"What's the plan?"

"See that yacht behind me?" I asked without looking. "The big one called the *Georgian Princess*?"

Natalia looked past me. About a hundred yards away she saw the boat with a figure on the top deck sitting at a table. At that range it was difficult, but she picked out the bald head of Pyotr Nikolov.

"I'm going to work on the engines while you languish there in the sun. Just press that button and point it at them. If they go inside, try and point it at the windows."

"Clever," she said dryly.

"Sometimes the simplest plans are the best ones," I said, looking at my watch. It was ten-fifteen, so we had some waiting to do. "Tell me who's at the meeting other than DiMarco or Nikolov if you recognize them, okay?"

"You got it."

I headed for the aft section of the boat, lifted both panels and fiddled with the hoses. About ten minutes later a voice came over their ear-buds. It was in Russian, but Natalia translated for me.

"The Italians are here, Mister Nikolov … and you should look at this." A large man in a gray suit stepped up to Pyotr and hand him something.

Pyotr laughed quietly. "Interesting," he said in English. Pyotr had a deep voice with a moderate Russian accent.

"Should I do anything about it?" the man asked in English.

"No. It could have its uses later. But maintain an Andropov protocol till the signal clears."

"Yes, Sir," the man replied.

"Now, send in those Italian clowns."

A minute later we heard the shuffling of footsteps and scraping of patio furniture, then their meeting began.

Big and Little Fish

Please, have a seat Mister DiMarco," Nikolov offered.

"Nikolov," Gino said, nodding as he sat down. Ricky and Tony-Two-Fingers took up positions standing behind Gino with their hands crossed in front of them. Nikolov sat alone, but there were men in gray suits scattered throughout the ship.

"Have you given any more thought to my proposal?" Nikolov asked.

"We're still working out how the numbers crunch," DiMarco offered, his New Jersey accent leaking through. "It's true that our volume and revenue would increase considerably, especially if we went global, and in spite of the significantly lower rates you quoted us. But a trade secret is a trade secret, know what I mean? And we're doing pretty well shipping to damn near everywhere west of the Rockies."

"I understand. Business decisions take time and careful thought." Nikolov took a sip of iced tea and changed the subject. "I understand you were unable to attend to Miss Voinovich. It was sloppy as well."

"She got lucky. We'll get it done," DiMarco assured him.

"Your first attempt made interesting reading in the L.A. Times, Gino. I prefer a much lower profile when attending to such things. Such mishaps can draw the attention of Federal intervention, and we would not want that, would we? Such a complication could jeopardize our business arrangement."

"Don't worry, Nikolov. I've got enough connections to keep the heat off while we get it done. We'd have to drop a bomb in the city for it to get up to the Feds."

"I'm trusting you, Gino. For now. Do not let me down. Thus far our relationship has been amicable. It would be a shame if I had to change that."

"Oh, I agree."

"I have one more thing to add to your calculations for whether to go into business with us or not," Nikolov added, his tone changing to a slightly threatening one.

"Yeah? What's that?"

"I had my organization look into what the chemist was working on for Miss Voinovich." Nikolov paused again, taking a long sip of iced tea. DiMarco's face was stoic, but he shifted a bit uncomfortably in his seat. Nikolov didn't miss the tell.

"It seems Mister Li was not working on fuel as we were led to believe."

"Really? What was he working on?" Gino was a good enough card player to make it look like he was ignorant.

"Are you sure that your motive for wanting them dead was an unpaid gambling debt?" Nikolov asked.

"Are you kidding me? The two of them were into us for three-hundred grand. They both had a taste for high-stakes poker ... they just weren't very good at it."

"I see," Pyotr said. "As to your question, Mister Li happens to have been working on something that could jeopardize your shipping methods with a competitive product. It is an interesting coincidence."

"I don't know what you mean," Gino said innocently, keeping up the façade.

"It's not important," Nikolov said. "What is important is that were Li's efforts to come to fruition, your business could be threatened. I tell you this out of friendship. We are, however, looking into his research and should be able to finish it. We would then control whether it saw the light of day or not."

"I understand, Nikolov," DiMarco said a bit tensely. Nikolov had threatened him in the nicest possible way without actually holding a gun to DiMarco's head.

Gino was the kind of mobster perfectly willing to make a deal with the devil if the money was good enough—so long as they stayed partners. If they weren't partners, it sounded as if Nikolov would have the ability to shut down DiMarco's production or shipping mechanism, essentially putting him out of business.

"So, based on that addition to your calculations," Nikolov said easily, "have you come to any last-minute conclusions regarding my proposition?"

"Now that you mention it, I think we could be persuaded to work with you, but we'd need to increase the cost per unit by two percent."

Based on what I'd read in an email to his assistant, he had been willing to go up three percent if absolutely necessary.

"I believe that my organization could manage one percent over the original figures and still keep our investors satisfied."

"Deal," DiMarco said sounding as if he'd achieved a victory. "It'll take me a few weeks to get everything ramped up and ready for you. Can you wait till then?"

"Of course, Gino. Take as much time as you need. You can contact me when you are ready."

I heard Gino start to get out of his chair, but Nikolov stopped him.

"There is one other thing, Gino." Nikolov's tone had changed from friendly to cold, bordering on dangerous.

"What's that?" Gino sounded nervous.

"I could forgive the sloppy attempt last night, save for one small matter." Nikolov sounded like a wolf preparing to pounce.

"And that is?"

"One of my soldiers did not come back to me." Nikolov paused, his voice turning deadly. "The driver your men killed was one of mine. You owe me one life, Mister DiMarco. And I expect payment in full."

Gino's expression bordered on horrified. "You can't be serious. It was an accident. He got in the way. Besides, we didn't even know," DiMarco's reply a mixture of defiance and thinly veiled fear.

Nikolov's tone was openly threatening. "I do not kid about such things. Even accidents must be paid for, and unpaid debts of this kind lead to wars." He stood up. "You could not win a war with me," he pointed out.

"What? Am I supposed to just hand someone over to you?"

"Precisely. Someone from your organization must be compensation for the debt you owe."

"And if I refuse?"

"Then the full weight of Solntsevskaya will be brought to bear upon your paltry family. Your brothers in New York will not help you, as it would be bad for their international interests. They know the cost. And all for one paltry man. It is a small price to pay for peace and good business. Do you not agree?"

"Can I think about it?" DiMarco said, beaten.

"No. You may not. Have the man delivered to me by sundown. Now go."

Show Time

Jesus, he's a tough bastard," I said quietly as I fiddled with the hoses.

"You have no idea," Natalia replied. "He's ruthless … and brilliant. He runs their U.S. operations for a reason, and I doubt he'll be satisfied with that." Natalia looked around the bay, checking out the passing ships. "I think we can go now."

"Let's wait a few minutes. I don't want us leaving the moment their conversation is over. Someone might have seen us pull up."

"Good point," she agreed.

We stayed put another ten minutes as I awkwardly hung half out of the engine compartment and Natalia languished in the sunshine. She seemed to be enjoying it. I suspected that her work didn't allow for much relaxation, so enjoying a few stolen minutes sunbathing made sense.

I closed the two hatches, moved to the cockpit, and started up the engines as she got off of the bow and sat in the seat next to me. I pulled the boat out slowly, throttled up and headed across the bay. She surprised the hell out of me with what she wanted to do next.

"Listen, I've got to get back to my house." Natalia's face was a mask, but I saw controlled fear and unwavering resolve in her eyes. She knew what she was asking.

I gave her an incredulous look. She was completely out of her mind. "DiMarco's probably got your place staked out," I said, putting it as lightly as I could, which wasn't much.

"Yes. Most certainly." She struggled with some internal decision and then sighed. "Look, Case, the uncomfortable truth is that I have little choice. I have to trust you with more than the rules allow, more than I would ever feel comfortable with under normal circumstances. Xen said you could be trusted, and that I could never ask for a better man to be in my corner."

"He said that, did he? That must have been hard for you to say," I smiled gently.

"You have no idea." She didn't look at me.

"They almost got you last night," I added, showing genuine concern.

"Yes, but they didn't, and it's because of you."

"And going to your house is important enough to risk us both getting shot?" I asked. "I hate getting shot, you know."

"I'm not all that happy about risking a bullet wound either, but I'm afraid I have no choice. You are my only option. I have to trust you."

"I'm the most trustworthy creature on the planet," I said seriously. "No joke. And we're still after the same thing ... the people who killed Xen." A flicker of pain danced across her face, but it quickly vanished.

"We are," she said coldly.

"Now we know who it was, but we still don't really know why."

"True," she said, looking into my eyes and struggling with what she wanted to say. "You seem to be a good man, Justin. Xen spoke very highly of you ... often ... and I don't think you're a threat to me."

"I'm not."

"I'm not what I appear to be," she added almost in a whisper.

"Don't worry. I know," I smiled kindly. I wanted to ease her mind, so I changed the subject to the task at hand. "Venice Beach, right?" I asked, referring to her house.

"Mmm-hmm."

"Damn, that's convenient," I said, laying the geography out in my head. I had seen her address when I looked up her data, but I hadn't really put it all together. "It's just down the road a ways. Like a mile or so."

"I didn't pick the house. SolCon did," she said matter-of-factly.

I'm sure an '*a-ha*' look crossed my face, because she gave me a curious expression.

"Did they, now?" I looked at her, and gears turned in my head … about whatever was on the device Nikolov's assistant had mentioned … and that Andropov protocol.

"I had originally been set up in a condo off Malibu beach, but they told me to move here about three months ago."

I did a quick calculation. I'd given the chemical data to Xen four months ago, so the timing would be about right.

The gears clicked into place as I thought about her pistol, Nikolov's protocol, and where her condo was located. "Can I see the Glock?" I asked.

"What for?"

"Something Nikolov said." I held out my hand as she reached behind her back and handed it over. I pulled the slide back and locked it, catching the round in my cupped hand. Then I ejected the clip and inspected both closely. I emptied the clip into my hand. Reaching into a pocket where my coat was draped, I dug through a number of tools until I felt the one I wanted. I extracted a long pair of slim, heavy tweezers that appeared to be made of glass. Pressing a button on the side, the tips glowed with bright light. I used them to push down the spring return inside the clip to see inside. As the return went down, I exposed a thin strip of black and silver metal that had the faint pattern of micro-circuitry on it. *A tracer.* "Damn, I'm good," I said, chuckling.

"What?" she asked, perplexed.

Grasping the strip with the tweezers, I pulled it out and lay it on the dashboard. "It seems that Nikolov is a cooler customer than I thought. He knew you were here. He's been keeping a very close eye on your whereabouts, but the range of these is a matter of miles. Hence the condo only a few miles from his yacht."

"Oh my god," she gasped.

I handed her the bullets and clip, and she started reloading it. Then I inspected the Glock. Looking inside the clip receiver revealed nothing, so I removed the slide. Stuck to the inside of the slide, hidden in a groove, was another tracer. I pulled it off and stuck it to the one on the dashboard. I inspected the rest of the

Glock thoroughly, making sure there were no other tracers. I put the pistol together and handed it back to her, a thoughtful look on my face.

"How did you know?" she asked, sliding the clip back into the pistol and chambering a round.

"Nikolov mentioned the Andropov protocol. It's something Yvgenny told me about a few years back."

"Yvgenny?"

"Hmmm?" I asked. "Oh, he's a violin player I know. Anyway, he said the Russian mob uses the Andropov protocol when they think there might be a snitch in the mix. When Nikolov said it, I thought he meant someone in DiMarco's crew. But when you mentioned how close your place was and who picked it out, it occurred to me it might be something else. He knew we … well, *you* were nearby. The only thing you had left from last night was the Glock."

She popped the clip and put the last round back in so she had a full load. "That son-of-a-bitch."

"What I can't figure is why he let us listen in. Shit," I muttered as I stood up. "Go change," I said. "I'm pretty sure you don't want to meet up with DiMarco's crew looking like that."

"You're right," she gazed down at her tanned skin and covered it up with the towel, prompting a disappointed look from me.

"Although, that outfit might distract them *considerably*," I pointed out.

"Cretin," she accused, feigning offense.

"Not at all," I said innocently. "Thinking tactically." With a lascivious smile, I pulled the earpiece out of my ear, dropped it in the bag and handed it to her. She removed hers, dropped the microphone after it, and pulled the drawstring tight. Without another word she headed down into the cabin.

I pulled the throttle back and got the boat moving at a slow crawl. Then I opened up one of the benches and pulled out a fishing pole and a role of electrical tape from the tackle-box. The line already had a brightly colored lure. Unhooking it, I let out some of the line and sat back down at the controls. I grabbed the two tracking devices, wrapped them around the line just above the lure, and taped them down. With a mischievous grin, I cast the lure into the water behind the boat and let it trail behind us. If I was really lucky, I'd catch something that stayed close to shore.

Natalia came up after a couple of minutes, and I felt her eyes boring into my back.

"What the hell are you doing?"

"Goin' fishin,'" I replied, turning my head and winking at her.

"Are you mental?"

I thought about it for a second, replying, "Yeah, but that has nothing to do with this. Look at the dashboard."

She did and noticed that the tracking devices were gone. She laughing lightly just as the fishing line went taught. I got a big smile, reached into the tackle box and pulled out a scaling knife. With a quick flick, I cut the line and watched it disappear into the water.

"We'll see if we can't send Nikolov on a wild fish chase," I said as I put the pole away. "Now let's get over to your place." I sat down at the controls and throttled up.

We crossed the bay in silence, ocean air and slapping waves providing a few brief minutes of serenity. All too soon for Natalia's taste, I'm sure, I pulled the boat in and cut the engines. I grabbed my coat, put it on quickly, and got the mooring lines tied down just as she appeared, wearing the clothes she had come in.

"Ready?" I asked.

"As I'm going to be," she said a bit doubtfully.

We walked down the pier, returned to the truck and got in. I fired it up and drove out of the marina. When we got to Washington Avenue, I pointed to the left, "This leads to the Venice Fishing Pier, right?"

"Yeah, straight down," she confirmed. "Why?"

"Oh, nothing ... just a thought," I said and turned on the radio. I hit one of the selector buttons and turned up the volume on Willie Nelson's "On the Road Again." I turned right onto Washington.

Wincing at the volume of the music, Natalia pointed up ahead, "There, turn left on Wilson. It'll be a quick left onto Harbor." She had to speak up to be heard over the blaring country staple as I made the turn. "It's Frey Street, the one right after Cloy. My house is half way up on the left." I slowed down to turn at the alley after Cloy.

"No, it's the next one," she corrected.

"Trust me," I said, smiling.

As I turned down the alley, we both spotted a black SUV parked in the alley. It was identical to the ones that had attacked us the night before.

"Get down," I ordered. Without hesitation, she leaned over and put her head in my lap. I looked down and enjoyed a fleeting but exceedingly naughty thought—or two—and then pictured Rachel again, feeling a strange sense of guilt. A man in a black suit, tie, and sunglasses stood in front of the SUV. He had the telltale bulge of a pistol under his arm. He leaned against the hood while another man, similarly dressed, sat behind the wheel, having a conversation on a walkie-talkie. "Why do all goombahs look alike?" I asked.

Natalia remained silent, assuming correctly that it was a rhetorical question ... albeit a good one.

"Howdy," I said with a southern drawl as I drove slowly by the SUV, nodding my head at the leaning goombah. I pointed at Natalia's head and winked. The man leaning against the hood saw Natalia's back and assumed the worst ... or the best as the case may be.

"Atta boy!" He flashed me a thumbs-up and smiled.

I grinned back wickedly and kept on driving. The driver was too engrossed in the walkie-talkie exchange to notice. I turned left and headed towards Frey.

"Did they see me?"

"One did, but he couldn't recognize you with your head in my lap." I started chuckling. "I think he might have gotten the wrong idea," I added.

I felt Natalia stiffen at the suggestion. She pinched my thigh ... *hard.*

"Owww! It's not my fault! Well ... not completely," I admitted, laughing even harder. "And I think you can get up now."

Natalia sat up and slapped my arm.

"I guess I had that coming," I said. I looked behind us to make sure it was clear then stopped the truck in the middle of the street.

"How did you know they'd be there?" she asked.

I turned professional in an instant. "Because these guys are hired help, DiMarco sent them, DiMarco lives southwest of Washington street, they're lazy, and their way to your house would have been the closest alley along the way that wasn't right next door."

"Isn't that kind of a reach?"

"Not really. How else would I have known they'd be parked there?"

"I want to argue with you, but I can't," she said. "And it bothers me. A lot." I shrugged at her with a *what-can-I-say* look and checked behind us again to make sure there was no one there.

"You know they're in there, right?" I said calmly.

"Yes."

"There's going to be between two and four guys, probably four. I'm also guessing that there's only one vehicle, but it's possible there are two. We'll have to risk it."

"Are we just going to walk up to the front door?"

"Do you have a door in the back?"

"Yes, and a patio on the second floor."

"Then no. We're going in the back. Does your back door have a window, and are there any other windows facing the alley?"

"A small window in the door, one over the kitchen sink and lots upstairs."

"Okay. If they see you at all, they won't till you get out of the truck. If they recognize you—and they probably won't with the wig—they'll be scrambling to get into position. If not … well, I have a plan to get in that should work. One question …"

"What?"

"Are you *absolutely certain* you need what's in there?" I had done this sort of thing before, and I was good at it, but I generally did it alone. Things like this usually got a little loud and messy, well, a *lot* loud and messy, and I'd prefer a different approach if I could find one.

"Absolutely." She showed concrete resolve.

"I meant two questions,"

"What's the other one?"

"Does your life depend upon it?" I was deadly serious.

"Yes."

"Okay … By the way, I lied. I meant to say three questions."

"What is it?" she said exasperated.

"What are you after in there?"

"My laptop."

I paused for a few seconds, pondering the answer. "Oh, okay," I said, satisfied. I looked at her sideways a moment later, a look of concern on my face. "We're not risking our lives for your music library, are we?" I found myself on the business end of one of the dirtiest looks I'd ever seen, and I'd had plenty thrown my way over the years. "I'll take that as a no," I concluded. "Could I just go in and get it myself? No need to risk both of us unnecessarily," I offered, smiling.

"No. It's in the master bedroom upstairs, but you can't get to it. Only I can. Thumb-reader," she said, holding up her thumb. Her tone was still a bit surly.

"That wouldn't happen to be detachable, would it?" I asked sincerely.

She shook her head slowly, the look on her face similar to the one Rachel had adopted over the years when I suggested the impossible. What neither of them realized was that where I came from, the impossible was often probable.

"It figures," I said fatalistically. "Quickly, what's the layout inside from the back door to the bedroom? Only the main rooms. And get it right. Our lives depend upon it."

"No pressure," she said sarcastically.

"Do you want your laptop or not?" I fired back at her.

"Okay, okay," she said, holding up her hands in submission. I closed my eyes and listened to her carefully. "The back door opens into a large kitchen. There's a breakfast nook immediately to the right, and beyond that it opens into a dining room. There's a short hallway on the right from the kitchen past the dining room the living room. On the left, there's a long hallway that ends at the foyer." She took a deep breath. "The living room entrance is to the right of foyer. There's an office to the left of the front doors and a bathroom to left of that. Stairs going up run back along left side of hallway. At the top of the stairs is a small sitting room that looks down on the living room and hallway. Straight back from the sitting room is the main hallway. There are two bedrooms on the right and a master bedroom on left. The door at the end of the hallway opens onto the patio. The master bedroom has doors opening on to the patio as well." She took another deep breath. "How'd I do?"

I opened my eyes and gave her a smile. "Perfect, I can see it."

A horn blared behind us. I put it in gear and slowly pulled ahead.

"Okay," I said, "I'm going to put on a show for these assholes. Play along and assume they don't recognize you, no matter what."

"You got it."

"Also, and this is *really* important, when I snap my fingers, you close your eyes *tight* until you hear a bang, understand?"

"Perfectly."

"Screw that up and they'll most likely kill you before I can get them. After the first bang, you move and shoot. You get the far ones with the Glock. I'll take care of anyone within ten feet."

"Okay," she said a bit doubtfully and checked the Glock on the back of her belt.

"One last thing …"

"WHAT?"

"Tile, wood, or carpet?"

"What?" She looked confused again.

"Tile, wood, or carpet?" I repeated slowly.

"Hardwood. Why?"

"This is gonna be messy," I said with a wicked grin, and I felt the old me gain a foothold in anticipation of what I was about to do.

"You're not setting off any of those burning thingamajigs, are you?"

"Don't worry. Those won't work in a situation like this. We'll all be mixed together … up close and personal. Remember to wait for the bang when I snap, and we'll be in and out in a jiffy. Start moving fast after it goes off, and they'll shoot where you were, not where you are." I turned left down the alley.

"There," Natalia pointed, "… with the trash cans."

"No recycle bins?" I scolded.

She gave me another dirty look, which I ignored. I came to a stop closest to the cans, blocking most of the alley. The patio stretched over the back yard, covering more than half of it and nearly reaching the alley. In the upstairs window, I saw a head attached to a black suit quickly pull out of sight. A moment later the flicker of a face appeared in the window of the back door. I reached into a pocket and stuck my arm in deeper than should have been possible. Natalia got a surprised look on her face, and to her amazement, I pulled out a bottle of beer. I twisted off the top and grinned at her.

"Show time," I said with a giant grin. I opened the truck door and took a swig of beer, "Ugh! Warm!" I stepped into the alley, leaving the door open and the engine running.

"Good luck," she whispered.

"Luck favors the prepared mind," I quipped, and let the predator loose. I staggered out of the truck like a drunk, fumbled with the gate and finally got it open. Twenty feet lay between me and the back door. As I stumbled up the sidewalk, I reached into another inner pocket and pulled out a bright orange sphere the size of a Ping-Pong ball that had two small black buttons on opposite sides.

In my best southern drawl, I shouted back at the truck as I stumbled towards the gate, "I'm tellin' ya, honey, God damn it! This is Billy's place, and he said there was more beer in the fridge!"

"I still say it's the next alley over, you mow-rahn!" Natalia yelled back from the truck in an equally thick drawl. "He said there was a key under a big black rock by the back door, didn't he? Do ya see a big black rock?"

I'll have to thank her for that later, I thought.

I spotted the rock to the right of the back door. "Yeeee Hawwww! I sure as hell do! Come on in, sweetie!" I flipped over the rock, grabbed the key and, stepping up to the door, quickly drove it home in the keyhole. As I did so, I palmed the orange sphere in my right hand and closed my fingers around it, making sure to depress both buttons. I twisted the doorknob. Through the window I spotted the black suit of a fat man standing behind the door.

Amateurs, I thought to myself.

I took a few steps into the kitchen and drifted right a pace or two towards the middle. I would need room to move, and I wanted to give Natalia as much space as possible. On cue a gun poked into the back of my head, and I stopped dead in my tracks.

"Don't take another step," a thick Brooklyn accent came from behind me. "You picked the wrong fuckin house, cowboy."

"Whoa!" I hollered, raising my arms. "Hold on there, partner." I saw a second man holding a gun step into the kitchen from the sunroom. I heard the footsteps of two people upstairs, one coming down the hallway and one coming down the stairs.

"Sweetie-pie, did you find the beer?" Natalia asked as she came in the back door. The man standing near the sunroom casually pointed his gun at Natalia, silencer attached, and pressed his index finger to his lips to get her to stay quiet. "Oh!" she yelped, acting surprised as she put up her hands. She put her back against the wall so no one could see her Glock.

"Vinny!" the man behind me hollered to someone upstairs. "Go back and watch the alley! That Russian bitch might still show up."

"You fellers know Billy?" I asked, keeping up the façade. "He sent us over for some beer, honest." The footsteps above us retreated back down the hall. I tried to drag things out. I wanted to at least get the third man in the room before starting anything.

"We heard you the first time, redneck," the man behind me said. "You're in the wrong fuckin' house."

"Is everything okay?" we heard from a walkie-talkie. A goombah appeared in the front hallway. He held a silenced pistol in one hand and a walkie-talkie in the other.

"We got this," the new man said into the walkie-talkie as he pointed his gun at me.

"What's going on?" the radio voice said. I recognized it as the goombah who had given me the thumbs up in the first alley. He must have taken the walkie-talkie away from the driver.

"Just a couple of drunk hicks. Stay where you are."

"Want me to call Joey in the other car?" the man on the other end of the radio said.

"NO! I said we got this," the goombah barked.

I cringed at hearing about the other vehicle.

"You want I should take 'em downstairs and get 'em outa' the way?" the man from the sunroom asked.

"Yeah, Guido, do that," the man with the radio confirmed. Guido took two steps towards me.

I released the bottle of beer and the orange ball simultaneously, and I snapped my fingers before they made it to my chest. "Shit, I dropped it!" I yelped.

The man with the walkie-talkie depressed the talk button, "We're gonna …"

Natalia and I closed our eyes while the three Italians naturally stared at both the bottle and the ball dropping to the floor. The beer hit first and shattered with a foamy crash. The ball, an instant behind the bottle, hit and went off like a gunshot, blinding all three gunmen with a brilliant flash of light. The Italians yelled in pain and covered their eyes with their hands.

Natalia and I leapt into action. She crouched and rolled forward along the floor. The silenced pistol of the Italian in the hallway thumped, and a blind shot hit the wall where Natalia had been. Faster than any human, I sidestepped and crouched down, reaching under the back of my coat in a single, fluid motion as I spun to my left.

The gun that had been pointing at my head thumped. The round harmlessly embedding itself in the wall behind Guido. The vlain gave off its high-pitched whine as my hand closed around it.

The weapon came out easily. I extended my arm, swinging the blade in a tight arc. The curved blade passed through the fat man's mid-section, slicing through skin, muscle, fat, and intestine. He grunted as his belly flopped open like a bloody, toothless mouth.

Natalia came up from her roll into a low crouch, the Glock in her hands. My backswing passed through the fat man's neck with a sickly-wet squelch, like a cleaver hitting a side of beef. Blood sprayed across the counters and sink as the blade opened his throat. His eyes went wide in surprised horror.

"What the fuck!" someone yelled from upstairs.

"Vincent, what happened?!" burst through the radio.

Natalia let off two fast shots, chest then head, which sent the man with the radio reeling backwards as he fell.

Guido shot blindly into the kitchen from the sunroom. I ducked down into a low crouch, taking two steps towards him as bullets sailed above me to the left and right. I came up as hard as I could, burying the stiletto blade up under his chin and angling it back into his brain. His head snapped back, and his arms swung down lifelessly at his sides. As I yanked the blade out, I heard the splat-spattering of the fat man's intestines spilling onto the kitchen floor behind me.

Without pausing, I leapt towards the hallway as both dead Italians thudded to the floor with loud thuds.

Footsteps hammered down the hall upstairs.

I reached into a pocket, pulled out another flash-bang and clicked the buttons on either side. I flashed past Natalia, leapt over Vincent's body, and ran down the hall, zigzagging left and right, pushing my weight off the baseboards.

A silenced thud sounded from above, and wood splintered near my foot. Without looking up, I hurled the flash-bang at the vaulted ceiling above and behind me as I kept running. It hit the ceiling and detonated, filling the hallway with light. I heard a yelp from above as the shooter was blinded. Shots rained down randomly into the hallway.

I grabbed the stair rail, let my momentum swing me around the post, and leapt from the bottom landing to the middle stair. Another leap propelled me to the top. The last gunman came into view, standing in the middle of the sitting room, holding his eyes with one hand and firing the gun with the other. My last leap, the vlain held high in the air, carried me the last six feet to the gunman. I brought the blade down across his elbow, with a thick *CHUCK!* as it passed through flesh and bone. Before he could scream, my back swing took his head almost completely off. The arm hit the floor with a squishy thud, and he crumpled in a heap, blood squirting across the hardwood floor. His head, attached only by a thin flap of skin and muscle, flopped backwards with the top of his head now resting between his shoulder blades.

"C'mon!" I yelled. "More are coming!" I ran to the back door and looked outside.

I heard Natalia get up, sprint down the hall and race up the stairs. She grimaced at the body lying on the floor and, leaping over the pool of blood, came back to the bedroom. I stepped up to the glass and looked out the glass doors onto the patio.

"Get it! *Fast!*" I ordered. I could see the upper half of my truck beyond the deck.

Natalia slipped the Glock into her belt and flipped the night-stand next to her bed onto its side. She then stepped up to a print of Munch's *The Scream*, pulled the painting off the wall, and threw it on the bed. She exposed a wall-safe with a combination dial, a handle, two small red lights, and a thumb-reader. She slid her finger over the reader, and one of two small red lights turned green. She quickly dialed in a combination, and the other light went green.

With a twist of the lever, she swung the door open.

Within lay a silver briefcase, a large Ziploc bag, a Glock .40, and four clips. She pulled out the briefcase, put it on the bed and worked the combination for both latches. They flipped open and she opened the briefcase, exposing a military-grade, heavy-duty laptop. She pulled the Ziploc out of the safe, and I could see it contained a stack of passports, six wrapped bundles of hundred dollar bills and three bundles of Euros. She threw the bag in the case, following it quickly with the Glock and three of the clips. She pulled the Glock she had been using out of her belt, ejected the partially used clip into the case and slid the fourth, fresh clip from the safe into the weapon.

"Let's go!" she said, gasping for breath as she closed the safe.

We both heard the sound of a big-block motor roaring down the alley and then tires squealing as a vehicle came to an abrupt halt behind my truck.

"Nice work, but we're not done yet," I said casually as I went over and locked the bedroom door. I wasn't even breathing hard.

Long Drive, Short Pier

I heard the man who had given me the thumbs-up yell, "Stay with the car, I'll check inside!" as he got out of the SUV. "Bennie's on the way!" he added and ran towards the house.

"Be careful, Dino," the driver cautioned, getting out and standing in the door.

Spattered with blood, I peeked through the glass patio doors from behind the wall. I thought I saw a MAC-11 in Dino's hand as he stepped out of the SUV.

That could be a problem.

The MAC-11 is basically a bullet hose. They're not very accurate past about thirty feet, and only good for short bursts, but *you* try standing in the middle of a hailstorm without getting hit. Everything in the house and yard would pretty much be within thirty feet, which made me quite worried about Natalia. I took a deep breath and looked at her. The plan I'd come up with for getting out in one piece was straightforward.

"When I go, you wait till I hit the end of the porch, then you run, jump onto the truck and get in the far side. If I buy it, drive off."

We both heard Dino yelling in a panicked voice from downstairs. "Holy mother of god!—Vincent!—Guido!—Frankie!—JESUS! What the fuck happened in here?" He paused, I'm sure when he saw the carnage I'd made of his buddies. "Vinny? YOU UP THERE?" I waited another ten seconds for Dino to make his way to the base of the stairs.

"Hurry, Dino! I'm hurt bad," I yelled in my best Brooklyn accent. I flipped the vlain around in my hand so the straight blade now pointed down. I smiled at Natalia, slid open the door, and leapt through it. It took me two strides to cross the fifteen-foot patio, and Natalia was moving the instant my foot hit the railing.

The man standing next to the SUV raised a MAC-11 through the open car window as my foot hit the railing of the patio. The Italian had good reflexes, I'll give him that, but he still wasn't fast enough. The barrel tracked me as I leapt into the air. A stream of gunfire filled the space behind me as I sailed over him. I flipped completely in a half-twist as the barrel banged into the window frame and stopped short. The burst continued harmlessly behind me.

The poor guy watched in terror as I came down hard on the roof of the SUV and drove the four-inch stiletto blade into his forehead. The hilt split his head open, and the impact drove his body down off the knife. He crumpled in a twitching heap on the ground just outside the open door. I heard Natalia's footsteps hammering across the patio. I turned to watch her hit the railing and jump.

She crossed the eight feet of open space easily just as the patio door erupted with bullets and flying glass. She came down hard on the roof, continued her stride, and dropped to the far side of the truck. I heard Dino kick the doorframe open. I realized immediately that I had to do something or he would hose the truck and kill Natalia.

I dropped to the ground and grabbed the MAC-11 at my feet. Dino crossed the fifteen feet of the porch quickly and raised his weapon.

"I got you now, bitch!" he hissed. Focused completely on Natalia, he didn't see me stand up and raise the machine gun. I hated to use the thing, but there weren't any options.

"Excuse me," I said as pleasantly as I could. Dino snapped a surprised look in my direction as I pulled the trigger. A quick, efficient burst caught him square in the chest, and he flipped onto his back, motionless. I dropped the gun on the ground and walked over to the open door of my still-running truck. I looked back down the alley and watched another SUV squeal around the corner, three men inside.

I spotted Bennie DiMarco in the passenger seat and sighed as I slid the vlain back in its sheath. I really hated that stupid, fat bastard. All I could think about was when we'd crossed paths the previous year. Bennie had put one in my lung with that damn, gold-plated Colt .45 of his. I was in the wrong place at the wrong time, which is why I never went looking for him. Checking the truck, I noticed Natalia wincing and holding her right shoulder.

"How bad is it?" I asked, calm but very concerned.

"Not bad. No bone. It went in and out."

"Okay. Buckle up. Now it gets exciting!" I yelled, the old me truly enjoying myself, and the rest of me feeling guilty for it.

"You're out of your mind, Case," she said, clearly appalled by my giddiness.

I yanked the back of my coat out of the way and pulled the vlain in its sheath off my belt. I normally would never take it off, but my plan called for a situation where I didn't want it to fall into the wrong hands.

I jumped in the truck and slid the sheathed vlain under the seat. Putting the truck in gear, I drove quickly but calmly down the alley. I looked behind me and saw the SUV still sitting there, waiting to see which way we went. Without hesitation, I turned left on Harbor back the way we came. The moment I turned, I caught a glimpse of the SUV backing up and turning the same way. I hammered the gas and flew down Harbor. Fortunately, there were no cars in the way. I reached Wilson in a matter of seconds and swerved around the corner to the right, heading back towards Washington. The SUV burst out onto Wilson three blocks behind us and careened off a red Volvo that swerved with the impact and drove into the bushes of someone's yard.

"I thought you hated guns," Natalia said calmly.

"I do. They're not any fun," I replied in all seriousness. She gave me a look that bordered on fear mixed with amazement, convinced of my insanity. "Would you have preferred I let him shoot his again?"

"Definitely not," she admitted quietly.

I saw a gap in the westbound traffic on Washington and bounced over the curb, turning hard to the right. The driver I cut off stood on the horn and stuck his hand out the window, giving me the universal suggestion for intercourse in the imperative. I waved pleasantly at the extended middle finger and stepped on the gas, heading straight down Washington towards the pier. I swerved left and right, weaving between slower cars and trucks while keeping an eye on the SUV swerving behind us.

"You were Spetsnaz, right?" I asked. She hesitated for a moment, still not certain how much she could trust me. "Come on. No games!"

"Close enough," she admitted.

"Good. Slide your hand under the seat." She did. "You feel that cylinder?" I asked.

"Yes."

"Slide your hand towards the door.... Do you feel *that*?"

She felt an oddly shaped piece of rubber. "Yes," she looked at me, understanding instantly.

"Use it." She looked towards the rapidly approaching Venice Fishing Pier and then back at me with wide eyes. "Trust me," I added confidently.

I floored the gas, the motor roared, and we accelerated hard down Washington. I had to slow a few times to keep from getting nailed by cross-traffic, and Bennie was gaining ground. I crashed through the wood barrier blocking the entrance to the pier and honked my horn to get people out of the way. I swerved around a hot-dog stand and a burrito vendor as we quickly started running out of pier.

"I have to try and find out what these assholes want, okay?" I said, motioning to our pursuers.

"Yes."

"*Au revoir*," I said. I opened the door and rolled out.

"Justin!" she yelled after me.

I came to a rolling stop just as the truck smashed through the railing at the end of the pier. The truck hopped up a couple of feet when it hit the lip and went sailing into the surf. I stood up and ran to the edge of the pier to see Natalia's body sagging limply towards the middle of the truck, hanging unconscious in the seat belt.

Seawater poured through the open windows, and her body swayed with the water filling the cab. I watched the truck, with Natalia still limp inside, sinking quickly.

"Natalia!" I shouted in horror.

Wheels screeched behind me, and I could hear sirens in the far-off distance—lots of them. I heard car doors open and heavy footsteps running up behind me. An iron grip clamped around my arm, and I winced at the strength of it.

"Get in the fucking car, Case." Someone jammed a gun into my ribs to emphasize the request. I turned around and saw the wide grimace of Bennie's biggest brute, Tommy at the other end of the vice-like grip. Antonio held the gun.

"Tommy … Antonio," I said sadly. "Long time no see." Bennie stepped up beside them both and looked out on the water where the truck had disappeared.

"She come up?" Bennie asked.

"No sir," Antonio said. "Nothing. It looked like she was unconscious when it went under."

"She must have hit her head," I said with a tinge of despair. People were starting to gather at the end of the pier.

"Good riddance, ya fuckin bitch!" Bennie said more loudly than he should have. He spat out into the ocean. Most of the gawkers turned and shot Bennie dirty looks. "Put him in the car, boys."

"Yes sir, Mister DiMarco."

Tommy turned and headed for the car, with me in tow. Tommy was so strong I might as well have been cuffed to a bull-dozer. Bennie watched for another thirty seconds to see if Natalia came up. Tommy threw me in behind the passenger seat and closed the door. Antonio, now sitting in the driver's seat, turned around and pointed his gun at my chest. We waited until Bennie was satisfied and then watched him walk back to the SUV, get in to the front seat, and turn around to face me.

"You're a real pain in the ass, Case," Bennie said as he opened the glove box. "You know that?" He pulled out something, but I couldn't see what it was.

"Yes, I know. You're not the first to say so, Bennie. Probably won't be the last."

"Don't count on that, asshole," he said, pointing a taser at my chest. "You're gonna love this. We have these made custom. Got 'em from the fucking Russians. They have … a bit more juice than your average taser. I just hope it doesn't kill you. I got something special planned for you."

"Oh shit," I said, meaning it. I don't handle electricity very well.

"Goodnight," Bennie said and pulled the trigger. I went stiff as Bennie let the current flow … and flow…. Thankfully, I only remember the first few seconds of it, and then the lights went out.

o o o

I woke to the sound of turbo-props spinning up and the realization that my hands were cuffed behind me. My shoulders were sore from leaning on them against the fuselage. My jaw ached, and there was the all-too-familiar taste of blood in my mouth. Someone must have hit me while I was unconscious. *Assholes.* It took me a minute to fully regain my senses.

"How we feeling, princess?" Bennie asked from across the aisle. The plane accelerated hard, and we shot down the runway. I ran my tongue over the side of my mouth to find a thick lump. I spat out some blood on the floor of the plane, not necessarily at Bennie, but not away from him either. "You made a real mess back at Natalia's. Most of those guys were friends of ours." The plane lifted off the ground, and we quickly gained altitude.

"Well, they started it," I said, sounding as petulant as I could.

"Tommy, when we level off, show him what I think of that."

"You got it," Tommy said cracking the massive knuckles of both fists. When the plane's ascent settled, the giant Italian stood up and stepped in front of me. "This is for Guido and Vincent," Tommy said and hit me in the ribs—left-right—with two heavy punches. I grunted and coughed as the air rushed out of my lungs.

Bennie and Antonio laughed.

After a few seconds I finally got my wind back. "Were they *all* friends of yours, Tommy?" I asked cautiously, thinking of the six bodies I'd left behind at Natalia's house.

Tommy nodded his head with an all-together unpleasant look on his face. "Yeah, they were," he added viciously.

"I was afraid of that."

"This is for Vinny and Al." He raised his right fist even higher than the first time and laid into my ribs with a monstrous right and then a staggering left. If I were human, I'm sure I would have heard a rib break when the left hit home. It took me even longer to catch my breath, and a sharp pain coursed through my right side with every inhale.

"No snappy come backs, Case?" Bennie asked chuckling.

"This is for Dino," Tommy said raising his right fist again. It came down across my jaw like a sledgehammer, knocking me over sideways on the bench. All I saw were stars for a few seconds. I felt Tommy lift me back up into place as I sat there shaking my head and blinking my eyes, trying to shake the dizziness.

"That's quite a right-cross you have there, Tommy," I managed to say as my eyes came back into focus. He really didn't do any permanent damage, but damn, he hit like a truck.

Bennie and Antonio laughed uproariously.

"Thanks, Case. They call the left one Mack … as in Mack truck … and *that's* the one you should be worried about. This one is for Frankie," Tommy said as he cocked his left arm.

"That's enough, Tommy," Bennie said, trying to gain control of his laughter. "I never liked Frankie. He was an asshole. Besides, we want Case here to fully appreciate his return trip to Mother Earth, don't we?" I finally took note of the fact that the three Italians were wearing parachutes. Coincidentally, only the guys with parachutes were laughing. Tommy went back to his seat, just out of my leg's reach.

"Tell me something, Case," Bennie said.

"Anything, Bennie," I said cordially.

"How the hell did you get mixed up in this … with Natalia? It just don't figure."

"Mutual friend."

"Mutual friend?" Bennie couldn't fathom whom I might know that Natalia would.

"Yeah. Someone killed him with a vat of chemicals recently."

"You're fucking kidding me!" Bennie said, and all three mobsters laughed again, even harder than the first time.

"That Chink was a friend of yours? Holy shit that's funny! Who woulda' thought?" Bennie kept laughing, having difficulty catching his breath. "Case … Case …" Bennie started, trying to control his laughing. "I put the contract out on him!" he finally managed, then laughed again. "Me, personally!" Antonio and Tommy added to his laughter.

"*You* had him killed?" I asked, with steel hardening into my voice.

"It gets better," Bennie continued. "The first try missed him. Some local guy tried to knife him in a parking lot, but, uhhh, apparently the Chink was too much for him. Broke his neck or something."

I smiled with a bit of pride. I had been training with Xen for almost two years, and apparently it had paid off. "I'm sorry to hear that."

"I bet you are," Bennie sneered. "Eh …" he continued, shrugging it off, "Contract killers like that guy are dime a dozen. You wanna hear the best part, though?"

"I do, Bennie."

"Whoever threw him in that vat of acid still hasn't come to collect. It's like … like Christmas for us."

"Why'd you want Xen dead?"

"He was a threat to our business," Bennie said suddenly very serious.

"So, what's your business these days?"

Bennie laughed sarcastically, "What, you think I'm an idiot?"

"Well, now that you mention it," I said under my breath.

"You think I'm just gonna tell you how we ship product?" Bennie continued.

BINGO! I thought.

"Bennie …" Antonio said, clearly trying to keep his boss from revealing anything else.

"Ehhh … fuck it. He's going out the door in a minute. Make of that what you will, Mister *Detective*…. while you still got time." He pulled out his .45, and Tommy slid open the door.

"You got a parachute in that fuckin' coat of yours, Case?" Bennie yelled over the engines and wind blasting through the doorway. The son-of-a-bitch casually pointed his .45 in my direction from across the aisle, smiling with that pudgy, piggy little face of his.

I did *not* have a parachute inside my coat. Even if I did, with my hands cuffed behind me, there wasn't much I could do with a parachute besides use it as a pillow.

Antonio and Tommy stepped up on either side of me, just out of reach. The wind blowing through the door made my trench coat flutter wildly. I looked at the .45 and then at Bennie.

I gave them a tired smile, sore jaw and all. I couldn't stand the sight of Bennie, which made staring down the barrel of that ridiculous, gold-plated Colt that much more intolerable. I decided right then and there that I'd have to kill him the next time I saw him. With the wind blasting, his jowls fluttered almost as much as my coat.

"Stand up." Bennie pulled the hammer back on the pistol. Malice oozed from his fluttering smile. I did as instructed, easily managing to keep my feet beneath me as the plane lurched slightly with turbulence. My balance—like my mohawk—was impeccable. I stared down on them … well, except Tommy, who had me by a few inches.

As the plane lurched, Bennie and the goombahs—*what a great name for a band*, I thought—all raised a hand up to steady themselves, grabbing one of two railings that ran the length of the ceiling. Bennie's gun, however, never wavered. Bennie was stupid, but he wasn't totally brainless. He knew what sort of damage I could inflict with my feet when the mood suited me, cuffs or not.

"Help him out boys," Bennie ordered.

Antonio and Tommy stepped in quickly, grabbed my arms and moved me roughly up to the open door. I didn't resist, I just stared at the .45. The wind howled by my face as they moved me into the doorway. I looked down at Hollywood, the hills spreading out beneath me covered with posh, mostly nouveau-riche neighborhoods aglow in late afternoon sunshine. Hollywood Reservoir lay a short distance ahead, and Universal Studios spread out beyond that.

"You know, Bennie," I said tiredly, "the only reason we're here at all is that I hate getting shot."

"Oh, yeah, that's right. I almost forgot." Bennie said, grinning. He clapped me on the shoulder like we were old friends. "Thanks for reminding me, Case!" His face turned vicious as he shot me in the thigh. I winced at the hot pain lancing through my leg, but I refused to cry out. I'd be damned if I'd give the pudgy fucker the satisfaction.

"Damn it." I said under my breath. "I *hate* getting shot."

"What was that, Case? I couldn't hear you over the gunshot," Bennie yelled, laughing. "Well, that and the engines!" All three Italians were laughing again.

Before they could do anything, I leaned out the doorway and let gravity work its voodoo. I wasn't going to give them the satisfaction of pushing me out. After all, I did have my pride … and an image to maintain. With my leg throbbing and the wind screaming past my ears, I plummeted towards the rapidly approaching Hollywood Hills.

Now, if I was from Earth, I'd actually be worried. This was still going to hurt like a mother-fucker, but the Hollywood Hills are a target rich environment. All I had to do was find the right spot … *there.*

I angled my descent and hoped for the best.

Unbelievable, I thought an instant before the impact. Another two-hundred yards north and I would have hit the reservoir. *Damn that Bennie.*

A Friendly Face

I hit the pool at terminal velocity, just over a hundred-and-twenty-five miles an hour. Water erupted like a bomb had gone off, and a deafening *CRACK!* of splitting concrete filled my ears when I hit bottom. A flash of gut-wrenching pain coursed through me before I blacked out.

When I came to, I was lying in a puddle with my face mashed against the concrete. The water had drained out through an impact-crater in the bottom of the pool as well as a three-inch crack that led from the crater up the side of the pool. The water had eroded the soil as it drained, pouring through the thin hillside dropping away towards the reservoir.

Having managed to pull my legs through my arms during the fall, I reached up with cuffed hands and pulled myself out. My whole body hurt, especially my face, which was a shade flatter than when I'd stepped out of the plane. My nose was a mess. I stood there dripping, looking around at the destruction Bennie had caused. Blood ran from my crushed nose as well as from my leg, although the bullet hole in my leg had mostly stopped bleeding on the way down. I was one big ache, pissed off from head to toe, with the puddle around my feet turning a cloudy pink. I reached up and pressed my fingers firmly together against the bridge of my nose to set it straight. My nose crunched slightly as I pushed what I use for bone back into place, and my eyes filled with tears.

I bent over, wincing at sore ribs, and pulled a large paperclip from out of my shoe. I straightened one section, put a kink in the end with my teeth and inserted the bent end into the keyhole of the cuffs. A single twist opened the left cuff. Another twist sent the cuffs clattering to the bottom of the pool, sliding and disappearing into the crack.

Like I said, if I were from Earth I'd have been worried on the way down. It's not like I'm invincible, although I am one tough son of a bitch. There are a number of ways to bring about my demise. It's all about the how. And how to kill me … well, that's my most closely guarded secret.

I let out a long, tired sigh as I rubbed sore wrists and reflexively reached into my jacket pocket. I pulled out a pack of Winston's, flipped it open, and tried to slide out a cigarette. The filter broke loose from the soaked paper.

"Idiot," I sighed. I wanted to kill someone. I calmly put the butt back in the package and placed the package back in my pocket. "Time to go," I said to myself. I reached into a front pocket, my fingers dipping into an inch of water, and pulled out my cell phone. A trickle drained out of it as I flipped it open, and I shook my head. God dammit. I reached into an inner pocket and pulled out my other cell phone, the one I kept in a Ziploc baggie just in case. I opened the bag, pulled out the phone and dialed Rachel. Limping up to the shallow end of the empty pool, I heard Rachel pick up on the second ring.

"Justin! Where the hell are you?" She sounded worried but not panicked. In my line of work I frequently disappeared for days at a time, but I always called in safe, or at least mostly safe.

"Hollywood," I said blandly. I walked up the concrete pool steps, limping slightly, and headed for the back fence. "Rachel, can you pick me up after dark on the east side of the Hollywood reservoir?"

"Of course. How will I find you?"

"Don't worry. I'll find you." I hung up, put it back in the bag and sealed it tightly. Slipping the bag back into my coat, I looked behind me one last time to see the flash of a woman's face in an upper window of the house beyond the pool. The curtain closed abruptly, and she was gone. I had to smile. She took that rather well. The cops couldn't be that far away, though. I hopped the fence, walked down the hill—now soaked with pool water—crossed Montlake Drive, and headed into the bushes to lie low until the cops were finished doing their cop stuff.

A Good Banana

I crouched beneath some thick scrub oak near the dam that formed the Hollywood reservoir. The evening was comfortably hot but not humid, and rain wasn't forecast till the following day. I saw the flickering, red-blue-white reflections of the last police car's light bar bouncing across the black-glass surface of the reservoir.

There had been police cruisers, fire engines, two police helicopters and four news helicopters around the house for hours. They probably didn't believe the woman's story, but the impact crater and empty pool would be impossible to deny. I could only hope they wrote it off as a meteor strike or something combined with too much wine.

I pulled a banana from my coat, peeled it and took a few thoughtful bites, and scratched the bump on my leg where DiMarco's bullet had gone in. I could feel the slug under the skin, wedged up against the bone, but it wouldn't work its way out for several days. The damn things always itched like crazy until they popped out.

Police cruisers had driven by the dam a few times, using their searchlights to see if there was anything or anyone unusual, but I was certain they wouldn't see me. When I didn't want to be seen, I simply wasn't.

A single, weak streetlight illuminated the small, dirt parking lot on the east side of the dam. Along its eastern edge ran a narrow, rough, dirt road, barely more than a trail, which led back to Montlake Drive and the house where I'd landed. The road continued on into the darkness, presumably into the Universal Studios property.

The sun had gone down only a few minutes before, so I scanned the area one last time to make sure the coast was clear. Then I stood up to stretch my tired legs and relieve my sore butt. My keen ears picked up the sound of something coming down the road, but it definitely wasn't Rachel's Porsche. In fact, it sounded a lot like bicycle tires crunching through dirt. I saw a small spotlight bouncing down the road towards the dam. The way it moved, I figured it was a helmet-mounted headlamp. Folding the banana peel over itself, I placed the banana back into my pocket, crouched beneath the bushes, and pulled out the Ziploc with the dry cell phone in it.

Opening both, I typed in "cops. Meet west side not east" then sent it to Rachel's phone. I would have to cross the top of the dam to get to her when she arrived. As long as I wasn't seen, though, I'd be fine.

A bicycle cop coasted into view, rolled through the parking lot and stopped at the base of the short flight of concrete stairs that led up to the walkway across the dam. He looked around for a minute or so, his headlamp flashing right over the bushes concealing me, and then mounted his bicycle and continued down the dirt road out of sight. I watched the headlamp bounce and jiggle through the darkness until it disappeared around a bend.

Minutes later, I heard the faint but distinct, six-cylinder purr of perfectly tuned German engineering. Across the hundred yards of dam, I saw a black Porsche Cayman S pull into the paved lot on the far side. The streetlight shone brighter on that side, and the car's sleek silhouette glinted in the light. My cell phone vibrated, so I opened it up.

"West side—NOW."

"I love ya, baby," I said quietly and grinned. I slipped the phone back into the bag, placed the bag in my coat and pulled out the banana. I scanned the darkness for another few seconds to be sure no one was coming, and then I stood up and walked casually down the short hill towards the weak light of the east parking lot.

Unfolding the banana again, I took another thoughtful bite and walked up the stairs.

There's nothing quite like a good banana, I thought. As I reached the top, I heard the bicycle coming back up the road at high-speed ... high for a bicycle anyway. It sounded like the cop was really humping it. After walking about ten yards across the top of the dam, I took one last big bite of the banana and dropped the empty peel at my feet. As I reached again into my pocket, I extended my stride a little in order to gain some distance on the cop without having to run. I pulled a transparent sphere about the size of a golf ball out of my pocket and dropped it on the walkway. When it hit the concrete it spread out into a thin, invisible film that coated the surface. The stuff would evaporate without a trace in about ten minutes. I was halfway across the bridge when I heard the cop's voice behind me.

"Hey! Hold it!" the cop yelled from across the parking lot.

I didn't turn around. Instead, I increased my pace a bit more but still refused to run. Running only excites the hounds, I thought. I was more than halfway across the dam when I heard the bike come to a skidding halt at the base of the stairs. The bike clattered against the concrete, and boot-clad feet stomped up the steps. I didn't look back. I kept walking towards the Porsche.

I heard him running as he yelled, "I said FREEZE!" Then he un-holstered his pistol. That's when I turned ... not because the cop said so, but because I wanted to see what happened next.

Just as he raised his pistol, he spotted the banana peel and stepped over the ridiculously vaudevillian trip-hazard. He planted his front foot squarely on the invisible coating I'd dropped and stepped forward at full speed. I grinned as his front foot scooted out from underneath him. He yelped in surprise, shot straight up into the air, and came down hard on the railing. He gave a second, pained yelp and rolled unceremoniously over the edge into the water ten feet below. I couldn't keep from chuckling when I heard the splash, but I turned and started walking again.

Splashes and yells rolled across the water behind me as I strolled down the steps, opened the door of the Porsche, and got in. Uncomfortably cool air from the AC hit me, forcing me to close up my coat. I'm not a big fan of cold.

"You may want to hurry," I told Rachel as I looked over my shoulder at the dam. "His radio might be waterproof." I couldn't keep from chuckling a little as I said it.

"What? Whose radio?" Rachel put it in first gear and hammered the gas.

"Oh, nothing," I said, still laughing a bit. "Let's just get back to my place. I've got some thinking to do." I finally looked at her, and a warmth spread through me.

"Is this all about that waiter?" she asked.

I nodded. "The waiter. Yeah, but he was just the tip of the iceberg. DiMarco's working on something big."

"Bennie?" Rachel was clearly perplexed by the notion of the dumb, fat mobster doing anything big. He was all clown-shoes and three stooges … like someone slipping on a banana peel.

"No. The smart one. The dangerous one," I corrected.

"Gino hasn't done anything for nearly three years. I thought he was retired."

"I thought he was, too. We all did. But something's got him pushing buttons again," I said, "… or still," I added thoughtfully.

Rachel's Porsche hurtled through the night. I said nothing so she could concentrate. The radar detector on the dashboard stayed dark and silent as she cornered hard, traversing Lake Hollywood Drive doing one-ten in the straights and seventy in the corners. We reached a T-intersection, and Rachel slid left around the corner like a professional stunt driver, which, of course, she was. I paid for the classes myself. She took the immediate left turn only twenty yards down the pavement and continued to chew through a dozen more corners, gravel spitting up behind us and tires squealing as she raced on down Wonderview Drive. The Hollywood freeway came into view, and she pulled onto the northbound ramp. She dropped down a gear and stood on the gas. I watched her savor the howl of the motor as we exploded onto the freeway.

"Okay, we should be clear now," I said. "There's no way he could have seen your car from the water."

"Awwww …" I knew she was disappointed that she didn't get to keep speeding. That was one of her favorite parts of the job. She eased back on the gas, and we dropped down from one-thirty to a sane seventy-five. "So, were you the meteor?" she asked, sounding like a lawyer who knows the witness is guilty.

I smiled innocently. "What do you mean?"

"A swimming pool? A crater? Some poor maid from Tijuana terrified out of her skull and yammering in broken English on the news about the end of the world?" She paused to take a breath after the tirade, hoping I would fill the void with something more than a smile. When the void and the smile remained, she filled it herself. "Any of that sound familiar?"

"Perhaps." I chuckled again.

"Are you going to tell me what happened, for Christ's sake? It's been twenty-four hours!"

"Just take me to the warehouse. And yes, I'll tell you at least as much as I can before we get there." I rubbed my still tender leg. "I have a lot of thinking to do tonight before O'Neil shows up in the morning."

"How do you know O'Neil is coming?"

"He watches the news just like you do, and there is the small matter of a meteor strike. And one of his bicycle cops does have to explain both a complete set of soaked gear and how the guy in a trench coat they were looking for got away." I rubbed the healed but still tender bridge of my nose. "O'Neil can add two plus two ... even more when you press him," I added.

"Well ... out with it!" she demanded. "Tell me what happened! Your place is only a few miles away, so we don't have much time."

"There's too much." I glanced over at the speedometer. "At ninety-five I'd barely get the first bit out." I patted her knee. "I'll give you the whole story tomorrow. I promise. For now I have to sort some things out, okay?"

Rachel spent the rest of the ride grumbling, but I was calculating possibilities and not paying attention. She pulled up to the loft—actually a warehouse—which was my primary place of residence. There were no cars along the empty, industrial street that stretched off in both directions. Distant street lights spilled pale orange islands of brightness on every other street corner. She pulled up to the curb quickly and hit the brakes hard like she was coming in for a pit stop at Le Mans.

"Thanks, Rachel." I opened the door and stepped out. "Like I said, I've got to get a few things straightened out in my head tonight and deal with O'Neil in the morning. I'll meet you for lunch around noon and give you the whole story."

"You're killing me, Case," she griped. "I hate waiting."

"I know, but you wouldn't have me any other way."

"Tease!" she accused.

"Oh … one other thing …" I leaned back into the car.

"What?" She glared at me, sounding more perturbed than I knew she actually was.

"Remind me to put a door out by the reservoir, will you?"

Not really knowing what I was talking about but accustomed to that feeling, she smiled and said, "I'll send you a memo."

I closed the door, walked around the corner of the building, and made my way down the alley. The engine roared and tires screamed as she peeled away from the curb, disappearing quickly into the night.

Home Sweet Home

I walked down the alley and stopped between an electrical panel and door set halfway along the otherwise blank warehouse wall. The alley continued on to a back street that ran between buildings. There were no lights, and this side of my two-story warehouse had no windows. Wide, floor-to-ceiling windows did wrap around the other three sides, but only on the second floor.

I looked left and right to make sure no one was around, more habit than concern, and slid up the rusty, dented Warning: High Voltage sign attached to the concrete wall between the doorway and fake circuit-breaker box. Concealed within the three-inch-deep space lay a plain, black plate and nothing more. I placed my hand on the palm-reader and lifted my thumb and fingers one-by-one in a well-practiced sequence.

Stepping in front of the door, I pushed on the side of the steel jam opposite the doorknob. The whole doorframe swung in, and I stepped into the second level of my home as ninety-degree air washed over me. I breathed a deep sigh of relief in that comforting warmth. Windows stretched away from me on all three sides. Although no lights were on, I could just make out most of the widely spaced furnishings and vehicles, cast in weak illumination trickling in through the street-side windows. I closed the door, and the city receded far behind.

"Lights," I said. Warm spotlighting came on, dotting the ceiling at regular intervals and shedding blue-tinted brilliance on each of the living areas. To my immediate right, on the street-side, sat a massive, red, sectional couch, an entertainment system with multiple monitors set up against the windowless, alley-side wall. The next pool of light along the street-side windows shone on a utilitarian office space with a wrap-around, steel desk, black leather office chair, and a credenza pushed up against the windows. A terrarium sat on top, and both of my snakes were curled up in opposite corners. The desk had three large computer monitors on it, with a keyboard, a mouse, and one of my silver interface circlets. To my left were the kitchen and dining areas. The kitchen shined with stainless steel and black granite. A tall kitchen table, also done in stainless steel, as well as two chairs stood alone on the far side the kitchen.

Four of the five hooks set into the wall between me and the kitchen held my spare trench coats. Three of them were identical to the tan one I wore, except for the bloodstains, of course. The fourth shimmered black and seemed to absorb light, making it impossible to discern the folds and seams along its dark surface. It was the only coat with a hood.

Removing the bagged phone from my pocket, I took off my coat and hung it on the second hook. The first hook held a jacket covered in dust, mud, and motor oil. I'd left it there a week earlier, not really feeling like cleaning it up. Cleaning my coats was always a pain in the ass.

I slipped my sneakers off bare feet and slid the shoes into the first, bottom cubbyhole of a low shelf that ran along the wall. Shoes and boots of every kind filled the shelving. What can I say? I'm a shoe-whore. I walked past the coats and into to the kitchen.

"Mag?" I called out. The lighting over my bed glowed softer and dimmer than the rest of the loft. "You awake?" She wasn't on the bed, so I figured she must be out hunting. Slipping my phone into a pants pocket, I opened the refrigerator and pulled out a jug of orange juice. I uncapped it and walked to my bed, taking huge gulps as I went. My bed sat on a low, wooden platform about twelve inches off the gray, industrial-tiled floor. There was a low table for a nightstand with a lamp on it.

I set the juice on the nightstand and removed my black t-shirt and jeans, dropping both on the bed. Standing naked in the warm air, I stretched out my arms, back and neck, going through a brief stretching routine to loosen up my stiff muscles. My ribs popped a couple times, and I winced as I stretched them out. The standing closet, doors open, lay between me and my van.

Beyond the van was a rectangular seam in the floor. Around that I had a black Chrysler 300, a Porsche Cayman identical to Rachel's, a cherry-red '67 Cobra AC and a white T-Rex auto-cycle. Beyond the T-Rex were three motorcycles backed up against a massive accordion wall that hid my workshop.

There was a large workout mat in the far corner of the loft, which made a reddish-gray ocean in the middle of the space. An assortment of exercise equipment stood along the windows beyond that, also mostly hidden by the darkness.

"Mat lights," I said towards the ceiling.

Bright spotlights lining the perimeter of the thirty-by-thirty foot gymnastics mat came to life, illuminating the back of the loft as well. As I walked by, I saw a dark gray and forest-green striped feline-like muzzle peering down from atop the standing closet.

"There you are, Mag. How are you girl?"

Bright orange eyes stared at me, unblinking, and her lips drew back into an unmistakable smile. At ninety pounds, she was the size of a cougar, but her sleek body, hidden by the closet she lay upon, was longer and thinner than that native, American feline—bordering on serpentine.

I reached up and scratched behind her ears. A loud rasping came out of her throat, her species' equivalent of a purr. It sounded more like tumbling gravel than anything else.

"Any mail?" I asked her.

She looked over at my desk and nodded her head. She can always hear the ding when an email arrives.

"Thanks, girl." With a last scratch behind the ears, I grabbed the orange juice and walked over to the computer. I entered my password and pulled up my mail. There was the regular assortment of junk, a few 'hellos' from old friends and other non-essential correspondence.

One sender, however, caught my eye. My heart skipped a beat. It was from Xen Li and dated that morning at one-thirty a.m., but from a Hotmail account, not Xen's regular one. At first I thought it was junk mail, but it was signed 'Kato,' my nickname for Xen. It simply read, "Trouble. Meet GDs. MND. Regular time -8." I smiled, let out a sigh of relief, closed my email, and locked up the computer. That was the piece I was looking for.

I walked to the center of the gymnastics mat and sat down cross-legged, resting my palms on my knees, I closed my eyes and breathed slowly. I walked my thoughts through every detail of the past twenty-four hours to put them in order and make as much sense out of it as I could.

Two hours later I stood up, walked to my bed, and slipped in under the covers next to Mag, who was now asleep on the comforter.

"All lights off." Everything went dark, only streetlight sifting weakly into the interior of the loft, and I quickly fell asleep.

Expected Guest

Sitting on my couch and drinking more orange juice spiked with several tablespoons of sugar, I watched Captain O'Neil on the bank of security monitors displayed on my big-screen TV. He walked cautiously up the alley towards the door, trying to be sneaky. I had to smile. Morning sunlight didn't make it down directly into the alley, but he had plenty of light to see what he was doing. He'd parked his unmarked police cruiser on the street at the end of the alley, blocking the entrance.

Another unmarked police cruiser was parked at the far end of the alley, and one of O'Neil's most trusted lieutenants sat inside, watching his boss with a moderately bored look on his face. His name was Grimes, I think, but I couldn't remember for sure. I knew he didn't like me, though. The lieutenant had never figured out why O'Neil liked me so much, or why he always went easy on me when everyone else at the station referred to me as "The Asshole."

Sure, I'd given the LAPD a long list of great collars, but I'm pretty sure they all resented having to clean up twice that many scenes where the bad-guys were just messy corpses. You can't arrest a corpse.

I watched O'Neil come up to the door and try the knob. As usual, he hoped to catch me by surprise. I kept smiling as I watched him go through the motions. He slipped his hand into his back pocket and pulled out a leather case full of lock-picking tools.

"Let's see if I still got it," he said under his breath. It came through loud and clear on my TV, giving me a chuckle.

He bent down, extracted a slim torsion wrench and S-rake pick from the case and went to work on the door. Thirty seconds later he twisted the wrench clockwise, and the lock gave way. A satisfied grin on his face, he stood up and put the tools away. Placing his hand on the knob, he pulled out a flashlight and opened the door. I was really enjoying the show. He stepped inside the first floor of the warehouse and closed the door behind him. His image was clear as day on a different monitor, which automatically displayed in infrared. I had turned off the electrics on the first floor years ago.

Without windows, I'm sure he couldn't see a thing except for a thin, floor-to-ceiling square outline of daylight along the back left wall framing a rolling garage door. He turned on his flashlight, walked into the warehouse a short distance, and cast the bright beam around the dusky interior, scanning the entire space.

There was nothing but steel support columns, dust and some trash scattered around. Aside from his own footprints leading back to the door, he didn't see any in the dust covering the floor of the entire warehouse. His flashlight illuminated an area along the street-side wall where a rectangle of different-colored bricks filled in what had been the original front entrance. I'd sealed it up when I first moved in.

I'm sure O'Neil was looking for stairs going up. He knew about the lift for my cars, and he'd even seen me go up a few times from the alley. I walked to the front door, opened it, stepped out into the alley and turned, giving a friendly wave to Grimes.

O'Neil had been inside a few of my other houses over the years, the newest one behind Xen Li's being the nicest. He'd even brought his family over a few times a year for barbeques and pool-parties, but he'd never been inside the loft, so he had no idea how else to get in.

"Case?" he yelled. The empty warehouse swallowed up his voice.

"Yes?" my quiet response came from behind him.

O'Neil spun around, startled to see me leaning in through the half-opened alley door, a huge grin on my face.

"You're up early," I said casually. "I wasn't expecting you until nine." I looked him up and down. He seemed both surprised and pissed off as I stared at him. "You went with the navy suit today," I added. "Are you upset about something?"

O'Neil's rugged frame was topped with thinning copper curls. His chiseled features, once considered handsome by the ladies, were covered with a thick, bushy moustache and wild eyebrows that he'd given up trying to tame years ago. Stern, deep-set eyes bored into me, accosting me with very un-policeman-like intent. *Well, maybe not so un-policemen-like*, I mused. He looked at his watch and walked up to me as I opened the door fully.

"How do you do that?" He didn't even try to hide the irritation in his voice. He was always surly with me. He'd never forgiven me for looking so young over the years while he continued to get older, balder, and wider.

"Do what?" I asked innocently. One of my greatest joys on Earth was messing with O'Neil's balding head. Besides, if he knew the truth about my phase doors, he might feel obligated to turn me over to the feds, and I'd end up in Area 52 or something.

"With the door … and me showing up … and coming in behind me…." he stammered, almost flustered.

"Good timing?" I asked brightly.

"I hate you, Case. You know that, right?"

"Of course I do," I replied, clapping him on the shoulder. We stepped into the alley and I pulled out a set of keys from my coat pocket. Pausing, I looked expectantly at O'Neil. "Would you like to lock it back up?" Mischievous delight filled my voice. "By the way, isn't breaking and entering illegal? I think I read that somewhere." I chuckled a bit then locked the door before he could answer. "Besides, this job wouldn't be the same if you didn't hate me." I turned, grinned again, and cuffed Captain John Spencer Dwight O'Neil on the shoulder again like the good friend he really was. "Let's go get some coffee and doughnuts," I offered. "Your blood-sugar looks low." I waved again at Grimes. "I'll buy."

"You sure as hell will." O'Neil shook his head in disgust. He motioned for his lieutenant to take off. "Why do you bother?" O'Neil indicated the locked door behind us. "There's nothing in there."

I chuckled wickedly. "For the sole purpose of keeping your life interesting, O'Neil. I would think you'd know that after twenty years."

We walked up the alley towards his cruiser. Behind us the lieutenant started his cruiser and pulled away quietly as we got into the car.

"Grady's?" O'Neil asked as he fastened his seatbelt, started up the engine, and pulled away from the curb with a lurch and squeal of tires.

I went over the top with "shocked and hurt" as I buckled in. "You have to ask?" More seriously I said, "You know Grady's has the best coffee and doughnuts this side of the Rockies."

O'Neil looked like he wanted to ask a question, so I reached into a pocket and pulled out my pipe, knowing full well I wasn't supposed to smoke in his car.

As I reached for the tobacco, he stopped my hand. "Not in the car."

"I could keep the window open," I offered helpfully.

"Not in the car," O'Neil gave me a tired smile.

"Awwww ..." I sounded like a kid being told he had to go to bed. With a depressed look on my face, I put the pipe back in my pocket and pulled out some gum.

O'Neil took a breath, looking again like he would ask a question.

"Want some gum?" I interrupted. I held the pack out to him, and he took a piece, popping it into his mouth. I did the same and put the gum away.

"There's something I have to ask ..." O'Neil started while looking straight ahead.

The unmistakable click of a switchblade stopped him. I held a brand-new switchblade with a beautiful elk-antler handle. I'd pulled it out when I put the gum away.

O'Neil slowly turned his head, looked at the knife for a few seconds, and then shot a stern, questing look at me before returning his eyes back to the road. "Those are illegal, you know."

"Yeah, I know ... illegal ..." I grinned. "Like breaking and entering," I gave him a maddening grin to mess with him.

O'Neil rolled his eyes. "So what are you doing with it?"

"Your kid's getting deployed, right? Afghanistan?"

"Yeah, in a couple of weeks." There was a mixture of pride and worry in his voice. "She's the best Apache pilot they have. Top of her class."

I closed the blade. "Here," I said and handed it to him. "This is for her. Tell her to tuck it away in a boot or something … you know … *just in case*." He took the knife and slid it into his own boot. "Tell her I said good luck," I added sincerely, "and to stay low and keep moving."

"Thanks, Case. I know she'll appreciate it." He took another deep breath to ask the question, but I beat him to the punch again.

"So what's cooking downtown these days?" I asked, leading O'Neil once again away from the topic that had brought him to my front door in the first place. I did my best to sound like a lovesick teenager and whined, "You never call me anymore."

Shaking his head, he cast me a sidelong glance. "These days? Well, as you may have heard, that T-Rex thing has been gaining momentum for a couple of years, but lately it's really been building up steam."

I nodded. "I've heard a few things about it. Some new designer drug, right? Supposed to be turning the coke-world on its ear or something."

O'Neil was all cop now. "Yeah. It's wicked stuff. It's a combination of coke, meth, and something else. I can't remember the name of the third compound. The stuff tests clean like coke, hits hard like meth, and has a smoother letdown than anything else out there. Perfect for parties, you know? Our lab guys keep working on it, and we're trying to track the source, but so far we haven't been able to pin anything down. It's double the price of coke, so the clientele is smarter, harder to stiff-arm, and has better lawyers. And the few we've questioned are scared … of something … or some*one*."

"Can't you put some under-covers on it?"

"We're trying, but this stuff isn't going through the normal dealers. Del Gato and the other Mexicans don't seem to be involved, either. It's weird. It's like it comes from nowhere." O'Neil looked at me again, the question hovering on the tip of his tongue, but he held back, thinking I would interrupt him again.

I couldn't believe O'Neil had restrained himself as well as he had so far. I'd expected him to hammer me with the obvious question the moment we got in the car, and when he didn't, I'd decided to take the opportunity to toy with him. What are friends for, after all?

O'Neil finally gave in. "I know it was you who demolished that pool, Case," he blurted quickly when he couldn't stand it any longer. The question had morphed into an accusation before he even started. What can I say? I have that effect on people.

"Pool? What pool? I have no idea what you're talking about." I smiled like the Cheshire Cat, minus the hookah—well that and a big, bushy tail. His face went crimson. After a few seconds I added, "And you can't prove anything. That maid was way too far away for a positive ID." I chuckled again.

He glared at me. "I knew it!" he almost shouted, and I couldn't keep from laughing. "You mind telling me how you pulled that one off?" he asked with harsh bewilderment. "You should be a bloody smudge on the bottom of that swimming pool.

"Aw, hell, I don't know. Blind luck mostly. I scooped some air with my coat on the way down and the pool *was* pretty deep. The water pressure must have cracked the concrete. Maybe there was a defect in the foundation when they first poured it. And we do have a lot of earthquakes around here. It's a miracle I wasn't killed … or *worse*."

"Yeah, sure," he said doubtfully.

"You tell me. I don't how I managed it."

"You've got nine lives, Case. And at last count, you used about forty of them." I started doing math on my fingers, trying to subtract forty from nine, and then threw him a *that-doesn't-make-any-sense* look. He didn't comment on the arithmetic.

"By the way," I changed the subject, "don't go too hard on the bicycle cop. He did everything right." I smiled as I pictured the poor guy popping into the air and hitting the water like a sack. "Well, except for not watching where he was stepping." I couldn't keep myself from grinning.

"Were you pushed, or did you jump out of the plane?" he asked quickly before I could lead him off track again.

"Is this O'Neil my *friend* asking or *Captain* O'Neil?" I queried carefully.

He sighed heavily, knowing immediately what the difference meant. "This is your friend asking." He'd known me long enough to know that there wasn't much room in my life for rules. I'd always given O'Neil the collars he needed, so he considered me a tool in his arsenal … Well, that and we'd been friends since shortly after he joined the Academy.

"Good!" I beamed. "Well, I actually jumped, but that was pride. I wasn't going to give them the satisfaction of pushing me out. You know me."

"Yes, I do," he said tiredly. "So who was it?"

"You have to promise me something," I looked a bit more serious.

Wary dread crossed his face. "Oh-oh," he said suspiciously.

"Yeah, oh-oh," I concurred, "I need you to promise to not even think about arresting anyone anywhere until I give you the go ahead, okay?"

"You're pushing your luck, Justin," he accused. "Seriously?"

My tone changed from my normal light-heartedness to deadly serious. "Very. You know I don't normally ask, but a friend's life is in the balance. When I do say go, though, I may need you to drop an anvil someplace, or a lot of places, get me? It'll be worth your while."

"You got it," he agreed warily. "I'm trusting you, though. You're gonna owe me a *big one*."

"It's a deal, and you know I'm good for it."

"True enough," he said sincerely. "So, what's this all about?"

"DiMarco."

"Bennie?" he asked as incredulously as Rachel had.

"No. The smart one … the *dangerous* one," I shook my head, marveling at how so many other people could put the same data together and come up with the impossible.

O'Neil knew exactly who I was talking about now, but he got a confused look anyway. "I thought he was retired."

"Déjà vu," I said under my breath. I looked O'Neil square in the eyes, "Not anymore, and I'm pretty sure he never was."

"Shit."

"Yeah … shit." I leaned back in my seat and looked out the window.

"I wonder …" O'Neil's voice trailed off.

"What?" I stared at him.

"Oh, it's nothing. I just had an idea, but I have to talk to some people first."

"Fair enough," I agreed easily. We'd been having these kinds of exchanges for two decades, and each of us shared and withheld what we needed to do our jobs. It was a nice arrangement.

O'Neil turned into Grady's already full parking lot. He pulled into one of the five spots reserved for police vehicles, and we both got out. We could see a full house through the wraparound windows covering the front half of the building. There was also a six deep line at the counter.

"Tell me what you can," O'Neil said, "and the meter's running on this one. The longer I go without a bust, the more you owe me," he added as he got out.

I winced at the thought of his meter. "I guess I better work quickly then, hunh?" I closed the car door.

O'Neil nodded like a dog eyeballing a steak. We walked into Grady's past a dozen crowded tables and got in line. The owner Marsha Callahan looked like a delicate southern belle but was about as tough as a Navy Seal. Like she always told people, her mamma taught her how to cook and be a lady; her papa taught her how to take care of herself. A series of hard-knocks hadn't kept her from making Grady's—her life's dream—a reality. I had a world of respect for her and had even helped her make the dream come true, but only a little.

Cards as Meditation

I can't tell you much up front," I told O'Neil as we got in line, "but I'll tell you anything that won't risk a friend's life." I stepped up to the counter and waited for Marsha to finish taking payment from the customer in front of us.

"I don't like being kept in the dark, Case, you know that," he said, "especially not when someone like DiMarco is up to something in my city. He's a tough son-of-a-bitch … and smart, too."

"I know. Pains me to do it, but I don't really have much choice right now." Marsha turned to us.

Flashing a warm smile, I asked, "Hey, Marsha. How's the leg?"

"Stitches come out tomorrow," she replied with a faint southern drawl that slid over the ear like water over glass. She stood five-foot-seven, had a crew cut of Irish-red hair, and a light sprinkling of strawberry freckles to match. She smiled at us both with jade green eyes that sucked customers in, and she had a physique to make any top-notch Vegas stripper envious. The common rumor had it that pole dancing was how Marsha had been able to buy Grady's, but I knew the truth. I'd been there when it all came down.

"I guess the guy didn't get you too bad, eh?" I asked.

She beamed with pride. "Hell, no! Ten stitches in the calf is all, and it barely touched the muscle, just a centimeter or two deep into the flesh. It was my own fault really," she said, berating herself. "I didn't get my leg up high enough out the gate. It clipped his knife as it went by when I kicked him in the jaw. Broke his jaw, though, so it was worth it," she added with a wicked grin.

"Nice work!" I cheered, laughing. I'd been teaching her martial arts for a few years, and she was a hell of a good fighter.

"We'll have to practice higher kicks in our next session," she said, "but it'll be a week or so before I can work the leg. That bastard and his two friends are a whole lot worse off, though. None of them are even out of the hospital yet, and the ringleader's still in critical. Internal injuries. Apparently, I ruptured his spleen when I kicked him in the belly. I almost feel bad about that ... *almost*," she added with another grin. "Thanks for the training, Justin." A look of sincere gratitude drifted across her face.

"It's my pleasure. I like Grady's way too much to see its owner get clobbered or worse by weekend punks."

"Stupid kids picked the wrong bitch." She smiled sweetly at us. "Now what can I get you boys?"

"Two apple fritters and two sicklys, please."

Marsha raised an eyebrow. "You got stuff to work out, right?"

"You know me well, honey. The place is jammed this morning, so we're heading to the back for some privacy, if that's okay with you."

"Go right ahead. I'll bring your order back when it's ready."

O'Neil and I walked to the back of Grady's past two dozen patrons cramming Marsha's fantastic food down their necks while they drank her flawless coffee.

We walked past the restrooms to a door with a sign that read *PRIVATE—DO NOT ENTER*. I looked behind me to make sure no one could see inside, and then I opened the door. We both stepped in quickly, and I hit the lights as I walked by. The door automatically swung closed behind us.

The fluorescents came on, exposing a nice but used-looking gambling parlor. Technically, the place was unlicensed, but O'Neil was the sort of cop more worried about protecting and serving than upholding the letter of the law. He'd never gambled there, but he turned a blind eye to the place.

Straight ahead were four large poker tables, two blackjack tables and, set aside from the rest, a roulette wheel for the suckers. To the left stood a fully stocked bar, and Marsha had put in a burgundy sectional conversation pit on each side of the door. Both pits faced multiple flat-screen TVs that hung on the walls. In addition to the gaming, she ran a little off-track and sports betting. I walked behind the bar and pressed the play button on the stereo. "Blues for Salvador" by Santana came on.

"God she has good taste," I muttered as I closed my eyes to enjoy the first few riffs. Finally, I turned back to O'Neil who stood there and smiled at me, waiting patiently. He knew all about my love of music. "Have a seat," I offered. We both sat down and leaned back comfortably in the worn leather seats.

"DiMarco never stopped running drugs," I said bluntly.

"I often suspected, but nobody could pin anything on him. How do you know?"

I pulled uncomfortably at my ear. "That's one of the things I can't tell you yet."

"Shit," O'Neil muttered as he shook his head.

The door to the parlor opened, and Kenny Schmidt, not Marsha, came in with a tray laden with two gigantic, hot apple fritters as well as two cappuccinos in the biggest cups Marsha used. At seventeen, Kenny had the skinny, emaciated frame of a habitual drug-user but the glowing face of a clean kid. He wore a Grady's t-shirt, overly long, torn blue jeans rolled up at the ankles, and ratty, black Converse sneakers.

"Hey, Kenny, how are you?" I asked.

"Great, Case. Things are finally going pretty well."

"Staying out of trouble, Schmidt?" O'Neil asked in his gentle but stern cop voice.

Kenny had been busted by LAPD the year prior on a minor drug offense and done sixty days. The target of the bust was a fairly well known street dealer. Most of the kids caught up in it rolled the dealer over, but Kenny refused to, not out of loyalty to the dealer, but because he wouldn't make someone else pay for his mistakes.

That was the reason I liked him so much. He'd told the arresting officer he was willing to do his time. That's what had caught O'Neil's attention. Kenny was a decent kid who got caught up with the wrong people.

"Yes sir, Captain. I am … thanks to Case here … and Marsha."

"Good," O'Neil and I said in unison as I reached into my jacket.

"Glad to hear it," O'Neil added.

Kenny set a fritter and mug in front of both of us. O'Neil reached for his and took a sip, wincing slightly at how sweet it was, and gave me a dirty look. I'd been waiting all morning for that wince … and that look.

"Here, Kenny." I pulled out a thick wad of hundreds and peeled one out. I handed the crisp bill to him. "Keep the change. Go get some clothes, okay? And art supplies. Spend it on anything else and I'll kick your ass."

"Thanks!" Kenny blurted, shocked at the size of the tip. "Thanks a lot! I really appreciate it."

"Just stay clean, okay?" I said in as close to a fatherly tone as I'm capable. "That's the deal."

"You got it Case," he said a bit sheepishly. He turned around and walked out, closing the door behind him.

It was going on two months since Marsha and I had walked out of my martial arts studio and seen Kenny run into a dead-end alley nearby with four gang-bangers hot on his tail. Being who I am, I naturally went after them, with Marsha trailing. It wasn't a contest, and the two of us came out of the alley with sore knuckles wrapped around the arms of a badly injured Kenny.

The gang-bangers were carried out of the alley in plastic bags a few days later.

O'Neil sat there grinning at me.

"You old … err … *young* softie." He sipped his sickly-sweet cappuccino, and I saw a hint of familiar jealousy as he once again looked at my young face. Not in a bad way, merely the mild, friendly resentment between friends when one of them wins the lotto. It irked him that my appearance hadn't changed in twenty years. I'd told him years ago that I suffered from an ultra-rare disorder called Lazarus Syndrome that prevented my features from changing much over time.

I blushed with youthful cheeks and smiled a little while O'Neil ran fingers through a receding hairline, surely wondering how he could catch Lazarus Syndrome.

"Kenny needed a break," I said quietly. "Marsha and I were there at the right place and time to lend a hand. He's a good kid, and he's got real talent. I didn't want to see it get snuffed out by gutter-bound assholes before it had time to mature." I pointed to a painting on the wall behind O'Neil.

He looked over his shoulder at a four by six painting of a blossoming L.A. sunset with the sun partially obscured by the Pacific. Full of deep yellows, reds, and purples, it brightened the wall to the left of the monitors.

"Kenny?" O'Neil asked.

"Kenny."

"You're right," he said, impressed. "The kid's got a gift." He took another sip of cappuccino and added, "You're okay. You know that?"

"Yep," I replied in my cockiest tone.

He gave me a sullied look. It wasn't dirty, per se, but it wasn't clean either. "I still hate you," he added.

"Anyway," I continued, undaunted, "as I was saying, I can't tell you everything I know, but I know he's trafficking … no proof yet. What you do need to know is that it's probably big, *really* big. More importantly," and I paused for longer than necessary, looking apologetic, "you won't get to arrest him."

"*WHAT?*" O'Neil coughed, foam shooting up into his face and onto his pants. He continued coughing and wiping himself off as I suddenly got a deadly serious look, the old me peeking out from the back of my mind. It was the look my few friends had come to know meant there was no changing my mind and no alternative.

"I'm going to kill him, O'Neil. And I'm gonna make it *hurt*."

Captain O'Neil stopped coughing and stared at me for long seconds. "Justin, sometimes I think you forget I'm a cop. You can't tell me that shit, man."

"I haven't forgotten, but don't pretend to be Gandhi. You're a great cop, but you're not squeaky clean. Besides, you know damn well you won't be able to pin anything on me, and the fact is that it'll be a public service. You guys have nabbed him, what, three times over the years? Four? And he *always* walks." My voice sounded almost accusatory. "Am I wrong?"

"No," O'Neil said quietly, not a little embarrassed.

"Then stay out of my way on this one and ship the body to the morgue when you find it. Splash the papers with it. I'm going to give you maybe the biggest bust this city has ever seen, shut down whatever DiMarco is doing, and finally end a career that never should have gotten started in the first place." I stared hard into O'Neil's eyes, "Can you think of one good reason why I shouldn't take his head off?"

"Aside from that pesky little thing called *the Law*, no, I can't."

"Look, O'Neil, in a nutshell, whatever DiMarco is doing is huge, and it has to do with drugs … *lots* of them. Maybe it's T-Rex. The more I think of it, the more it makes sense. He sure as hell didn't go legit like he tells the papers. He found subtler ways to do more business. And apparently he did it completely under everyone's nose, including yours … and *mine*."

"You think VeniCorp is a front for all this?" O'Neil asked.

"Looks that way. You can run taps on anything you want wherever you want to get a feel for what's going on. Just make damn sure you don't let him know you're watching, okay? What I have to do requires that they don't see it coming for a while."

"Could any of our surveillance mess you up? Possibly expose you?" he asked with a bit of concern. We'd done this particular dance many times in the past.

"Not a chance. Don't worry about me," I assured him. "Just don't act on anything till I say go. *Please*."

"Okay, Case. You always seem to know what you're doing … at least so far. And I owe you … hell, the city owes you. I just hope you don't screw up, or it'll go bad for you one way or another. You get caught, and I won't be able to protect you, understand me? I can't help you if you fuck it up."

"Hey," I said, smiling and as cocky as ever, "it's *me*."

We both heard his phone vibrate. He pulled it out of his pocket and answered. "This is O'Neil."

I always got a kick out of when O'Neil put on his official "captain" voice. *He really is a good cop*, I thought to myself. I couldn't make out what the other person was saying, but he got a serious look on his face.

"Right." He nodded. "Got it. I'll be there in fifteen. Lock it down and don't let anyone in or out till I'm there, understand?" He closed his phone. "I have to go," he said, crisply. "Bank heist went south downtown … two cops and one asshole dead. Three more assholes are hiding in a What-A-Burger … with hostages, including a baby. You got a ride?" he asked as he got up. He took a few more gulps of his cappuccino, wincing again at the sweetness, wrapped the fritter in a napkin and headed for the door.

"Yeah, don't worry about me. I'll have Rachel pick me up when I'm done here. She and I are going to lunch later anyway. Go take care of business, and no prisoners, right? The only good asshole is a dead asshole … except for me, of course."

"Well, hard to argue with you on either count, but I have to follow the rules, Case, at least in public. It's my *job*, remember?" As O'Neil opened the door, I stopped him.

"Hey, O'Neil?"

"Yeah?"

I did my best imitation of Sergeant Phil Esterhaus from *Hill Street Blues* and said, "Let's be careful out there."

He sighed and shook his head. "I hate you, Case."

"I know," I said, laughing, "Be careful anyway, okay?"

"Right."

We smiled at each other like old comrades, and O'Neil walked out. The door closed slowly behind him, leaving me alone with my thoughts. I picked up my sickly and fritter, walked over to one of the poker tables, and sat down as the song "Shape of My Heart" by Sting started. The words "He deals the cards as a meditation …" sifted through the speakers.

"Hmmm … good idea," I said to the empty room. I reached into a pocket and pulled out a tarot deck wrapped in a scarf. I unwrapped the cards, shuffled quickly, and laid seven down from left to right. One by one, pausing at each card, I flipped them over and stared blankly at the picture before me. The door to the gambling parlor opened without me noticing, and Marsha watched me go through the exercise a few more times.

"I wouldn't have thought you were into tarot, Case," she said, but I was only peripherally aware of her. "They have tarot wherever it is you hail from?"

Marsha had asked me a few times over the years where I'd been born, but I always tap-danced around the answer. She'd finally given up and simply considered me a competent man of mystery with a heart of gold … although I know she suspected something was very different about me. She knew more about me than most.

Without responding I picked up the cards and laid down another seven.

"Case?" Marsha injected, raising her voice a bit.

"Hunh?" I looked up, surprised, finally realizing that Marsha had been watching me. "Oh … this," I said, smiling as I scooped up the cards. "I'm not, and we don't. I was just thinking about something, and this occupies the front side of my brain. I have no idea what they mean." I wrapped the cards up in the scarf again, slipped the bundle back in my coat, and stood up. "Marsha, can you do me a favor?"

"Anything, Case," she said. I knew she meant it.

"Never say 'anything' before you know what I want," I scolded her, but I had a smile. "Can you be closed Monday night? And let me have the keys?"

"You mean shut down the *back* of the place?"

"Yeah."

"Sure. I've been meaning to take a break, and the crew wants to hit Vegas for a night or two. I'll post it in the usual spots. You'll have the place to yourself." She hesitated a moment and then asked, "What's this all about?"

"I can't tell you anything other than that a friend is in trouble." She knew what that meant, because she had been a friend in trouble once. When my friends were in trouble, it usually wasn't for very long, and the people causing that trouble never fared well. She could attest to that personally. "Thanks, sweetie," I said. "I owe you one."

"We'll work it out in trade, mister," she said, smiling a bit wickedly. "Maybe I'll bring a friend." I knew she had always batted for both teams, frequently inviting me to join in, but I'd never taken her up on the offer. I'm old, and a bit old-fashioned, even for where I come from. There, people are particularly rigid, and I'd inherited quite a bit of that before my hasty departure.

"We'll have to see about that," I said, grinning. "Speaking of friends, how's Sasha?"

"Sasha? Didn't you hear? Fling of the month for both of us. She's dating a Hollywood exec these days."

"No kidding? You crazy girls. I could never keep up with two like you."

"I'm thinking you probably could if you put your mind to it." She leaned in half-seductively and half-jokingly. She ran her hands over my buttons, plucking at them gently. She raised a suggestive eyebrow.

"I'll get here around eleven," I said, holding my ground, "but I may not be done till one or two. I'll lock up when I leave. You won't even know I was here."

She disengaged, laughing at me with her eyes. "That sounds fine." She kissed me on the lips lightly and walked to the door, opening it. "Are you going to take very long back here?"

"A few more hours, and then Rachel will pick me up. We're having lunch."

"Do you need me to bring you back anything?" she asked.

"Nope. If I get hungry, I'll hit the fridge behind the bar."

"Make yourself at home, then. No one should be coming back here except Kenny and me until later tonight. And we'll leave you alone unless you call."

"Thanks, Marsha. You're the best."

"You say that to all the females in your life."

I considered that for a moment. "True," I said finally.

"Even that weird cougar of yours," she added.

"Also true," I added, grinning from ear to ear.

She closed the door, leaving me alone with my thoughts once again.

I pulled out my phone, selected Rachel's number and typed in "Grady's 11am back room please." I pressed SEND and reached into my jacket, pulling out the leather pouch and the pipe. I packed it, lit up, and pulled out the tarot deck again. Unwrapping it, I sat down and went through the motions of dealing. For two hours I robotically dealt cards while my brain continued to sort out the plan for learning everything else I needed to know about DiMarco's operation and, more importantly, how to bring an end to DiMarco himself.

Everybody's Not Dead

Rachel opened the door to the gambling parlor and peered in. I still sat at one of the poker tables, dealing tarot cards like a robot, my unlit pipe stuck in my mouth. She watched me go through the motions as she walked up behind the bar, poured herself a cola and walked back to the nearest of the two conversation pits. Reclining back and facing me, she straightened her slacks, crossed her legs, and waited patiently through another round of cards.

"*Ahem!*" she said loudly as I picked up the cards and prepared for another deal. My hand stopped in mid-motion, and I looked at her.

"Hello," I said cordially.

"You know, one of these days that's going to get you killed." She shook her head. "I will never understand how you can be so intuitive, observant, brilliant, and everything else and yet be so totally and completely *not there* when you're focused on something."

"Any complaints about my flaws should be forwarded to the manufacturer," I said calmly. "Besides, it would be impossible for me to get killed like that."

"And why is that?" she asked dryly.

"Because, I only ever never notice my friends. Everyone else shows up on radar." I grinned mischievously.

"What about that waiter?" she asked.

"I blame the mai-tais … and your dress," I added, winking at her. I looked at my watch. "Eleven-o-five …" I twisted my face into a scowl. "You're late," I chided.

"I'm exactly on time," she admonished, holding up her drink to emphasize that she'd been there a while. "You're an airhead."

I thought about that one for a few seconds. "Oh yeah," I finally conceded, unable to argue with her. I quickly wrapped my cards in the scarf and stood up from the table. Slipping the bundle into my coat, I walked over to the bar, leaned over it, and pressed the intercom. "Marsha?" I called.

After a pause, "Yeah?"

"Could you send back another sickly?"

"Sure thing."

I turned to Rachel. "You want a sickly?"

"You know those things make me barf. They're like, half sugar. Besides," she added holding up her drink and juggling it in front of me again, "I have something. *Remember?*"

"Oh yeah," I replied and chuckled slightly. I turned back to the pickup and pressed the button. "Thanks, Marsha."

"No problem, sweetie."

"Now that beverages are attended to," Rachel said slowly, "would you mind telling me where the hell you were for twenty-four hours?"

"Yep," I said as I walked over to the conversation pit. "I mean, yep, I'll tell you, not yep, I mind." I tapped my pipe out into a giant, multi-colored, seventies-vintage ashtray on the coffee table.

"I know what you meant," she said with mock irritation and covering a laugh. "Get on with it, would you?"

"Let me give you the *Reader's Digest* version—"

That's when Marsha walked in with my sickly-sweet. Rachel got a frustrated look on her face as Marsha winked at her, like they knew something I didn't. I wondered about it but didn't ask. Instead, I reached for my leather tobacco pouch.

"We should tell him," Marsha said.

"Tell him what?" Rachel gave an almost worried look.

"What we were just talking about."

"You don't mean—"

"I do." Marsha turned to me. "Justin, *you* have a conundrum." She walked up and put the sickly in front of me.

"Marsha ..." Rachel said, clearly uncomfortable.

I gave her a thoughtful look and finally said, "I know. That's why I came in here."

"Not *that* conundrum, you blockhead." She put her hands on her hips. "Another one."

I put the cards down. "Okay," I said slowly. "Tell me about my other conundrum."

"Well, when Rachel first came in, we had a chance to talk. She'd asked me about Sasha."

"To which you replied, 'Old hat,' I'm sure." I had no idea where this was going.

"That's right. Sasha and I are still friends, but she has her sights set on money."

"Which isn't what *you* want," I guessed.

"Right," she confirmed.

Rachel cut in, "And I asked her if I should be sorry or happy to hear it."

"Definitely happy." Marsha said, with a grin. She turned her eyes to me, searching for something. "And then I asked if *you* and Rachel had anything going."

My eyes got a little wider. "Uhhh ... what?" It takes a lot to blindside me, but I have to admit, she could have hit me with a thirty-pound haddock and I wouldn't have been more surprised.

Marsha clearly enjoyed my shock. "You know what she said?"

"Uhhh ..." was all I could manage.

"She said, and I quote, 'No, but lately things have been ... oh, I don't know ... evolving. I can't explain it.'" Marsha gave me a quirky smile. "And then she asked me if you and I were an item."

I looked at Rachel, and I could tell she was afraid of the answer—not Marsha's answer, but my reaction to all of this.

"I told her, 'No, sweetie, but only because he's never asked.'" Marsha got a concerned look on her face. "I think there's something you need to do, Justin, and you don't know what it is."

I looked at Rachel's face and saw the feelings there. I guess I'd known for a while. Hell, I was working through some strange feelings myself, but I really had no idea what to do.

"I … ummm …" I started.

"You're so cute when you're speechless," Marsha added. She pinched my cheek like I was a chubby five-year-old. "I just thought you should add that little bit of information to whatever it is you're working out." Marsha picked up my empty cup and walked towards the door. She gave Rachel a smile and said, "He's all yours." She leaned over and kissed Rachel on the lips, holding it a bit. I knew the two of them had enjoyed a fling the previous year—a girls' night out, a couple of pitchers of Margaritas, and then a cab-drive back to Marsha's because they were both too drunk to drive. It hadn't happened again—that I knew of, anyway—but I also knew both of them remembered it fondly. They'd become close friends over the years.

I could only sit there blinking at them. They parted and Rachel glanced at me, a funny sort of look on her face, like when someone spots a bewildered puppy with its head cocked sideways. She squeezed Marsha's shoulder and then changed the subject to give me an out. "I meant to ask you," she said to Marsha, "how's the leg?"

In that instant, my respect for Rachel went up a few more notches, which is saying something. She'd taken Marsha's ploy in stride, let the message get across, and then given me an out so I didn't feel like my nuts were in a vice. I added that little fact to the long list of reasons Rachel is my favorite human.

"Stitches come out tomorrow," Marsha replied as if nothing had happened.

"Nice!" Rachel cheered. "What about the other guys?"

"Still in the hospital, one in critical," Marsha said with pride.

I finally came back to my senses. "She might be better than you are, Rachel," I added quietly as I lit the pipe and took a few puffs. I gave Rachel a wink.

"*What?*" Rachel blurted, her pride clearly stinging. Marsha remained silent, but a wicked smile lit up her face. "We'll just have to see about that!" she challenged. "I smell a showdown." She sent a steely, almost predatory look at Marsha. "When did the doctor say you could train again?"

"A week," Marsha replied, grinning confidently, "maybe less, but I'll need a week to get back in shape after that if we're going to scrap. That means training four or five nights straight, Justin. You up for it?"

"If I'm not working, sure. To be fair, you both should be training together." I'd actually baited Rachel deliberately, knowing this was exactly where it would lead. The people I was dealing with all-too-frequently went after friends and family, and I wanted to make sure that both of them were as lethal as I could make them.

"Head-pads, full contact," Rachel said boldly.

"You're on!" Marsha replied. "And you ref, Justin."

"Nope." I rejected the suggestion seriously as I sipped my cappuccino. "No ref. This is the real deal. All I'll be doing is counting points. You both go all out, and may the best woman win … no broken bones, though. Okay? I need you both in one piece. Well, one piece and one piece," I added awkwardly, pointing to both of them, "not both of you attached."

They looked at me a little wide-eyed at the suggestion, then they stared at each other with slightly narrow eyes, sizing each other up like the predators I'd been training them to be.

"Deal!" they said simultaneously. It warmed my heart … among other things. I couldn't help but think to myself that the whole thing was kind of … *hot.* I almost felt guilty about it … almost.

"I have to get back to my customers," Marsha said, heading for the door.

"Did you park in the back, Rachel?" I asked.

"Don't I always?" she replied.

"Good girl," I nodded to Rachel. "We'll go out the back, Marsha," I called as she opened the door.

"Take care … *both* of you," Marsha said and walked out.

I sipped my cappuccino thoughtfully and then put the pipe back in my mouth. Rachel watched my face for a few moments, seeing the gears turning. She'd worked with me long enough to know when a plan was shaping up in my head.

There was, a dangerous one that would put both magnificent women in considerable danger, but I was increasingly certain they could both handle it. I came back to the moment and looked at Rachel.

"Okay. So where did I leave off?" I asked her.

"You hadn't started, dammit."

"Right." So I told her about the limo and Natalia. Then I mentioned what Natalia had said about Xen being dead.

"WHAT?" Rachel cried. "Xen's dead?" She looked horrified.

"No, no, no," I said, holding up my hands. "It's okay. Xen's alive," I added quickly.

"Alive?" Rachel's voice filled with joy. "But you said—"

"She *thinks* he's dead. So does everyone else, and we have to keep it that way, okay?"

"Of course," she assured me.

"I got an email from him. *After* the Natalia said they found his remains in that vat. Xen's no dummy. Whatever happened, he saw it coming. I'm betting he faked the whole thing himself to keep from getting killed. I may just give him my job. It seems I still have a best friend. Well, best guy friend," I corrected. "You're my best friend," I added, winking at her.

I swear she almost blushed.

"Let's go get some lunch," I said, interrupting what little of the story I'd started. I got up and walked towards the back door.

"Are you serious?" Rachel asked in disbelief, but she followed along.

"Yeah. I'm hungry." I opened the back door onto an alley where she'd parked her Porsche up against the wall.

"But what happened next? Damn it!" she fumed. I'm *always* doing this to her.

"I'm too hungry to finish," I said, smiling. I got a thoughtful look. "Chinese or burgers?"

"Bastard," she said quietly, convinced that I wouldn't continue until I got food in my stomach.

"Do you read Russian?" I asked as we got into the car.

"No, only French, Spanish, and Latin," she replied with a just a trace of venom. "I'm still mad at you." She hated when I left her hanging. I had what she considered a filthy habit of dragging stories out simply for the tease value. She called it *taleus interruptus*, and she considered it to be almost as bad as the coitus kind, with a significantly lower possibility of lung cancer.

"Don't worry, I'm gonna keep talking while we're in the car, I promise. But before we get lunch, I need to see a busker downtown."

"What the hell is a busker?" she asked.

"Street musician." I gave her a look like she should already know that sort of thing. Then I winked at her and smiled. "In this case a Russian busker … Head for the six-hundred block of South Fairfax. Got a piece of paper and a pen in here?" I asked.

"You don't have one in your coat? You have everything else in there." She smiled sarcastically.

"I had an accident," I mumbled a bit sullenly. The pen and paper had been in my front coat pocket rather than one of the inner ones when I hit the swimming pool. Believe me, it makes a difference. Both my $200 fountain pen and the notebook became … inoperable.

"In my pocketbook," she said finally, enjoying a rare victory as she started up the car. As I turned my body to grab her purse, she revved the engine and dropped the clutch, squealing down the alley. My head bounced off the headrest as I struggled to get my hand on the pocketbook.

Without looking at me she said smugly, "You had that coming, you know."

"Yes, I did." I nodded, and we both laughed. I finally got my hand on the bag, opened it, sifted through the short list of items within—including a small Berretta—and easily came up with a small spiral notebook and a ballpoint. *Rachel always keeps a tidy purse*, I thought. I flipped open the notebook and scrawled some Cyrillic characters on it. I held it up so she could see.

Церковь дом бога

"What does it say?" she asked.

"I don't know … that's why we're going to see the busker."

"Where did you see it?"

"I was just getting to that."

So I told her everything that had happened right up until after Xen's house got remodeled by the Italians and I texted her.

"Why didn't you call me?" she asked as she pulled away from a stoplight in downtown L.A.

"Didn't need to. I knew we'd have this conversation eventually, and as long as you knew I was safe, you wouldn't worry."

"That's something, at least … jerk," she added and hit my thigh, but she had a smile on her face. She nodded in the direction of the street ahead of us. "There's six-hundred south."

I scanned the block quickly, looking for someone. "Turn right here," I said. She did as instructed, and we drove slowly down the block as I continued searching.

"Pull in wherever you can," I suggested, seeing that the metered spots along the street were all full.

"Okay." She turned quickly into a pay lot.

"C'mon," I said as she pulled into the closest spot. We got out and headed for the pay-board. "The guy's name is Yvgenny Gershovich." We stepped up to the pay-board, and I slid a folded ten-dollar-bill into the slot for our parking spot. "You'll like him," I added with a broad smile. "He gives me all kinds of shit."

"Really?" she asked, her face brightening into an eager smile. She was clearly interested in meeting anyone who gave me a taste of my own medicine.

Second Hand Lion

"Over there." I pointed at a group of about ten people standing around something in front of a Russian teahouse. The sound of a violin drifted over us, and I quickly identified the song as the opening to *Fiddler on the Roof.*

We crossed the street, pausing briefly as a black Audi with opaque black windows passed by. It drove by a bit too slowly, as if someone was scoping us out, so I looked for the plate number as it went by. It had a temp tag in the back window, barely visible through the tinted glass. I could make out a big white three—March expiration—but the rest of the tag was too small for me to read. The car did have one small patch of red paint on the lower left-hand portion of the front bumper. That was something, at least.

We stepped up onto the curb and walked directly up to a crowd gathered around an old man sitting in a blue, nylon camp chair. He was the one playing the violin as he smoked a long Meerschaums pipe carved in the shape of a lion's head. He'd placed an old, ragged hat on the ground in front of him that had a sizable pile of money in it, mostly ones, but with a few fives and tens scattered throughout.

"That's him … with the violin," I said. "He plays beautifully, but he can never get his gerunds right."

Rachel stepped closer and moved to the side of the crowd to get a better look at him. Yvgenny looked to be around sixty with a thick shock of long, wild, white and gray hair. A thick, scraggly beard with the same coloring covered his face, and his weathered, grizzly features looked like they'd seen decades of harsh sun. He was burly, like a wrestler, and I knew none of it had turned to fat. His eyes were closed as he played. The old-timer wore patched blue jeans that bagged around ancient, tan work-boots. He also had on a dingy gray t-shirt mostly covered by a faded and threadbare blue work shirt that had the sleeves rolled up on his thick, muscular forearms. His arms were covered an assortment of blue-black tattoos, most of them utilizing Cyrillic characters on, in, or around them.

We all stood enthralled as the he effortlessly made his violin sing to us. Few people get to hear a violinist of such talent, and the emotion he poured into the instrument almost brought tears to my eyes. I actually saw a little moisture welling in the corners of Rachel's. Yvgenny brought the song to a close with a flourish of the bow and bowed deeply from his chair as everyone applauded and cheered.

"Thank you all, my friends," he said in a deep, scratchy voice, thick with the sounds of Russia. "You honoring me with your accolades." The grizzled face looked up and, scanning the crowd, spotted me. He smiled with all the joviality of Santa Claus as I winked at him. "And with that, I must ending show. These old bones are weak, and I am seeming tired. Thank you." He bowed his head graciously.

The crowd started to disperse, most of them dropping a one or five-dollar-bill into the now overflowing hat. When the last of them walked away, he bent over, placed his violin into an open case, and then closed and latched it. He picked up the hat, scooping up the bills that were still on the concrete.

"Not a bad morning," he muttered, talking mostly to himself.

"You sure can work that Stradivarius," I offered. "I never tire of listening to you, old man."

Yvgenny mashed the bills into the hat and pulled the hat tightly over his head. His wiry hair stuck out from underneath it, and the wad of cash made the hat ride too high on his skull, making him look a bit ridiculous. Out of the corner of my eye I saw Rachel cover her mouth to keep from laughing and, after a few seconds of momentous struggle, managed to force herself to look more serious.

"Ahh … Justin Case. Such a nice boy. Do you having on your rubber underpants?"

"No, Yvgenny," I replied with an understanding tone. "No underpants at all, in fact," I added, chuckling.

Rachel blurted out a laugh she simply couldn't hold back any more.

"Pity. Should you wet yourself as usual, everyone will be knowing it." Yvgenny chuckled. "Embarrassing, no?" he added, laughing even harder. My old friend finally noticed that Rachel had not left with the rest of the crowd and deduced that she was with me. He looked her up and down, puffing on his pipe and leering like a dirty old man not ashamed to admit it. I knew with perfect certainty that he was just too old and too ornery to care. "And who is being this delightful creature with you? Is she your baby-sitting today?" Rachel got a sparkle in her eye, and I could tell she liked Yvgenny already.

"Yvgenny, this is Rachel Devereaux." I turned to Rachel and said, "Rachel, may I present one Yvgenny Gershovich."

She offered her hand. The old man clasped her hand and drew it to his face. He inhaled deeply, sniffing her perfume as he kissed her knuckles lightly. He held the kiss perhaps a tad bit too long to be entirely gentlemanly and then sighed as he released her hand.

"You are having lovely perfume, miss. It is pleasing me to meeting you."

"The pleasure is all mine, Mister Gershovich," she said and bowed her head slightly.

"Call me Yvgenny. It is also pleasing me if you do."

"Thank you. I like anyone who can dish grief out to Justin as good as he dishes it to others."

"I'm having boots older than this child, Miss Devereaux. I should putting him over my knee and spanking him. Why do you consorting with such an *infant*?"

She smiled and looked me up and down like she was inspecting a side of beef. "I'm not sure, Yvgenny. That's a damn good question."

"So, boy," he asked, taking his eyes off Rachel. "What is bringing you to see me this time? It's been quite a while."

I pulled out the piece of paper I had scrawled the Cyrillic characters on and handed it to him. "What's it say?"

"Hmmm …" Yvgenny looked at it briefly, clearly recognizing the words. He handed the sheet back to me.

"In tourist translating book it is saying *Church is the house of God.*" Yvgenny let out a low, rumbling almost evil laugh.

"What does it say in *your* book, Yvgenny?" I asked pointedly.

"Heh … it says Prison is the house of thieves."

"Are you sure?"

The old man turned to Rachel with a look of utter disbelief on his face. "He doubts me, Miss Rachel. Such a foolish boy," he added, shaking his head. Yvgenny turned back to me, unbuttoning the top two buttons of his work shirt. His eyes never left mine. He reached up with both hands and pulled down the collar of his t-shirt, exposing the very same Cyrillic characters tattooed on his chest in a curve over the top of three castle towers. "I was having mine when I was fourteen years old in Moscow. My first, and in the organization, one is never forgetting. We are all having them, Justin … well, most."

"Does anyone ever leave the mob?" I asked, fairly certain of the answer.

"No. No one does … at least not breathing. Not even poor old men playing music on street."

I reached into my pocket and pulled out the thick stack of hundreds I'd separated from what Victor had given me in the limousine. I folded it and slid it into Yvgenny's front shirt pocket. "For the kids. Compliments of SolCon."

"You're a good boy, Justin…." and then Yvgenny smiled wickedly as he added, "No matter what people saying about you!" Yvgenny and Rachel laughed heartily at my expense while I smiled as tiredly as I could. Yvgenny finally stopped laughing and looked first at me then Rachel. "Come, you are having lunch here, no?"

"Well, we were thinking about Chinese or burgers," I said.

"You insult me!" Yvgenny accused.

"*He* was thinking about Chinese or burgers," Rachel corrected. "I've never had Russian cuisine before."

"Please. Come. It is being on me," he said, patting the wad of money in his shirt. "I insist. I am recommending borscht."

"Yvgenny, you know I can't stand that shit."

"I am knowing this, Justin. You should still eat it. You are scrawny child. It will making you grow up big and strong. Just like me," He tapped his chest with bravado. "*Please*," he added sincerely.

"*We'd* be delighted," Rachel said, grabbing my arm and pulling me towards the front door of the teahouse.

"Alright, Yvgenny," I said, realizing I was out-manned and out-gunned. "Thank you. I'm not having the borscht, though."

"Suit yourself … *weakling*," Yvgenny smiled as he bent over and grabbed his Stradivarius. He stood up, towering over Rachel. He was well over six feet tall and built like a bear. Despite the baggy clothes hanging on him, it was clear that his sixty years hadn't seemed to weaken him much, if at all. Yvgenny grabbed his camp chair, folded it and walked into the teahouse with us close behind.

The interior was done in dark wood and separated into three different sections. The right side had been dedicated to a teahouse with several small café tables, a long counter, some tall copper water heaters with levered spigots, and a high row of shelves with endless boxes, bags and jars of different teas. A young, pretty girl of maybe nineteen or twenty, with distinct Eastern Bloc features stood behind the counter, reading a book with Cyrillic characters on the spine. Several patrons sat at the café tables, drinking tea, chatting, or reading.

The left side of the place had a series of very comfortable looking easy chairs done in a clearly European style. Along that wall were jars and jars of different tobaccos. Old books, predominantly classics from around the world, lay scattered about on shelves and a few end tables. There were two older men, also with Eastern Bloc features, sitting in chairs in the far corner, talking quietly enough to not be heard by anyone else.

"How is business, *vnoochka*?" Yvgenny asked of the girl behind the counter. She looked up and smiled.

"Quiet, grandpa," she said in perfect English.

Yvgenny said something is Russian.

"Still getting straight *A*'s," she replied. "Don't worry *dedushka*. Medical school is a shoe-in."

"You make us *proud*, Alisa. Your father would be bursting with joy if he was here."

"Thank you, *dedushka*," she said and smiled.

Yvgenny motioned to Rachel and me. "Alisa, Justin you know. This beautiful creature is being Rachel Devereaux."

"Hello Rachel," Alisa said extending her hand. Rachel and Alisa shook hands. Alisa turned to me with a more-than-bright smile and added with a bit more enthusiasm than necessary, "Hi Justin!" Nobody missed the crush Alisa clearly had on me.

Yvgenny frowned slightly.

"Hey, Alisa. It's good to see you again," I said quietly.

"Come, let us going to eat," Yvgenny interrupted, looking suspiciously at me. I shrugged and looked as innocent as it's possible for me to look … which, admittedly, isn't that much.

"It was nice meeting you, Rachel," Alisa said with a bit of disappointment in her voice as her grandfather walked towards the back of the house.

"It was nice meeting you, too, Alisa," Rachel said warmly. "Good luck in school."

"Luck is not a factor," Alisa said confidently. "Bye, Justin!" she added cheerily.

"We'll see you around, Alisa," I said, smiling as I turned and followed Yvgenny. Rachel fell in step next to me as we walked towards the back portion of the teahouse.

Yvgenny pulled aside thick curtains hanging in the doorway to expose a nicely decorated dining area with eight tables in it. Six of them were occupied with couples of varying ages. At the back of the room ran a long counter separating us from kitchen. A single waitress, who appeared to be about the same age and appearance as Alisa, walked back into the kitchen. On the right-hand side of the room stretched a well-used flight of stairs going up to what I knew was a patio.

"Galina," Yvgenny called to the retreating waitress.

"Yes, *dedushka*?" the girl replied as she stopped and turned.

"We will being upstairs, please."

"*Be*, grandpa. 'We will *be* upstairs,'" the girl corrected, smiling as she greeted us.

"Oh. Da. We will *be* upstairs," Yvgenny repeated, bowing his head slightly to thank her. "Please come up when you have time. We will having lunch." Galina shook her head, smiling at yet another in an endless line of gerund infractions, but she said nothing.

We walked up the stairs and stepped out into a beautiful, open patio with six tables surrounded by a garden of different flowering plants and shade trees, including several bearing fruit. A small fountain gurgled and splashed in the middle of the patio, and string lighting surrounded the entire area. To the left of the patio, a door broke up the wall of the next building over that I knew was the only entrance to Yvgenny's home. The back of the patio dropped away to the alley, and the right-hand side opened up onto a parking lot below.

"Please, pick a table. Galina will be up shortly to taking your order, and I will not disturb you. I have my crosswords to do."

"Thanks, Yvgenny. Rachel and I have some stuff to talk about." I headed to the far back corner table under a full, blossoming orange tree, pulling Rachel along as I walked. Yvgenny walked over to the door of his home, pulled out an overflowing key ring, selected a key, and unlocked the steel door.

"Oh … and Justin," Yvgenny called back.

"Yeah?"

Smiling, he said, "If you ever touching one of my granddaughters, I'll snap your neck."

"I know," I said between laughs. "Don't worry."

"Good boy," Yvgenny added as he stepped through the door and closed it behind him. We were alone again and sat down in the shade. I habitually took the chair in the corner so I could see the entrance to the patio.

"You were wrong," Rachel said.

"About what?" I asked with a confused look on my face. I didn't think I'd made any slip-ups recently … not since the pen and paper fiasco, anyway.

"I don't like him …" she said, which caught me by surprise. "I *love* him!" she almost shouted. "Where on Earth did you find that man?"

"Yvgenny and I sort of … found each other … a long time ago," I said fondly as I picked up one of the menus propped between a flower vase and condiments in the middle of the table.

"Will he get in trouble for giving us lunch?" Genuine concern traced its way across her delicate features.

"Trouble? You kidding? He's not the manager here. He owns the place. He pretty much owns this block."

"But the music, the money …" she said slightly confused.

"He's a busker because he enjoys it. He dabbles in quite a few enterprises. He's actually quite the philanthropist. He also runs a home for wayward kids north of here, and that's where the money goes."

"What an interesting man," she said. "He looked like he could still hold his own, despite his age."

"Don't ever underestimate him," I said seriously. "He'd give me a run for my money if he got one of those paws on me. He's been kicking the shit out of people for a *long* time."

"Really? What did he do for the Russian mob?"

"Kicked the shit out of people … and he was *really* good at it."

The door we had come through opened, and Galina walked up carrying a tray with two glasses of water on it.

"Hi, Justin. Long time no see," Galina said.

"Galina. It's been what? Two years?" I asked.

"A little less. Grandpa still giving you a hard time?"

"With a vengeance!" I admitted, smiling. "Galina, this is Rachel Devereaux. Rachel … Galina Gershovich, another one of Yvgenny's granddaughters."

"Hello Galina," Rachel said.

"Miss Devereaux," Galina said nodding her head. "So what can I get for you two?" she asked hurriedly. "I've got a full house downstairs."

"We'll both have the Stroganoff, Galina," I said and turned to Rachel. "It really is fantastic. You'll love it, I promise."

"Sounds good to me," she said hungrily. "I'm famished."

"Thanks, Galina. And could we get a couple of sweet teas?"

"Sure thing." Galina walked away and left through the door down to the dining room.

"So, did Natalia come knocking at your door in the middle of the night?" Rachel asked, not being able to bear waiting any longer for the rest of the story.

"Hmmm?" I asked, confused by the absentee segue. After a second I realized what she was talking about. "Oh, yeah, the rest of the story."

She looked like she wanted to slap me.

I tried to focus and cleared my throat. "Actually, no. We both got a full night of sleep."

Yvgenny's apartment door opened.

"Justin, I need to speaking with you," Yvgenny said very seriously from the opened door. He had a crossword book in his hand, and horn-rimmed glasses perched on the end of his nose. "It is important. It is *business.* Is she knowing about business?" He nodded, indicating Rachel.

"Rachel and I have no secrets, Yvgenny," I said honestly. "Well, not many, anyway. I don't know who she lost her virginity to, for example, and I still have a few secrets I haven't shared with her."

She gave me a dirty look.

"Good. Secrets are being such a terrible thing." Yvgenny walked up and sat down next to me, also with his back to the wall.

"Bennie DiMarco is just asking me to kill you," Yvgenny said abruptly. "He has putting contract out on your life."

I spoke slowly as I asked, "Did you take the job?"

Rachel looked at me sideways, clearly concerned that I sounded a bit too serious for her comfort. She shifted in her seat uncomfortably and placed her hand on her purse. I spotted her fingering the pistol she kept in there.

"No need to being nervous, Miss Devereaux," Yvgenny said, chuckling. He looked at me and grinned like the Devil himself. "DiMarco was not having enough money!" Yvgenny guffawed, and I laughed with him.

Rachel looked at us like we were both crazy.

"Besides, I could never kill my friend," he added more seriously. "Who else could I abusing so ruthlessly, no?"

Yvgenny stopped laughing and looked at me like a concerned father. "Seriously, Justin. Being careful. I know who has taking the contract, and he is not one to be trifled with."

"Anyone I know?"

"No. He is only recently coming to America, the land of opportunity." Yvgenny grasped me by the shoulder in a very concerned way. "This one is rogue, though. Not to following the code of thieves. Also, Justin ... he is being most unpleasant, even by *our* standards," Yvgenny referred to the brutal methods of the Russian mob. "Do not getting caught with trousers down. Understanding me, *young* man?"

"Yeah, Yvgenny. Thanks. Got a description?"

"He is in thirties. Shorter than you, and thicker. Short, black hair and goatee like beatnik."

"That'll help. Thanks again, Yvgenny. I owe you one."

"No. It is still I who is owing you." Yvgenny looked at me fondly as he stood up. "Now, I will let you get to your lunch." He walked to the opposite corner of the patio and sat down at the table closest to the door leading downstairs. "Did Galina come to take your order?" he called back to us.

"Yep."

"Justin?" His eyes crinkled mischievously.

"Yes, Yvgenny?"

"Did you order your baby's bottle of mother's milk with nipple on it?" Yvgenny laughed heartily, and Rachel laughed right along with him.

"No, Yvgenny," I answered dryly. "I've been trying to cut down."

"I'm sure," he said with a grin before returning to his crossword puzzle.

"So, you were saying that both of you got a full night's sleep?" Rachel prompted, sounding a bit suspicious. I know she wanted me to get on with the story, and there was the matter of a beautiful European woman spending the night in my house. She took a sip of the sweet tea Galina had set down on the table only moments before.

"Right," I agreed. "*Nothing* happened between us. Then I did some research into SolCon before she got up … in one of the *spare* bedrooms. When she did get up, I made her breakfast."

"What happened to Xen's house?" she asked. "Did it burn down?"

"No, they saved it. I heard the cops and fire engines show up just as we went to bed. His house was still there in the morning, so they obviously got there in time." I grabbed my own glass of sweet-tea, added six packets of sugar, stirred it, and leaned back in my chair. "Xen has been talking about remodeling the kitchen for a few months anyway. Now the insurance money will cover it," I said brightly, taking a sip.

"And the demolished entry way? Was he planning on remodeling that, too?" she asked a bit condescendingly.

I sobered a bit. "Well, no, actually. He hadn't mentioned that." My tone bordered on embarrassed, but I kept it from crossing over the line. I tried to keep a straight face for a few seconds, but I finally lost it and started laughing. "Oh my god, Rachel, it was so jacked up. Xen is going to kill me when he sees me." I kept laughing.

"And don't forget the charred bodies and wonderful smell they must have left."

"Eh ... abatement services are dime-a-dozen in this town." I dismissed the notion with the wave of my hand. "And *also* paid for by insurance, I might add."

Rachel rolled her eyes at me. "So what happened, handyman? Tell me everything."

I reached into my jacket and pulled out my pipe and tobacco. I stuffed the pipe and lit it with a lighter from another pocket. Placing the pouch and lighter on the table, I took a deep breath and leaned back thoughtfully.

"Well, let me see...." I said and started into the story.

Sunshine and Debts

I got as far as going fishing with Pyotr's tracking devices when Galina set plates of beef Stroganoff in front of us, interrupting my story with a smile. "I'm sorry it took so long," she said apologetically, "but we're really busy downstairs." Yvgenny stood behind her, casting a concerned look at me.

"Don't worry about it, Galina. We're in no hurry," I said and smiled. "When you get a chance, though, could you bring us two glasses of the house burgundy?"

"It may be a bit. I'm really in the weeds," the young girl said, wiping a bead of sweat from her forehead.

"Don't worry, Galina," Yvgenny said from behind her. "I'll get it. I have something I am needing to talk to Justin about. Go on." Yvgenny placed a caring hand on his granddaughter's shoulder and guided her towards the door. "Have your mother work the front of the house and get your cousin to helping you with those who are eating."

"Yes, *dedushka*," she said with relief. "Thank you."

"That's a good girl. Off with you!" Yvgenny ordered, smiling compassionately. Galina hurried towards the door to the lower level.

"Eat up, my friends. I will returning with bottle of our best burgundy. We have something to discuss."

I cast a questioning look his way.

"Soon, Justin. I will be back momentarily. Please. Eat." And with that, Yvgenny followed Galina out.

"What was that all about?" Rachel asked when the door closed behind him.

"I don't know," I said perplexed. "But he's got something on his mind." I looked down hungrily at the meal before me. "But who am I to disobey orders?" I picked up a starched linen napkin, opened it with a flourish, and placed it in my lap.

"You don't take orders," she said. She set her own napkin in place and inhaled deeply. "This smells wonderful."

"Yvgenny's daughter does most of the cooking ... at least she used to. It's all her recipes, anyway. Best Russian food in the city, if you ask me."

"And you wanted to eat burgers?" she accused me. "Foolish boy!" she said in her best impression of Yvgenny. We both laughed and dug into the thick, rich sauce and chunks of beef poured over perfectly cooked egg-noodles.

"Oh my god! This is fantastic!" she squealed around a mouthful. I simply kept eating, making an occasional yummy sound. We'd finished about a quarter of our meals when Yvgenny reappeared. He carried three glasses in one hand and a dusty, opened bottle of wine in the other. He stepped up to the table, set the glasses down and filled each about halfway. I caught the label out of the corner of my eye.

"Yvgenny, that's a Pétrus?"

"What's a Pétrus?" Rachel asked.

"They're like, I don't know, a thousand dollars a pop, or something," I said, truly impressed Yvgenny had brought up something special.

"Closer being to three, actually," Yvgenny said, smiling, "but naming price of bottle is insult to vintage." He winked. "Simply drinking and enjoying, my friends." Yvgenny shifted his chair to rest between us and filled our glasses before sitting down. He picked up his glass and held it up to toast.

We picked up our own glasses and touched them together with a pleasant ring of fine crystal.

"To friends old and new, yes?" Yvgenny said.

"*Budem*," I added sincerely, which translates roughly as *stay healthy*.

"*Budem*," Yvgenny said rather seriously.

All three of us swirled the wine in our glasses a bit and sampled the bouquet. The fragrance was magnificent. We each took a sip and savored the spectacular vintage. We returned the glasses to the table, and Rachel and I dug back into our Stroganoff.

Yvgenny pulled his pipe out from a pocket. "Will this ruining your meal, Miss Rachel?" he asked, holding up the pipe.

"Not at all. I've always liked the smell of Justin's."

"You are rare woman. Were I younger man, I would stealing you away from this child." He chuckled while Rachel blushed slightly. "Please, finishing your meals, and then we will talk." Yvgenny opened my pouch of tobacco, stuffed his pipe, and lit it with an ancient Zippo lighter he produced from the same pocket the pipe came from. He stared at me, taking a series of long, thoughtful puffs while we ate.

We finished up our Stroganoff and wine, perhaps a bit more quickly than we otherwise would have were we not curious about what Yvgenny wanted to say. We leaned back in our chairs and looked at the old man expectantly. Yvgenny took a deep breath to take up his story when the door to the stairs opened and Galina walked up to us.

"Ah, Galina, your timing is perfect," he said smiling wickedly. "Please clearing plates." He looked at us with a mischievous grin, enjoying the opportunity to draw out what he had to say.

"Yes, *dedushka*." Galina picked up the plates and silverware and then walked out.

"You enjoy doing that almost as much as Justin does, don't you?" Rachel knew *taleus interruptus* when she saw it, and Yvgenny wasn't even trying to hide it.

"I couldn't possibly knowing what you refer to, Miss Rachel," he said chuckling a bit. But the smile in his eyes told her he knew exactly what he was doing.

I leaned over to her. "Where do you think I learned it?" I whispered in her ear.

After tapping his pipe out into the soil under the tree next to him, Yvgenny repacked it and lit it up, staring at me once again.

"Forgiving me, Justin, but I couldn't help overhearing several things. Of Natalia and SolCon? And *Pyotr.*"

"Yes," I said slowly. Yvgenny shook his head. "How much did you overhear?"

"Not much, just names, but those names carry significant weight within the circles I travel. What have you getting yourself into, boy?"

"That's what I'm trying to figure out," I said, scratching the back of my head.

"Is it possible you were, perhaps, being in limousine two nights ago? And perhaps it was parked in less-than-traditional location. Say, for example, someone's living room?"

"You heard about that, hunh?" I smiled knowingly and with not a little pride. I truly enjoy the mayhem that is a natural result of my work, although I'd never say so out loud.

Yvgenny guffawed. "Justin, there isn't gangster or cop in city who hasn't hear of that. Seven dead, including one *innocent* Russian driver and six Italian soldiers, three of them burned to death. You are dangerous man."

I smiled evilly. "You already knew that."

"*Da*," Yvgenny conceded. Over the years, the two of us had inflicted a delightful amount of damage upon both the suspecting and unsuspecting scum of Los Angeles … every one of them more than having it coming to them. "Fortunately for you, there is no one but you and me knowing that Natalia and Victor were not alone in limo. Those who knew are now dead."

"You wouldn't be obliged to tell anyone, would you?" I asked slowly.

"I am not telling what no one is asking. And no one will ask tired old street musician, especially not without reason. I am being far from such things for years … thankfully. I am … how do they say … second-hand lion." Yvgenny leaned over to Rachel as if to tell her a secret, but his voice didn't lower as he added with pride, "They used to call me *unbreakable*."

"You're still the best of them, Yvgenny," I said sincerely, raising a glass of wine. "Old school."

Yvgenny raised his own glass, and we drained them. "If it is pleasing you, Justin, continue with story."

So I did while Rachel finished off the last of her wine. I got to the point where Natalia and I were about to go into her house when Rachel asked, "Do you really think DiMarco was after Natalia and Xen because of gambling?"

"Unlikely. Xen is a shitty card player. *You* could beat him," I said smiling at Rachel, who returned in kind by sticking her tongue out at me. "But I doubt he would ever get in the hole, and certainly not to the tune of three-hundred, let alone three-hundred-*thousand* dollars."

"So why were the Italians trying to kill Natalia?" she asked turning serious. "And why would the Russians let them? Pyotr clearly wanted her dead. Sounds to me like he was using the Italians to do his dirty work for him."

"Yep." I smiled. "I have a pretty good idea you're right, but I can't pin anything down yet. Pyotr said Xen was working on something that was a threat to Gino, although, how dry-cleaning could be a threat to anyone is beyond me. This Pyotr is a smart customer, though. He's a real chess-player by the feel of it. It all has to do with chemicals … and smuggling. Yvgenny?" I cast a questioning look to my old friend, hoping that he knew or had heard something that would help make sense of it all.

"This I am not knowing, but there is something important I do know."

"What's that?"

"Natalia is Interpol." Yvgenny waited for a surprised look on my face but was disappointed.

"No she's not," I said calmly.

"She is. I am having ways to knowing these things."

"She *was* Interpol."

"What do you mean?" Rachel and Yvgenny both asked simultaneously.

"I was just getting to that." I paused, contemplating what I should and shouldn't say. With Yvgenny there, I didn't have much choice, but with or without him, it was better to go the safe route. "Natalia's dead."

"Dead?"

"Yeah. In the surf." I told them about the house, the chase, and the pier. I wrapped up with Bennie, the plane, and the swimming pool.

"You pretty much know the rest," I said, pouring the last few drops of the second bottle of wine into my glass.

"Poor Natalia," Rachel said.

"My fault, too. She must have hit her head and gotten knocked unconscious. I thought I had it all worked out." I leaned back and sadness flickered across my face. In my line of work people die, but I'd never gotten used to when people I was responsible for didn't make it. I hope I never do. The old me took it as a matter of pride, and the new me simply feels gutshot by it.

Yvgenny spoke up. "You were doing what you could, Justin. The woman chose a dangerous profession, no? And going after her laptop was reckless. Had it not being for you, she would have certainly been killed the night before."

"I still feel responsible," I said sincerely, "but you're right."

"You are honorable man." Yvgenny placed his hand on my arm.

"Thanks."

"So, what happens next?" Rachel asked with a mix of concern and confusion.

"A little bit of good-old-fashioned private detective work to start with. Then I play cards with an old friend," I said slowly.

"Xen?" Rachel asked.

"Xen. And wait for a hit man to come calling. Right, Yvgenny?"

"Da. I'll call you if I am hearing anything else."

"Thanks," I said as I stood up. "Let's head back to my place, Rachel. I want to go over an idea I have."

"Sounds good."

"Don't say that," I cautioned. "You haven't heard the idea yet, and it could get you killed, too."

"Great," she said, utterly devoid of any enthusiasm.

PART TWO

CATALYST

Den of Iniquity

"So, did you see that article about the UFO sighting over Helsinki?" I asked as I poured Rachel another margarita. We reclined in lounge chairs on her back patio, having said goodbye to the sun an hour earlier. She still hadn't brought up the conversation with her and Marsha. She acted as if nothing had happened, and I was grateful for it. I didn't know how to react, though, and she was either wise or scared enough not to chase me down about it.

She wore a simple tank-top and shorts. Her hair was up in a ponytail, and I realized that I considered her beautiful no matter what she looked like. For the first time in my life, I was more interested in knowing a woman than anything else. And I had no idea what to do about it. Up until now I'd had friends—didn't matter what gender—and I'd had trysts with women when sex seemed like the right thing to do. But I'd never had someone occupy my thoughts the way Rachel did. And frankly, this was uncharted territory. How could I get involved with a woman, I mean *really* involved, without either lying to her for the rest of our lives or risking becoming a freak show if I told the wrong woman what I was. Hell hath no fury, etc. … I had visions of divorce court and gasps when a crazy ex screamed "ALIEN!" in court or on the news.

So I'd posed a question about UFOs to get the lay of the land. I needed to know her stance on alien visitors. I also figured now was as good a time as any to find out if she was up for a more active role in my work. Ultimately, they would go hand-in-hand. A glimmer of a plan was taking shape, and for it to work, I'd need her actively involved. It would also require showing her the phase doors and programming the network so she could use them. Knowledge of them would require her knowing pretty much everything else about me. I *had* to be sure.

"Helsinki? Yeah," she said and took a pull from the glass, licking some salt along the way. "Saw some footage, too … I forget what channel. Pretty compelling stuff, though." she added, taking another drink.

The thought of revealing my origins unsettled me quite a bit. I'd spent twenty-seven years keeping that particular secret, but it was wearing on me. Don't get me wrong. I trust Rachel—with my life, in fact—and I knew she felt the same. But there's a difference between the trust two good friends share and having her know my whole story. I couldn't afford to have her freak out on me. There was too much at stake, and I wasn't in an easy position to disappear if it came to it. I didn't feel like becoming the talk of the town on late night television, either, right before government spooks came looking to part me out and put various pieces under a microscope. Only one human on Earth knew for certain who and what I was, and he'd tried to do just that the last time we were in the same room together. It's a long story, and I did *not* want to repeat that particular fiasco.

"You sound like a believer," I mused, testing the waters.

"In UFOs?" she asked, raising an eyebrow in my direction. "Yeah, I do. There's too much information—hell, going back all the way to the Stone Age—that supports extraterrestrial life. Granted, most of the stuff we see is pretty shabby, but when you add it all up, it can't *all* be fake. It comes down to numbers, if you ask me."

"How do you mean?" This might not be as bad as I had feared, I thought.

"Well, think about all the stars we can actually see. Add to that all the new planets they're finding with the Kepler Telescope. Then take into account all the stars we can't see. There has to be more out in the whole of the universe than just this tiny little planet with life on it. And fifteen billion years is a long time for civilizations to rise and fall."

"Hard to argue with you there." I took a healthy swig from my margarita and gave her a mischievous look. "So, umm … what would you do if you met one?"

"If it was a he and he was a hunk, I'd take him to bed just for the bragging rights!" My eyes got wide with disbelief, and she started laughing … clearly at my expense. I gave her a smile.

"No, really," I prompted, trying to sound at least a little serious.

She sobered a bit. "Oh, I don't know," she said thoughtfully, "probably pee my pants and run for the hills." She chuckled. "There's just no telling what an alien might want with me."

"That's a fair point," I agreed. "And if it turned out that it meant you no harm?"

"Well, I guess it'd be like meeting anyone from a foreign country. You get to know them."

I was satisfied she could probably handle it, mostly because the alien would be me … but there were still no guarantees. It would still come down to the difference between talking about aliens over a pretty good margarita buzz and sitting across the table from an actual alien, but I couldn't have asked for a better response from her. It was time for the next piece.

"Enough about aliens. It's not like they're gonna show up any time soon and introduce themselves." I paused and changed my tone. "There's something I've been meaning to ask you."

She knew my business voice. "What is it?"

"This DiMarco thing. I wanted to know if you might be interested in doing more than research and driving the car." Suddenly the thought of Rachel involved directly in what I did—and the risks that went along with it—filled me with a great deal of anxiety. I worried about all my friends when they got involved with my cases, but having her even more in harm's way and the possibility of losing her stirred up a feeling in my chest I didn't quite understand.

"You mean, field work?" she asked. "With you?"

"Yeah, pretty much."

"That sounds fantastic!" she shouted.

"It's not all fun and games," I warned. "It didn't work out so well for Natalia," I reminded her.

She sobered up quite a bit at that. "I've been thinking about Natalia … and the people you've killed. I mean, people die around you all the time, don't they?"

I paused, took a deep breath and let it out slowly. "Well, there's no denying that I've left a fair number of corpses in my wake, but not many of them were people I was working with." I looked into her eyes and felt that feeling again, that worry for her safety. It occurred to me that the old part of me, that part that always rose to the surface when the killing started, he'd never cared what happened to anyone. For him there was always just the job, and the rush of killing. But the part of me that cared for Rachel ached at the thought of something happening to her. Was I crazy to even suggest bringing her into the fold? I had similar feelings for Xen, Marsha, and Yvgenny, but they weren't nearly as intense as they were for Rachel.

"Could you have done anything for Natalia?" she asked, searching my face.

"I did everything I could to protect her," I added sincerely. The image of Natalia sinking beneath the waves filled my thoughts, and a strange twinge hit my guts. The truth was, if I'd gone in after her, Bennie and his thugs would have killed her anyway. I still held out one slim hope, but it was a long shot. "There's always risk in this game, and she accepted that risk years before she ever met me. That's the choice you're making here, Rachel. You're accepting the risk, but know that I'll kill anyone whoever even tries to hurt you. I can make that one guarantee … the rest is up to the universe."

She looked at me for several long seconds. Maybe it was the tone of my voice. Maybe it was the allure, the excitement of doing the things I do. She pulled her gaze away and stared up at a starry sky.

"Okay. I'm pretty sure I'm in," she said quietly, "but I want some time to think about it." She sounded resolved, and I'd expected to hear at least a little fear in her voice, but there was something else in her tone that I couldn't put my finger on.

I nodded my head. "I understand. You've got a few days to mull it over."

When it came right down to it, my plan would probably require her and Marsha as well as Xen, and possibly Yvgenny, to make it all happen, and anyone involved would have to be exposed to some of my story, which scared me not a little. But if I couldn't trust these people, I might as well chuck it all in anyway. As I'd gotten older, I realized how isolated I was. Not lonely, per se—I had lots and lots of friends—but none of them knew who and what I really was. I guess somewhere along the way I decided I needed to change that. It was strange. The old me, tucked deep inside mocked me for my weakness. But Mag just wasn't enough anymore, and I got the sense she might be feeling the same way. We'd always been alone.

The rest of the evening turned into the simple, very comfortable sort of chat only long-time friends can have over a few pitchers of margaritas. I'd never felt so comfortable around a person, and I had been tempted to make a pass at her. I'd gotten the sense that she wanted me too. Maybe that's what I'd heard in her voice, but the truth was, an affair now would only complicate things if I decided to tell her everything. *One step at a time*, I thought to myself.

o o o

I woke with cottonmouth at four in the morning. I lay in my bed and felt the thud of a mild headache. Mag wasn't around, so I figured she had gone hunting. I rubbed my temples to clear the headache. *Not bad for eleven margaritas*, I thought. Rachel's seven had put her down completely. When she had finally fallen asleep in her lounge chair, I'd put her to bed, tucked her in, and used the phase-door connecting her bathroom to my front door.

"Lights," I said, and the main area of my loft filled with light. I threw back the comforter, got out of bed, and walked over to the refrigerator. I opened it, pulled out a jug of orange-juice, a glass, and a large, stainless steel container of sugar from the counter, I poured an inch of sugar into the glass then filled it with orange-juice. Half of the orange juice went down in big gulps, and then I paused to swirl the contents around and get the rest of the sugar. A few more gulps finished off the mixture, and I set the glass on the counter.

As I reached the desk, I heard the cat-door in the back of my closet swing open. I turned to see Magdelain slink halfway out of the closet with a limp monkey in her mouth.

"What are you doing?" I asked with a mild but accusatory tone. "You know you can't bring that in here." Mag stopped just outside the closet doors and looked at me. "Is it still alive?" I asked.

She nodded her head.

"When that thing wakes up, it's going to freak out. You know what happened the last time. It got crap all over the place, and you don't have hands to hold the broom and dustpan. Monkey shit stinks!" I added in a scolding tone. "Go on, put it back. We're leaving soon."

Magdelain got a dejected look on her face and hung her head low.

"Awwww … don't look like that, girl. We're going to go *play*." Mag's face brightened into a smile wrapped around the unconscious monkey, looking more like a snarl. She spun around and leapt into the closet. I heard the door swing open. A few seconds later she came bounding into the room without the monkey. "Thanks, girl. Let me check my mail, and then we'll get going."

I sat down in front of the computer. She followed and walked around me, rubbing her face on my legs. I pulled up the email client, scrolling by mostly junk. There was one from Rachel dated the previous morning. I opened it and it simply said, "MEMO: Put door out at reservoir … whatever that means."

I chuckled, remembering my request.

"Right," I said to myself, smiling. I scrolled through the rest of the email and, not finding anything of import, locked down the workstation.

"Slight change of plan Mag. One errand and *then* we're going to play. Will that work for you?"

Mag smiled and rasped happily.

I scratched her behind the ears, and the rasping increased in volume.

"Good girl." I stood up and walked towards the front door. "Go on, get in the van. I'll be right there. Can't go out like this, can I?" Mag looked at me, smiled and bolted for the back of the loft. I walked over to the coats hanging on the wall and grabbed the next clean one in line. The first two were still filthy. It would take me all day to clean them up. "On the seventh day … I did laundry," I said to myself, shaking my head. I put on a pair of baggie, black pants and a black t-shirt, and added a pair of lightweight, black boots. Grabbing my black trench coat, I stepped around the closet to where my vehicles were parked and walked to the driver's side of my van.

I got in, dropping the black coat between the seats. Mag sat in the passenger seat, having slipped her head and body through the shoulder strap of the seat belt. She turned and looked at me expectantly as I buckled in.

I fired up the motor and rolled up the darkly tinted windows halfway. Pulling forward onto the rectangle area of the floor, I lowered the visor and hit the remote. The twenty-by-thirty slab of flooring dropped slowly and silently through the floor. Halfway down I hit another button, and the garage door slid quickly up. I pulled into the dark alley, headlights slashing at the darkness, and hit both buttons of the remote. I watched the platform rise as the door came down.

Exiting the alley, I rolled down empty streets, not surprising at four in the morning. It took us twenty minutes to return to the reservoir where Rachel had picked me up two nights before. Pulling off Montlake Drive, I drove slowly down the dirt road and into the small parking lot. Thankfully, the lot was empty.

When I'd first stepped onto the dam, I'd seen an old steel door on the east side, partially obscured by a tall bush about twenty feet to the right of the steps. My headlights briefly illuminated the rusty, steel door set in the side of the dam as I turned the van around and backed up to it. I cut the engine and got out. The weak streetlight overhead was even darker than I remembered, barely illuminating the parking lot.

"Watch the road, girl."

Mag jumped over to my side, slid out the door and slipped around the front of the van. As she did, her coat rapidly changed from the normal forest green and gray stripes to a rusty-gray color almost perfectly matching the badly lit parking lot. I lost her blur quickly in the shadows as she darted across the parking lot and disappeared into the shrubs near where I had hidden.

I walked to the back of the van, opened the windowless doors and hit a switch just inside. The interior lights came on a row of cabinets on each side of the van, with an aisle wide enough to crawl between. I stepped in, opened one of the cabinets and pulled out a fifty-foot length of coiled, gray cable that seemed to shimmer dully from within.

Next to that sat a small device that looked like a cross between an electric shaver and a screwdriver. It had a broad, rectangular head on one end and a double-set of prongs sticking out the other. I grabbed both the cable and the device and got out. Opening a panel on the end of the cabinet, I looked behind me at the old steel door. To the right of that, mostly hidden by the bushes, I spotted a faded, rusty NO TRESPASSING sign bolted to the wall.

"Perfect," I muttered, delighted I wouldn't have to jury rig anything.

I grabbed one of the standard palm-readers from the cabinet. It was rectangular, three inches deep and several inches narrower than the dimensions of the sign. Slipping the palm-reader under my arm, I walked over to the sign, pushed the branches out of the way and dropped the cable on the ground. Using the small device, I pressed one of the two actuators on it. The prongs glowed and hummed. Placing the prongs on each bolt, the tips glowed more brightly, causing a small metal hiss. I repeated the process on each bolt. When I cut the last bolt, the sign—with all four bolt-heads fused to the metal plate—fell to the ground.

I grabbed the palm reader, flipped it over and pressed a small gray button on the back, removing my hand quickly. The surface glowed, increasing in brilliance. Holding the reader in both hands, I centered it on the wall inside the pale outline the sign had left and pressed the reader against the concrete. There was a faint crackling of energy when the panel touched the wall. I pressed it into the concrete, watching it slowly sink into the surface with an electric hiss until the outer edge was flush with the brick surface.

Grabbing the dimly glowing cable, I uncoiled about twenty feet and pressed it into the corner between the wall and the jam. I ran my finger along the cable, tracing it all the way round. It adhered itself to the surface as I went. With the entire doorframe outlined in the cable, I grabbed the pronged device from my pocket and pressed the other actuator.

It began to hum, and the flat, rectangular tip took on a deep blue glow. I touched the tip to the end of the cable stuck to the doorframe and quickly ran it along the cable all the way around to where it touched the ground again. As I did, the cable flashed with pale white light. I placed my hand on the newly installed palm-reader and lifted my fingers in a new combination for this door, committing it to memory. The cable around the door flashed white again, accompanied by a soft, electrical crack. The cable returned to its normal dull glow, and I pulled it off of the frame, coiling it neatly.

I placed my hand on the panel again and ran through the combination for my loft. Pushing in on the door-jam on the opposite side from the handle, it swung inward. A wave of ninety-degree air washed over me. Swinging the frame all the way open, I looked in on my living room.

"Easy peasy," I said out loud. I stepped over, picked up the sign sitting on the ground and pressed it onto the lip of the palm-reader. Releasing it quickly, it stayed in place, held there by a gravity field. Pressing with my thumbs, I pushed on the bottom of the sign, and it slid upwards, stopping at the upper lip of the reader. Sliding the sign back down in place, I gave a sharp whistle.

I put everything away, closed the back of the van, and stepped up to the driver's side as Mag came trotting up out of the shadows. She leapt into the cab and slid under the seatbelt. I fired up the van and pulled out, turning right on Montlake. It didn't take long to get back to the highway. I turned on the radio and "Space Cowboy" by Steve Miller came on.

"I love this song, Mag. It always puts a smile on my face." We both nodded our heads in rhythm as I headed east out towards the desert.

It took me an hour to make it out to the VeniCorp facility. I drove about a mile past the plant and turned off the highway onto a dirt county road. A sliver of burgundy creased the eastern horizon, and a low, hazy pink glow swelled out of the deeper reds as sunrise began its ascent.

I'd actually looked up the layout the of the VeniCorp chemical plant the previous year on a different case. That's when I'd crossed paths briefly with Bennie. The job had never brought me to VeniCorp, but the location and the general layout were still tucked away in my head. I drove down the dirt road for almost a mile and finally spotted the tips of the highest heating and storage towers of

DiMarco's plant. A dune rose in the desert between the plant and me, and since the towers didn't have catwalks that high up, no one would be able to see the van. I couldn't see the highway behind me anymore, so I stopped the van, got out and let Mag slither past me.

"Game-face Mag. Range out and hunt all you want, but don't get too far. If anyone comes calling, don't let them know you're here unless I say so."

She looked up at me, nodded her head, and disappeared as her coat turned the same color as the terrain around us. She slipped out into the dawn, and I quickly lost track of her. I took off my tan trench coat, threw it on the seat and grabbed the black one. As I slipped it on, the surface shimmered slightly and faded from shifting black to hues matching the van and the desert. I stepped around to the back of the van and, opening several cabinets, grabbed a large backpack made from the same material as the black coat. I grabbed the cable I'd used at the reservoir, the device to set doors, four palm-readers, a pair of black goggles, a vlain, and what looked like a long, coiled-up zipper made of thick, gray, smooth plastic. It was called a splitter and had a fob to pull on but only a seam where the teeth would be. I clipped the vlain to my belt, on the side this time rather than the back, and slipped the goggles around my neck. Everything else got stuffed in the backpack, which slid easily over my shoulders. It shimmered and took on the surrounding colors as well.

Closing the doors, I bent over and grabbed straps attached to the bottom of my coat, securing them to my ankles so that the jacket wouldn't flutter behind me as I moved. I checked my gear one last time and jogged across the desert towards the rise that hid the facility. I crossed the distance quickly, crouching low as I approached the top of the rise. I crawled the last twenty yards and stopped when I could see the whole thing. I put the goggles on, pulled the hood over my head, and lowered the facemask as the sun peaked fully over the horizon. The goggles allowed for considerable magnification, adjusting to whatever object I focused on.

I spent the entire day watching the plant as two pair of guards circled the facility slowly. Laying in the sand, moving from bush to rock, I looked just like another piece of the desert. The plant had a twelve-foot electrical fence around the perimeter with Warning High Voltage signs every thirty feet or so. There was a small, two-level office building on the east side, a wide variety of storage and processing towers inside a massive main facility, and a row of thirty-foot chemical tanks along the fence-line closest to me. The structures around the compound would make perfect places to move undetected. A large warehouse squatted in the far southwest corner of the property. Three stories tall, it had a twenty-foot concrete wall around it with a sliding, steel gate that faced north between the building and the main facility.

The entrance of the plant was on the west side and had a manned security building. The building had windows all around and several computer terminals that I could see. Two men occupied the building at all times, and there had been a switch of guards at ten a.m. I saw an M-16 come into view more than once throughout the day. Roughly every two hours a tanker truck would leave the plant and one would enter.

As vehicles came and went, the security guards would check IDs, taking note each time, and then hit a button in the security building to lift the gate. Most of the people I saw appeared to be regular workers—mostly hard-hats, gray overalls and boots—but a few suits and regular folks came and went. They were going about the business VeniCorp was known for, namely chemical production.

My initial vantage point was on the north side. I shifted my position several times throughout the day, quickly running from spot to spot and making a clockwise circle from the north side. I moved every couple of hours or so, and I didn't see or hear Mag the entire day, but I knew she would stay within easy reach of me no matter where I went. She was a better hunter than I would ever be. When it came right down to it, I sometimes got the sense that I worked for her, and she only needed me for my opposable thumbs … well, that and to drive the van.

As the sun drifted down towards the horizon and most of the overall-clad employees had left, I found myself lying behind a tall, spiky agave cactus. I'd identified a number of locations inside the facility that looked promising for the work I had to do that night and committed them to memory. Details of the building in the southwest corner caught my attention. A catwalk ran along the upper level of the west side, with a door in the middle and stairs that lead up to the roof on the northwest corner of the building.

Each corner of the roof had a raised portion of wall. I hadn't thought much about it until I saw four men in desert cammies come out the door. Three of them had M-16's and the fourth sported a German DSR-50 sniper rifle. All four weapons had scopes on them.

Money, I thought. Whatever they kept in the building was worth having snipers on the roof. That meant drugs, money or both, unless Gino had gotten into government defense contract work, which was about as likely as me being elected President of the United States.

The four men walked along the catwalk and up the stairs. Three of them crouched and moved across the roof. Now that I knew where to look, I saw the camouflaged heads of three men on the roof peeking from behind the raised walls at the corners. As each new man got to his corner, he exchanged a few words with the guard already in position, and then they changed places. The replaced guards made their way to the stairs, descended, and disappeared into the building.

As the four entered the building, I saw a VeniCorp truck pull away from the main facility and drive over to the guard post at the front gate. As they had done that morning, two men went in and two went out. I looked at my watch to see it was six p.m.

"Eight hour shifts," I said out loud. I heard a rustle behind me and reached for the vlain. Turning over slowly, I saw the faint outline of Mag and her exposed, grinning muzzle coming towards me.

"Hey girl. Having fun?" She nodded, her muzzle was tinged with the blood of some animal, and stepped up to me. I looked around, enjoying the heat of the day and the dry air.

"It's kind of like home out here, isn't it?" I said a bit wistfully. She nodded and rubbed her muzzle on my leg to comfort me.

"Thanks girl. I sometimes miss it, you know?" She pawed at my boot and started rasping. "You're the best," I added. I sat up and scratched her behind the ears, setting off another round of intense rasping. "Go on. I've got to wait here a while before we go in, okay? Think you can amuse yourself for another couple of hours?" She nodded again and ran off. I watched for another hour as the sun went down.

With dusk fading into darkness, I caught sight of three sets of headlights moving towards the main entrance. The three vehicles stopped at the security post, and I could finally identify them as white, unmarked vans illuminated in the bright island of light around the guard building. None of the vans had windows behind the cabs.

Both guards inside the building grabbed M-16's and stepped out. One of them walked around to the driver's side and said something to an obviously Hispanic driver and passenger. The driver nodded, and the guard moved around to the back of the van. He opened the back doors and then closed them a few seconds later. The other guard hit the button inside the building for the gate, and it lifted quickly out of the way, allowing the first van to pass through. They repeated the process for each of the remaining two vans, and I noted that all of the van occupants were Hispanic. I memorized license plates as they passed through the gate.

When all three were in, they drove through the middle of the facility, their progress illuminated by a row of dim streetlights that followed the road. One of the guards pulled out a walkie-talkie, said something, and put it away. I lost sight of the vans for a minute, but as I suspected, they drove up to the steel gate in front of the walled building. The driver of the first van waved at someone inside, and the steel gate rolled back. The vans drove in to the well-lit area behind the wall and out of sight. I saw the light of a garage door opening, and thirty seconds later it closed.

The desert cooled quickly as the sun went sun down, and I needed to move to keep warm. Pulling my hood lower over my face, I stood quickly and ran through the desert night, making my way towards the fence-line. As I approached I heard the garage door opening again. I lay down in the sand and watched as headlights lit up the steel gate. It opened slowly, and the three white vans drove out and through the compound. I noticed a larger gap between the tires and the wheel-wells, so this was a delivery, not a pickup. After a minute they reappeared at the guard post. They were stopped, searched quickly, and allowed to pass through the gate into the night.

"Let's get to work, Mag."

She silently stepped out of the night, virtually invisible, and I could just make out her tail twitching in anticipation.

Bump in the Night

I waited for the last white van to disappear down the road before I moved again. Nothing seemed to be going on inside the compound, but even with my coat and hood making me virtually undetectable across the spectrum, the snipers on the roof might see something when I went through the fence. I needed a better spot. I faded back into the darkness of the desert. Mag paced me about twenty yards off, and we skirted back around the way we had come. My goggles allowed me to see perfectly in the darkness.

The large containment tanks came into view as I made it around the southeast corner, and I cut a diagonal across the sand to reach them. Thirty feet of open dirt lay between the fence and the tanks. Fortunately, the few lights on the forty-foot structures only illuminated about half of the ground between the tanks and the fence. I walked up to within twenty feet of the fence and stopped, scanning the entire compound one last time to make sure it was clear. With the guards walking the perimeter, I had a pretty good window of time to get through.

Whoever ran their security was probably counting on the fact that no one on the outside knew what was going on at the plant. Add to that the tighter security on the walled building, and the guy probably wanted to keep costs down. Most people don't know this, but bean counters are the biggest boon to cracking security than any other job title in an organization. *God bless 'em.*

I slipped the pack off, pulled out the coiled splitter, and waited for the next pair of guards to walk by as I slipped the pack back on. When they turned the far corner, I sprinted to the fence line. Grabbing the loose end of the splitter, I snapped my arm, uncoiling the splitter like a whip. I carefully placed the top end of the splitter about seven feet off the ground and slid my thumb down the whole length, pressing it into the chain-link fence. Each time the splitter came in contact with the fence, it elicited a quiet crackling sound, and the gray material seemed to meld into the metal of the fencing.

Taking one last look, I grabbed a fob at the bottom of the splitter and pulled it up. It noiselessly came up in my hand, separating the fence links. The thing works like a phase-door, connecting two points in space regardless of how far apart they are. To the security system, electrical current flowed through it uninterrupted. Pulling the seam apart, I stepped through and held it open for Mag who leapt through the opening and dashed into the shadows between the two nearest storage tanks. I considered taking the splitter with me, but this area of fence-line was dark enough that someone would have to shine a light directly on it to see the thing. Closing it, I left it in place in case I had to make a quick getaway.

I dashed into the shadows next to Mag, and we crept between the double-row of storage tanks towards the two-story office building. The front doors of the building faced south towards the plant and away from the fence. Between the building and me lay a forty-yard open area of dirt with several pick-up trucks and a parking lot beyond that with a red Lexus coupe parked next to the building. I scanned the area for a few minutes and, certain no one was looking, sprinted across the opening at full speed. Mag followed close behind.

I ran straight for the back corner of the building and dashed behind some bushes where I waited for the next pair of guards to pass buy. I'd need every second to finish what I had to do before the next pair came around. My target was the back door of the building, facing the fence. The guards in the security booth couldn't see it, although the snipers atop the walled building might see the light.

Two guards came into view as they passed the storage tanks and started their slow approach along the fence line. Like the previous two, they both had M-16's slung over their shoulders. One smoked a cigarette, and they appeared to be talking as they walked towards the building. Just as they were about to pass me, the one with the cigarette stopped.

"Hold up," he said, grabbing the arm of his partner. "There's something wrong."

His partner un-slung his machine gun and looked around quickly. "What's could possibly be wrong?" He scanned the area, looking for trouble.

I held my breath.

The first guard took his nearly finished cigarette out of his mouth, held it up and then dropped it into the dirt, twisting it out with his boot. "I need another," he said, chuckling at his nervous partner.

I stopped holding my breath and took my hand off the vlain.

"You asshole," the non-smoker grated, then he laughed with his partner while the guy pulled out a cigarette and lit up. "You know, you're not doing yourself any good," he scolded.

"Fuck you. This place will kill me before these things do."

"You're probably right. Have you seen how much of that stuff they have stacked up in the lab?"

"Hell, yes. I don't like even going near that building anymore. It scares the shit out of me. Someone's going to fuck up, and this whole place will blow sky high."

"Just hope it's not on our shift." The guy shouldered his M-16 again. "Come one. Let's get going before Thompson comes around the corner. You know what a prick he is."

"Yeah. He's been like that since Marty gave him a promotion." They started walking again.

"I have it on good authority that he's actually spending weekends blowing the god damn foreman." He made a fellatio motion with his hand and mouth.

"You're just jealous," the smoker said, pulling out the cigarette and waving it in his partner's face. "Everybody knows *you* wanted to be the one to go down on him, princess."

"Fuck you!"

They both laughed again and walked around the corner of the building.

Grateful the two comedians had moved off, I took a deep breath and focused. Sliding along the wall, I paced them as silently as a shadow, heading for the recessed back door of the building. I wouldn't have much time before the next pair came around the far corner. I pulled off the pack and extracted the palm reader, cable, and phase door tool. I quickly got to work and went through the sequence with a feverish speed. I had the door installed in forty seconds and the palm reader installed in another thirty. I set it behind an Emergency Exit—Do Not Block Door sign on a side wall in the entryway. I tucked the cable and tool back in the pack then slipped it on just as the next pair of guards came into view. Both of them had their M-16s unslung, and one of them had his hand to his ear. Someone must have seen the light from the light form the phase door.

"*Freeze!*" I hissed, and Mag stopped dead in her tracks. "Slow and easy."

We both glided across the open area like ghosts, making our way towards the tanks in silence. I checked the tower and spotted three of the snipers scanning the building behind me. I could finally hear one of the perimeter guards talking. He and his partner had stopped and hovered in a deep shadow on the outside of the fence not far from the splitter.

"No, tower, we don't see anything. Quiet as a church over there." He raised his rifle and peered through his scope. "The back area is clear. If there was someone, he could be inside by now.... Clyde, hold up on the south side. We're gonna check the back of the offices while Jim's team checks the building. Keep your eyes open.... No, Jim, I don't give a shit if it's not your shift. Take a couple of guys and check out the offices. Unless you'd like to call up Gino and cry to him. Maybe he'll be feeling generous and let you get some more beauty sleep ... That's what I thought. Now get going ... Copy that, tower. Heading to the back of the building."

The two guards started moving again, and I heard a door slam open over by the front guard building. Light shone from a door set into a structure that was part of the main processing facility. Three men hopped into a car and drove across the compound.

"Now, Mag," I whispered. Everyone in the area would be watching the car. We dashed to the storage tanks and slipped between them. "Now it gets interesting." I looked at Mag. "You know the drill. Cover me from shadows and corners," I whispered.

I peered out from the shadows, looking for any movement directly across from the compound. The three in the car were just getting out. Otherwise, the coast looked clear. "I have a general idea where I want to place these, but anything is possible once we get up into the superstructure."

I patted her head, took a deep breath, and sprinted across the compound, my feet patting against the ground as lightly as raindrops. The superstructure of the chemical plant loomed above me, much of it illuminated in bright lights. I ran into a recessed area that had stairs leading up into the plant where I found a double-set of doors with an Authorized Personnel Only sign on one of them and a single door to the left with a High Voltage sign on it.

"Watch the yard, girl."

Ensuring I wasn't in the line of sight to the office building, I went to work on the High Voltage door. I installed that phase-door just as quickly as the last one and set the palm-reader directly into the door under the High Voltage sign. Mag didn't make a sound as I worked. I gathered my gear and headed up into the infrastructure with two more doors to install. I spent the next two hours working my way around most of the facility, looking for the right spots. Mag and I easily avoided the few plant employees going about their business, and I found the next spot at an upper utility closet door. It was about halfway up the superstructure on the side facing the security building at the main gate. I installed the phase-door slowly, making sure nobody could see.

I placed the last phase-door in the highest location I could find. It faced east, and the sign next to it simply said Maintenance Access. I'd seen workers in gray overalls go in and out during the day, all of them wearing standard tool-belts. Looking down at the three-story building below me with the guards on the roof, I realized I would have to be very careful. If any of them looked up, they might see the soft flashes of light that a door-installation caused. I switched my goggles to thermal and scanned the rooftop below, easily making out the hot silhouettes of each guard. One appeared to be sitting with his back against the wall. His head at a slight angle, I figured he was asleep. The other three were sitting upright in the remaining corners looking out into the desert. I'd have to risk it. This spot was prime real estate for the plan that was taking shape.

I moved quickly, installing the door in record time. I checked the guards several times, but none of them ever looked upwards. I hoped this would be the only door I needed, but I'd put the others in as a safety precaution. Packing up my gear, I figured I was done for the night. I moved down the stairs along the west side of the tower. A glimmer near the highway caught my eye, easily seen from my vantage point. The vehicle came down the road and stopped at the gate as one of the guards came out to greet what I could now see as a stretched limousine. I enhanced the magnification and zoomed in. I briefly saw the coarse features of Gino DiMarco flash in the streetlight as the mobster said something curt to the guard and disappeared back into the car. I ran as silently as I could down the steel steps, Mag a silent shadow trailing behind me.

The guard hollered to his partner in the booth, and the gate swung up just in time for the already moving limousine to pass through. Before the gate had come down, I covered three of the eight flights of stairs to the bottom. "Mag, get back to the storage tanks," I told her as I rounded another flight of steps and raced down. "I want to see if I can learn anything from DiMarco."

It took us another twenty seconds to make it down the rest of the stairs. We leapt down the last flight, hitting the dirt and running without breaking stride as the limousine pulled into the parking lot next to the Lexus. I paused, crouching in an island of darkness in the middle of the compound, and waited for DiMarco to get out. The driver got out, moved to the back door and opened it. DiMarco stepped out, lighting a fat cigar as he stood up straight. Two of the perimeter guards disappeared around the corner of the building. DiMarco didn't acknowledge them, and they didn't wave. I'm sure they knew better.

"I don't know how this fucking guy does it," DiMarco said to the driver. "He never sleeps. Good thing I ain't paying him by the hour … and he sure has made me a mint, hasn't he?"

"Yes, sir, Mister DiMarco."

"Leave the motor running. I won't be long, and I want to get back to the house. I don't want to miss *CSI*. I fucking love that show. Who says T.V. can't be educational?"

"Yes, sir."

DiMarco walked towards the front of the building, and I bolted from my spot, sprinting as silently as I could. I ran around the trucks in the dirt lot and slipped into along the darkness near the fence-line. The driver neither heard nor saw me as I passed by. My objective was in sight. The guards were out of sight around the corner of the building now, making their way along the north side of the compound.

Running parallel to the back of the building, I cut a sharp left as I approached the dumpster. I'd have one shot. I leapt up and in one stride cleared the edge of the dumpster. My left foot came down on the edge hard with a loud *BANG* as I jumped up. My momentum carried me forward and up. I hit the wall with my right foot and pushed up as hard as I could. Reaching up with both hands, I caught the edge of the building and pulled, my momentum carrying me the rest of the distance. My feet cleared the edge of the building by a foot. I came down, rolled forward and stopped in a low crouch. The guards on the north side stopped when they heard the noise and stared at the building.

"What the hell was that?" the driver yelled.

I heard the limo door open and close as I approached a roof access door. It stood near the edge of the roof on the parking-lot side, leading down into the building.

"I'll take a look, guys," the driver hollered at the two guards.

"Roger!" one of the guards shouted. I heard him say something quietly, undoubtedly over his radio, and I could feel sniper-eyes scanning the rooftop for any signs of life.

I had to move slowly around several patio lounge chairs and a picnic table as I crossed the roof. If they saw any part of my outline, they might shoot first and apologize to DiMarco after. I heard footsteps below walk up to the corner of the building and stop. I peered down over the edge. I saw the driver peek around the corner with a Beretta in his hand. I moved back to the door, reached into a pocket, pulled out my lock-pick set and prepared to work on the lock. Fortunately, the stairwell entrance lay between me and the snipers. I pulled out a torsion wrench and S-rake and then paused, turned, and looked at the patio furniture then back at the lock. Doing a double-take, I turned again to the patio furniture, thinking about why they were there. I cocked my head to the side, reached out my hand slowly, and pressed down on the door lever. It twisted easily in my hand, already unlocked, and the door swung open for me.

"Sweet," I said, smiling. I slipped the tools back into the case, the case back into my pocket and stepped quickly into a dimly lit stairwell. I closed the door behind me and slipped down the stairs. There was a door on the second level, and the stairs continued down to the first floor. Gambling that whoever DiMarco was here to see had an upper-floor office, I turned the lever and silently pulled it open a few inches. None of the lights were on, but light from the streetlights outside was enough to see by.

There was no one in sight, so I stepped in quickly and sank down into a low crouch, sneaking up to the edge of a short hallway. A low-walled expanse of small office cubes filled the central part of the second-floor and a row of offices lining the north wall that continued all the way around the building. Most of them had their doors open. In the far corner I spotted the back of a small man with a long, black ponytail. He had on a black t-shirt and worked in a doublewide cubical along the south wall. A half-dozen monitors glowed before him in the corner where he sat.

He appeared to be switching between tasks on all of them. He worked like I did. I zoomed in on the screens I could see. They displayed a mix of chemical data, engineering diagrams, and some scheduling and volume data measured in thousands of gallons. I moved quickly down the aisle between the offices and cube-farm, stopping when I heard the elevator doors chime and start to open behind and to my left. Trusting my camouflage, I turned the corner and snuck down the aisle directly behind the man in the cubicle.

"Jackie, baby! What are you still doing here?" Gino hollered as he entered the cube-farm. He held a pistol in his hand as he scanned the area, obviously looking for an intruder. I stopped at an open door two offices away from Jackie and disappeared into the darkness. He never turned to look at Gino. "I've been trying to get ahold of you since Thursday," Gino added sternly.

"I know, Gino. I was ignoring you."

Gino raised a fist at Jackie's back and forced a smile. "Ha! It's a good thing you make me so much money, kiddo. And what the hell are you doing in the dark?" Gino walked up the aisle and stopped behind Jackie.

"Please don't turn on the lights."

Gino scowled again. "Have you seen or heard anything in here tonight?"

"Some guards came in looking for something a couple of hours ago. Aside from that, it's been quiet."

"You sure?"

"How could I not be sure about something like that?"

"Right …" Gino looked like he wanted to slap the guy, but he kept his tone calm. "Did you get my message?"

"Yes."

"And?" Gino asked expectantly.

"I'm crunching the numbers now."

"And?" Gino asked again, a bit more impatience in his voice. I gotta hand it to the guy, whoever he was. He didn't seem to fear DiMarco. "I've committed us to those god damn Russians, and, believe me, they don't fuck around," Gino added quietly.

Jackie sighed and stopped what he was doing. He paused for a few seconds, looking at his computer screens. He slowly turned around in his chair to face Gino. I finally got a look at him. In his late twenties or early thirties, he had a clean-shaven, boyish, Asian face. Black, horn-rimmed glasses sat on a flat nose, and he had dark eyes that, to me, looked just plain mean. He wore leather sandals, blue jeans, and a t-shirt with a logo on it made up of four colored boxes stacked in a diamond pattern: white, blue, red, and yellow. The text read *Unstable: May explode at normal temperatures and pressures.* I almost laughed.

Funny shirt, I thought, considering the guy's job and demeanor. I made a mental note to try and find one of those.

"Gino, you only have one thing to worry about," Jackie said. "The plant can handle the volume. Based on what you gave me, we'll need to increase production by four-hundred percent. We'll also need to shut down or severely reduce the hydrogen and liquid nitrogen production, but they're not really making you any money anyway, so it's a huge net gain. As you suspected, you don't have enough storage right now. I figure you'll have to triple the number of tanks you have out there," Jackie added, indicating the tanks where Mag hid in the shadows. "Fortunately, you have the space, but they'll take time to build." Jackie leaned back in his chair and sized Gino up for a moment. "The real problem is Del Gato. Are you sure he can deliver? I can't make something from nothing, and he'll need to increase deliveries by four-hundred percent as well."

"You let me handle that," Gino said with a bit of an edge. "Del Gato says he can handle it, and I'm sure as hell paying him enough."

At least I know where the drugs are coming from. I could tell DiMarco wasn't accustomed to his people talking to him like that, but Jackie was probably a certified, wacko genius. He was the sort of tool a guy like DiMarco couldn't afford to lose ... at least not yet, anyway. "As long as you're sure you can get it done here, I'll get what we need from Del Gato. And I can go to other vendors if he comes up short."

"Alright. I'll have the report and the project plan to you tomorrow with everything we have to do on our end. We'll be able to get everything set up and ready to rock in about three weeks."

"That's perfect, Jackie my boy. Just email me the specs ... make sure they're clean. I think I may have someone on my back."

"You got it," Jackie said, turning back to his monitors. "Oh, and if you want to review any of my data, it's on the internal network at corporate. You won't be able to access it from home or anyplace else outside. You'll need to log in at the downtown office."

"Why the fuck would I want to look at that shit?" Gino asked. "That's what I pay you for. Besides, it makes my head hurt." He turned, walked back down past the rows of cubicles, and then stopped at the end.

"Right," Jackie said, devoid of any interest in Gino at all.

"Oh, and Jackie?"

"Yeah?"

"Take a few days. Enjoy yourself."

"Thanks, Gino," Jackie said without turning around. "I already booked a flight to Vegas for tomorrow night and reserved your penthouse at the Venetian."

I watched Gino's face stiffen as he glared at the presumptuous little chemist. He raised the pistol as if he was going to shoot the kid in the back of the head. He took a deep breath, lowered the weapon, turned, and strode back to the elevator. I waited till I heard the elevator open and close before slinking out of the office and back the way I had come. Jackie, his attention focused on the monitors, never moved.

I silently opened the stairwell door and went upstairs into the cool, desert night air. The stars twinkled above, much more visible than they were back in the city. I stood there a few minutes, thinking about home. I waited for the limousine to drive back towards the highway. When the taillights were out of sight, I walked to the edge of the building, checked to see that there was an adequate gap between guards, and stepped off. Hitting the ground effortlessly, I jogged across the parking lot. I crossed the dirt field, returning to the shadows of the storage tanks and felt Mag brush up against my leg.

"Let's go, Mag. We're done here."

The two of us returned to the fence, went through it, and I removed the splitter from the other side. I took a quiet, calm stroll back to the van, put my gear away, switched coats, and drove home.

Parking the van back it its slot, I shut off the engine and looked at Mag. "You want to sleep sea-side tonight? Maybe you can find that monkey again."

Mag looked at me, smiled, and rasped her agreement.

I grabbed the black coat and got out of the van. "Go on girl. I'll be there in a couple of minutes. I have to go grab a few things."

Mag darted past me through the open door and around the corner of the standing closet, and I heard her door open and swing closed. Walking past my bed and up to the row of coat hooks, I hung up the black coat, brushed the dust off of it, and then hung up the tan one I'd been wearing. Grabbing the two dirty ones, I draped them both over my shoulder, stepped up to the front door and placed my hand on the palm reader. Running through the appropriate finger sequence, I pushed open the door and stepped into the living room of my beach house. Humid air and the smell of the ocean filled my nostrils.

Without turning on the lights, I walked through the dark living room, down the hall, past the kitchen and bedrooms, straight back to the double-sliding glass door. Unlocking it, I slid it open and stepped out onto my patio. The sound of the ocean filtering through the jungle behind my house made me smile. The patio glowed enough in the moonlight for me to make my way to one of the lounge chairs along the low brick wall that surrounded it. Mag had already curled up on one of the other lounge chairs, looking at me. I threw the coats on the long, glass patio table, sat down, reclined the chair all the way back, and was asleep in seconds.

The Seventh Day

I woke to the sound of screaming monkeys. I looked at the now empty chair where Mag had been sleeping. The heat and humidity of the mid-morning sun soothed me, and I lay there for a while, simply enjoying the sights, sounds, and smells of the jungle. There isn't much jungle where I come from. It's mostly desert and cityscape, although I'd visited plenty of jungle worlds over the years. The canopy stretched overhead, and I watched a troop of monkeys playing tag through the branches high above. The orange blossoms of the elequeme trees that fenced in the sides of my patio and ran around the front of the property gave the air a subtly pleasant perfume. They were part of the reason I'd kept the place, a gift from an old friend on his deathbed. And no, before you ask, I didn't kill him.

As I stood up, I noticed an iguana on the low, stone wall at the back of the patio, lounging on one of the gateposts. I stripped down, leaving my clothes draped over the back of the chair, and walked through the gate down the path towards the ocean. The soft earth and dead leaves felt good under my bare feet. The sound of the surf grew as I reached the end of the tree line. I walked down the beach and waded out into the surf. I spent an hour swimming and diving deeply, both for the training and the mere pleasure of it.

The sun drifted to a position straight above, and it was time for me to get to work, so I walked back to the house. As I approached the gate, I noticed the iguana was gone but Mag was back. She sat there inside the gate, licking blood off her paws and muzzle. She must have decided to put iguana on the lunch menu. I opened the gate, stepped over Mag, and grabbed my clothes.

"Did it taste like chicken?" I said chuckling. Mag never stopped cleaning.

I walked into the house and took a long, hot shower. I dried off and walked into the kitchen where I grabbed a couple cans of peaches, a spoon, and a can opener, setting everything on the counter-top. I opened the cupboard and pulled out a gallon bottle of clear liquid and a toothbrush that was on the shelf next to it.

Walking into the living room, I hit a few buttons on the stereo and heard music start playing out on the patio. I returned to the kitchen, gathered everything up in both arms and walked out to the patio. Setting it all on the table next to my coats, I sat in one of the upright chairs. Latin jazz played while Mag continued to clean herself. Most pleasant, I thought as I opened one of the peach cans and spent the next few minutes enjoying the sweet fruit slices. When I finished, I set the spoon and empty can aside, moved one of the jackets out of the way, and laid the other one out flat in front of me.

I twisted the cap off of the gallon jug and poured a small amount of the liquid directly onto one of the blood-spatters on my coat. The fluid had a tangy smell to it, reminiscent of almonds, oddly enough, considering the fluid didn't originate on Earth. I replaced the cap, set the jug aside and, picking up the toothbrush, scrubbed at a blood spot on my coat. As I pressed the brush into the fabric, moving in small circles, the liquid slowly evaporated. After a few minutes of working the area, the blood spot disappeared. I poured the liquid on another blood spatter and worked the brush.

I worked for several hours like this and finally finished the first coat. I stood up, draped the now pristine coat over the back of my chair, and stretched out sore muscles. At some point during the process, Mag had crawled up on a lounge-chair behind me and gone to sleep. I had to wonder if the iguana had similar levels of tryptophan as turkey. She always seemed to sleep more after eating one of the lizards than she did when she got hold of a monkey.

My thigh itched, so I scratched it and realized that Bennie's bullet had finally made it to the surface. I scratched a bit harder, removing a few layers of skin over the hard lump in my flesh. The bullet broke through the surface. Squeezing with both fingers, I pushed the slug out and caught it as it fell. With a spurt of blood, the skin quickly closed up over the declivity left behind. I let out a sigh of relief, dropped the flattened-out slug into the empty peach can, then grabbed the opener and another can. It was time for supper. I opened it up and enjoyed a fifteen-minute break of peaches and ocean air.

As I set the second empty can next to the first, my phone rang. I heard the ring coming from both the coat on the table and the one draped over my chair. I grabbed the dirty coat on the table, reached into the appropriate pocket and pulled out the phone in the baggie. Opening the bag, I pulled out the phone, and answered.

"Hi Rachel."

"Are you at the zoo again? I hear monkeys."

I looked up at the trees and saw several monkeys screeching and throwing fruit at each other. "Yeah, I'm at the zoo." I smiled but felt a little guilty at always having to lie to Rachel about where the house was. I really need to fix that, I thought. "You know I like it here. Needed to think."

"Well, I've been doing some thinking of my own."

"I figured. It's not an easy decision to make."

"I'm in. I talked to my sister about it for hours yesterday. At first she had me convinced I shouldn't, but by the end we both agreed this is what I want. Besides, why should you get to have all the fun?"

"I hoped you'd say that. You're just about ready. I'll know for sure when you and Marsha have your match-up." I paused, choosing my next words very carefully. "I love you, you know." I meant it in more than a friendly, respectful sort of way. I heard Rachel breathing on the other end, but she didn't say anything. "It takes guts and real mettle to want to get into it like this. And like Yvgenny said, you are a rare woman," I added, doing my best impersonation of the big Russian. "And a hell of a lady," I said truthfully.

Rachel laughed. "Thanks, Justin…." A long pause settled between us before she added, "I love you, too." The phrase was careful, platonic even, without any emotion coming through. "When will you be done at the zoo?" she asked. "I was thinking we could go to dinner."

"Oh … uhh … actually, I've got to finish up something," I said looking at the second coat. "Then I'm going to hit the sack. I'm still pretty strung out from yesterday."

"Yesterday? What happened yesterday?"

"Oh, yeah … I forgot to tell you. I went out to the VeniCorp plant and did some snooping."

"I wish you'd tell me this stuff," she said laughing lightly. She had gotten used to me going off and doing dangerous things in the way other people go to the grocery store, but I knew she would rather know what's going on.

"I know you do. Sorry about that."

"No, you're not."

"Well …" I said evasively. "I might actually surprise you one of these days."

"I won't hold my breath."

"As long as I'm in the dog house, can I ask you to do me another favor?"

"You always do," she said dryly.

"Can you try to dig up anything on an Asian chemist that goes by the name Jack or Jackie? Works for VeniCorp. I think he's Chinese, but I'm not certain. I'd do it myself, but I won't be near my computer tonight."

"You're not going home?"

"Not tonight. I feel like sleeping on the beach."

"Got a hot date?"

"You know I don't. Not unless you count Magdelain," I said chuckling. The cat raised her head and looked at me. "I think we're heading into a rough one with DiMarco and all, and I want to get one last good night's sleep before we do."

"I understand. Get some rest." I caught an unusual trace of real disappointment in her voice.

"I'll take you to dinner this week, how about that?"

"Deal," she said a bit more brightly. "So the name is Jack or Jackie?"

"Right."

"And he works at VeniCorp."

"Right."

"I don't suppose you have anything more for me to go on?" she asked with a bit of exasperation.

"Yeah, he's an Asian chemist, remember?" I pointed out innocently.

"Yes, I do remember. I mean, do you have anything more than that? You can be such a lunkhead." I could hear her smiling.

"Well … not really," I said a bit apologetically.

"That dinner better be spectacular," she warned me, "Like surf and turf or something … you hear me?" She laughed a bit.

"Deal. I'll figure something out," I assured her.

"I'll talk to you tomorrow."

"*Hasta*, sweetie. You're the best."

Resigned, she said, "You say that to all the women in your life."

"Yeah, but I always mean it."

"Good bye, Justin."

"Bye, Rachel." I sat there for a few minutes thinking about her. I knew she looked at me as more than a good friend. "I definitely need to do something about that," I said to nobody but myself.

Good Kids

Monkeys woke me for the second morning in a row, and it pleased me. *Maybe I should let Mag keep one of those monkeys around the house,* I thought to myself. Coming to my senses, I rejected the idea, thinking of all the monkey crap, and headed back into the house. I showered and got dressed quickly. With my jackets in hand, I walked through the front door in Costa Rica and stepped back into my loft. A rumbling stomach sent me in search of coffee and fritters, so I naturally ended up at Grady's by way of my Victory V-twin Hammer.

I peered over my coffee at Kenny and his sister Abby as they walked into Grady's café. I waved at them, and they waved back, giving me great big smiles. Smiles like that were what I considered icing on my daily cake. If I didn't get smiles from the people in my life, I probably wouldn't bother getting out of bed … or off the beach … at all. Smiles are intoxicating to me, and I'm a card-carrying junkie for them. Kenny broke off and headed for the back office to clock in. It was the beginning of his shift. Abby, however, came straight at me. As usual, the place was filled with the drone of people joining in the universal celebration of coffee, breakfast, and pastries to start the day.

"Can I join you?" she asked a bit hesitantly as she stepped up. She and I had never really spoken that much—a few hellos and goodbyes when she picked up or dropped off Kenny.

"Of course. Have a seat." I moved an empty fritter-plate and the newspaper I had been reading out of her way as she sat down. "Can I get you anything?"

"I don't have enough time. I'm headed to my other job."

"Hold that thought," I said, holding up my hand. "Marsha!" I hollered, waving at her behind the counter. She looked at me between customers and gave me a pleasant what-do-you-need look.

I held up my coffee with one hand, raised my index finger for "one" with my other and then pointed at Abbey and made a walking motion with my fingers. "STAT?" I asked.

Marsha nodded with a smile.

"And a fritter in a bag!" I added.

She nodded again and said something to Kenny I couldn't hear.

"I got ya covered, Abby," I said smiling. "Consider it payment for the smile."

"Hunh?" she said a bit bewildered.

"Nothing," I said warmly, brushing it aside. "What can I do for you?"

"I wanted to thank you," she said a bit nervously.

"For what?" I couldn't remember having done anything for Abby ever, let alone lately.

"Kenny would be dead or in jail, or dead in jail if it weren't for you."

It was my turn to smile. "Well … I had some help. Marsha's the one who gave him the job. He'd probably get killed working for me. Or worse!" I added, grinning. We both laughed lightly.

"No, really, I mean it. You know my dad left after Kenny was born, right?"

"Yeah. Kenny mentioned it a while back. Sorry to hear it."

"Not your fault. But when my mom overdosed a few years ago, it was just Kenny and me. Having to work two jobs meant I couldn't spend much time with him. I blame myself for him getting into all that drug shit."

"Never blame yourself. Even a kid makes his own choices, and Kenny made some bad ones. All Marsha and I did was give him an opportunity to make some good ones. That's all."

"You really have no idea, do you, Mister Case." It was a statement, not a question, and there was something in her eyes that humbled me. "I wanted to thank you."

"Call me Justin. All my friends do … well … most of them, anyway." I gave her a big smile, and she returned it in kind. I wanted to make her do that more often. She was good at it. "And I just do what I do."

"Thanks just the same. Whether you want to admit it or not, you saved him." Kenny walked up with a refill for me plus a to-go cup and a paper bag.

"Thanks, Kenny," I said. I finished off my original coffee and poured a healthy amount of sugar in the new one. It already had cream. Then I pushed the to-go cup and the bag at Abby. "For the road. Working two jobs must kick your ass."

Abby blushed. "Thank you, Mister … uhhh … Justin," she said a bit shyly.

"Don't mention it. Just keep doing what you're doing, and things will work out. I'm sure of it, okay?"

"Okay." She stood up, grabbed the coffee and bag. Kenny and I watched her head out the door to their beat up Ford Bronco. Kenny turned halfway.

"Kenny?" I said, stopping him in mid-stride.

"Yeah?"

"Your sister's alright, you know that?"

"Yeah, I do. I don't know what I'd do without her."

"Don't ever forget that, kiddo. Now get back to work!" I ordered, laughing.

"Yes sir!" Kenny walked off smiling. It must be a family trait, I thought. They were both good at smiling.

I looked out the window at Abby's Bronco. She was still trying to start it. It finally turned over, and a thick cloud of smoke blew out the tailpipe. I watched her put her head on the steering wheel for a few seconds. She raised her head, and I thought I saw tears on her face. It occurred to me that I might just have to help them out a little more. I picked up the newspaper, stirred my coffee, took a sip, and went back to reading the movie section of the paper. It's all about the smiles, I thought to myself.

One Mystery Solved

I selected Rachel's speed dial, typed "Can I stop by at 2?" and hit SEND. I'd spent the whole morning at Grady's, drinking coffee and reading an assortment of theatrical rags from Marsha's newsstand. I was wired from the highly sugared coffee and planned on skipping lunch after the three fritters I'd downed throughout the morning. I had to get to a bookstore, because what I needed I hadn't programmed into my system yet. The process took a few days, and I just hadn't spent the time.

My phone dinged as a message came in. "I'll be here."

I typed in "See you then" and sent the message. Putting the phone back in my pocket, I dropped a couple twenties on the table, scooped up my reading material and headed to the newsstand. I put back the magazines I'd read and headed for the door. The Lieutenant who had come with O'Neil the previous day stepped up to the door as I stepped out.

"Here," I said cheerily and handed over the newspaper. He reflexively grabbed the newspaper and gave me a mild scowl. I get that from most of the cops that work for O'Neil. They'd all had to cover for me at one time or another at the behest of O'Neil, and I'd gotten the sense that most of them really resented it. I'd have to do something nice for the department to keep them smiling. I walked out into the parking lot, hopped on my bike, and headed for Hawthorne Books on the south side of Griffin Park. Ironically, it was only a few miles from the swimming pool I'd demolished.

Once there, I went straight for the Italian language section. It had occurred to me that a time might come while dealing with DiMarco's men that a working knowledge of Italian might be handy. I grabbed a copy of *Italian for Dummies* and went over to the reading area. Taking a seat, I opened to page one and dug in.

o o o

My phone dinged with a new message, so I set the half-consumed book down and saw that the message was from Rachel.

"You coming?"

I looked at my watch to discover it was three o'clock. "Oops!" I said out loud. The people on either side of me looked up from their books. "I'm late," I said apologetically to them, and they returned weak smiles before returning to their reading. I typed in "Sorry … Got distracted. On the way" and hit SEND.

I walked to the counter, paid for the book and headed back to my bike. Slipping the book into one of the leather side-bags, I hopped on and headed for Rachel's. With traffic it took me another forty-five minutes to pull into her driveway.

I shut off the motor and walked up to her front door, rapping on the screen door. When she didn't answer, I opened the door and stepped in.

"Rachel?" I yelled into the house.

"I'm on the patio!" she called back.

I walked through her house and out through the open sliding screen door to the patio. She lay face down out on a lounge chair, and wore a bikini. God damn she looked good. And there it was again. That feeling. A stack of printed pages sat on the small table next to her. She rolled over and looked at me through dark sunglasses, and it really put the hook in me. All I needed to do now was figure out how to … well … I guess I needed to figure out *what* I needed to do and then I could figure out how to do it.

"You're late," she said, scowling.

"Yeah, I know. I'm sorry. I decided to pick up Italian and lost track of time at the bookstore." I took off my coat and t-shirt and sat down in the chair across from her.

"That's funny. I decided to learn Italian, too," she said, smiling. I raised an eyebrow, once again impressed with her attitude of tackling things head-on. "I figured I'd need it if I'm going to start getting more involved with these guys."

"Smart," I said through a wide smile.

"There's iced-tea in the fridge."

"I'm okay. I've got about a gallon of coffee in me. In fact, could I …" I motioned to the bathroom.

"Go ahead," she offered.

I stood up, headed back into the house and took care of my bursting bladder.

"I think I found some useful data on that guy you wanted me to dig into," she hollered from the patio.

In the three years I'd known her, my admiration for Rachel never stopped going up. I finished up and headed back out to the patio. There were two glasses of iced tea on the patio table, one within easy reach of both of us.

As I stepped out into the sun, she reached over to the stack of paper and held up what appeared to be a county mug shot, orange jumpsuit and all. "Is this him?"

"Bingo," I said, recognizing Jackie, despite the close-cropped hair in the photo. "So, he's got a record?"

"Meth-maker. Busted the first time at the age of twenty-two. Served four in Federal. Two at Terminal Island and two at Metro, downtown. Guess who his bunkie was in Federal."

"Who?" I asked, but I had a pretty good idea.

"Tommy Molfetta. He's one of Bennie DiMarco's guys, right?"

"Correct."

"I called Sandy at the parole board and got some pretty good info. The guy's name is Jack Shao. Born in '78, raised here in L.A. graduated a year ahead of schedule with a B.S. in chemistry, summa cum laude. Then kicked out of the UCLA grad-program a year later. Couldn't find out why."

"Wait. He would have graduated in '02. And Grad-school in '03 at UCLA?" An interesting possibility occurred to me.

"Yep."

"Xen got his PhD in '03."

"Think they knew each other?"

"Maybe … it's a big school, but aren't the super-stars in programs like that pretty well known in University circles?"

"It was like that when I went to school," she confirmed.

"I'll have to ask Xen about that when I see him tonight. Go on."

"Well, Jackie disappears for a year and then gets busted on a minor possession. The case is thrown out for improper search, and his parole officer gets him a job at VeniCorp in '06. He's been there ever since."

I sat there thinking for a bit. "It's starting to come together, Rachel. God, I love this job." I looked at her with open admiration on my face. "Nice work, by the way."

"Don't be too impressed. It wasn't that hard. When do you see Xen?"

"Eleven. Grady's."

"Want me to come?"

"Not on this one. He's on the run, and there's no telling what might happen. However, a job well done deserves a killer dinner. How about the Sunset Grill?"

"You got thrown out of an airplane the last time we went there."

"But I like the food."

"I feel like Italian, and I want to get into character. You're taking me to the Ago." She smiled mischievously, knowing the Ago to be one of the nicest and most expensive Italian bistros in the city.

"Am I?"

"You are," she looked at me greedily. "Like you said, you owe me."

I sighed, resigning to my fate and a $500 dinner tab. "Deal. You're worth it. But you can't go like that," I pointed out, eyeing her up and down. "I don't have time to get into any fights defending your honor. The way you look, I'm certain someone would want to besmirch it."

"Besmirch? Me?" she asked, grinning wickedly.

"You know what I mean."

"I think I do. I'll go get dressed. You going like that?"

"Don't I always?"

"One of these days I'm going to get you dressed up. I've never seen you in a tuxedo."

"And you probably never will."

"It's a bet." She practically leapt out of the lounge chair and rushed inside.

Uninvited Guests

I sat at the bar in the back room of Grady's, thinking fondly about my dinner with Rachel. I sipped a cup of tea with '40s big band music playing in the background. I'd dropped her off at her place around ten after a really wonderful meal, a couple bottles of really good wine, and positively soothing conversation. Without a doubt, Rachel was my favorite person on Earth, and I'd become increasingly more comfortable being around her, especially in the past few months. However, despite enjoying myself as much as I did, something at the back of my mind kept eating at me.

I had a weird feeling about the meeting with Xen all through dinner. I'd learned to trust my instincts early in my existence, so I'd stopped at my loft on the way to Grady's, trading out my motorcycle for the Chrysler and bringing Mag along. As Marsha had promised, the place was closed down, and there were no cars in the parking lot. I parked the Chrysler in the alley, and the two of us went in through the back door using the keys Marsha had given me. Once in, I unlocked the front and fixed myself a cup of tea.

I told Mag to hide behind one of the sofas closest to the front door and stay there camouflaged unless there was trouble. She wouldn't move unless I said so. Xen knew I had a cougar and had even seen her a few times, but I was hoping it wouldn't be necessary to show him her true form yet. Luck favors the prepared mind, and I didn't want to get caught with my pants down. Besides, if it came down to it, I did trust Xen at least enough to walk through the routine I'd come up with about Magdelain being a genetic mutation of a cougar and how I'd found her during a case years earlier. The story had worked before with Marsha and a few others.

I went behind the bar and poured myself another cup of tea just as the little hand closed in on the eleven. As I sat back down, I heard the doorknob of the back door turn. I leaned way over sideways so I could see the back door. I saw Xen's face appear and disappear through the barely open door. He was bald and hadn't been the last time I saw him. The clock showed eleven o'clock sharp. As usual, Xen was right on time.

"It's okay Xen. It's just me," I called out. "Come on in." I headed towards the back door as he stepped in and closed it quickly behind him. Xen is a not-thick-not-thin five-foot-seven and had taken to my training like a fish to water. He wore black boots, black jeans and a black long-sleeve pullover. I noted dark circles under his eyes; eyes that held fatigue, fear, and something else I'd never seen before—resolved strength. The past week and a half had clearly changed him. We met halfway and gave each other a huge hug.

"It's good to see you, man," I said.

"It's good to be seen," he replied, slapping me on the back as we released.

"C'mon. I'll pour you some tea," I offered.

"Bourbon," he said like a veteran drinker.

"You don't drink."

"After killing a hit man downtown and living on the run for a week, I started. *Bourbon*," he repeated firmly.

"Okay." I stepped behind the bar, got a couple of tumblers and pulled down a bottle of Wild Turkey. I poured two fingers worth into each glass and pushed one over to Xen. He gulped down a finger's worth, set the glass down and stared at me for a few seconds. I waited for the gasp-cough from the bourbon burning down's his throat, but he didn't even flinch.

"What the hell did you get me into?" Xen asked with a taint of anger. He'd obviously pieced together that his troubles began when I'd given him that data.

"I swear, Xen, I didn't know," I pleaded. "And I'm only starting to piece things together now." I gave him an impressed look. "Good work with the faked death, by the way. You scared the hell out of me, you know."

"Scared the hell out of you? I haven't slept in a week."

"I bet."

"And there's more. I'd met someone … and she doesn't know either. I didn't know if I could trust her."

"Natalia?"

"Yeah, she's … how did you?—"

"She's the one who told me you were dead. Listen, Xen. About Natalia …"

"What?" he asked, suddenly fearful.

The back door opened, and four, thick-built men walked in. Cold murder filled their eyes, and every one of them had eastern-bloc features. Xen and I looked at each other and back at the men without saying a word. A few seconds later, the front door to the parlor opened up, and three more walked in.

"Can you take two?" I whispered to Xen, nodding to the two guys at the front door.

"I'll bloody well try, but there's three," he said with more confidence than I expected.

"You just have to worry about two of them." He gave me a worried look. "Trust me," I added. "If they have guns, follow my lead. If not, stay alive and kill them if you can. Get behind the bar," I added under my breath. I faced the four at the back of the parlor. "Hi!" I said brightly, as if they were old friends I hadn't seen in years. I stepped around the bar towards them. "The place is closed tonight. You must not have gotten the message." One of the men stepped up and caught me with a fast right across the chin. No one else moved. I straightened up, running my tongue over my teeth.

"So, it's going to be that way, hunh?" I concluded, still smiling.

"Bennie DiMarco sends his regards," the man said with a slight Russian accent. "He paid us extra to take our time in beating you to death."

The three men at the front door headed for Xen who had stepped back behind the bar. I moved towards the middle of the parlor, and the remaining four carefully moved around me.

"I don't suppose we could make a deal, could we?" I asked hopefully. "I'm rich."

The man simply shook his head.

"I was afraid of that." I sighed tiredly as I positioned myself, putting the one who had clocked me to my right.

"Mag?" I said loudly and clearly. The four men looked at each other, not understanding. "Front door. NOW!" As I heard an ear-splitting snarl, I spun with blinding speed to my right. I drove my elbow as hard as I could into the throat of the man who had spoken. I felt his larynx collapse, crushed completely with the impact, and he flew back through the entrance to the bar. In the same motion I kicked out with my left leg, hammering my boot into another man's crotch, catching him completely by surprise. He grunted once and staggered back into the hallway towards the back door, bent over and gasping for breath with his hands grasping at his wrecked testicles. Did I mention I don't fight fair?

The man with the collapsed throat smashed into a tall rack of wineglasses and fell to the floor, holding his throat as he turned blue. A man's screams filled the room, and there was a horrible snarling sound as Magdelain tore into one of the men who had come in the front door.

The two left on Xen came at him fast, but with Xen behind the bar, only one could really get at him. Xen went into a defensive stance, using the bar as protection. The two left around me kicked at my mid-section. I blocked one kick and grabbed the leg of the second man. I crouched down, spinning as I went. My back leg swept under the legs of the first kicker who tumbled to the ground. Turning, I dragged the captured leg with me, completed a full rotation, and heard a sick popping sound as his knee dislocated. I sent him flying headfirst into one of the large TV monitors beyond the conversation pit. Sparks flew as his head shattered the screen and he slumped to the floor, motionless except for one leg twitching.

I took a quick look behind the bar. Xen was doing okay, mostly blocking the attacks of the first man, but the second had leapt up onto the bar and dropped down behind Xen.

"Xen!" I yelled.

Without looking Xen shot out a back-kick that caught the man in the chest just as he landed on the floor behind the bar. Grunting and staggering back, he tripped over the legs of the still-choking man and fell directly into a rack of wine bottles that shattered as he collapsed on top of my first victim. He was down but not out, and started to get back up, albeit slowly.

The man I had tripped came up cautiously, approaching me with something in his hand. We were both in solid fighting stances, and I had no doubt every one of these guys was a pro. I heard a loud, metallic click as the blade came out of the guy's cowpuncher, a switchblade of particularly deadly design. I looked at the knife and then at him, a subtle smile on my face.

He held the knife with point outward in line with his thumb. He might be a pro, but I knew immediately that he wasn't a knife fighter. The good ones hold the blade pointing down, away from their pinky fingers. I shook my head as we closed. I calmly stepped back from the first slash and then the back swing, waiting for my opening. I widened my hands, inviting a stab.

Taking the bait, he came in low and fast, trying to catch me in the belly. My hand moved down in a flash, grabbing his hand in an iron grip. I raised his hand, twisting his arm outward and opening him up. He was already leaning forward, and my knee came up into his belly like a piston, picking him up off the ground and forcing the air out of his lungs. As I looked past the man doubled-over in front of me, I saw the guy I had first kicked in the balls straightening up and pulling out a Makarov from his shoulder holster. He'd finally gotten his wind back and seemed intent on shooting us rather than beating us to death.

I tore the knife away from the man in front of me, spun him around, and using him as a shield, charged full speed at the guy with the pistol. I glanced at Xen and realized he was in trouble behind the bar. One of the killers held him from behind, his arms pinned, while the other worked Xen's mid-section with fast punches. Then another snarl filled the parlor.

Gunshots rang out as the man fired the Makarov. There were more screams, this time from behind the bar as Mag tore into another one of them. I pressed my living shield into a hail of bullets. At full speed and with every ounce of strength, I smashed the two men together into the back door of the parlor. The eyes of the man with the gun rolled back in his head as he slammed against the steel door. In a fast motion, I slit the throat of my shield, finishing the job the gunman had started, and then buried the switchblade deep into the dazed left eye of the shooter.

Hearing screams and snarls from behind the bar, I spun. I stepped out to see Xen being held firmly by the last man and dragged backwards towards the wall of TV screens. Xen stopped struggling, planted his feet and came up with a heel directly into the crotch of the man holding him. The guy yelped and let go. Xen spun, crouching as he did and caught the guy with a palm-strike in the solar plexus. The man doubled over, helpless. Xen grabbed the guy's hair in both hands, raised his head up and then brought the guy's face down hard into an up-coming knee. He grunted as he put everything he had into it. The guy's face exploded, his nose and cheeks caving in completely. He flew up and back, his feet lifting off the ground, and sailed into the TVs mounted on the wall behind him. He fell to the floor with two monitors following him down, crashing on top of his lifeless body.

The room went silent except for the dripping of wine from a few bottles hanging precariously in the broken rack. Mag came out from behind the bar, her muzzle and claws covered in blood. One of her eyes had swelled shut and she walked with a slight limp. Xen wordlessly walked behind the bar, slammed down his remaining finger of Wild Turkey, and grabbed my half-full glass.

"You okay?" I asked as he stepped away from me. He glared at me over the Wild Turkey as he leaned back against the bar and held his ribs with one hand. I walked up to the bar, exploring Xen's face. He downed the drink fast, gasping a bit, and shook his head at me.

"I'm pretty goddamn far from okay," he said, his eyes a bit wild and adrenaline poured through his system.

I looked him over and realized that he'd done more than held his own against two professional killers. "Not bad Xen. Not bad at all," I said quietly.

I took off my coat and laid it over one of the bar stools. Grabbing the bottle of bourbon, I poured myself a drink and downed it. Then I set the glass down on the bar next to Xen's.

A shot rang out from the front door, and I heard Mag howl in agony. I spun to see a dark-haired man a bit shorter and thicker than me, wearing a black suit. He held a gun in one hand and a gasoline can in the other. He had a black goatee.

The Russian, I thought, remembering Yvgenny's warning.

"Impressive, gentlemen," he said with a harsh Russian accent. I looked at Mag who had collapsed on the floor, panting heavily. Blood oozed from the bullet hole in her side. Rage filled me, the old rage, the one I try to keep bottled up so no one can see what I used to be ... what I was created to be. I didn't care what Xen saw. I stepped away from the bar and moved towards the Russian.

Two more shots filled the gambling parlor, catching me in the chest. I felt the bullets tear through me and heard them shatter a mirror behind the bar. Pain screamed through my body. I coughed up a mouthful of blood and collapsed mid-stride, lying motionless on the floor with my face turned towards Xen, eyes open. Xen's glass slid from his hand and shattered behind the bar, his eyes wide with terror.

Wide Eyed

Shaking slightly from fear and shock, Xen froze as the Russian walked up to the bar and set the gasoline can on top of it. The gun never wavered as he tipped the can over and slid it down the bar, gasoline pouring out and spilling over onto the floor. All Xen could do was watch. The Russian reached the end of the bar and left the can there to empty out. He stepped back and faced Xen as gasoline fumes filled the air.

"Xen, yes? The chemist?" the assassin asked.

Xen nodded his head almost imperceptibly.

"You are one DiMarco's thinks dead?"

Another tremor-nod.

"I think you should have stayed dead. Better than this, yes?" He nodded towards the gasoline on the bar.

"How did you know we were here?" Xen asked, finally able to speak.

The Russian smiled confidently.

"Had man on roof across way, waiting for that man." The Russian pointed a thumb over his shoulder at my motionless form. "Now I not have to pay lookout. You killed him for me." The assassin nodded to the corpse to Xen's left with the TVs on top of the body. "My thanks. Maybe I just shoot you and not burn to death. You like this?"

Xen's eyes grew impossibly wide, but not at the Russian's question. I'd risen behind the Russian and wiped the blood off my chin.

"You missed me, asshole," I growled, letting the old me loose. I spat out a mouthful of blood.

It was the Russian's turn to look scared, and I had a feeling his own eyes grew wide. But he was a professional, after all. He spun around, the gun swinging quickly in a tight arc, but too late. The gun came round directly into my perfectly placed snap kick before the Russian could train it on me. The impact shot the Russian's arm straight up, and the gun fired harmlessly into the wall and then went flying out of his hand.

I stepped in and hammered my elbow into left side of his jaw. He dropped down onto all fours but didn't go all the way to the floor. In a flash, he snapped his hand down to his right ankle and pulled out a small Beretta, raising it quickly at me.

I was ready for it and snapped a front kick before he could point it at me. The gun sailed from his hand with a shot, but the bullet went wide, tearing a hole in the carpet and ricocheting off the concrete underneath.

"I figured you had a hideaway." I smiled like the devil. "You should have waited to pull it." I breathed heavily and spat out another mouthful of blood, this time on the Russian. "You shot my cat." I let the fury take control as the Russian rolled back and jumped quickly to his feet. Xen had never seen me like this, had never seen the *thing* I used to be before coming to Earth. "Now I'm going to take you apart, one piece at a time."

The Russian said nothing. He moved into a fighting stance, hands raised and flexing a jaw already starting to swell.

I closed in slowly, my own hands raised but held open, loosely. The Russian circled to my left, away from the bar. By the Russian's stance, I could tell he knew how to use his legs. He shifted his weight and came up fast with a snap kick. I leaned back a bit and blocked it lightly with an open palm, waiting for the follow-up punches. They came an instant later, right on queue—a fast flurry of left-right combos that I easily blocked, moving back a step with each punch.

The Russian pulled back for an instant, creating the opening I needed. I let fly a quick right-jab, faster than he could see, landing it squarely on the swollen bruise that had formed on his jaw. As his head swiveled with the impact, I cocked my left leg and brought my foot around hard into his forward knee. The knee bent badly, shooting sideways in a direction knees are not supposed to go. He sank into his stance, trying to regain his footing, but he toppled. Rather than collapsing, however, he rolled to the side and came up immediately, favoring the leg. I smiled with grim satisfaction.

"Stings, don't it?" I asked. "Now an arm." I saw Xen move towards the Beretta on the floor between us. "Stay where you are, Xen," I growled without looking, and the icy tone was an order, not a request. Xen froze, looking almost as afraid of me as he had the Russians.

The Russian went back to circling with his oh-so-satisfying limp. I shifted into the drift and let fly a fast left-right. The Russian blocked quickly and came around with a right aimed at my head. I leaned out of it and followed with a left that grazed his right cheek. The Russian leaned back and came up at my mid-section with a snap kick using the bad leg. It connected, but not hard enough to do more than slow me down. I stepped back, and the Russian smiled. I stepped in quickly and shot a weak kick at his face. He sidestepped and pivoted all the way around to his right. He hoped to catch me with a backhanded left.

Most men couldn't pull off a punch like that quickly enough, but the guy was *really* fast, I'll give him that. At least I knew why Yvgenny had made a point of warning me. It had probably connected plenty of times before for the guy, but not this time. I saw it coming, tilting my torso and raising my left hand just in time. I caught his wrist in an open hand and clamped down. I pulled in his left hand hard towards my body and, using my right forearm, smashed it into the Russian's straightened elbow.

A sick, wet cracking sound filled the room as his elbow snapped, bending back ninety degrees in the wrong direction. He howled, but I didn't let go. I kept pulling with my left and pushing with my right. He spun forward, losing his footing. I heaved with all my strength and sent him flying into the roulette wheel headfirst. He sailed into it, and the big wheel snapped off with a crash. Man and wheel bounced off the wall and toppled to the floor.

I stood where I was, almost casually, and waited for him to get back up. "You alive back there," I called out. "Come on … I heard you Russians were supposed to be tough. Someone even warned me about you. Imagine that."

He got to his knees, supporting his weight mostly on his right arm and leg. He looked at me with blood coming out of a broken nose and cut lip. He moved with fatalistic fury. He knew what was coming, but he got to his feet and stood, glaring at me. His left arm hung limply at his side. He grabbed it with his right hand and tucked his left hand into his belt, wincing as he did.

"You know what. I'm going to cut you some slack," I said. "Stay there." I backed away from him and, keeping an eye on him, went over to the two bodies piled by the back door. I bent over, pulled the switchblade out of the eye-socket where I'd left it and wiped the blood off on the corpse's coat. I strolled back towards the Russian who went into a wary crouch, thinking I would come at him with the blade. Instead, I stopped at the end of the broken roulette table and lay the knife down. I took a few steps back, giving him plenty of room.

Narrowing his eyes, calculating if he should pick up the knife or not, he realized it was his only chance. He stepped forward. His twisted knee held his weight a little better, and he picked up the knife with his good hand. He spun it around so that the blade pointed down, away from his pinky.

I nodded as I went into a crouch. The Russian came at me slowly, steadily, without any fear. We both knew this was the endgame. He either killed me here and now, or it was all over for him.

He never slowed down. The instant he got within range, he popped forward with a fast kick to my knees and slashed at my face with the blade. I stepped back and let it sail by. His back swing was lightning fast, and I had to leap back another step to avoid getting a C-section. As his arm swung out, I popped up in the air and hammered a tight roundhouse into his broken elbow. He stumbled sideways with the impact and screamed in agony.

I pounced like a cat, dropping a hammer-fist across his good forearm. The impact broke his arm, and the knife dropped to the floor. My momentum carried my arm down right on top of the blade. I grabbed it, spun in a low crouch and slashed down to the bone across his right knee. His leg buckled as the severed tendons gave way and shot back up into his leg. I came around behind him and grabbed him by his hair.

I leaned in and whispered into his ear. "How many helpless people have you killed? How does it feel to be one of them, hmmm?" And there it was again. Someone could easily ask *me* the same question, with the same kind of rage for the things I'd done back home.

The Russian closed his eyes and waited for it. I wondered if someday I'd be in the same position, waiting for someone else's killing blow.

I jammed the switchblade through the back of his neck. The tip of the blade came out through his throat, and he made a quiet gurgling sound. I let go of his hair. His eyes went wide, and he gurgled again, trying to say something, but only blood came out, pouring down his chin. He fell forward and never moved again. As his life expired, I felt the rage start to dwindle, and the one inside me who owned it faded as well.

I stood and walked over to my coat. I picked it up and reached into an inner pocket, pulling out a smooth, oblong device the size of my palm, concave on one side and convex on the other. I walked over to where Magdelain still lay on the floor, panting. She had reverted to her natural gray and green coat. I looked at Xen who now stared at Magdelain, his eyes still wide.

"It's okay, girl. You'll be fine," I whispered "I'm sorry that bad man shot you," I added as if talking to a child with a scraped knee. I placed the device over her wound. It glowed momentarily and then went dull-gray again. I reached under her, running my hand along the other side, feeling for any blood. "Did it get past these ribs, girl?" I asked, placing my hand gently on the device.

She weakly shook her head.

"You'll feel fine in the morning. I'll get you some Kobe beef. How does that sound? Would you like that?"

She nodded her head with a little more vigor.

I stood up and walked back to the bar. Grabbing the bottle of Wild Turkey, I filled the tumbler half full, set the bottle down and picked up the glass. I looked at Xen who stared blankly at me, speechless.

I raised the glass. "Budem," I said and downed the whole thing. I set the empty glass back on the bar, staring into it. The silence dragged by like a corpse in a procession. I could feel Xen staring at me. "Owwww …" I finally said, rubbing my chest where the bullets had gone through. I rubbed at it like other people rubbed recently whacked funny bones. Collapsing onto one of the barstools, I looked down at the wood and sniffed the gasoline. Xen stared at me, then at Magdelain for a few seconds, then back at me.

"What the hell is that?" Xen asked a bit fearfully, pointing at Mag. "I'll ask you why you're not dead later. I don't think I could handle the answer right now."

"That's Magdelain. You know, my cougar," I said matter-of-factly without looking up.

"Cougar, my ass. What the hell is it?"

"It's a … cat," I said without conviction.

"Justin, I told you about my schooling, right?" Still mostly in shock, Xen's scientific training got the best of him.

"Yeah. You said you had three PhDs." I thought he showing remarkable calm, considering everything that had happened. I figured it was only a matter of time before he popped … and went around the bend a bit.

"Did I tell you what in?" he asked slowly.

"No, we never actually got around to that, but I'm assuming one was chemistry."

"Chemistry," Xen counted them off on his fingers slowly, "botany … and … *biology*, with a focus on mammalian life, coincidentally." He pointed at Magdelain and said, "*That* doesn't exist. Mind telling me how I'm looking at one?"

Mag lifted her head with a bit more strength and stuck her tongue out at him.

I looked at Mag with compassionate eyes. "Of course she exists. Look. He didn't mean that girl," I soothed. I turned back to Xen, rubbing my temple, "And it's a long story. How about I tell you later?"

"I'd rather you tell me now." I picked up a trace of frantic desperation in Xen's voice. He was on the verge of popping. I could hear it is his voice.

I looked around the room, taking in all the destruction. "Shit," I said to change the subject.

"What?"

"I told Marsha she wouldn't even know I'd been here."

"You do seem to be getting into the habit of wrecking other people's places. It's bad for your Karma. Which reminds me …" Xen stepped up and hit me in the arm … *hard.*

"Owwww! What the hell was that for? I've just been shot … remember?"

"That's for my front fucking doors! For my fucking living room, and for my fucking kitchen!" Xen shouted, genuinely pissed off.

"Oh, yeah," I said sheepishly. "That. Sorry. I may have to light one of my own houses on fire just to fix my Karma. How about I let you bring marshmallows?"

"You're on," Xen said way too seriously. "You know, you should be dead," Xen added with a scared tone in his voice. The shock was wearing off. I could see it in his face. "How long have we known each other?" he asked.

"I don't know … a little over two years,"

Xen's face showed a mix of fear and fascination, bordering on a total freak-out. "Yeah. Well, I've known you long enough and seen and heard enough things to piece together that something isn't normal about you. In fact, a whole lot of somethings. I'm not an idiot. But this?" he said motioning around the room. "This puts it way, way beyond impossible.…" He stared at me for a few seconds. "What the actual fuck?"

I sighed. "Fair question," I said quietly and poured another glass of Wild Turkey. I would have to come clean with Xen, at least a big piece of the story, anyway. But I couldn't right there and then. I reached into a coat pocket and pulled out my phone. "Look, can we talk about it later? I have to get this cleaned up." My eyes pleaded for a break.

Xen hesitated for a moment, desperate for some sort of explanation. He looked around the room, took in the carnage and finally realized that there were eight dead bodies on the floor.

"Yeah. Later." He reached behind the bar and pulled out a fresh tumbler. He filled it to the top with Wild Turkey and took three long gulps. Then he went into a coughing fit while I tried not to smile at him. I took a stiff belt of my own. Between coughs he said, "But we're *going* to talk about it. You're not getting off this particular hook. You hear me?" I heard steely resolve in his voice. Something I wasn't used to.

"Alright, man. I guess I owe you that."

"You *do*, and keep in mind … I'm a *scientist*. I'm pretty objective about things when I can see and touch them. And I've seen and touched quite a bit tonight. You know what I mean?"

"I think I do, Xen. Thanks," I added sincerely. I selected a speed dial and hit CALL. Putting the phone to my ear, I waited for an answer.

Yvgenny picked it up almost immediately. "Da?" he said.

"Yvgenny, it's Justin."

"Justin! How are you my boy?" he asked, laughing lightly. "Isn't it past your bed time? Or maybe milk and cookies have keeping you awake. What trouble are you getting into this evening?"

"Funny you should ask that," I said not at all innocently.

Yvgenny picked up my somber tone. "What's wrong?"

"I need a mop up. Fast. No questions. The guy I normally use is on vacation … in Norway," I added with not a little disgust.

"Normally use?" Xen asked incredulously, shaking his head. He realized there was a *lot* he didn't know about me. I held up my hand to shush him. Xen was always interrupting phone conversations.

"Norway?" Yvgenny asked.

"Yeah, his mother died."

"Did *you* kill her?" Yvgenny chuckled lightly.

"NO! Yvgenny! Come on, this is serious," I said, but I finally had a smile on my face. The old rage was, thankfully, gone. Yvgenny always managed to crack me up.

"How many?" Yvgenny asked.

I hesitated, "Uh …" I twisted my toe in the carpet like an embarrassed child.

"Two?" Yvgenny prompted.

"Well … you see …"

"Three?" Disbelief grew in his voice.

I sighed. "Guessing will take too long...."

"Christ, Justin! How many?"

"There are eight bodies in here ... most of them bleeding out."

"Good God! What did you do?"

"Well, they started it," I said like a child in trouble.

"I'm thinking you are saying that a lot to people these days."

"There's more, Yvgenny."

"What?" the old man asked with a touch of anxiety and suspicion in his voice.

"Well ... you see ..." I cleared my throat nervously. "They ... they're not Italian."

"Really? Then what are they?" Yvgenny asked in a deadly serious tone.

"Well, you know that Russian hit-man you warned me about?"

"Da ..." he said slowly.

"He ... he sorta' brought friends."

Yvgenny was suddenly very calm. "Before we continue, I need you to go to one of them. It is not mattering which. You may have placing me in difficult position." I picked up the tone in Yvgenny's voice and got a knot in my stomach.

"Alright," I said carefully and walked over to the one Xen had killed by the TVs.

"Can you seeing any of their arms?" Yvgenny asked.

"They're all wearing long sleeves."

"Pull one up ... a left sleeve."

I leaned over, holding the phone between my ear and my shoulder, then unbuttoned and rolled up the corpse's left sleeve. "What am I looking for?"

"Tell me what you are seeing on his wrist, on the palm side."

"He's got an iron cross, like those German ones, and some Cyrillic characters under it."

Yvgenny let out a sigh of relief and quietly said something in Russian.

"What'd you say?" I asked.

"I said, 'This boy will being the death of me.' You are being most lucky these men are not part of our organization. Our crews only work together, and they all have double-skulls on left wrist. If they were ours, I could not help you."

"I understand. So do you know anyone?"

"I can't using one of our people. It would get … *complicated*."

"I hear ya. Look, Yvgenny … I need these guys to disappear." I changed my voice to one of a teenager in double-dutch. "I mean, when mom gets home, she's gonna be *pissed*." There was a pause, then Yvgenny and I both laughed, but Xen lost it completely. His laughter started out normal enough, but it quickly shifted into a slightly higher-pitched, nervous, frantic sort of cackle.

I heard an imaginary pop in my head as the weight of what happened hit Xen full on. His laughter was the kind people make when they're straddling the fence between sane and … not so much. I turned my head away from Xen's laughter so I could hear Yvgenny a little better.

"I am knowing a man, but he's not cheap."

"Can I trust him?" I asked cautiously.

"I do," Yvgenny said with complete certainty. "We usually keep things in-house, but he's worked for me before. He is professional, although, he is being sort of oddball."

"If you trust him, I will."

"How much do you have on you?" Yvgenny asked.

"Just shy of four grand."

Yvgenny started laughing. "You'll need five times that, and that's if he is being in good mood when I *wake* him."

"Make the call. Tell him to meet me at Grady's in forty-five minutes … and to come in the back. If he wants, he can have their car or cars. I don't know how many they came in."

"That is … how do you say? S.O.P.? It will not change price."

"I know. Just get him here. It's eleven-thirty. If he's here in forty-five, there's an extra ten grand in it for him, okay?"

"That will most certainly putting him in good mood."

"Thanks, Yvgenny."

"Of course. And Justin."

"Yeah?"

"Try not to kill anyone for rest of day. You are having thirty minutes before midnight, and if you are trying really hard, I think man like you can make it." Yvgenny started laughing definitely *at* and not with me this time.

"I'll do my best," I said dryly.

I hung up the phone and looked at Magdelain. "Can you walk, girl?" She still lay on all fours.

She nodded her head and slowly got to her feet.

"Come on, Xen. We're going back to my place."

"Un-hunh." Xen had finally calmed down and had a blank stare on his face. He took another gulp of bourbon, stepped around the bar and walked mechanically towards the back door.

"Wait up," I called from behind him. "Let me go lock the front doors." I went to the front of the place and found that the Russians had thankfully picked the lock rather than smashing the door. I locked the doors, hit the lights, and returned to the parlor. I looked around and still couldn't believe all the damage. Marsha was going to flip out. I hoped a stack of cash would be enough to keep her from killing me. If not, I'd take it like a man. I walked past Xen who had stopped just short of the two dead bodies blocking the back door.

"Here, help me move them," I said quietly. A series of short laughs snuck past Xen's lips, and he covered his mouth to get hold of himself. "You okay?" I asked, real concern in my voice. He nodded quickly with his lips pressed firmly together. We each grabbed a body and pulled it a few feet away from the door. Stepping over the corpses, we walked into the alley. I opened the door of my Chrysler for Mag and closed it after her.

"What a night," Xen said with complete disbelief.

"Mmm-hmmm."

We drove back to my loft in silence, you know, that weird silence that only comes after you kill a bunch of hit men with your bare hands. Parking on the street, we got out and walked down the alley. I was about to lift up the sign but stopped myself. "Xen?" I asked cautiously.

"What?"

"Steady yourself, okay?" I tried to reassure him with a calm tone.

"What? Are there more bodies in there?" he asked a bit frantically.

I chuckled. I couldn't help myself. "No," I said still chuckling. "No bodies. Just steady yourself. Your world is about to get a little bigger."

Xen had never been to the warehouse, just the place I have behind his. I slid up the sign beside the door, laid my palm on the reader and ran through the combination. Then I pushed open the door jam. Mag slithered between us and into the loft.

I stuck my head through the door. "Lights," I called out, and we were both bathed in the light from inside. "After you," I said to Xen, ushering him in.

Xen stepped through the doorway, took a few steps and looked around. Then he stopped dead in his tracks. "Wait a minute…." He turned around with a baffled look on his face and stared at me. The alley was clearly visible behind me. Xen looked at the window again and could see a streetlight not far off, almost at eye level.

"It gets better," I said smiling. "Hold on to your hat." I closed the door and placed my hand on the panel next to it, using a different combination. I opened the door again, and it opened into my beach-house living room.

"Fuck me!" Xen yelled.

"You okay?" I asked worriedly.

"Yeah, I'm fine," he said, but his voice was full of everything except fine.

"Look, I have to get back to Grady's. If you go through that door, no one in the world will know where you are except me. I'm going to send Mag with you, okay?"

"Okay." He was stupefied and seemed to be merely going through the motions. I probably could have told him to cut his own arm off and have gotten a positive response.

"If you go straight through the living room and kitchen, there's a patio in the back. Down the path behind the house, there's a nice beach. Make yourself at home. Get cleaned up and get some rest." I looked at Mag. "Stay with Xen, okay girl?" She nodded her head and walked through the doorway.

"It'll be okay, Xen. I swear. If you need to reach me, your cell phone won't work. Only mine does down there. Use one of the phones around the house. If you can't reach me, call Rachel."

"Okay," Xen said numbly.

"Oh, one more thing. If, for whatever reason, you absolutely, positively think you have to come back to the warehouse, tell Mag. She'll lead you back, although you'll have to crawl through her kitty-door. It's big enough for her, so you should fit fine."

"Okay," he replied with a bit of unease.

I gently placed my hand behind Xen's back and guided him through the door.

"Call me when you wake up," I said to his retreating back.

"Un-hunh … one question." Xen said quietly, stopping and turning around in my living room.

"What's that?" I asked.

"Where the hell am I?"

I locked eyes with him. "Costa Rica." I winked and closed the door on Xen's wide-eyed face.

Couple of Clowns

A wave of fatigue and some dizziness hit me as I closed the door. Even I have side effects from blood loss. I walked over to the fridge and grabbed a half-empty bottle of orange juice. Uncapping it, I poured in about a cup of sugar from the dispenser on the counter, turned, and opened one of the cupboards, pulling down a container of protein powder. I poured in a healthy amount and recapped the juice, shaking it vigorously to mix everything up.

Uncapping it again, I gulped the thick mixture, finishing it in seconds. Setting the empty container on the counter, I walked over to the standing closet, dropping my coat down on the sleeping mat along the way. I kicked off my shoes, pulled off my bloody shirt and slacks and threw them in a pile on the floor. I ran my fingers over the slightly red, swollen entry-wounds on my chest, wincing slightly as I touched them. They were still tender but had sealed up quickly during the fight. The exit wounds on my back were larger and hurt even worse.

"At least they came out," I said to myself.

I grabbed a fresh shirt and some jeans, slipped them on and then put my shoes back on. I headed to the back of the loft between the cars and gym-mat. "Mat lights." The back area lit up.

I opened one of the wide, eight-foot-tall double-doors along the back wall, revealing a twenty-five-foot hallway wide enough to drive a van through. There was a door a short way down the hall on the right, leading to my bathroom and shower. A second door further on opened to a utility and storage closet. A palm-reader was installed between the two doors. I walked in and put my hand on the reader, going through a lengthy and complex finger-sequence. I heard a loud metallic *THUNK* and then a hissing sound as air-pressure equalized between the two separate environments. A massive door the size and height of the hallway swung towards me with the quiet sound of servos. I quickly stepped through the widening gap before the door finished opening and walked across a cluttered cargo hold.

There were stacks two and three high of blue boxes three feet on a side made of something resembling dull plastic. The floor and walls were a uniform, egg-shell-white cerametal, and gray lockers lined both sides of the compartment. A single, closed door at the far end of the thirty-by-fifty-foot area had a palm reader beside it. Every locker had a small square made of the same material as the palm readers set in one side at chest-height. I walked up to one of the middle lockers on the right side and placed my left thumb on the reader. There was a soft click, and the door swung open. Inside were eight stacks of plastic bags, each one of them filled with ten wrapped stacks of hundred dollar bills. I grabbed a bag, closed the door, and headed back to my loft. As I walked past the cargo-hold door, the servos whined and the door closed behind me. With another metal clunk, it finished the cycle. I closed the double-doors behind me. "All lights off," I said, and the place went dark again.

I returned to Grady's via a phase-door connected to the men's restroom. The smell of blood and gasoline hit me hard, and I coughed once to catch my breath. I dragged the two bodies by the back door around the corner out of sight, and then I counted the rest to make sure all eight corpses were still there. One never knew, and I'd had bodies disappear on me before. I came up with the right number and walked behind the bar to the cooler. Opening it, I pulled out a pale ale, twisted the top off and walked over to the nearest conversation pit, taking up a position with a good view of both the front and back doors.

It was 12:10 a.m. and I suddenly craved a cigarette. I pulled a pack out, tapped it a few times to compress the tobacco, removed one and lit it up. Closing my eyes, I leaned my head back and relaxed while I had the chance. The beer went down like ambrosia, but the cigarette tasted like shit. I put the cigarette out after only a few drags. I'd have to thank Yvgenny next time I saw him for turning me on to the pipe. A few minutes later someone knocked on the back door.

"Come in!" I hollered as I stood up. I was on my guard, but frankly, I was tired enough that I didn't care what came through the door. I was ready for anything.

A clown stepped in through the back door and looked at me.

Except that, I realized in an instant. I lost it completely. I couldn't help it. I laughed so hard, I collapsed onto the couch. The guy had big red shoes, carnival-striped baggy pants, big red suspenders, a frilled blue collar, the classic white-painted face, and a great big red painted smile. He carried a small backpack, and if he'd wanted to kill me, he wouldn't have gotten much of a fight. It occurred to me later that such a ploy might come in handy in the future.

"You the guy who wanted the clean-up?" the clown asked with a slight smile when I finally got ahold of myself. He was a clown, so I guess he was used to people laughing at him.

I looked around the room slowly, deliberately. Then I looked the clown dead in the eyes with a wry grin and a light staccato of chuckles. "I don't know, what do you think?" I asked, my voice filled with irony.

The clown walked in and examined the parlor … and the carnage within. His eyes got a little wider as he slowly counted up the corpses. "I guess you are," he answered flatly. We looked at each other and laughed like the couple of clowns we were.

"You're not at all what I expected," I said dryly, still laughing.

"I know, I know … the outfit." He hadn't stopped smiling. "I had a gig … some rich kid's birthday party. I wanted to make your deadline. Ten grand is ten grand. The kid's dad was nice enough to let me bail before the party was over."

"No worries, man. I actually needed the laugh. It's been a hell of an evening."

"I can see that. Mind if I wash up?" he said, indicating his face paint.

"Go right ahead. You can use the sink behind the bar. Grab a beer out of the cooler if you want."

"Thanks, don't mind if I do." He moved behind the bar, set his backpack next to the sink, and pulled out some face cream. "This stuff leaves kind of a mess," the clown warned.

"I'm pretty sure this place couldn't look any worse if we slaughtered a hog in here," I said, taking another tired swig of beer.

The clown looked around again, and I think he frowned, but I couldn't tell through the red smile.

"Good point," he replied. He remained silent for a few minutes as he continued to clean the grease paint off his face. "You do all this?"

"I had some help," I said a bit evasively. The clown nodded his head. "Is your help one of these guys? I normally don't ask details, but some people want special treatment for their … *help*."

"No. He's gone. I mean, he left. These guys are garbage."

"Two of you did this?"

I nodded tiredly.

The clown raised his eyebrow, clearly impressed. "Remind me not to piss you off."

"It takes a lot," I reassured him, smiling. "I'm kind of an animal lover." The guy raised a questioning eyebrow, but when I didn't elaborate, he went back to cleaning his face. The last of the paint came off, and he rinsed his face one last time.

I looked at him and something occurred to me. The guy looked just like a young version of Leonard Nimoy. "Hey, you look just like …"

"Yeah, I know," the guy said grinning. "I get that all the time. No relation."

"You working like that?" I asked, referring to the clown-suit.

"No choice. I didn't bring a change. I was headed home right after the party."

"Okay. How do we work this? You want to just haul these bastards into your truck. You did bring a truck, right?"

"Van," he corrected, "and let me go get some bags. Some of these guys are still damp."

"Alright."

He walked out the back door with his backpack over his shoulder. He returned a minute later with an armful of black body bags. He walked around the room and dropped a bag on top of each corpse, stopping at the Russian hit man with the goatee. He got a curious look on his face and flipped the guy over with his big red clown-shoe.

"Hey, I know this guy. I just did some work for him a few nights ago."

"No shit? Friend of yours?" I asked cautiously.

"Hell no. He was a prick. The fucker even stiffed me five-hundred bucks." The clown kicked him with a big red shoe. I had to control a burst of laughter.

"He *was* a prick," I added, smiling. I had to marvel sometimes at some of the things I'd seen over the years. A guy in actual clown shoes kicking the corpse of a hitman was definitely one for my diary … if I kept one.

"You know, wasting this guy was a public service," the clown said, nodding at the body.

"I think so, too." I got to thinking about the rest of the mess. There were probably a few gallons of blood soaked into the carpet, and the room reeked of gasoline. "Hey, do you do abatement?"

The clown's face brightened. "As a matter of fact, that's one of my day-jobs. This work is a perfect lead-in for it."

"Makes sense. What would you charge to replace the carpet in here and do a full clean up? Down to the concrete."

"Oh," he rubbed the back of his neck, looking around the room, "Figure about six-grand plus materials. I even know a bonded interior designer who knows how to keep her mouth shut. She does good work. She's listed. Even done a few movie-moguls."

"Hypothetically speaking, how much would it be for a house that might … just possibly … have had a few bodies catch fire inside? Living room and kitchen would need some work, too."

The guy gave me a sidelong glance with a raised eyebrow, looking just like Spock when somebody says something illogical. "You *have* been busy."

"Long story."

"I bet," he replied, not wanting to know any more.

"I'd have to see it first to spec it out. Here's my card." The guy reached into the inside of his clown pants and produced a card. He walked over and handed it to me.

"You have a card?" I asked, wondering if it said, *Fast, Reliable Body Disposal While You Wait* on it.

"For abatement services, I do, plus a few other things." He paused and looked around the room. "This kind of work," he pointed to the bodies, "is word-of-mouth only."

"I bet." We laughed, and I looked at the card. *Stanley-Fast Abatement Services* was printed across the middle with a phone number below it. "Stanley. Is that you?"

"In the flesh," he said and gave me a big grin. All I could see in my head was the painted red smile that the guy had walked in with. "Yvgenny said there was eight. You got anything else around here needing disposal?"

"Naw. This is it."

"Okay, then let's get to work." We spent the next thirty minutes wordlessly filling the bags with their grisly contents and stacking them near the back door. We searched each body and emptied their pockets, placing everything on the bar. We found three sets of car-keys, and all the corpses had wallets, but the wallets were empty except for small amounts of cash.

"Hey … that's weird," Stanley said.

"What?" Justin asked.

"Only two of them had guns?"

"Looks that way. They said they were supposed to make it hurt. Guess our asshole over there," I indicated the goatee, "didn't think they could keep their hands off their guns if they were carrying."

"Lucky you."

"You got that right. If they all had guns, it probably would have been my friend in a bag with these guys."

The clown looked at me funny, thinking about what I had just said. "What, are you bulletproof?"

"Oh, I meant me and my friend," I corrected quickly. "Not thinking straight after all this."

The clown nodded his head. He walked to the back door, opened it and kicked down the doorstop so it would stay open.

"Well, let's load 'em up," he suggested.

We each grabbed an end of the top bag and carried it into the alley where he'd parked a white van with a large AC unit on the top. The clown backed in through the open rear doors with me trailing and unceremoniously dropped the body on the steel floor. The space was wide enough to get three bodies side-by-side. I felt cold air pumping hard and fast out of a vent in the ceiling and noticed that there were shelves of commercial heating dishes.

As I stepped out of the van, I peered around the open door and looked at the side of the van. In big colorful letters I read, *Stanley-Fast Catering and Clowning—Parties, Weddings and Bar Mitzvahs.*

My jaw dropped open, and I turned my head slowly at the clown retreating back into the building. The implications were a bit unnerving. I thought about the bodies and that big word *Catering.*

"You do catering, hunh?" I yelled into the building with a mostly veiled look of suspicion on my face.

Stanley laughed. "I get that a lot, too. Don't worry. My cargo never ends up in the kiddies."

I let out a sigh. "Glad to hear it," I added, truly relieved. We finished loading up the rest of the bodies. "Well, that's the last of them." I reached into a pocket as we headed back into the parlor to the bar. I pulled out three stacks of hundred dollar bills and set them on top of the wallets and keys. "It's all yours," I said smiling.

"Mind if I count it? I'm leery after dealing with that asshole," he added, pointing his thumb back at the bodies in the van.

"Wouldn't expect anything less," I replied.

The clown reached into his pants and pulled out a yellow marker, the kind they use in banks to check counterfeit money. He thumbed through the bills, marking about every fourth or fifth one. The money and the number of bills checked out.

"It's solid," he said. "Got a bag?"

"Lemme check," I replied, stepping behind the bar. I looked under the sink and came up with a small, clear plastic trash bag. "This ought to do it."

"Thanks. About the cars …" Stanley said, placing the cash, wallets and keys in the bag, "I saw three black Lincolns in the parking lot behind the building next door."

"I reckon the keys fit the cars," I speculated. "They're all yours."

"Thanks. On the way home I'll drop the keys off with a guy I know. The cars will be gone in a couple of hours, no sweat." The clown grabbed the beer still on the counter and finished it.

"Perfect," I said.

"Where's your car?" he asked.

I smiled. "I've got alternate transportation. It's all arranged."

"Gotcha," Stanley said holding out his hand. "Well, it's been a pleasure doing business with you."

"Same," I said simply.

"You know," he said slowly, "I've got my hands into a few pots. I'm also a Notary Public and do accounting. Let me know if you need anything."

I smiled and shook my head. "You're quite the entrepreneur, aren't you?"

Stanley smiled back. "You have no idea. I don't sleep much, rare disorder, and it all keeps me from getting bored. Have a good night," he said and headed for the back door.

"Hey, Stanley," I asked.

He stopped and turned with a raised eyebrow. "Yeah?"

"If you don't mind me asking, if the bodies don't end up on your menu, what do you do with them?" I'd always wondered about that but never asked anyone.

"No, I don't mind. I know a guy. Has a farm right on the border. Few hundred acres near the Tijuana River."

"Yeah?"

"Pig farmer."

"Oh," I said, the brutal truth that pigs will eat anything dawning on me with gruesome clarity.

"Yeah. Handy that. Best bacon you ever tasted, though."

"I'll bet," I replied slowly. "See ya around. I'll call you tomorrow about the abatement stuff."

"Thanks," he said, smiling. He closed the door quietly behind him.

I looked around the place again, taking in the damage. Even with the bodies gone, the place looked like hell. "God, Marsha's gonna be pissed," I muttered.

Determined to do the right thing, I walked through the front door of the parlor into the diner. As I stepped through the door, I saw a black Audi in front of the building. It squealed away, leaving rubber on the pavement as it left. I paused for a moment, contemplating the implications. Oddly enough, I wasn't as concerned as I normally would be. It was the second time I'd seen a black Audi, and this time where it shouldn't have been. There had to be a connection. Either they wanted to kill me or they didn't. If they did, I'd know soon enough, and if they didn't, it wouldn't matter that much.

I walked into the diner, turned the corner and went into the kitchen. I went into the office, turned on the light and sat down. Grabbing a pen and paper, I quickly wrote a note.

Marsha,

I know I said you wouldn't know I was here, but I was a victim of circumstances beyond my control, just like that time at the Maltese. DON'T go back into the parlor without calling me first. Here's some money to pay for the repairs. I'm also working on finding the folks to do the job and will arrange everything tomorrow.

I'M REALLY, REALLY SORRY!

Justin

I reached into my pocket again and pulled out the rest of the cash I had gotten from the storage locker. I laid the seven stacks down on the desk in two even piles, setting the oddball on top on its end. I propped the note up against the stacks, stood up and left the office, turning off the lights as I went. I could only hope that Marsha went into the office first. It was a safe bet, but if she did, it would ease the shock and reduce the likelihood of her cracking me over the head with an iron skillet … a number of times.

I left her keys beside the cash register where she had told me, walked outside and memorized the plates on the three black Town Cars. I went home, logged into my computer and did some fast research into the license plates of the Lincolns as well as the white vans that had gone into the VeniCorp plant. As expected, the Russian plates got me nowhere: registered to the occupants under phony names, I assumed. However, the white vans were registered to a daughter company of Zapata Tequila, and Zapata traced back a couple layers to a major drug cartel run by the particularly nasty drug lord named Del Gato, whom DiMarco had mentioned. I yawned, planning on digging into Del Gato later. I shut down the computer and headed to Costa Rica.

O O O

I arrived at the house about the time the sun was coming up. I stripped down and showered on the patio, hoping not to wake Xen. The showerhead stuck out onto a corner of the patio and was perfect for keeping sand out of the house. I dried off and lay down on one of the lounge chairs, letting the sound of the jungle put me to sleep.

Xen slept till three in the afternoon, which was about six in LA. I had seen that sort of thing a few times before; the body produces so much adrenaline during a fight like the night before that people simply crash afterwards. *Rachel and Marsha will go through it, too, if things kept going the way they are*, I thought.

When Xen got up, I grabbed the cooler, and we headed out to relax in the sand. Xen had on trunks. I didn't. Neither of us said a word, letting the surf and the monkeys do the talking. We whittled twelve ice-cold beers down to three, with Xen responsible for most of the whittling.

Finally, with the sun about half a beer off the ocean and well on its way to taking a swim in the Pacific, I asked, "How much can I trust you?"

He paused for a moment, looking at me out the corner of his eye. "If you're worried about me telling someone about all this, I have no one to tell. You know that." He finished off his beer, set the dead soldier next to its comrades. He grabbed another, twisted the top fiercely and taking a long swig. "You're my only real friend in the States besides Natalia. Everyone else is back in China. I told you I was from a village, right?"

"Yeah," I said, upending my own bottle before lying back in the sand.

"Well, I was being generous. It's nothing more than a few shacks surrounded by gardens and rice-patties. They'd never believe any of this. I'm having a hard time believing it myself. But seeing is believing, right?"

"Right," I said quietly.

"I guess when you tell people you're not from around here, you really mean it, don't you?"

"Yep." I sighed. "You're the first person to really know since I got here. Well, that's not entirely true. There is one other guy."

"Friend of yours?"

"Quite the opposite, actually."

He looked at me out of the corner of his eye. "You going to tell me your story?"

"Yeah," I agreed, "but not till Rachel is here, okay? She deserves to know, too, and I might as well only tell the story once."

"I can wait. I'm still wrapping my head around all *this*." Xen waved his beer at the beach and the house behind him, and then his eyes lingered on the two bullet wounds in my chest. He remained silent for a while, listening to the surf roll in. "Does it hurt?" he asked.

"Yeah. A lot. I *hate* getting shot. Happens quite a bit. But what can I do? It's the life I chose ... well ... more like was chosen for me."

We sat there like that, just enjoying the feel of the air, the warmth of the sun, and the sound of the surf.

"You said that Natalia came to get you," Xen finally said, breaking another silence. "Where is she? Is she safe?"

I hesitated and bit my lip. I had thought about what I would tell Xen since the moment Natalia sank beneath the waves in my truck. Both routes I could take would cause harm: one had risk and the other had pain. I made up my mind, dreading the inevitable conversation later.

"She's not, is she?" he asked quietly. I shook my head slightly, not looking at Xen. "DiMarco?" he asked.

I nodded slowly. "I have to tell you ... what happened to you and Natalia was technically my fault, but I had no idea any of this would happen. It still doesn't make sense ... yet. But I'll figure it out, Xen. I swear." I looked over at him and saw tears rolling down his cheeks. "I'm sorry."

"If you didn't know, you didn't know," Xen said tightly, barely controlling his wavering voice. "How's your cat?"

"Dratar."

"What?"

"She's called a dratar. She's not a cat. And she'll be fine. She's asleep around here somewhere. I pulled the triage unit off her when I got in last night. She'll probably sleep till tomorrow while she finishes up healing. She takes longer to heal than I do." I rubbed my eyes.

"Oh." Xen was really struggling with everything. I had said it all so matter-of-factly, expecting him to roll with the punches.

"Think you could stay here a few days?" I asked cautiously.

"I'm not likely to get shot here, am I?"

"A lot less likely than in L.A., I can tell you that much."

"Then I'm staying."

"Good. I'm heading back tonight. I have to set a few things in motion. I'm going to take care of this, okay?" I reassured him.

"I believe you. Is there anything you can't do?" Xen asked with a trace of awe in his voice.

I chuckled. "Lots of things." My voice was full of a lifetime of struggle. I'd always come out on top, but there were plenty of mistakes and inadequacies along the way.

"You gonna kill DiMarco?" Xen asked quietly, but with hope in his voice.

"Yep."

"Good. Can I help?" There was that iron resolve in Xen's voice again, and I was still getting used it. Xen had crossed a threshold and become something more than he was before this all started.

"Yep," I replied simply. "When I get back, I'll probably have Rachel with me. You'll get the whole story. And then we'll work on killing DiMarco." It was my turn with the iron resolve.

"Deal."

"Hey, I meant to ask you," I prompted, changing the subject. "Do you know a guy named Jackie Shao? He was in the same program as you, just a couple years behind." In all the chaos, I had nearly forgotten about DiMarco's chemist.

"Jackie? Yeah, I remember him. That guy was nuts."

I grinned. Not only did Xen know Shao, he knew him well enough to assess his sanity. I love it when pieces of a puzzle fall together. "Nuts? How do you mean?"

"He was sharp … smart, you know? *My* league." Xen wasn't bragging, merely pointing out a fact. Xen had been head of his class for a reason, and for him to equate Jackie's IQ to his own meant something. "But he liked to make drugs … more money in it up front for him, I think. He was an impatient sort. Got caught working with cocaine in the lab at school … trying to make it better."

"If he was so smart, how'd he get caught?" I asked.

"I ratted him out," Xen said simply.

"Oh." I said quietly. "So, he's a friend of yours." I smiled.

"Not bloody likely," Xen added. "Shao and I were oil and water, not peas and carrots. Is he involved in all this?"

"He works for DiMarco. He met one of DiMarco's guys in prison, and they hooked him up at VeniCorp when he got his parole. Do me a favor."

"Name it," he offered.

"While I'm gone, try and remember everything you can about him, okay? It may come in handy later. We'll trade stories, and you can tell me and Rachel what happened to you."

"If it will help bury DiMarco, I'll tell you anything you want."

"It will," I said, standing up. "You'll find a bag of money under my bed. Down the road about a mile is a small market. How's your Spanish?"

"Passable."

"Good. Get anything you want. About two miles past the store there's a hotel with a casino. If you get bored, you can head there. Tell them you're my guest, but don't take more than fifty from the bag if you go. Don't worry about blowing it all. It's disposable income." I smiled sympathetically. "I know how lousy you are at cards." I smiled. "Always tip heavy if you win."

Xen gave me half a smile. "We'll see. The beach is about all I can take right now." He leaned back in the sand and closed his eyes.

"I understand. Like I said before, if you need anything, call my cell from the house phone. Just keep cool, okay?"

"I'll do my best."

"Your best is better than just about anyone I know. It should work out." I headed back into the house and through the front door into my loft.

Rule Number One

I stepped up to Rachel's front door and rang the doorbell twice, following it with a rapid knocking that I didn't stop. Holding a large bundle of roses in front of my face, I waited for the peephole in the door to go dark. I only exposed the dozen red roses, dark sunglasses and curly blond hair. I hoped she liked the dark blue pinstripe suit I had on.

"Who is it?" she asked through the door.

I spoke with a proper English accent. "I have a delivery for the lady of the house from one Justin Case." I'm sure she thought it unlikely I would send her roses, although we *had* been growing closer. She unlocked the door and opened it a crack, leading with a taser so she could give me a once over in safety. Although the roses covered my face, she could see both my hands: one holding the roses and the other a fedora and a silver-topped walking stick. I clearly had no weapon, unless she wanted to count the cane, so, keeping an eye on me, she closed the door enough to remove the chain and let it swing open. The taser stayed pointed at my groin, however. *Nice touch, that.*

I lowered the roses and placed the hat on my blond curls so she could see that I had a trim, blond mustache. "Hello, my good woman. No need for the electrical appliance," I said, indicating the taser. "I was simply wondering if you would like to come out and play. Hmmm?"

Rachel stood there staring at me, blinking her eyes. Then it slowly dawned on her.

"You're wearing a suit," she said smiling lightly.

"Quite right. It's the only civilized attire for the discriminating gentleman en route to visit corporate America. You couldn't expect me to wear that drab little trench coat. What? They'd never take me seriously … and might be inclined towards the most uncouth behavior. Gunplay and whatnot."

Her smile grew as I continued to put on the show. "Come on in before the neighbors start to gossip," she said brightly. She opened the screen door, and I stepped in. "I was out back," she said indicating the patio. "I take it I'm going with you?"

"Of course, madam! Such an adventure into a den of evil would not be as entertaining on one's own, would it?"

"Den of evil?" she asked, raising an eyebrow and stopping in the kitchen.

"VeniCorp, of course … the corporate offices downtown."

"Really?" she asked eagerly.

"Yep," I said, using my normal voice. "Here, these really are for you." She blushed and accepted them.

"Thank you," she said only slightly flustered. "Let me get something to put them in."

"Here," I added, pulling out a small packet. "Pour that in the water. It'll keep them fresh longer. That's what the lady said, anyway. I've never actually bought roses before."

She gave me a funny look and then opened a tall cupboard, pulling out a beautiful crystal vase. She filled it, took the packet, emptied the contents into the water, clipped the ends of the roses and gently placed them into the vase.

"So you want to go?" I asked, my voice full of hope and a twinge of devious temptation.

"Are you kidding me?" She grinned like a kid. Changing to an English accent, she added, "It sounds positively delightful!"

"You sound just like Mary Poppins," I complimented, "but you'll need a costume. They can't recognize us."

"I'll return in a jiffy," she continued with the accent. "Would you be so kind as to amuse yourself out on the terrace? Fix a spot of tea if you like."

I went out to the patio and reclined in one of the lounge chairs. Setting the cane against the table, I leaned back and propped the hat over my eyes, and enjoyed the sunshine. About thirty minutes later I heard her step out onto the porch.

She cleared her throat. "Excuse me, sir, but have you seen a Miss Rachel Devereaux recently? It's my understanding she resides in this domicile."

I pushed the hat off my face with my index finger and took a long look at her. She wore black, metropolitan glasses, had added a mole to her right check and blue contact lenses that covered up her normally brown eyes. Beige, low-healed, Italian pumps adorned her feet. She'd changed into a silky, lavender blouse opened wide at the collar, and she had obviously put on a serious push-up bra that exposed a healthy cleavage. Over that she wore a beige ladies' business jacket and matching slacks. Her auburn hair lay hidden beneath wig of shoulder-length, curly blonde locks almost identical to mine. We looked like brother and sister.

"Perfect! You look better than I do." I stood up, placed the hat properly on my head and grabbed the cane, slapping it firmly under my left arm. I held out my right arm in proper, gentlemanly fashion. "May the gentleman have the privilege of escorting the lady?"

"Certainly! You flatter me, sir." She held out her elbow and we linked arms. We both laughed as we walked into the kitchen.

"We'll take my car," I said normally.

We got into my Chrysler and headed for the highway.

"By the way," Rachel said, "I think I'm being followed. I've seen this black …"

"Audi?" I interjected quickly. "Yeah, I've seen it, too … and in the damnedest places."

"Any idea who it is?"

"Not really. When did you first notice it?"

"Yvgenny's, I think."

"That's right. Very good," I said, impressed. "How many times since then?"

"Twice: once last weekend on the highway and then again yesterday as I came home from grocery shopping."

"I wouldn't worry too much. If they were hitters, they'd have done something by now. This feels like surveillance … someone just sniffing around."

"How did things go with Xen last night?"

"Oh … hit and miss, I guess."

"What happened?" she asked, figuring the worst.

"The guy Yvgenny told us about … the psycho … well, he showed up. He'd staked out Grady's and was waiting for me."

"Oh my god! Are you both okay?"

"I'm fine, and Xen didn't get hurt too badly. He handled himself really well in there, I gotta admit. Xen surprises me more and more every day." I smiled.

"You are pretty predictable about that, by the way. Grady's, I mean."

"The thought occurred to me, too … anyway, we sorted out our differences with the Russians the way I like to, and that was the end of it. Xen was pretty shaken up by the experience though. I put him in a safe house I know about."

"Where's that?" she asked.

"I plan on showing you later on. With things heating up, I want both of you safe."

"Awwww … how sweet!" she said putting her hand on mine.

"I need you," I said simply. I decided to bait her a little. "I mean, where else could I find someone with your qualifications: a stunt driver who speaks three languages, does decent research, can kick the crap out of most men, and looks that good in a dress?" I gave her a sideways wink. "You're not exactly dime-a-dozen, are you? It would take me at least a week … maybe two to replace you."

"Cretin!" she yelled and smacked me in the arm.

I laughed and then got very serious. "No, really," I put some emotion into my voice, "the truth is that I need you. Life wouldn't be the same without you." I smiled affectionately at her.

She paused for a moment, smiling slightly. "You're forgiven." She leaned over and kissed me on the cheek.

"Awwww …" I said, mimicking her.

She slapped my arm again, but lighter this time and with more affection.

"Brute," I added with a mischievous grin. I turned on the radio, and we were silent as I drove us downtown.

It took us another thirty minutes to get into the city, and I pulled into a parking garage one building away from the VeniCorp offices. We got out, exited the garage at street level, and walked up the street towards the office building where VeniCorp had its HQ. There was a wide pay lot full of cars between the buildings. As we approached the end of the lot, I stopped dead in my tracks and looked to my left.

"What?" Rachel asked, bumping into my shoulder.

"Look," I said, motioning to a car parked one row in.

"Ah." she said, seeing it immediately. "It's a black Audi. And I'm sure it's the only one in the city," she said a bit sarcastically. "This is, after all, Los Angeles. How many black Audis could there be?"

"Rule, number one: it's all about the details. What do you see in the back window?"

"Temp tag with a 3, for next month. That narrows it down, sure. But what are the odds?"

"And do you see anything on the bumper?"

Rachel peered at the bumper, not seeing anything at first. "No, I …" Then she spotted a small red patch of paint on the lower left portion. "The red paint?"

"The red paint," I said with certainty.

"What's the Audi doing here?"

I narrowed my eyes, mulling over the possibilities. "I'm thinking someone had the same idea as me. Do you see anyone inside the car?"

"Hard to tell through the tinting, but I don't think so."

"Me either. Walk with me," I said and stepped over the low-hanging cable that encircled the parking lot. I casually approached the car with Rachel right behind me. I scratched my head and *accidentally* knocked off my hat. I stopped by the back window, picked up my hat, put it back on my head, and used the black mirrored surface to look at myself, adjusting it to a rakish angle. I also memorized the license number, date of purchase and engine ID. Satisfied with the angle of my hat, I walked past the Audi and exited the parking lot through a gap in the wire. We walked towards the front doors of the building we wanted.

I switched to the English accent. "Alright, madam—we're here as sales representatives of Livingston, Inc. Reginald and Margaret

Livingston, proprietors. Siblings, not spouses. If anyone asks, we inherited the business from our father, Sir Jonathan Livingston. We're here to discuss exporting rare gases such as xenon and argon for VeniCorp's commercial use. Our flight home leaves in the morning. Have you got all that?"

"Indubitably, sir," she replied with her Mary Poppins impersonation.

I tapped the hat on my head, opened the door, and motioned for her to go in. "After you, madam."

"Thank you ever so much."

There were no security cameras or gates in the main lobby, but a couple of rent-a-cops occupied a wide information desk in the middle of the brightly lit space. We approached with as much British pomp and circumstance as we could muster, my cane clicking loudly as we walked up.

"Excuse me, gentlemen, but I wondered if you would be so kind as to direct me to the offices of VeniCorp?"

The one in front of us answered, "Third floor. Elevators are down that hall." The guy pointed behind him with his thumb.

"Thank you very much, my good man. Ta." I doffed my hat, and we both strolled down the hallway. We stepped up to the elevator doors, and I pushed the UP button.

A few seconds later the doors opened, disgorging a mild assortment of office workers leaving for the day. We stepped in once the elevator emptied. I smiled when I heard "Mack the Knife" coming over the elevator speakers and pushed the button for the third floor. The doors closed, and I whistled along with the tune, snapping my fingers with the rhythm. Rachel turned her head slowly and gave me a mildly irritated look of disbelief.

"What?" I said innocently, but I stopped whistling and snapping.

The elevator chimed our arrival. "Game faces," I said. As the doors slid open, we both stared directly into the face of Ricky Petri, Gino DiMarco's financial advisor. We were practically nose-to-nose.

"Can I help you two?" he asked.

Xen's Discovery

Xen sat bolt-upright in the lounge chair and yelled. He had dreamed of the fight at Grady's, and the image of the gangster hitting him in the ribs woke him up. He shook his head, trying to lose the memory, but it stuck with him. Mag sat near him and stared. "It's alright, Mag. Just a bad dream." She licked her paw and cleaned her ear.

"Didn't Justin say something about a casino?"

Mag stopped cleaning, nodded her head and looked north. She nodded once more and then looked back at Xen, cocking her head to the side.

"Up that way, hunh?"

She nodded. Xen suddenly felt strange having a conversation with her, but he wasn't going to mention it. He stood up, headed into the house and back to a bedroom. He remembered Justin's comment about cash under the bed. He got on his knees, pulled back the comforter and looked.

"Holy shit," he said, face to face with a sleeping bag stuffer, and the only thing under the bed. It had bulges here and there that had to be bound stacks of cash. He pulled the bag out, set it on the bed, released the pull-string and opened it.

His jaw dropped. It was full of hundred dollar stacks. He did a fast calculation ... more of a wild-ass-guess ... of how much he was looking at. "There's got to be over three million in here." Xen looked around the room, suddenly feeling very guilty and having no idea why. What was it Justin had said? Xen thought to himself as he tried to remember … "Don't take more than fifty out of the bag," the words echoed in his head. "He couldn't possibly mean …" Xen muttered. He looked at the money on the top. There were only hundreds.

He up-ended the bag and poured it out, digging through the pile and looking for tens, twenties or even fifties, anything smaller than a hundred. Nothing. All C-notes. Xen gulped and put the money back in the bag. He could do math, and fifty had to mean fifty thousand dollars. It was the only possible answer. "Okay," Xen said out loud, smiling gleefully. He left five bound stacks on the bed and slid the refilled bag underneath it.

He went to the closet and spotted a fanny-pack. He grabbed that and threw it on the bed. Taking a blank t-shirt, some shorts and sandals that were too big for him, he got dressed, clipped the bag around his waist and headed out of the house, turning north towards the casino.

English Propriety

"How do you do, sir?" I took off my hat and extended my hand. "My name is Reginald Livingston, and this lovely woman is my sister, Margaret. Livingston, Incorporated. Proprietors. At your service, sir."

"Richard Petri," Ricky said as we shook. "Pleased to meet you both, Mister Livingston, Margaret," he said, shaking her outstretched hand as well. "Look, most of our people have gone for the day. I was headed that way myself."

I looked at Rachel, and she didn't miss the queue.

"Oh, that is unfortunate, Mister Petri," she said taking him by the arm and walking towards the receptionists desk just inside the elevator. A young, shapely woman in her early twenties watched us. We stood in a small, contained lobby. A closed pair of tall wooden doors stood on the left of the desk, and I saw one camera over the receptionist's desk and one behind us over the elevator. There was a stairwell door directly across from the receptionist's desk. "Our flight leaves in the morning, and we were hoping to make one more stop during our tour."

"Did you folks have an appointment?" Ricky said, smiling at Rachel … and her cleavage.

I jumped in, "No, actually. We've been discussing our intentions all day with a number of corporations in your line of work. One of them had accidentally mentioned VeniCorp in a rather negative light—something about you beating the trousers off them or some such. I can't say whom, of course, but if you are successful in the industry, then we'd like to consider doing business with you ... and not them."

"You're a perceptive man," Ricky said a bit slyly.

"Oh, I absolutely pride myself on it, sir," I said, bowing my head slightly.

"I'm going back in, Paula," Ricky said to the receptionist. He reached into a pocket and pulled out a card-key, passing what I recognized as a Prox II card over the reader. The door clicked, and he opened it, motioning for Rachel and me to enter. "Why don't we talk in my office?" Ricky offered.

Rachel and I stepped through the door, smiling at each other. I winked at her when Ricky couldn't possibly see it.

"So, uh. What is it you're into?" Ricky asked.

"Rare and noble gases," Rachel said enthusiastically.

"Correct," I added. "Neon, xenon, argon, and their applicable derivatives. We even produce halon for several security firms in Great Britain."

Richard walked into the office space. Offices lined the outer wall, stretching from the door all the way down about seventy feet. Small and large cubicles filled central area, and the far end of the office space lay behind floor-to-ceiling glass, a laboratory containing an assortment of equipment, several desks, and some computer terminals.

"It's a lovely space, Mister Petri," I said. "Is this all of it?"

"Thank you, and yes, it is." Turning back to Rachel, he said, "We don't have much use for gases like that, at least not today."

"Perhaps not," Rachel said, taking Ricky's arm again. "But think about the future." We walked towards the corner office.

"I always do, Miss. It's my job."

"Of course it is. And we understand completely that you might not require our products or services at this time. We're mostly laying the groundwork for an international expansion."

We stepped into his open office. Ricky took a seat in a big leather swivel chair behind his desk, while Rachel and I perched on the end of upright chairs set in front.

"What a coincidence," Ricky said, smiling slyly. "So are we."

"All we're asking is that you consider our organization for your future needs."

"Of course I can do that. I don't close doors. Do you have a business card I can keep?" Rachel looked at Justin.

"Unfortunately, we've nearly wall-papered the city with cards today," I said smoothly. "We ran out two offices ago, terribly sorry. Perhaps I could pull up our website on your terminal there. At least you would have that." I stood up so I could see Ricky's hands on the keyboard.

Ricky typed in a password, brought up a browser, and stepped aside.

"There ya go. All yours."

I sat down and typed in an IP address. "They're in the process of moving the servers for our site, so we have to use the IP for a few more days. You can go to LivingstonInc.com eventually. Decent IT help is so hard to find," I lamented.

"Eh … you ain't kidding," Ricky added, understanding completely.

I finished the URL and hit enter. The cursor churned for a few seconds and then the screen came up with a "Page Not Found" error.

"Bloody hell!" I blurted then regained my composure. "I'm sorry, Mister Petri. They were supposed to have this work complete over the weekend." I closed the browser and stood up, stepping back to stand next to Rachel who remained seated. "At least you'll have the URL once they have the site back up."

"Like you said … bad IT guys are dime-a-dozen, good ones worth their weight in gold." Ricky sat down and locked up his terminal.

"Agreed, sir." I nodded in affirmation. "I say, do you have a card? I'd like to contact you upon my return to Britain, if that's alright with you."

"Certainly, Mister Livingston."

We shook hands, and I put my hat back on as I gently grasped Rachel's elbow. "You've been more than kind, Mister Petri. And please, call me Reginald."

"It's Ricky, and it was my pleasure."

"Thank you, Ricky," she said as she stood and held out her hand. "We really do appreciate you speaking with us after business hours. We were told that Americans would be a bit uncouth, but we've encountered nothing but kindness all day."

"Like my daddy used to say, don't believe everything you hear." He lifted her hand up and brushed her knuckles with a kiss.

She bowed her head. "Lesson learned, Richard. I'll have to keep that in mind. Ta," she added as she extracted her fingers.

We stepped out of the office, and turning I said, "We'll show ourselves out, Ricky. Thank you again for your time. Cheerio." I tipped my hat and quickly followed behind Rachel. I opened the main door for her, and we stepped into the elevator. "The Girl from Ipanema" played on the way down, and I almost started whistling again, but thought better of it. We quickly walked back to my car, noting the Audi had disappeared.

The moment the doors closed on my Chrysler, Rachel hugged me from across the seat and kissed me on the mouth. She was flushed with excitement, and I found myself feeling some odd stirrings in places not previously stirred by Rachel.

"That was fantastic!"

I smiled and licked my lips, tasting her lip gloss. I'd never think of strawberries the same way again. I cast her a sideways glance and started the motor. "And useful. He gave me an easy in."

"The URL?"

"Yep. I'll show you when we get to my loft." I pulled out and exited the garage, merging directly into a traffic jam.

She paused. "You're taking me inside?"

"Yep."

"Justin, you *never* let me into your loft, only your house and the martial-arts school. You said it was private."

"That's right."

"And now it's not?" She sounded rather suspicious, but excited, too. "What's the special occasion?"

"Last night," I replied vaguely.

Confused, she asked, "What do you mean?"

"Well, because of what happened last night, I had to show Xen a few things … things nobody knows … things I never considered telling anybody until recently. You deserve to know, too. You should have been first, but it didn't work out that way. I figured I better fix that."

"That sounds so ominous," she muttered, raising an eyebrow at me. I forced my way into a crack between two taxies and waved at the middle finger raised by the driver behind me. Then I pulled out my phone while we were stopped at a light and handed it to Rachel.

"Dial Yvgenny. The locking code is 2273."

She opened the phone and keyed in the code. She hit the Contacts button, scrolled to Gershovich and hit dial, handing the phone back when it rang. I grabbed it and put it to my ear. Yvgenny picked up,

"Da?"

"Yvgenny, it's Justin."

"Let me guess … you having killed some Mexicans this time … or perhaps Americans … and you are needing my help." Yvgenny didn't laugh this time.

I practically whined, "No … nobody's dead, Yvgenny. But I do need your help. It's an easy one."

Rachel shot me a questioning look and mouthed, *What happened?*

"Sure it is," and this time Yvgenny laughed. "It is always being easy with you and your *requests*."

I mouthed the word *Later*, to Rachel. Talking into the phone again, I said, "Do you have any Prox cards handy? Prox IIs, to be specific. Every place I can think of that would have them will be closed."

"I'm sorry, but I'm not having any here. However, man I am knowing uses courier service. He could probably have them here in forty-five minutes if you're needing them today. And he only charges retail. He is actual vendor."

"Perfect. It'll take me that long to get to your place with this traffic. Think he would have a card imprinter as well?"

"Probable. I will asking him. Shall I hang up phone and calling him?"

"Also perfect. Thanks." We both hung up.

"So, what was that about no one being dead?" Rachel asked, bursting with curiosity.

My phone rang. I held up my finger, prompting a dirty look from her as she endured another bout of *taleus interruptus*. I looked at the phone and cringed. "Oh, shit! I forgot to call the abatement guy." I was tempted not to answer it, but I knew I would only be prolonging the inevitable, and Marsha would get angrier the longer I waited, and she'd been waiting all day.

"The what?" Rachel asked, baffled.

"He's the guy who came for the bodies last night." I answered, trying to ignore the blank stare Rachel held on me. "Hi, Marsha!" I said brightly.

"*WHAT THE FUCK DID YOU DO TO MY GAMBLING HALL?*" I winced and pulled the phone away from my ear.

"Curiosity got the best of you, did it?" I asked her quietly and a bit nervously.

"Don't tell me about fucking curiosity!" she hollered. "My place is demolished!"

"I'm *really* sorry, Marsha. But it wasn't my fault."

"Yeah, sure," she accused. "Trouble follows you like stink on shit."

"It's not like I invited them in. *They* followed *me*. And besides, they started it."

Rachel had to cover her mouth to keep from laughing out loud. She was clearly enjoying me on the defensive *way* too much. And she knew as well as anyone that someone else always started it, and someplace usually got demolished afterwards.

"It looks like a football team came in and wrecked the place. And there's blood everywhere! I mean *everywhere!*"

"Well, actually, it was more like a Russian baseball team," I corrected. "There were eight of them."

"Eight?" she said, stunned. "Are you okay?" she asked, genuine concern in her voice.

"Yeah. I'm fine. And thanks for asking," I said, delighted to hear the calm, loving Marsha again. "Xen's okay, too. He's had a little trouble, and he wanted to meet there. He picked your place, not me. But he had no idea people might be following me. If you need more money to cover the damage, I'll cough it up gladly. Tell me how much." I paused, and an idea popped into my head. "How about we *really* renovate the place? Do it the way you always dreamed. On me."

Her tone changed to friendly, "You sure know how to sweet talk a girl."

"I try," I said and smiled at Rachel. "Look, I've even found an abatement guy for you. He has a designer and everything. I was just about to call him when you rang me. Honest." I crossed my fingers at the fib, and Rachel slapped my arm. "I'll have him call you either tonight or tomorrow. The deal is, you want it, you get it, okay?"

She didn't even hesitate. "Deal," she said firmly. And by her tone I could tell I was in for a pretty big bill.

"Hey, something just occurred to me," I said.

"What?"

"The lot next to yours is still for sale, isn't it?"

"As far as I know," she asked with a curious tone.

"You want a business partner? I might be able to scrape up some investment capital, and you could double your square-footage or more. Build whatever you want. How does that sound?"

"I don't know. Let's talk about it." I could tell she was interested, but she was also smart enough to be cautious, even with friends.

"You're on," I agreed. "I have to sort a few things out over the next few days, but we'll work out a deal when things calm down, okay?"

"Okay."

"Oh, and we'll start training in the next few nights. You and Rachel still have your showdown."

"Don't worry," she said, "I haven't forgotten. The leg is just about ready for some action, and I'm jonesing for it," she added eagerly and with a bit of an edge.

"Good. Oh, and this abatement guy … He's sort of an oddball. When I first met him, he had on a clown suit, so don't be surprised. He's quite the entrepreneur."

"I'll wait for his call."

"Thanks for understanding, Marsha. And I'm sorry about the hassle."

"We'll work it out, mister." We hung up. Realizing I had left Stanley's card on my desk, I handed Rachel the phone. "Dial 411. Ask for Stanley-Fast Catering and Clowning."

"The guy who picked up the bodies also runs a catering service?" she asked, appalled. I laughed as she dialed, but I didn't answer. She said "L.A." when asked by the 411 system, following up quickly with the business name. She paused for a minute and then handed me the phone. "It's ringing."

I waited for an answer. "Hello?" said a recognizable voice.

"Is this Stanley?" I asked.

"It is."

"This is the guy from last night."

"Oh, hey! How are ya? Those packages have been dropped off. They're a memory."

"Perfect, and thanks. I love working with professionals."

"Me too," Stanley agreed.

"Look, you still interested in the abatement gig?"

"Hell yes!" he said enthusiastically.

"Okay. Here's the deal. Got a pen?" There was a pause.

"I do now."

"I want you to call Marsha Callahan." I gave him the number. "She's expecting your call, either tonight or tomorrow. Get hold of her and work out the details."

"You bet."

"One other thing," I added. "She was pretty pissed off about her place."

"I bet she was."

"Yeah. Well, to keep her from killing me, I'm paying the tab. Carte blanche. She asks for it, she gets it, okay?"

"You got it. I'll need half in advance, once we spec it out."

"No problem. She's got seventy grand on her for that. Get me a shopping list on an invoice. I don't want to pay more than about ten percent over wholesale for materials, okay?"

"Deal. I'll call her tonight."

"Thanks, Stanley."

"Hey, I didn't catch your name."

"Case. Justin Case."

"Like in the movie?"

"Yeah, you saw it?"

"I own it," he said matter-of-factly.

"Now that's funny," I said, smiling. "I didn't think anyone even remembered it. Look, I gotta go, but I'll get hold of you in the next few days. Call me if you have any questions."

"You got it. Ciao!" We hung up.

"Eight?" Rachel asked, a bit of awe in her voice.

"Mmm-hmm," I replied quietly.

"So," she hesitated, "what does a caterer do with dead bodies?"

"You know, I asked that same question."

"What did he say?"

"He said he knows a guy who's a pig farmer."

"Hunh?"

"Apparently, pigs really will eat anything … even dead Russians."

She got a disgusted look on her face. "Ewwww …"

"He also said it was the best bacon he's ever had," and I grinned viciously as she turned green. "Come on … let's get to Yvgenny's."

Stolen Identity

Rachel and I walked into Yvgenny's teahouse to find the dining room full despite the early hour. We got past Alisa with a quick hello, stepped through the curtain, and headed for the stairs to the patio.

"I'm sorry, but the patio is closed until eight," Galina called to us from the kitchen. She and another waitress were putting together a large order for a table of eight who sat laughing and drinking on the far side of the room.

"It's us, Galina! Justin and Rachel," I said, waiving my finger at both of us.

Galina peered at me closely and then finally recognized our faces. "Nice outfits," she said, laughing lightly.

"Thanks!" we both said as we continued up the stairs.

As we reached the top, the door opened and a young, skinny kid around Galina and Alisa's age stepped out. He had on bicycling gear and a satchel over his shoulder. "Excuse me," he said as he passed by us.

I walked through the door and saw Yvgenny in the right-hand corner of the patio. A last patch of evening sunlight shone brightly on the old man. He wore flip-flops, cut-off jean shorts, a clean white t-shirt, and the same dingy blue shirt over that. His pipe stuck out the corner of his mouth, with a lazy stream of smoke drifting over his head. He had a crossword book in one hand and a pen in the other. His glasses were perched on the end of his nose. A brown-paper-wrapped package sat on the table in front of him.

Yvgenny watched us walk onto his patio and pushed the glasses from the tip up onto the bridge of his nose. He set the crossword book down and took the pipe out of his mouth. "Good evening. How am I being able to help you? We normally don't open …" His voice trailed off, and he narrowed his eyes, examining us closely as we wordlessly walked up to the table. Yvgenny put the pipe back in his mouth and puffed thoughtfully, a smile growing across his face. "Halloween is being in October, yes?"

We all laughed.

"How could you tell?" I asked.

"The eyes, my friend. One never forgets your eyes."

"That's true," Rachel added thoughtfully.

I smiled. "Is that my package?"

"Da."

"I owe you one."

"You owe me many," Yvgenny said slowly.

"Hard to argue with you," I said a bit sheepishly.

"It would being foolish to try. I'll probably breaking your bank when I collect."

"That's about the size of it," I agreed. "What do I owe you for this?" I asked, hefting the package.

"Two hundred."

I reached into my pocket, pulled out my wallet and handed over the money.

"Would you like to stay for tea and supper?" Yvgenny offered.

"No thanks. We have to get back and do some research."

"I understand. It is too bad. I would love to knowing where both of you have been in such costumes."

I reached up and pulled off the hat and wig, scratching my scalp in a few places. "Whew! That's better. It's actually a short story, for a change."

"What a pleasant surprise. You normally rambling like senile old woman," Yvgenny said, prompting a wide grin from Rachel.

I rolled my eyes at him. "I wanted to go digging around the VeniCorp office and find a way to go back when it was empty. I found out they've got an internal network, which isn't surprising, and what I'm after is on it. I could always crash the place, but there's a greater likelihood I'd leave a trace going in blind like that. This way I'll be able to make it look like business as usual as far as they're concerned."

"So, when do you go back?" Yvgenny asked.

"Not sure yet. Maybe tonight, maybe tomorrow. I'm still sorting details."

"As always, be careful," the old man warned.

"I will. Thanks again. We've got to head out."

"It was pleasure to seeing you again, Miss Rachel."

"Good bye, Yvgenny. Good to see you, too."

We walked out as Yvgenny went back to his pipe and crosswords. When we hit the street, we turned right and walked down the block. The pay lot across the street had been full when we arrived, so we parked in a parking garage a few blocks away.

O O O

I swung down the visor and hit the remote button as I entered the alley. The garage door rolled up, and we waited for the lift to come down. Rachel shifted a bit nervously in her seat, adjusting the bag of Chinese food we'd picked up on the way home. I could almost feel her anticipation. I pulled past the entrance and then backed onto the lift.

"Look, it's just my loft. It's not that big a deal," I said smoothly. I hit the remote again and the lift rose.

"I've waited over two years to see this place. I never thought I would."

"It's still just my loft. You know, kitchen, living room, desk, bathroom, like everybody else …" I paused, thinking for a moment. "In fact, that's something you should really keep in mind. I'm just like everybody else … well … mostly."

"You're pretty exceptional, Justin. I've seen some of the things you do. You're far from normal." As the lift stopped, she saw that it was mostly dark inside. The setting sun cast an orange haze that soaked into the dark interior. She started to get out, but I placed my hand on her arm and shook my head.

"That's not what I mean. All I'm saying is that you need to always think of me as just another person … like everyone else. Okay?"

"Of course," she said confidently. I smiled gently at her. *You have no idea what you're in for*, I thought.

We opened our doors, I grabbed Chinese food, and Rachel grabbed the package from Yvgenny's. "Where's the light-switch?" she asked. "Damn! It's hot in here!" she added.

"All lights," I said to the darkness. The lights came on, and Rachel got her first look at my real home. "And I like to keep things warm."

"Apparently. And that light thing is nifty." She walked behind the car and looked around.

"The bathroom is through those doors." I pointed towards the big double-doors at the back of the loft. "The door inside on the right."

"Okay," she said and walked towards the middle of the loft. "You're right. It's no big deal," she turned and smiled at me, "but thanks for bringing me here."

"See, I told you. A loft like anybody else's. Hungry?"

"Famished!" she said and headed for the kitchen table.

"Let's eat." I followed her to the table and tore the bag open.

Rachel laid everything out.

"I'll get us some plates," I added.

"Okay," she said, and bit off the end of an egg roll.

"Beer?"

"Mmm-hmm," she said around a mouthful.

I got plates, two beers, and spoons for the rice. We sat down and wordlessly wolfed through pork lo mein, sesame chicken, and Mongolian beef. We washed the last of the rice down with the last of our beers. I got up and grabbed two more, twisting the tops off each and handing Rachel one.

"Let's get to work," I said, grabbing the package. She took a pull from the beer and followed me over to my desk.

"Hey! What's in the tank? Are those snakes?"

"Yeah, a couple of king snakes … a scarlet and a California. That reminds me. I have to feed them."

"What do they eat?"

"Mice."

"You keep mice?"

"Sort of. These are frozen." I walked towards the kitchen. "Hey, open the package, will you?"

"Sure," she said and tore away the brown paper. I opened the freezer and took out two small plastic bags. I grabbed a bowl from the cupboard and filled it with hot water. Tearing open the packages, I dropped two small, frozen, white rodents into the steaming water to thaw them out. Then I headed back to the desk. Rachel laid out the card imprinter and a stack of ten Prox II card keys.

"USB, right?" I asked.

"Yep," she held up the long white cord.

"Open the door there beneath you and plug it in," I said as I came around the desk.

She opened the door and saw a small panel with a series of different inputs on it. She pushed the jack into a USB port as I sat down.

I moved the mouse, and the monitors came to life. The desktop on each screen was identical to the one displayed on the computer in my bedroom: green logo, strange green characters and all.

"Interesting desktop," Rachel said. "What are those letters, *Klingon*?" she asked sarcastically.

I smiled. "Something like that," I said and put the circlet over my head. I caught her giving me a curious look. "Search: VeniCorp." The VeniCorp site came up on the far left screen. An access-point box appeared in the middle. "And bring up the access ping from this afternoon on the right, maximum security protocol." An instant later a standard operating system desktop appeared with the login prompt in the middle of the screen. The username field had the letters PETRIR, and the cursor blinked in the password field.

"Holy shit," she said.

"You ain't seen nothing yet," I replied mischievously. I pulled the keyboard to me and typed in Ricky Petri's password, having seen him type it upside down, and hit the ENTER key. I pushed the keyboard away and went to work.

While the website didn't change at all, Rachel stared in awe as I raced through data on both screens. My head shifted back and forth between the two active displays. She could tell from glimpses of the images and words screaming by that I was digging into Ricky's files on the right while simultaneously hammering through all sorts of network and user data on the left.

The middle screen stopped flickering, and a small box of data in the lower left-hand corner came up. "Stat max user login by hours, past two weeks," I commanded. A graph appeared in the middle monitor with a list of about sixty names across the bottom. She could see that the left-hand margin indicated the number of times users had logged in. The graph looked fairly level across the top of the screen, fluctuating between eighty and a hundred times, except for one noticeable trough.

I turned to her. "This is the number of logins at the corporate office for the past two weeks. Look," I said and pointed to the name below the valley.

"SHAOJ," she said. "Jackie."

"Yep." I turned back to the monitors. "Stat user login past eight weeks by hour for SHAOJ." The screen flickered, and I saw what I'd hoped. "What does that tell you?"

Rachel looked at the report. The left hand margin went from seven a.m. at the bottom to six a.m. at the top. The bottom had the date, and scattered across the screen were numbers of logins. Although the numbers were all over the place, the middle of the report had the highest concentration of twos, threes, and fours. Almost ninety percent of the logins had occurred between seven p.m. and one a.m., and they were scattered across every day of the week without a pattern. "Jackie goes there at night, and there's no telling what night he arrives or leaves."

I smiled with admiration. "Exactly. That's our in."

"How?"

"Easy. Watch," I said and looked at the screens. The middle screen flickered with data again.

Rachel picked up a list of names, the same names that had been on the first report. One flashed green with SHAOJ in the user field and stayed lit.

"Slide one of the cards into the imprinter," I said to her as my eyes shifted to the left-hand screen.

She watched as I burrowed through Petri's email. She grabbed one of the Prox cards from the stack on the desk and slid it into the slot of the imprinter. "Okay," she said.

I turned to the middle monitor, and the name flashed again. The light on the front of the imprinter blinked a few times and went dark. "Another," I said and turned back to Petri's email.

She pulled out the first card and slid home a second. "Okay."

I shifted my attention back and forth between setting up the Prox cards and reviewing Petri's emails. The name flashed for the card, the imprinter light blinked, and I turned back to the email. "One more."

We repeated the process, and when the lights on the imprinter stopped blinking, I slapped the desk, yelling "Yes!"

Rachel jumped.

"What?"

"Rule number two," I started, and then I got a thoughtful look on my face. "Well, more like rule ninety-something. Finance execs everywhere … and marketing execs, too, for that matter … are usually lazy when it comes to IT security. I figured Ricky was one of them, and I guessed right. Look," I said, pointing to an email.

"What's it say?"

"It's an email from one of their junior network guys telling Ricky that his bridge to one of their inner networks is complete, plus how to access it. According to this, the guy's director would kill him if he found out." I grinned like a big kid. "Hang on a minute," I said and focused back on the monitors. "Swap screens left and middle." The two monitors flickered and their images switched places.

An icon flashed On Ricky's desktop, then an interface filled the screen with a login prompt. I pulled the keyboard again, typed in PETRIR in the user field and then Ricky's password. The UI changed to a standard drive listing with a series of enumerated folders. "Shit," I said quietly. "File count?" I asked. A small box appeared in the upper right-hand corner, and a count scrolled by rapidly, stopping at over eighteen million. "Hmmmm …" I said, leaning back in my chair and thinking furiously. I snapped my fingers and leaned back in intently. "Search left: molecule for cocaine." The left hand monitor flickered, and sixteen boxes appeared on the screen, each with an internet page. "One and nine," I said. Two of the screens expanded and filled the screens. One was text about the chemical chain for cocaine, the other a diagram of the molecule. "Capture data." The characters and images flashed briefly green. "Search middle: match captured data to files." The number on the upper right-hand corner scrolled back to zero. "Shit," I said, frustrated.

"What does it mean?" Rachel asked.

"Well, we know that Mister Shao goes there frequently and that he's a drug maker. We know that Ricky has access to the internal network. We have to assume that Shao uses a computer to do at least part of his work. What does that add up to?"

"Shao has either a separate network," she said slowly, "a stand-alone computer, or he uses an abacus like no one else alive," she added, smiling.

"That's right. Looks like we're going in."

"When?"

"Still not sure yet. I think I want to take Xen along for this particular ride, so we'll have to ask him."

"Where is he?"

"He's in a safe place. In fact, we'll be going there shortly. But first, let's see what we can find out about our friend in the black Audi."

"Thank god. That's really been bugging me."

"Clear screens," I said. They went back to the strange-looking desktop. "Okay … middle screen … Los Angeles Department of Motor Vehicle … search on three fields." A box appeared in the middle of the screen with three text boxes and a blinking cursor. I typed in the license number, hit tab, typed in the date of purchase, hit tab again and then typed in the engine ID and hit the ENTER key.

A second later a small box appeared with the words "No data."

"Damn, I was afraid of that. He just bought it. It hasn't been processed yet."

"Can this thing search LAPD records?"

"Yeah, why?"

"Well, you're assuming that he's a law-abiding citizen. Maybe the guy's a lead foot."

"Hunh?"

"Maybe he speeds a lot."

I looked at her, impressed again. "Good idea. Search middle: LAPD, same three fields." A second later one record popped up with a name, date, and city in it, and the violation had occurred the previous week.

"See?" Rachel said with a knowing grin. "Widen the search."

I looked at her with a *What for?* expression on my face.

"Maybe he's from out of town," she offered.

I looked at the screen. "Same search: all of California."

Two more records showed up, but these were in Sacramento, one each in the previous two months. "Sacramento?" I asked. "So he's not from around here."

I looked at the screen, blinked at the most recent record, and it expanded to fill the screen. I read out loud, "Six-point ticket issued to Albert Zajac. Eighty-four in a sixty-five … this guy drives like you do." She punched my shoulder, and then I continued. "Weird, he's a Polish national on an international driver's license. Sacramento address. He's on an extended travel Visa that checked out."

I leaned back, looking at the data with a confused look on my face. "Now that just don't figure … Polish?" I looked at Rachel and asked, "You piss off anyone from Poland lately?"

"Not that I know of," she said, equally confused.

"Me either."

My phone rang. I pulled it out and recognized the Costa Rican prefix but didn't recognize the number. I opened the phone. "Hello?"

"Justin! It's Xen!" Xen had to holler over the sound of slot machines ringing and gamblers talking in the background. "I'm in trouble, and I need your help."

"Are you okay?" I asked, immediately concerned.

"I'm fine, I'm fine!" Xen said over the noise.

"You burned through all the money, didn't you?" I said, smiling. I figured he would. Xen really is a shitty poker player.

"Well, about that …" Xen said a bit evasively. "I have a little problem, and I need your help. Can you meet me at the casino?"

"Sure. Right now?"

"As soon as you can. I can sit tight till you get here."

"I'll be there in thirty or forty minutes, okay?"

"Sounds good. Thanks!" Xen hung up.

"What was that all about?" Rachel asked.

"Xen. He says he has a little problem. So we have a change of plans … well, an acceleration of them. Lock console," I said, and the screens went black. I took the circlet off my head. "Feel like taking a little trip south of the border?"

"How little?" she asked suspiciously.

"Oh … I don't know … about …" I paused and did a quick calculation in my head, "three thousand miles."

"What?" she blurted. "I'll need to go get some clothes … and my passport."

"No you won't," I said simply, a subtle grin blooming on my face.

"Justin, three thousand miles south of the border is Central America!" she clarified, speaking as if I were an imbecile.

"Trust me," I said.

Secrets

"Follow me," I said as I walked over to the kitchen. Rachel followed closely but with a curious hesitation in her step. I opened a cabinet and pulled down a bottle of tequila and a shot-glass. I topped the glass off and handed it to her. "Shoot it."

She looked at me with a bewildered look on her face. "Why?"

"Shoot it," I insisted.

She grabbed the shot glass and downed it easily, not showing any reaction at all. We'd spent a number of evenings doing shooters of the stuff, so she was accustomed to it. She looked at me expectantly. I took a deep breath, preparing for the worst.

"You know when I say I'm not from around here?" I asked quietly.

"Yeah?"

"I really, really mean it. And that story about having Lazarus syndrome that I told you last year, and how I don't appear to age like normal people?"

"Yeah?" she asked, clearly wondering where I was going with all this.

I shook my head.

"Come on." I grabbed her hand and walked to the front door, stopping before it and grabbing her gently by the shoulders. I looked squarely into her eyes. "After we go through this door, nothing changes between us, okay? Promise." For the first time in nearly a hundred years, I had butterflies in my stomach. I didn't know what I'd do if she freaked out on me.

"What is this all about, Justin?" She sounded confused, with a tinge of fear.

"Promise me. Nothing changes."

She looked into my eyes, and I could see something there … for me … something she had kept pushing down. She kissed me gently on the cheek. "I promise," she said sincerely.

I stared at her for a handful of heartbeats, suddenly afraid that I might lose her but desperately wanting to trust her for reasons I was only just beginning to understand. I wanted to kiss her then, kiss her and hold her. But I didn't know how things would go. Maybe after, I thought.

"Okay," I said a little nervously. She'd never seen me act like this, perhaps even a little vulnerable. I walked back to the kitchen, grabbed the bottle of tequila, and returned to her, putting my hand on the palm reader and running through the combination. My eyes never left hers as I pushed the door open. "Go on."

She peered through the doorway and saw the living room. She got a confused look, her head cocked sideways, and disbelief gradually replaced the confusion. She stepped in and looked around a living room three thousand miles away. It slowly dawned on her that it simply could not exist where it was. She looked to her right and saw a window that looked out onto a tall, verdant-green hedge spotted with orange flowers highlighted in silvery moonlight. She looked around the door to her left and saw another window exposing a crushed seashell driveway leading to a wide gap in the shrub. A dirt road intersected the driveway, and she watched in disbelief as a flatbed truck drove down the road out of sight.

She stepped back into my loft and looked for the windows where they should be in the wall. All she saw was a blank wall full of coats on one side and my TV screens on the other. Her mind struggled with the impossible. She looked at my face, wide-eyed, not really comprehending. I handed her the bottle. She uncapped it and took a healthy swig, this time coughing as the tequila went down her throat.

"Go on," I said, motioning her to go through. My face was immobile, a gently hopeful look frozen there. Is that fear I'm feeling? My insides felt like a tornado as she stepped through the doorway once again and walked all the way to the middle of the living room. I stepped through the doorway behind her and closed the door. She slowly turned around, taking in the rattan furniture with burgundy cushions, the walls lined with bookcases. She saw a statue of a matador and bull on an old wooden coffee table, an empty coffee cup beside it. There were two rattan end tables, both with lamps on them, and a hanging basket chair in a corner with the chain bolted into the dark-brown rafters exposed on the pale, textured ceiling. She could see a kitchen down the hall with a light on, and a closed back door—all where my alley should be.

"It's impossible," she said quietly. I opened the front door. She turned and watched me step onto a brick porch and walk out into the middle of a coarse, dark green lawn. I turned my gaze up to the sky, my back to her.

She followed me out, hesitating briefly at the door, and then stepped up beside me, looking at a full moon and a dark sky dotted with bright stars she would never be able to see in a Los Angeles sky.

I put my arm around her and looked into her eyes. She took a long pull from the bottle of tequila and stared up at me.

"Welcome to Costa Rica," I said. "I hope you can you keep a secret."

Wonderland

Having left Rachel on the beach with the bottle of tequila to sort out her new reality, I handed the keys of my old, gray Land Cruiser to the casino valet and slipped the claim ticket into a pocket. I walked up the stairs into the wide, red-carpeted entrance of the hotel and was bathed in a cacophony of dings, buzzes, claps, cheers, yells and every other sound that comes out of a well-populated casino. I scanned the crowd, hoping for the long shot of spotting Xen amongst the throng. I walked towards the cashier's booth straight back from the entrance. I figured I could have Xen paged, but then a motion caught my eye.

Under the entrance to the baccarat room, holding four trays of chips in one hand and waving wildly with the other, stood an excited, almost frantic Xen wearing my clothes. I waved unenthusiastically and then just stood there watching as he walked up to me, cradling the trays in both hands like they were nitroglycerin. As he approached, I took note of the winnings, and my eyebrow went up. All three bottom trays and one row of the fourth had yellow chips, which I knew were thousand-dollar chips. The rest was a mixed bag of smaller increments. I also noticed rectangular bulges in the pockets of the shorts Xen wore.

Xen's face split into the largest, shit-eating grin I have ever seen on a human. It even rivaled one of Magdelain's best smiles.

Calmly I said, "I may be a terrible judge of situations, Xen. Lord knows I've missed the mark more than once in my time, but I seem to distinctly recall you saying that you were in some sort of *trouble*.... something about a little problem, if memory serves, and it usually does. That," I pointed at the chips, "does not look like a little problem to me, unless you took a million out of the bag and that's all that's left. Still not really a crisis, as there's more where that came from, but I'm wracking my brain here to see where the problem is. How much is there?"

"Three hundred and twenty-three thousand dollars!" Xen tried to whisper it, but it still came out loud enough for passers-by to hear him over the noise of the casino.

The thought occurred to me to place a bet with the casino on whether or not Xen would simply explode right there on the spot. I figured I could get even odds. I'd never seen him, or anyone else for that matter, so excited.

"Oh, here, hold this," he said, almost calm, and handed over the chip trays. "I have your money." I barely grabbed the chips in time as his hands shot into his pockets. He pulled out five stacks of hundreds and jammed them into my coat pockets. I could only smile at him.

"What'd you do? Rob the place?" I looked around to see if any security guys were edging in to make a grab for us. I'd been in a South American jail before—long story—and it wasn't a place I wanted to return to.

Xen took the chips back and cradled them like a newborn. He stepped in close, his eyes going wide, and looked around, as if he had the secret of the ages. "Baccarat," he whispered into my ear. "I'm a natural."

"No shit?" I asked a bit dubiously. He was the worst card player I'd ever seen, no exceptions, but the proof was there in his hands and my pockets.

"I play steady and make a slow grind on betting on the bank. When it gets near the end of the shoe, I hit the stand-offs three out of five times. I can see the cards, Justin. They're all in my head. At eight and nine-to-one, I clean house," Xen whispered. "They finally asked me to leave the table." Xen calmed down a bit and looked thoughtfully at me. "The trick is not giving a shit, isn't it?"

"That's right," I said a bit more seriously. "Well, sorta'. At least not caring about *yourself*." I clapped him on the shoulder. "I'm proud of you."

"Thanks!"

"But you haven't answered the original question."

"What?" he asked with a confused look on his face.

Slowly, I asked, "Where's the problem?" I looked at him expectantly.

"Oh, yeah," he said, finally coming at least a little bit back to the real world. "There were these guys watching me … big guys in suits. I didn't want to walk back to your place with a bag full of money and get robbed or something. I'm a little drunk and would have gotten my ass kicked."

I started to fire up a snappy comeback, but upon thinking about it said, "Good thinking. You're absolutely right. Come on. Let's cash you out and head home … unless you want to hit the tables some more?"

"No," he said, almost relieved. "I think I'm done for the night. Besides, I don't think they'd let me come back." He chuckled like a villain.

I nodded, smiling. "You're probably right." We turned and walked towards the cashier's booth.

"Wait a minute," I said, grabbing Xen's arm. "Let's go next door."

"For what?"

"You'll see." Around the corner from the cashier's booth stood a small shop that sold all sorts of expensive vices, two of which were my favorites. We walked in and wove our way through a smattering of tourists looking at imported bottles of liquor and boxes of cigars.

"Julio!" I yelled over the noise towards the back of the shop. A small Hispanic man, well past sixty, and wearing a white button-down under a blue apron, looked up from an *Aficionado* magazine.

"*Hola, Señor Case!* Good to see you again, amigo!" Julio looked at Xen's stack of money, did a fast calculation in his head and gave Xen a raised eyebrow with an impressed smirk.

"Good to see you, too, Julio," I replied. "Could you please get us three boxes of Esplendido's, the real ones, not the counterfeits, and two bottles of Elegancia?"

"*Mui bueno!*" Julio said enthusiastically. "Watch the shop for me while I get the cigars from the back, okay?"

"You bet," I said and turned around to watch the tourists.

A minute later, Julio came out with three boxes of Cohiba cigars and two boxes with scotch bottles in them. He set them on the counter.

"Will there be anything else, Señor Case?"

"No, that should do it," I replied calmly, delighting in these sorts of purchases. I reached to the top stack of chips and pulled out two yellows, thousands, and a green one, a five hundred. I placed them on the counter. "Will that cover it?"

"Si, Señor!" I knew it was more than enough.

"Keep the change, Julio, and thanks." I turned to Xen who had just shy of a hurt look on his face. "Interest on the fifty thou you borrowed." I winked.

He smiled and chuckled a little, realizing that twenty-five hundred was a pittance.

"Good point," he admitted.

We cashed in Xen's chips, just over three hundred twenty thousand. As the cashier put the stacks of hundreds into a white, canvas bag, she reminded both of us that we were required to claim all winnings at customs and pay all applicable U.S. taxes upon re-entry. "Of course we will," I said, winking. The cashier smiled, and we walked out to get my car. The valet brought it up, and we got in.

"I brought Rachel with me," I said quietly.

Xen's face went from the perma-grin to a sober realization of what that meant. He looked at me with a concerned look on his face. "How'd she take it?"

"What did you do when you woke up yesterday morning in Costa Rica?" I asked.

"I went out on the beach, got drunk on your beer, and contemplated the nature of a brand new universe."

"I believe you and Rachel have set the standard. That's exactly what she's doing … well, except that she's using tequila."

"Why didn't I think of that?" Xen asked.

"I didn't have any," I said bluntly.

"Good point."

O O O

Xen followed me down the path behind the house and out onto the beach. We both had blankets draped over our shoulders. The beach was a mottled strip of silver and gray in the almost-full moonlight, everything set against a black backdrop of ocean and sky. Small white-capped rows of black waves, highlighted by the moon, crumbled against the sand in steady, soothing echoes of contrast. Rachel's back was to us. She had pulled her knees up to her chest, the bottle of tequila stuck into the sand. I noticed that she hadn't touched much since I left for the casino.

We walked up behind her, and I draped my blanket over her shoulders, taking a seat cross-legged in the sand next to her. We sat in silence for a few minutes.

"I feel like I just went down a rabbit hole," Rachel said finally.

"You did," I confirmed quietly. "How do you like Wonderland so far?"

"It's not real yet."

"It will be when you wake up," Xen said. "That's when it really starts to sink in."

"You okay?" I asked, concerned.

"Yeah," she replied with a certainty that surprised me. "Knowing what I know now explains a lot of things over the past couple years."

"It's been my experience that the mind has a way of explaining away the impossible, or at least improbable, no matter what planet you're on, unless someone smashes you over the head with it."

She laughed nervously. "I bet."

"It's funny how that works, isn't it?" Xen added.

"Yep," I said quietly. We were silent for a few more minutes while Rachel continued to ponder the new world she'd been brought into.

"There's someone I want you to meet," I said.

"Who?" Rachel asked a bit nervously.

"The only true friend I ever had up until today, somebody who knows everything about me." I saw Rachel's shoulders tense a bit and then relax after a few seconds. "Mag!" I hollered into the jungle over my shoulder. I saw her slowly glide out of the tree line about twenty yards up the beach. I put my hand on Rachel's arm and pointed at the approaching feline form. "Over there," I said pointing.

"Jesus!" Rachel blurted and squirmed back in the sand a few inches.

"Don't worry. She's a friend," I reassured her.

"You told me you had a *cat*," Rachel reminded me.

"She's called a dratar, actually—where I come from, at least—but cat is close enough."

Magdelain came trotting up to me and rubbed her head against my knee. Rachel leaned back into Xen a bit, away from Mag.

I scratched Mag behind the ears, and the rasping started. "Magdelain, this is Rachel. Rachel, this is Mag."

Mag raised her head and slowly moved a few steps towards Rachel.

"If you scratch her behind the ears, you've got a friend for life."

Rachel slowly put out her hand and gingerly touched the back of Mag's furry skull. She scratched the way I had, and the rasping increased in volume.

"See?"

"She's beautiful," Rachel added, smiling. "Is that a purr?"

"Sort of," Xen added. "She's smart, too. Like … *people* smart."

"Really?"

"Yep," I confirmed. "I trust her with my life. She's saved my ass … hell … I've lost count of how many times. We were made for each other. Literally."

Mag smiled at me but let Rachel keep scratching.

"Was … was that a … smile?" Rachel asked slowly, uncertain she had seen what she saw.

"Yeah," I said affectionately. I patted Mag's side warmly. "I don't know what I'd do without her."

Rachel looked at me closely, searching for something in my face. "You said that about me, too."

"Yep," I said but didn't look back at Rachel. "Meant it, too."

There was a minutes long silence. Mag lay down in with her head in between us.

"Ahem!" Xen cleared his throat and then forced a yawn, stretching his arms. "Well, I'm about ready for bed," he said a bit too loudly. "I think I'll hit the sack and let you talk about …

whatever. . . .” His voice trailed off. He stood up and laid the blanket out flat on the sand. “Good night, you two.”

“Good night, Xen,” Rachel said quietly.

“You need anything?” I asked, calculating how much he’d been drinking the past two days.

“Where’s the aspirin? I have a feeling there’s a hang-over with my name on it waiting in ambush somewhere.”

I chuckled lightly. “Bathroom cabinet. You can’t miss it.”

“I’ll just curl up in the guest bedroom and pass out. Goodnight.”

“Goodnight, Xen,” I said with a smile.

Xen nodded to me, winked once in the darkness, and walked back up the path through the jungle.

Magdelain raised her head and looked at Rachel and me. A few seconds later she got up and followed Xen, leaving us alone on the beach, bathed in Costa Rican moonlight.

“Why’d you show me this?” Rachel asked after a few minutes. “You didn’t really have to.”

“Yes, I did.”

She looked at me again, searching for what she clearly hoped was there. This time I turned and stared into her eyes, showing her what she wanted.

“Somewhere along the way you became more than just important to me. Seems to me you feel the same way.”

“I do.”

“If we wanted to explore that, then you needed to know who … and *what* … you were dealing with.” I shifted a bit uncomfortably in the sand. “I mean, it seems to me you have a right to know if the person you’re with is a … a …”

“A what?” she asked grinning a bit too gleefully, delighting in my discomfort.

“There’s only one word for it. . . .” I said and paused again.

“Yeah?” she asked expectantly, knowing the answer and refusing to say it. She was actually enjoying seeing me squirm.

I let out an exasperated sigh. “An *alien*,” I finally blurted, laughing a bit nervously. “God, how I hate that word!” I said, and we laughed together at a truly bizarre situation.

"You're still Justin to me, you know. I don't care about the rest." She put her hand gently on mine. Our fingers intertwined. "There's something I want to ask you."

"Oh-oh," I said, a bit of the nervousness coming back. "What?"

"Well, I mean … you look like us … like a human … a man."

"Yeah," I said, not certain where she was going.

"Well … are you like a man … in *every* respect?" She looked at me and raised her eyebrow, smiling a bit wickedly.

My eyes grew wider as it dawned on me what she was talking about. I stared at her, and a grin spread across my face. That wasn't the only thing that got bigger.

"There's really only one way to find out, you know." I leaned in and kissed her, gently at first, but our lips parted, and our breathing got heavier.

Her hand untangled itself from mine and slid up over my thigh. She found what she was looking for and ran her hand over it. "Oh!" she said.

I chuckled and pushed her gently over onto the blanket Xen had so thoughtfully spread out in the sand. "God bless Xen," I said into her mouth.

"Amen," she whispered.

Alarm

"So, you going to give us our Q & A?" Xen asked expectantly as he unwrapped one of the cigar boxes.

I took a deep, controlled breath, as if preparing for something I'd never done before. Giving them the whole story scared the hell out of me. I had no idea how they were going to react. But I owed it to them both. Xen sat behind me at the small kitchen table with the cigars and scotch in front of him. I had fried up a mix of diced bacon, onions, chilies and tomatillos and was scrambling eggs into the mix. I'd also set a pitcher of orange juice on the table and three glasses.

"Once Rachel gets out of the shower, we can all get into it," I said as I threw some cheese on top of the eggs. "How's the juice?"

"Freshest I ever had."

"Yeah, the locals squeeze it themselves. It's a perfect setup here. The loft is my home, but this is my sanctuary."

"How'd you find it?"

"It was a thank you gift, actually … about fifteen years ago … I helped someone, and he expressed his gratitude by giving me this."

"*Gave* it to you? Anyone I know?" Xen asked, sniffing the cigars. "And is he interested in adopting a son?"

"No … and no."

"What happened to him?" Xen asked.

"He died."

"Did you kill him?" He sounded a bit too serious for my comfort and then went to work on one of the boxes with the scotch inside.

"No, damn it. Why does everyone ask me that?"

Xen raised a *Why do you think?* eyebrow at me.

I sighed heavily, resolved not to let things like that get to me. "Time," I finally said simply but with a great deal of thoughtfulness. "Time got him."

"Hunh?"

"He was old. Juan de la Vega … the last of the great Spanish gentlemen. He died in his sleep. Hell of a guy, too. I miss him." I felt wistful as I thought of the old man. "I only hope have that kind of class and poise when I'm in my golden years … if I ever have golden years, anyway."

"How'd you meet him?" Xen asked, pulling the cork slowly out of the scotch bottle.

"His granddaughter had been kidnapped in L.A. He needed help finding her. I helped him." I was lost partway in the memories of those events.

Incredulously, "And he gave you *this*?"

"Yep. Drop in the bucket for him, though."

"Still, it must have been some help."

"Vega thought so. He almost died alone, you know." I said sadly. "I was the only one there. All Vega wanted was to pass this world with a loving family around him. His money made that impossible with those kids. Shitty brats, every one."

Xen looked at me thoughtfully. "You know, sometimes you have more humanity than most of humanity."

Rachel's sweet voice interrupted my reverie. "That smells wonderful," she said as she walked in wearing one of my robes and drying her hair with a towel. *All the sweeter this particular morning*, I thought.

"Kitchen or patio, you two?" I asked, shaking my head to shoo a few lingering, long forgotten ghosts out of the corners of my mind. "And we can let the interrogation begin."

"Patio!" they shouted in unison, but Xen kept looking at me thoughtfully.

"I'll bring this," I said, holding the eggs. "Rachel, grab the plates, sugar, and silverware. Xen, you get juice, glass and cigar detail." I walked out onto the patio and waited for them. They collected what they were supposed to, followed me out and set everything down on the patio table.

As they sat down, I dished out the scrambled eggs and set the still-hot skillet on the brick wall behind me. I sat down, grabbed the sugar and poured a healthy amount into my orange juice, stirring it with a table-knife. Xen and Rachel were perched on the edges of their seats looking at me expectantly, almost like buzzards circling.

"I'll start," Rachel jumped in as she dug into her eggs. "What's with putting a ton of sugar into everything? Orange Juice not sweet enough for you? And those sickly-sweet cappuccinos? God! They're awful!" They both started eating, expectant looks on their faces.

I smiled, intrigued at her choice of beginnings, and massaged the back of my head. "That's not where I thought we'd start, but okay." I set the knife down and drank half of the juice. "Sugar for me is like five shots of espresso for you … crossed with really mild hemp and a touch of speed."

They both stared at me a bit wide-eyed, their mouths stuck around the food they were chewing.

"You mean you're *high* all the time?" Xen asked, incredulous. Rachel looked shell-shocked.

I chuckled. "Well, high is a strong word … more like a really good buzz. It's how my metabolism works."

They looked at each other and laughed.

"Unbelievable!" Xen added finally.

"No wonder you never take anything seriously," Rachel said, shaking her head.

"It certainly explains your attitude," Xen added.

"I guess it does," I replied, laughing along with them.

"Okay," Xen started, with a more serious look on his face. "My turn. Why do you look like us?"

"I was kind of wondering that myself," Rachel added quietly, hiding a suggestive grin from Xen. I'm pretty sure I actually blushed.

"I mean," Xen continued, "you're from another planet, right? Let's get this shit out in the open. I want to hear you say it."

I paused, still hesitant to actually let the words cross my lips. I took a deep breath. "Yes." I nodded once with a resolved finality that seemed somewhat cathartic. "I'm from another planet." It was a huge relief, and the depth of the feeling caught me by surprise.

"So, how can you look like us? It's statistically impossible, unless that's a possessed body, a copy, a construct, costume or something else I can't think of." Xen looked at me with a serious, almost accusatory look on his face. He was a scientist, a good one, and his understanding of biology and natural selection simply didn't have room for such genetic synchronicity across the stars. "Impossible," he concluded with certainty.

"No, it's not," I said, smiling lightly.

"What?" Xen erupted. "Come on! Are you saying that all life around the universe looks like humans? I'm almost insulted."

"Of course I'm not saying that," I conceded with a *Don't-be-silly* look on my face. "What I am saying is that a large portion of the sentient races look like us. Like you and me. There are a few other archetypes, but about sixty-five-percent have this body-type."

"How is that even possible?" Xen was actually getting worked up. He didn't want to accept it.

"Well, I'm not a scientist, and I didn't really study it. They had me studying other things. It has something to do with stars and the life that evolves around them. Stars of one type create people like us, and stars of a different type create different archetypes. As I understand it, they were just beginning to identify a network of both communication and something like consciousness between solar bodies. But that's about all I know."

Xen had a thoughtful look on his face as he contemplated the possibilities and *plausibilities*. "Interesting," he said finally.

"Why are you here?" Rachel asked suddenly. And she nailed me down with an exceedingly serious look of her own. Although Xen didn't pick it up, I also heard the between-the-lines question of *Will you be going?*

I'm sure my face looked a little sad as I remembered my egress from home and the unpleasant circumstances surrounding it. "Well, I'll kill two birds with one stone on that one, because you both also want to ask *what* I am, why I can do the things I can do."

"Yes," they both said.

"When I said that people look like us all over, I meant it. They make love and babies just like you do. Babies of all kinds are born every day out there," I said somberly. "But I wasn't one of them." I paused and took a drink of juice. "I was an … experiment … a … a weapon," I added with both sadness and even shame coming into my voice.

"What do you mean?" Rachel asked with a look of genuine concern on her face. She placed her hand on mine. I looked up and smiled at her.

"I mean, a group of people, some of them tyrants, drew up a specification for me, hired and forced people to create me, and used me as a weapon to do their dirty work. I killed … a *lot* of people in those days … some, maybe most of whom didn't really have it coming. My father, if I had such a thing, saved me … well, helped me save myself."

"What happened?" Xen asked.

"I asked questions … asked *why*. The powers that existed at the time needed a weapon that went where it was told and did what it was told. Asking those questions, was beyond my specification, a sign of anomalous behavior. They decided they were going to fix me, make me more compliant and less inquisitive. It's the only thing that ever scared me to death, so I left. I stole what I could, including my transport, broke into a phase facility, programmed it for destinations unknown, and ended up here. My father blew the console to wipe the destination just as the troops blew the doors. I didn't even get to say goodbye to him."

"Fix you?" Rachel asked.

"Wipe my mind. The body is what they needed. A consciousness could be recreated and all the training re-implemented." I wasn't looking at them anymore. I was staring at my past, remembering everything that had happened in my life before Earth. Tears welled up in my eyes, and when I realized it, I came back to them, cleared my throat, and smiled. The tears disappeared quickly. The tenderness in Rachel's eyes almost made me start bawling again.

"Shit," I muttered, wiping my nose.

"How long have you been here?" Xen asked.

"Since eighty-three." I silently thanked Xen for changing topics.

"Justin?" Rachel interjected. "You said something last night that I didn't really understand … about Mag." I looked at her expectantly. I knew immediately what she wanted to ask. "You said you two were made for each other."

I nodded. "She was created along with me. She even shares a lot of my DNA. She's kind of like a sister. That was the other part of their plan, but she couldn't be wiped. They would have terminated her and grown a new one to match the new me." The old killer in me, the one full of rage, added, "I couldn't allow that." Then the rage faded and the sadness took hold.

Xen and Rachel saw the melancholy welling up, and neither of them ever would have thought me capable of it. I'm sure it drifted there on my face like a tide-pool, swelling and then receding quickly as I got my control back.

A smile popped onto my face, and whatever sadness had been there disappeared in a flash, replaced with elation. "Xen, break out some of those cigars! This is a big day for me." Neither of them could tell if my happiness was natural or forced, but they rolled with it, not wanting to press me. "You two are the first people I've ever told any this stuff to. I'm not as alone as I used to be." I smiled at them both as warmly as I could. "Thanks," I said sincerely.

"For what?" Xen asked.

"For letting me trust you. You don't know what it's been like all these years."

Rachel squeezed my hand. "So, nobody else knows anything?"

"Well, Yvgenny knows something is odd about me. He's known me since I first got here … literally. I haven't changed in appearance in all those years. At first, he bought the story about having Lazarus syndrome, why I didn't appear to age. But like you, he's seen and heard enough to know something's up. He's just too polite to call me on it. Like I said, we sort of found each other."

"Sounds like you really trust him," Rachel observed.

"With my life. But he does work for who he works for. Knowing would do him no good, so there wasn't any reason to say anything."

"Is there anyone else?" Xen asked, handing me a cigar.

"There is one," I said a bit ominously as I pulled out a cigar cutter and lighter from my jacket. Xen and I unwrapped our cigars.

"Hey!" Rachel interjected. "Don't leave me hanging. I love Cubans." We looked at her with raised eyebrows and then smiled at each other.

Xen pulled out one more cigar and handed it over. We passed around the clipper and then the lighter. Wisps and streams of smoke drifted into the jungle, carried mostly intact through the trees.

"So, who's the other one?" Rachel asked as she leaned back, pulling on the cigar like an aficionado.

"A spook." My voice went cold, and both Rachel and Xen saw a brief glimpse of the cold-blooded killer that I keep hidden away within. "This was just before 9/11." I looked at Xen. "Me and this guy had a night similar to what you and I just went through. I thought he was a friend. Turns out he cared about was sending me to a fucking lab … in pieces."

"Is he still alive?" Rachel asked carefully.

"He was when I last saw him. I barely got out of that one. That's one of the times Mag really pulled my bacon out of the fire."

The three of us spent the rest of the day talking about my home world and what life was like there. I avoided talking about the work I used to do, saying I didn't want to remember, which was true, but anything else they wanted to know was fair game. As the conversation evolved, what became clear to both of them is that life is pretty much the same all over. There are good people and bad. Some have power and some don't. They all eat, sleep, fight, love, and make babies.

"It's a universal constant," I said during a philosophical moment, "an endless sequence of events that brings joy and despair to every living creature … life and death. All you can really do is give and get as many smiles along the way as possible before you check out. That was the last lesson my father taught me."

O O O

I poured them each a snifter of the Elegancia and prepared to talk about what came next. I looked at Xen. "There's something I've been meaning to ask you."

"What?" Xen peeked over his snifter.

"After I sent you that chemical data, how did you get hooked up with SolCon?" I avoid the topic of Natalia.

"An acquaintance gave me a list of companies that took proposals for grants and research projects. I sent it out to a few of the bigger ones. Dow, PetroChina, and SolCon were among them. A few weeks later, I got a bite from SolCon. It came from Natalia personally."

"When was that?" I asked around a freshly lit cigar.

"It took me a week to review your data and formulate some options, and another couple of weeks to put together the proposal. She called me about a week later."

"And they set you up at the SolCon facility in Paramount?"

"Yep. They've got a pretty big operation there. Much bigger than DiMarco's. I had a lab to myself, and only talked to Natalia about the project. I started working only a few weeks after she first contacted me. That's why you didn't hear from me during that time. You know how focused I get."

"Yes I do," I said, smiling. I did some quick figuring in my head. "And I'm guessing that Natalia moved to her new house a couple of weeks after that, right?"

"That's right. How did you know?"

"The timing works out. It also means a few troubling things."

"Like what?" A look of concern crossed his face.

"Well, it means that even if we get DiMarco and shut him down, we may have an even bigger problem."

"What?" Xen was openly scared now. He was having a difficult time coming up with anything worse than hired killers gunning for him.

"Pyotr Nikolov."

Fear shifted to confusion on his face.

"The U.S. head at SolCon?"

"Yeah. You know him?" I was hoping he'd crossed paths with the Russian. I wanted … needed … any information on Nikolov I could get at this point. My guts told me DiMarco wasn't even a small fry compared to the Russian.

"I only met him once, and only in passing. At a corporate dinner. He seemed nice enough to me, although a bit impersonal. Cold even."

"We'll, let's just say that SolCon is just his day-job. I'm thinking he knew all along about Natalia. I'm also pretty sure that he's the one who put things in motion to make you both dead, but he didn't seem to care that much when it didn't happen."

Rachel flicked some ash off her cigar. "Knew what about Natalia?"

I scratched my head, putting things together. "I think he knew all along Natalia was Interpol."

"*WHAT?*" Xen shouted. He looked like a deer in headlights.

"You didn't know?" In the back of my mind I heard a cat dash out of a bag and run for parts unknown. I guess there wasn't any reason he should. I took a sip of scotch and watched surprise churn in Xen's features. He blinked in disbelief and shook his head silently. His mouth kept opening and closing as he tried to say something, but no words came. He looked at Rachel, seeking wisdom, but she only shrugged at him. "I wish I knew what game Nikolov was playing," I continued. "This is all starting to feel like a chess board now, and Nikolov's moving all the pieces."

Xen's shoulders slumped, accepting the revelation, and he finally found his voice. He decided to get down to business. "There is one thing, Justin. Like I said, I only talked to him that one time, but I got the sense that he was smart ... like smarter than me ... smarter than everyone in the room. That kind of smart ... *scary* smart."

"Yeah, I know," I agreed. "Rachel? You ready for VeniCorp?" I changed topics to avoid something I wasn't ready to deal with yet. I looked at her with a mix of concern and affection. I needed to get used to the thing growing between us, and it wasn't in my pants.

"Hell, yes." She squeezed my hand again.

"Xen, how about you? Think you're up for a little sneak and peek at VeniCorp?"

"Is it going be like Grady's?" Fear edged into his voice.

Magdelain appeared out of the jungle and curled up in the sun on the patio behind me. She could smell a good sneak and peak a mile away.

"Well, I can't promise it won't be, but it's unlikely. It should be rent-a-cops, if anything, and a little breaking and entering. I doubt there will be anyone there."

"I don't know." Xen slowly shook his head.

"If you don't want to go, I understand. I wouldn't ask at all, but we're going to hit Jackie Shao's PC. It's on a disconnected network. It may just be a standalone, and while I have a good idea of what we're looking for, you'd be able to dig deeper and faster than I will. You guys are both chemists. You think the same way."

Xen thought for a bit, and we watched him go through an internal debate. "Jackie is a piece of why they came after me and Natalia, right?"

I nodded. "Pretty much. It's not a straight line. Hell, Jackie may not even know about you, although I doubt it. But it's all part of the big picture, and I can't be certain all the loose ends get tied up unless we go in there."

"Okay, I'm in." He looked at me and smiled. "But if I get killed, I'll never forgive you."

We all laughed.

"Don't worry," I assured him confidently, "I won't let anything happen to either of you."

Xen's face went serious again. "I hope you're right, Justin … I hope you're right."

"Okay. Let's go back and get ready." I turned around and looked at Mag who sat up and looked at me expectantly. "Why don't you stay here tonight Mag? We'll be out on the streets, and this is no big deal. There's no point risking you getting seen, okay?"

She nodded her head, but with some disappointment.

I looked back at my two human friends. "Formal attire, if you please."

"What?" They said in unison.

"Everyone wears black tonight. It's etiquette. And evening gloves."

Back-Up

We walked out of the parking garage, down the street, and approached the building. As I had hoped, the streets were clear. We crossed through the parking lot where the Audi had been and went up to the main entrance. I pulled the Prox II card out of my pocket and swiped it over the reader. The light went green, and the door-latch clicked. I pulled the door open and motioned for them to go inside. We walked quickly across the lobby, and as we entered the hallway, Xen and Rachel grabbed their hoods and pulled them over their faces. I slipped the pack off, slid my coat on, then replaced the pack. As my features dimmed to near invisibility, my companions stared at my visible head perched six feet above barely visible shoes. The rest was like looking through a pane of distorted glass.

"What the fuck?" Xen blurted.

"Nifty," Rachel cooed.

"Business suit," I said to both of them and pulled the goggles and hood over my head. I pressed the UP button. The door dinged immediately, we stepped in, and I pressed the three button. "Jeepers Creepers" by Tony Bennett played over the speakers.

Rachel and Xen looked at my goggles—the only thing really visible on me. They looked at each other, looked at my goggles again and started giggling. I could only shake my head, the goggles appearing to sway with a life of their own in mid-air, which made them laugh even more.

"Alright, alright. Game-faces. Let's pretend this is serious, shall we?" My goggles shifted back and forth, glancing at both of them a few times.

Xen put a thoughtful finger to his temple. "I'm reminded of the story of a pot, a kettle, and shades of obsidian," but he and Rachel stopped laughing and sobered up a bit.

I pulled down the facemask, and the goggles disappeared. I palmed the Prox card in my hand. "This should be easy."

The door opened, and we stepped out into the empty reception area. If anyone was actually watching, this would get hairy fast, but corporate offices, even those owned by goombahs, rarely have twenty-four-by-seven eyes on security cams. I walked up to the door and swiped the card over the reader. The latch clicked, and Xen opened the door. As we stepped in, our motion set off the detector above the door and a loud, piercing *BEEP! BEEP! BEEP!* erupted above us.

"Shit!" he cried an octave higher than normal. Then he turned and bolted for the still-open elevator.

Rachel and my shifting outline calmly turned in the doorway and stared at Xen as he practically dove into the elevator.

"Xen," I spoke quietly and calmly as the poor guy hammered at the down button over and over again. "Hold up a second." I stepped into the office, put in Jackie's code on the panel just inside the door, and the alarm stopped. The elevator doors began to close, but Xen stepped out before they did, a slightly embarrassed look on his face.

I leaned out into the office doorway and looked at him. "SOP," I explained in a friendly, almost parental tone. "You get thirty seconds to disarm the system before anyone is notified. You okay? Need to change your shorts or something?"

"I'm fine, damn it." He walked past Rachel who was unsuccessfully trying to keep a straight face. "Nobody says another fucking word," he added with venom.

Rachel motioned, locking her lips and throwing away the key, but she shook slightly, trying to hold in the laughter as she followed Xen inside.

"The good news is that nobody is here, otherwise the alarm would have been off." The door swung closed behind us. "Our luck is holding so far."

I headed to the left towards the glassed off area at the back of the mostly dark office. We walked up to the door that opened into the lab. I slid the Prox card again, opened the door, and we stepped in. Rachel hit the light-switch, and fluorescent lights flickered to life, exposing a fairly elaborate lab facility with a half-dozen desks and a wide array of equipment.

"There it is," Xen pointed to a large cubicle in the far corner.

"How do you know?" I asked.

Xen walked over to the wall of the cubicle, slid out the nameplate from the bracket on the wall and held it up. It had JACK SHAO printed on it. "See?"

"Smart ass," I said with a smile on my face.

"I learned from the best."

"Gee, I wonder who that could be," Rachel added. Xen and Rachel stared at me deliberately, and they both chuckled. Rachel and I walked up behind Xen who had already sat down at the desk. There were two workstations in the cubicle.

"Just as I thought. That one," I pointed to the one on the left. "No network cable or antennae."

Xen moved the mouse, and the screen sprang to life. SHAOJ was in the user-field, and the password field was empty. "What's his password?"

"I don't know," I said simply.

Xen and Rachel turned to me slowly with stunned looks on their faces.

"What?" I paused. I was toying with them and let the seconds tick by. "Don't worry, I have a plan." I reached into an inner pocket and pulled out a small gray box with a cable attached to it. "Here, this will do the trick, but it could take a while."

"How long?" Rachel held her hand out so she could examine the device.

I handed it over. "Well, there's good news and bad news."

"What's the good news?" Rachel looked at it closely.

"It can take as fast as a few seconds."

"What's the bad news," Xen asked.

"It can take as long as thirty minutes to run through the permutations." I almost sounded apologetic … almost.

"Thirty minutes?" Xen was appalled.

"I'm afraid so."

Xen shifted in his chair. "We can't stay around here that long, Justin. I'm barely holding it together as it is."

"Wait a minute," Rachel interrupted and reached between them to pick up a sticky-note hanging from a calendar on the cubical wall. "What's this?" She held it out for them to read. In printed letters it spelled out *A-U-F-V-R-0-9*. "Could this be it?"

"Only one way to find out," I said. "Try it, Xen." Xen looked doubtful, but he typed in the capitalized letters and hit the ENTER key. The screen prompted: *The Username or Password is incorrect.* "Try lower-case." Xen typed it in and got the same response.

"Wait a minute," Xen said. "Let me see that." Rachel handed him the sticky-note, and he looked at it for a minute, thoughtful furrows creasing his brow. His head cocked to the side and then a clever smile crossed his face. He turned to the keyboard and typed in some characters. He turned to us both and hit the ENTER key with a flourish. The login prompt disappeared, and the desktop came up on the screen.

"How'd you know?" Rachel asked.

"Think of it like a license plate," he suggested, smiling.

She went through the options. "O-fever … aw-fever … ah-yu-fever … I don't get it."

Xen enjoyed watching her go through the puzzle. "Think like a *chemist.*"

Rachel's head turned to the side as she wracked her brains for the answer. I was motionless for a few seconds, then I turned to a periodic chart of the elements on the wall.

"Gold fever," I said quietly. "Nice work, Xen."

"What?" Rachel was still confused. I reached over and pointed at one of the elements on the chart.

"AU is the symbol for gold," I explained.

"And all caps," Xen added, "just like it is on the sheet."

"Start digging, Xen," I said, putting the now unnecessary hacking device back in my pocket.

He grabbed the mouse and started in. He spent a few minutes running through folders and opening files, not really knowing what he was looking for. He'd zeroed in on a PROJECTS folder, but there were dozens of folders within.

"This would go a lot faster if I knew what I was looking for," Xen said with a touch of exasperation, and then he double-clicked on a folder named KING.

I spoke up. "It has something to do with cocaine and meth. That's what I …"

"Wait a minute," Xen said, interrupting me and leaning in towards the screen. He opened a document and started reading. He clicked a few links in the document, and a series of three-dimensional molecule diagrams appeared in another program. He clicked through them, and the shapes appeared to morph from one structure through to another in a progression of four steps. "But that's not possible … Is it?" he said to himself quietly.

"What have you got?" I leaned in.

"Well … I think this is it. It starts with cocaine and meth then a series of chemical processes and a reagent. I'll have to read all the material to see what the catalysts are and how they're being processed, but this has got to be what you're looking for."

"Are you sure?" I asked as I reached into a pocket and pulled out a thumb-drive.

Xen nodded. "Pretty sure."

"Here," I handed him the drive. "Copy the whole thing."

"There's a lot here, will it fit on this?" I nodded. Xen grabbed the drive, slipped it into a port and dragged the folder over. We all watched as about ten gigabytes of data was copied. Xen pulled the drive out and handed it to me. "I don't suppose you have a copy of ChemPen on your PC at home, do you?"

I shook my head. "Do they sell it on line?"

"Yeah," Xen confirmed.

"Done deal, then. Close everything down, and let's get out of here."

Xen did as instructed, and we headed out. Rachel turned off the lights as Xen opened the front door and waited for her. I stepped up to arm the security system, and they stepped through the door. I heard a brief scuffle in the lobby, and someone whispered a "Shhh …" that I'm certain wasn't meant for my ears.

Shit … We've been made. Fear clutched at my insides, something that had never happened before. I'd been worried about friends in trouble, but the thought of Rachel out there terrified me. I had to fix the problem, but barging in would lead to shooting, and I couldn't afford to let that happen. I needed an opening.

I backed up against the wall a few feet away from the panel, completely camouflaged in the darkened room. I watched the barrel of a gun come slowly around the corner. I held perfectly still as an Italian face I didn't recognize looked around the corner right at me. The man stepped up and put his back against the security panel, scanning the room for a couple minutes.

"Al, the video only showed two people," another man's voice said from the lobby. "Let's go take them to Mister DiMarco."

"Something about the video is bugging me … shut up a minute." The man reached behind him while still looking into the room, and he turned on the lights. He circled the cube farm slowly, watching and listening. "Hmmph," he finally said, shaking his head. He turned off the lights, turned to the panel and set the system. I began counting down from thirty. I could still set off the alarm if I was in the room when it reset. The man walked out the door at twenty-five seconds. The door closed at twenty-two seconds

"Let's go," someone said from the lobby.

I stepped around the corner and up to the door. The elevator door opened at seventeen seconds. I placed my hand on the doorknob and heard people being pushed into the elevator at twelve seconds. The elevator doors began to close at seven seconds and finished at four seconds. I opened the door and closed it behind me at zero, but I didn't hesitate. I didn't have much time. I couldn't take them in the building but had to get them before they got into their vehicle.

I leapt across the room to the stairwell entrance and pulled out the vlain. I opened the door, stepped into the stairwell and jumped down the first flight, landing like a panther. I turned, leapt again down the next flight, careened off the wall, and kept going. I made it down the three floors of stairs almost as fast as if I had been falling. I stepped up to the first-floor door and silently opened it a crack. I'd beaten them down.

Stepping through, I closed it silently behind me and crouched behind a large potted plant in the hallway. I found myself at one end of a long hallway near the back of the building. Halfway down, a short hallway led to the elevators. Straight ahead, at the other end of the building, an exit emptied out into the parking lot.

The elevator doors opened and I heard Rachel ask, "How did you know we were here?" She sounded scared but in control. She knew I was out here somewhere. I hope she knew I would never let anything happen to her.

"Mister Shao is working tonight … at the *plant*. When we got the door login here, an alarm went off with the double entry, so we checked the video. When we saw you two going into the office, we decided to surprise you."

Crap, I thought. It should have occurred to me. *I must be getting rusty*.

"Why didn't you call the cops?" Xen asked. *He* sounded scared.

"We're not a big fan of the legal system," one of the guards said, laughing. "We handle things our own way … you know … *without* cops or lawyers. Shovels are a lot faster … and *cheaper*. We got a van out back, and we're all going for a little ride."

"No-no," one of the other men said. "Not the front door. Back that way." I heard them walking towards the hallway where I stood, and then they came into view. There were three goombahs, two of them jammed Rachel and Xen's arms up behind their backs and held guns at the backs of their heads. The third trailed behind them. Neither Rachel nor Xen had their masks on.

"Hey Al, think we should have told Ricky about this?" the man holding Rachel asked.

"Nah …" Al replied confidently. "We got this. Besides, why wake him up? Maybe Gino will give us a bonus for bringing them in ourselves."

The group turned away from me and walked down the hall towards the far door. Xen and Rachel were both looking around, searching for me, do doubt. I crept back to the stairwell entrance and opened the door as quietly as I could. I closed it behind me, went to the door leading to the alley, opened it and peered out. I could see the back of a black van at the far end of the building to my left. There were dumpsters between me and the van, so I quickly opened the door, stepped into the alley, closed it behind me, and ran to the dumpsters. I peered around the corner and spotted a face in the driver's side, rear-view mirror. The back of the van lay fifteen feet away.

"Nice!" the driver hollered through the window. "You got them."

"Piece of cake," Al said as the group finally came around the far corner of the building. The two men holding my friends walked along the van as Al and the driver exchanged a few words.

Xen and Rachel scanned the alley, fear in their eyes. They stopped at the back of the van, and then Al came around and opened the doors for them. "Get in," Al said.

The two men shoved Xen and Rachel into the van, and they tumbled onto the hard, steel floor. Once they were locked inside, I could make my move.

I heard a car come around the corner behind me. I turned quickly and identified the shape of a black Audi as it pulled completely into the alley and stopped with the motor running, blinding us all with its headlights. I barely saw my own outline illuminated in the bright glare.

"What's this happy horseshit?" Al asked as he stepped away from the back of the van. He walked along the dumpsters with his arm raised to shield his eyes. "Go on, get the fuck outa here," he shouted at the car. "Keep those two covered," he ordered over his shoulder. He turned back to the car in front of him. "Motherfucker," Al said under his breath as he stepped up even with the end of the dumpster where I hid. The car door opened, and a shadowy figure stood there looking down the alley towards us.

"I suggest you go about your business, asshole! You don't want a piece of this. You have no fucking idea who I am!"

The shadow moved, and we both saw the silhouette of a rifle come up in the driver's hands. Al's hand went inside his pocket, and I heard the thump of a silenced shot come from the Audi. The man guarding Rachel tumbled to the ground. Al yanked his gun out just as a second shot went through the head of the man guarding Xen.

I moved in a flash, swinging the vlain through Al's arm as leveled in front of him. He got a confused look on his face as he watched his arm fall away, severed between shoulder and elbow, the pistol still in hand. "I know who you are," I whispered in his ear.

Al inhaled ready to scream as he turned a horrified face towards me. The stiletto blade of the vlain entered his throat, cutting off the scream … and Al's life.

"What the fuck!" the van driver yelled and flung open the door. He stepped out of the van and aimed his pistol at my shape, shimmering in the Audi's headlights. I saw a flash from the bushes across the parking lot. The driver's face blossomed into a red rose as the bullet passed through his head from behind. He crumpled silently in a heap. I pulled the vlain out of Al's throat and let him drop to the ground.

I turned to face the Audi, motionless. Highlighted in the headlights as I was, if the driver wanted to drop me, there wasn't much I could do about it. I tried zooming in with my goggles to get a look at the person holding the rifle, but the glare made it impossible. The best I could make out was a like a tall, well-built man.

The driver stared at me for several seconds, lowered the rifle, and got back into the car. He put it in reverse and backed out of the alley, turning down the street and slowly driving away. I turned back to the van and walked up to my friends. They both had blood-spatters on their faces, and the inside of the van had the same crimson patterns of goombah blood, bone, and gray matter. Rachel and Xen sat motionless in the back of the van, surprised looks on their faces, staring at my outline.

I pulled the hood back and lifted the goggles off my eyes as I stared at them for a few seconds. "You two alright?" I finally asked.

They blinked a few times and slowly got out of the van.

"Are you alright?" I repeated.

"*Who was that?*" Rachel shouted.

"That," and I turned my head down the alley, "was our friend Mister Zajac. And he wasn't alone."

"What?" Xen asked, finally breaking his silence.

"Look," I said, pointing around the corner of the van at the dead driver.

They did. "Oh my god!" they said in tandem. "So, who got him? I only saw the one guy."

"I don't know. It came from across the parking lot. Could be anybody…." I got a thoughtful look on my face. "Well, not any of us, obviously. That would be metaphysically absurd, unless time travel were possible, which I happen to know for a fact is not. But it could be anyone else, and they sure do know how to shoot." I flicked a glance at Rachel to see if she'd put it together.

Rachel got a funny look on her face, smiling knowingly. She looked at Xen and gently put her hand out on his shoulder. "They sure do," she added as she looked at me. I winked at her and then shook my head slightly.

"Come on, help me load these guys up," I said as I turned to grab Al. "Get the driver." I tucked Al's arm inside his coat, dragged the body back to the van, and quite un-gently threw his body inside. We stacked the rest of the bodies on top.

Rachel and Xen retrieved the guns from two of the bodies before closing the doors. I started wiping blood off the side and roof of the van. It couldn't be seen in the dark, but if a cop pulled me over and brushed up against it, it could be a problem.

"You kept your cool," I whispered in Rachel's ear. "I'm really proud of you."

"I knew you'd come for me." She smiled and kissed me on the cheek, which got my insides doing flip-flops. I suddenly realized just what I was getting into with her. My work would be putting her at risk, and a pang of *guilt? Worry? Fear?* ran through me. This wasn't a game anymore, I couldn't help wonder if having Rachel in the mix might compromise my composure.

Clearing my head of doubt, I said to them both, "Head back to my van. There's a jug of water in the upper right-hand cabinet all the way in. Clean up, lose the gloves in a sewer and get moving. I want you to meet me a block west of Natalia's place. You know the way, right Xen?"

"Yeah," Xen said quietly, a slight look of pain flickering across his face.

I put my arm on Xen's shoulder. "I'm sorry, man."

"It's alright. I'll be fine."

Rachel put her hand on Xen's arm again and gave him a comforting squeeze. She shot a questioning look at me again, and I shook my head again almost imperceptibly but firmly.

"Okay, go on," I ordered. "Turn signals and speed limit only, and don't forget to wipe the blood off your faces." They walked off towards my van as I got into the black one. I pulled onto the highway in a matter of minutes. As soon as I hit fifty-five, I set the cruise control. The clock on the dashboard said it was one a.m. I pulled out my cell phone and hit an all-too-familiar speed-dial. I was not looking forward to this phone call.

"Hello," a tired but familiar voice said in a whisper.

"Did I wake you?"

"No, Case," O'Neil whispered into the phone. "I always stay up till the wee hours of the morning waiting for the phone to ring. Hang on a minute." I heard O'Neil get out of bed, go to another room, and close the door behind him. "What do you want?"

"Well, I have a gift and a favor. Which do you want first?"

"Don't fuck with me Case. I have a gun and a badge. I'll shoot you and make it look like self-defense. There won't even be much paperwork."

"I hear you…." I said, knowing that tone all too well. "Here's the deal. I've got that chemical data we were talking about last week, and I'm having someone really good dig through it. I'll send you all the data in the morning…." I paused for a reaction. "You forgive me for waking you up?"

"Barely," but O'Neil didn't sound tired anymore. "I did some digging myself. If it will help your guy, I found out what's in T-Rex."

"What?"

"It's a mix of coke, meth and tetra … tetra …" O'Neil paused and then yawned.

"Tetrachloroethylene?" I asked with surprised disbelief.

"Yeah! That's it … tetrachloroethylene. How'd you know?"

My voice remained calm, but that was a big missing piece. "Because it's what they use for dry cleaning. I'll be damned. That's what KING stands for."

"What?" O'Neil asked, confused.

"King," I said clearly. "It's the name of the folder where we found the data. And Rex means king in Latin."

"Where'd you find this folder?" O'Neil sounded suspicious. "And, now that I'm thinking about it, what's the favor?"

"Oh … yeah … about that." I tried to sound completely innocent of wrongdoing and not evasive, but I failed, and O'Neil knew it.

"Oh shit," he said.

"No … it's nothing bad … well … mostly nothing bad."

I pictured O'Neil holding his forehead in his hand. "What happened?"

"Well, we broke into VeniCorp tonight."

"You did what?"

"We broke in to VeniCorp." I might just as well have said we went shopping.

"Who is *we*?"

"Me, Rachel, and Xen."

"Xen's alive?"

"Yeah."

"Justin, you gotta stop calling me in the middle of the night. You're killing me, man."

"Yeah, I know. I'm sorry." I even sounded appropriately apologetic. "The thing is we sort of got caught."

A weighty silence stretched out on the other end as O'Neil went through all the possibilities in his head, each one worse that the last.

"O'Neil?"

"I'm here. Keep talking." His voice was surly. He knew this wasn't going to be good.

"Well, when we came out, there were three guys waiting. They sort of ended up … dead."

O'Neil sounded suddenly terrified. "Please tell me these weren't rent-a-cops. If they were rent-a-cops, you're going to jail for fucking ever."

"No-no-no … there were these three goombahs. They were going to take Xen and Rachel off to bury them in the desert." I paused for a moment and realized something I wanted to clarify. "And besides, *I* didn't kill them!" I said defensively. "Well, that's not entirely true. I killed one of them. But somebody else killed the other three."

"You said there were three guys. That's *four*!" I think O'Neil really would have shot me if I was in front of him. In the leg or something, but there would have been gunfire.

"Three goombahs and a driver. I killed one, this guy who's been following me killed two, and somebody else killed the driver."

O'Neil was just about at his limit. "Justin?" he asked calmly.

"Yeah?"

"Are you on any medication?"

A thoughtful pause later, "Not that I know of."

"Maybe you should be. You're making about as much sense as crack head at a political debate. I want to go back to bed and forget this conversation till morning. Get to the point and tell me what you want?"

"You know that house where those six Italians got it a few days ago?"

"Yeah. By the way, that definitely looked like your work."

"It was," I confirmed easily. "So, anyway," I continued without missing a beat, "these four will be in the alley behind that house in about twenty minutes. Can you keep them on ice for me?"

"You want me to store bodies for you?" O'Neil was stupefied.

"Yeah."

"What the fuck for? I should just charge you with murder and sleep for a week."

"You don't mean that," I said.

"The hell I don't!" O'Neil paused and then asked the obvious question. "Why keep them? You could have just dumped them."

"Well, the people who killed the other three, I still don't know whose side they're on, or what they're after. I'm pretty sure they're good guys, but you know I like to keep my options open. If it comes down to it, these guys are evidence."

"Is there anything else?"

"No, that should just about do it," I said matter-of-factly.

"Then goodnight," he said, and I could almost hear the headache forming inside his skull.

"Goodnight, O'Neil. And thanks."

"Oh, and Case?"

"Yeah?"

"I hate you."

"I know."

We both hung up.

When we got back to the loft, I'd logged on and used my system to hack VeniCorp and replace the lobby images of us walking in and getting captured. Then I erased our User entry in the logs. If Al hadn't been lying, then all anybody would know is that the three goombahs disappeared in the middle of the night. I had to hope that was the case, although it was unlikely DiMarco's organization would ever call the cops.

I escorted Xen and Rachel to Costa Rica, explaining that my father had taught me it was customary to kick back after a night on the town. Xen was grateful for the opportunity to get out.

My loft was, as he put it, "Fucking hot in here."

As we left, I handed him a laptop with the VeniCorp data, and told him to start going through it. I needed to know how the whole thing worked as quickly as possible now that things were heating up.

Rachel and I undressed, crawled into bed, and were asleep before we could even kiss. It had been a long day.

PART THREE

CHEMICAL BURN

School Day

Rachel and I had spent the morning in the surf while Xen worked on the chemical data. At lunch, we put together a few edibles and a cooler full of beer. Rachel and I were dying to know what had happened to Xen when this whole thing had started off. When we finished lunch, we lit up three more cigars and relaxed.

"So … uhhh … Xen?" Rachel pulled on a cigar, enjoying watching the smoke drift up into the trees.

"Yeah?"

"How'd you manage to fake your death, anyway?" She blew a smoke ring up into the air.

Xen grinned at her, his lips stretched to their limits, and held it for a few seconds. Through clenched teeth he asked, "What do you see?"

Rachel got a confused look on her face, wondering if it was a trick question. "Your teeth?" she said slowly.

He gave her a victorious look. "Wrong."

"What?" she asked, perplexed.

"These aren't my teeth."

Rachel looked at his face, still perplexed. I stared at Xen for a few seconds and then smiled knowingly.

"You kept them, didn't you? Your teeth, I mean, and had the new ones installed some place abroad." I turned to Rachel. "Those are implants," I clarified for her. The truth dawned on her as she figured out what we both meant. "Tell us everything."

"The night I disappeared, I'd just finished up at the lab," he said, "when this guy comes at me in the parking lot." He took a long pull from his beer. He shifted a bit uncomfortably in his chair, trying to get out of the hot sun.

I leaned back in my chair, moving further into the sun as monkeys screeched above us, and sized up my friend. To look at Xen, you'd never think that he'd be able to hurt a rabbit, let alone take out an armed killer.

"Wait a minute," I said. "Back up … to the beginning of that night."

"Tell us everything," Rachel said, intently staring at Xen.

So he did.

O O O

Xen logged off his computer and unplugged the external hard drive containing his finished research. Natalia had left the lab on her way to Sacramento only a few hours earlier. She'd apologized, since they normally went out on Friday nights, but she told him it was an award dinner for a co-worker … employees only.

She had asked about his progress before she'd left and said she was very anxious to get a finished product from him. He could have told her he'd wrapped it up, but he wanted to surprise her with a printed and bound version of his work. He'd decided to hold out on her, saying he nearly finished. He'd kissed her before she left, the kiss turning into a short but intense round of lovemaking right there on his desk.

They didn't have to worry about spectators. His lab was tucked away in the back of one of the larger buildings at SolCon. Where he worked, only maintenance personnel came in after hours. The one chemist who worked in the lab next door was on vacation, so on a Friday night the place was a graveyard.

He patted the drive and smiled, proud of what he had done, and in such a short amount of time. It represented some of his best work, even if the idea had come from someone else. He'd worked through the entire project mostly from his external PC. Every couple of weeks, when the SolCon checks cleared, he would upload large bodies of data to the location Natalia had given him and provide a status report to her. However, as one of his doctoral instructors had taught him, he always kept the last bit of the data until the last check cleared. He had certainly come to love Natalia, but business is still business … as is chemistry.

He slid the drive into his backpack, added his folio and zipped the pack closed. His plan was to work on the final report from home for the next couple of days, finish the molecular modeling, and then have it printed up. He would give the bound, full color report to Natalia on the following Friday night at dinner.

Slinging his pack over his shoulder, he got up and headed through the warren of pipes, tanks, and equipment that separated his work area from the rest of the facility. It was a long walk through SolCon, a truly massive facility, and after a few minutes of walking and waving to a few employees and security guards, he exited the building and made his way to the top level of the parking garage where he'd parked his Jetta. He always got lousy parking spots because he came in late, but he saved an hour or more a day on his commute, and he considered it to be one of the advantages of being a contractor. There were only a handful of cars left in the garage and only two others on the top level. A green, eighties-vintage Riviera he'd never seen before was parked next to his.

Probably another contractor, he thought as he pulled his keys out of his pocket. He hit the button to open the trunk, and it lifted it up.

He stepped up to the trunk and jumped when a skinny man in a black, hooded sweatshirt stood up on the other side of the Riviera. Xen froze as the man came around the back of the car and headed straight for him. A long knife gleamed in the stranger's hand.

Terror gripped Xen like a vice, and the copper taste of fear filled his mouth. His heart raced in his chest, and his breathing picked up to a rapid pant. Adrenaline pumped through his system. He felt hot and his face flushed red. He couldn't move. The stranger approached and stopped just out of arm's reach.

"Wallet, asshole," the guy said. Xen didn't move, and his eyes went wide with fear. "Gimmie your fucking wallet!"

Xen watched his free hand move of its own accord and pluck his wallet out of a back pocket. His arm lifted and held it out to the thief. The stranger reached out, grabbed the wallet, and slipped it into his jacket pocket.

"Now the bag," the stranger said with venom. Xen's hand automatically gripped around the shoulder strap of the backpack, reflexively not wanting to give over his work.

The guy sneered, his eyes shrinking to narrow slits. "If I have to ask you again, they're carrying you out of here."

A few more heartbeats of paralysis passed, hammering at Xen's chest. The guy cocked his head and raised an eyebrow expectantly. He raised his arm and held out his hand, palm up, waiting for Xen to hand the pack over. Slowly, Xen lifted the strap over his head and held out the pack. The man's hand closed around the strap, and he set the pack at his feet. His eyes never left Xen's. Then a cruel, toothy grin appeared on his face.

"Thanks … saved me the trouble of taking it off you." Xen's brow furrowed, and he got a confused look on his face, not really understanding what the stranger meant. "I wonder how long it will take for them to smell your body in the trunk up here," he added and lunged with the knife.

Xen's still outstretched right arm moved exactly as he had been taught. It stiffened into a hard ridge, and the bony bottom of his hand came down hard on the guy's swiftly moving wrist. The blade would have entered Xen's mid-section, but the blocking blow hammered down, knocking the man's hand into the lip of the trunk and sending the blade clattering down to the concrete. Xen reflexively spun around with the momentum of the block, swinging his left elbow hard into the man's surprised face.

"*KIAI!*" he shouted as his elbow struck home. The force of the blow knocked the man down, and the upper-half of his body slammed into the floor of Xen's trunk. Stunned and nearly unconscious, the guy slid back out over the lip. Xen jumped up and brought the trunk down with all of his strength just as the guy's neck crossed the lip. There was a sickening *CRACK!* The trunk bounced back up, and the man collapsed on the concrete in a heap, his head flopping badly.

Xen stared down in horror at the corpse he'd just created. Gasping for breath and panicked nearly to the point of madness, his head swiveled around frantically as he looked to see if anyone had seen. He was alone on the parking roof. His mind raced as he tried to figure out what he should do next. Fear drove him … and shock.

He bent over and searched the corpse. In a front pocket, he found an irregular lump that felt like keys. Grimacing, he flipped the body on its side, reached into the pocket and pulled them out. One of them had a Buick logo on it, so Xen rushed over to the trunk of the Buick and tried it. It slid in, and with a twist, the trunk came up. Inside, he spotted a black plastic bag and a small shovel underneath. Not thinking about the contents of the killer's Riviera, Xen put the keys in his pocket and went over to the body.

Grabbing it by the wrists, he dragged the body to the trunk and spent the next few minutes grappling and dancing with the cadaver, the head flopping wildly with every adjustment. Finally victorious, Xen plopped the whole body in the trunk with a thud. He looked down, pushed in the leg hanging over the lip, and stared down at his handiwork. A surprised look was frozen on the guy's face, his eyes still wide open.

A strange sense of pride came over Xen as he stared into his assailant's lifeless eyes. A nervous laugh escaped Xen's lips, and he slapped his hand over it to keep from losing it completely. "I guess they'll be carrying *you* out of here, won't they, asshole?" he said quietly.

Using his elbow, Xen closed the trunk. A quick scan of the parking lot again showed that he was alone. A short wall ran behind him, separating the lot into two sections. Cars rarely had to park that far up, and an idea popped into his head.

He pulled the keys out of his pocket and went to the driver's side door, careful not to leave fingerprints. He unlocked it and slid into the seat. He stuck the key in the ignition and fired it up. Pulling his jacket sleeves down over his palms, he put it in reverse. Palms on the wheel, he backed out slowly and pulled the car around to the far corner of the lot in a slot up against a dead end wall. He cut the engine, pulled the keys, and made sure all the doors were locked. Stepping out, he closed the door, wiped off the door handle and walked back to his car.

His heart pounded in his chest, but a strange sense of elation filled him. He tried to think of anything that might trip him up. The whole thing was clearly self-defense, but the American court system is less than perfect. And he was Asian, after all. The corpse was Caucasian. He'd seen too much just to take it on faith. He had just killed a man, and the possibility of prison terrified him beyond rational thought. He looked around the light poles of the parking lot and made sure there were no cameras. He hadn't left any prints, and his skin hadn't ever touched the guy's flesh.

A flash of fear hit Xen like a wave, and his hand slapped down against his butt where his wallet should be.

"Shit!" he yelped. He ran back to the Riviera, opened up the trunk, and pulled his wallet out of the thief's front pocket. Quickly closing the trunk, he jogged back towards his car. Along the way he saw an open storm drain at the corner of the wall. He pulled the Riviera keys out of his pocket and meticulously wiped every surface with his shirt, making sure he didn't touch them again. Then, with the keys dangling over the welcoming black hole below, he looked back at the Riviera, wondering if he'd forgotten anything else. Certain he hadn't, he dropped them in with a sigh of relief.

There were several clatters as the keys bounced off the sides of the pipe and then a final clank as they hit bottom far below. He was in the clear. He went back to his car, picked up his backpack, placed it in the trunk, and closed the lid. His car started up smoothly, and he put it in reverse. Confident he'd thought of everything, he backed out and turned towards the exit. A glimmer of light on the concrete caught his eye. He stopped the car and stared. There, glinting in his headlights, lay the thief's knife.

"God damn it!" he shouted and slammed his fist down on the dashboard. He put it in neutral, set the brake, got out, and went over to the knife. With his jacket pulled over his hand again, he picked it up and ran back to the drain, adding the knife to the waiting oblivion with a loud thunk. He got back into his car and stared at himself in the rearview mirror. His eyes were wide, almost crazed, and he realized he was panting. He placed his hands in his lap, closed his eyes, and tried to calm down. Taking long, controlled, deep breaths, he forced his heart to stop racing.

There was a tap on the window.

"Shit!" he yelped again and leapt away from the window, his bladder giving way with the shock.

"Oh, god! I'm so sorry, Mister Li. I didn't mean to scare you … Are you okay?"

So much for calming down, Xen thought to himself as he looked through the window at a familiar face. Jennifer. Jennifer Bates from accounting. She's the one who handled his checks.

Xen rolled down the window. "I'm … I'm fine. Just had a long day and was clearing my thoughts."

"I had a long day too, working late to get ready for the audit."

Xen smiled but said nothing.

"Well, I best be on my way home. My cats are probably starving by now. You have a good night, Mister Li." She turned towards her car.

"You too, Jennifer." Xen stared silently at her retreating back. He closed the window, put the car in gear, released the brake and drove home as slowly as prudence allowed without getting pulled over. His hands shook the whole time, and when he got home, he took off his damp pants and underwear, jumped into the shower, and stayed there for an hour crying like a baby.

o o o

"Don't feel bad, Xen. Most people lose it like that after their first kill. And you did a hell of a job." I nestled back in the sand and put the rolled-up towel over my eyes. The sound of the Costa Rican beach washed over all three of us.

"Near as I can tell, you covered everything.… Not that you really needed to," I added, smiling. "You could have just called the cops. If there was ever a clearer case of self-defense, I never hear of it."

"Yeah. I thought about that, but you're not Asian, you know? I don't have much faith in the courts, and can you picture me in jail? I was running on pure fear and adrenaline till I passed out at home." Xen nodded to Rachel and held up his empty beer bottle.

Rachel opened another beer and handed it to him, taking his empty and dropping it in the cooler. She took a long pull from hers and stared at him. "I'm really impressed, Xen. You're hell on wheels when you get going, aren't you?"

Xen blushed and looked at the sand between his legs. "Yeah, I guess," he said quietly.

"Trust me," I injected, "Xen took to fighting like a fish takes to water," I said to Rachel. "And that cleanup was pretty tight."

"Who knew?" he added in disbelief.

"It surprised me, I'll tell you that for nothing," I said, chuckling.

Rachel slapped my leg, admonishing me, but we were all laughing. We sat in the sun, simply enjoying the day after the tension of the previous night at VeniCorp.

"So what happened next?" Rachel asked.

O O O

The morning after the attack, Xen jolted out of bed at the sound of the man's neck breaking. His dream was a replay of the previous evening. He sat there shaking for a minute, and then he threw back the covers and got out of bed. He jumped in the shower, took a quick rinse and brushed his teeth.

As he put the toothbrush away, something popped into his head—body bag and a shovel. He closed his eyes and remembered opening the trunk of the Riviera. There had been a body bag and a shovel in there. Then he ran the whole thing through his head. The thought dawned on him that it wasn't a random mugging. For starters, there was no reason in the world for someone to drive all the way up there, in the industrial sector of the city, just to mug a guy. And then, why mug Xen? If the guy was waiting for someone, why not wait for a small woman? Xen realized the guy never had any intention of leaving him alive.

There were only three possibilities. One, the guy was there to kill Xen. Two, the guy wanted Xen's work. Three, both one and two together. He hadn't recognize the man, and it was unlikely he worked for SolCon, at least not at the offices. A sick feeling clutched at Xen's guts, and he turned pale at the realization. Someone wanted him dead. An even worse thought crossed his mind. What if Natalia was in on it? She was the only person at SolCon he'd ever talked to about the project.

He had to disappear, at least for a while, until he could figure everything out. He'd go to Justin as soon as he felt certain that no one could find him, but if they knew Xen well, they'd know about Justin, too. He wanted to disappear off the face of the Earth for a week in hopes they'd lose track of him. Then he could see about trying to figure out who wanted him dead.

But how? he asked his reflection. The answer was right there behind him in the reflection. On a shelf across from the mirror he saw a three-inch green tin. He turned around and grabbed it. It rattled as he picked it up, sounding as if it was full of pebbles. He had gotten implants three years earlier while on a sabbatical to England. A bicycle accident had knocked several out. His real teeth had been somewhat irregular to begin with, and he'd always wanted them straight. The orthodontist had told him how long it would take to repair and then suggested another option—full implants.

Xen smiled at the memory, opened the tin and looked down at a mouth full of teeth, fillings and all. A plan was forming. He spent the next hour running through his house, grabbing things he thought he might need. He'd never been on the run before, but it wasn't all that different than when he'd come to America. When he had everything, he got in his car and drove off. Next, he had to get some cash. He'd need a pretty good chunk to stay afloat.

He did business with three banks and spent the next two hours going to each of them, withdrawing five-thousand dollars from each. He figured that fifteen-thousand would be enough. Each teller had asked him the same question: why the withdrawal. "Going on a trip," was all he said. He stopped at a department store next. He went in and bought a few items from the sporting goods and women's departments. He hit a Wal-Mart on the way out and bought a few other items, including a half-gallon of orange juice and a box of protein bars. He chain ate the protein bars on the way to the university, chasing them with orange juice. On Saturday most of the place would be empty.

Fortunately, he'd been teaching classes for three of his old professors and even gave talks on bio-chem when the university hosted conferences. They had given him a set of keys to the department so he could come and go as he pleased. He parked his car and threw the bars and orange juice into his backpack. He then got out, locked up the car, and walked a short distance across campus with the backpack over his shoulder, entering one of the science buildings. The halls were empty save for one student on the way out who Xen didn't recognize.

He made a few turns in the halls and stopped at a door marked *Medical Sciences—H7*. Reaching into his pocket, he pulled out a thick key ring full of brass keys, sifted through them, and found the one he wanted. Inserting the key, he opened the door quickly and stepped in. The main area looked like several hospital operating rooms all put together into one. Equipment lay everywhere. A hallway with rooms jutting off to the left and right at regular intervals stretched beyond the main area, each room separated by curtains hanging in the doorways for privacy. They were for students and patients during classes.

He went to one of the near cabinets, unlocked it, and pulled out several empty blood bags, some surgical tubing, a bottle of alcohol, cotton balls, and tape. Then he locked it back up. From another cabinet, he grabbed several hypodermic needles and a stack of heart needles with the largest syringes he could find.

Throwing everything into his backpack, he headed to the last patient room on the left. He pulled the curtain closed as he went through, stepped around the gurney and turned on the small light over a desk inside. Setting everything down on the desk, he opened a cabinet to his left and pulled out a blood extraction needle and a bottle of saline.

He'd done it many times before in class, just never on himself. He stripped down to his boxers, washed and disinfected his hands, and then sat down at the desk. He quickly set up the saline drip and inserted the needle into his left arm. Raising the stand to its highest position, well over his head, he grabbed another needle. Hooking it up to one of the blood-bags, he laid the bag on the floor and stuck the needle into his right arm. Wincing slightly, it only took him two tries to get the needle into a vein. "Now for the hard part," he said, looking at the stack of large syringes and heart needles. He stood up, closed his eyes and breathed deeply for a while, trying to focus.

This is going to hurt like a motherfucker, he thought.

He unwrapped one of the syringes and attached a big heart needle. Holding the needle in his right hand, he grabbed his right pectoral muscle, squeezed slightly and then pressed the big needle sideways into the flesh, through it and down into the fatty tissue he knew lay just under the skin. He groaned with the pain but kept going.

The thought of another killer coming for him drove his motions without mercy or hesitation. He spent ten minutes probing tissue and slowly extracting a mixture of blood and cellulite, filling the syringe with a cloudy, reddish liquid with gelatinous blobs suspended within. Once he filled it, he set it down carefully on the desk and put a cotton ball over the wound, taping it down. He switched to his left pectoral, and this one seemed to hurt a little less, but it took longer to fill the syringe. Looking down, he saw that the bag was full, so he set the second, fatty syringe next to the first, disconnected himself, sealed the bag up and carefully placed it in his backpack.

He repeated the process with big needles going into his abdomen, which almost made him scream in pain. Both butt cheeks, then both thighs, gave him a total of eight. He grabbed another blood bag, unsealed it, and emptied the syringes into the bag, quickly sealing it up and slipping it into the backpack.

He looked up and saw that the saline was empty. Disconnecting it, he laid it on the desk, grabbed a gallon ziplock he'd brought and put the saline drip and the blood extraction tubing into it. The empty syringes followed, and the whole thing went into his backpack. There wasn't anything left, so he slowly stood up, feeling only slightly dizzy but hurting like hell in each place where a needle had gone in.

He put everything he needed back into his pack, except for the orange juice and two protein bars. Looking around the room to make sure that he hadn't left anything, he headed out to his car. A light rain had rolled in, the day cool for a change. By the time he got to his car, both protein bars were gone and the orange juice container empty. His head felt like it was full of helium. He got in, opened the cooler he'd bought, and scooped the ice out of the way, putting the two full blood bags inside. Feeling more and more light-headed with each passing second, he figured he'd just close his eyes and rest for a few minutes to regain his strength.

He woke to the dark of night, and the rain had stopped.

Breasts and Drumsticks

My phone rang just as Xen started the rest of his story. I held up a finger to stop him, picked up the phone and looked at the number. It was O'Neil.

"Hang on, Xen. I gotta take this one." I answered brightly, "Hi, O'Neil!"

"Don't 'hi' me, Case. Let's have the rest of that conversation now that I'm awake and your four bodies are on ice in the morgue. They all check out by the way. Goombahs. All federal rap sheets, three with warrants, and one who just got out of the lock-up. What would you have done if they'd been rent-a-cops … or *real* cops?"

"Knocked them out, tied them up, and run like hell."

"That would be a first," O'Neil said snidely.

I thought about it for a minute. "You may be right. So where'd we leave off last night? I'm kinda drunk."

"Drunk? And what is that I hear in the background?"

"Monkeys," I said, implying it was the most natural response in the world.

"Why the fuck would there be … Never mind," he said curtly. "I don't want to know. You said something about dry cleaning last night. What were you talking about?"

"That's how they're shipping, delivering, and distributing … at least I'm pretty sure of it. My guy's already working on it."

"Xen?"

"Yeah, but leave him dead for the time being. He faked his own death to avoid a second attempt on his life. As long as the world thinks he's dead, there's no heat. And I think you'll find another body in the parking lot at SolCon."

"Green Riviera?"

"That's the one."

"We already found it. Someone smelled the guy the other day and called LAPD rather than Oakland. Our homicide's got it. Turns out the guy was a local douche-bag hitter, barely above amateur."

I nodded. "It was self-defense, O'Neil, plain and simple. Xen ran because he panicked. From what I heard, it should be a clean scene. Nothing to connect him to it. Can you turn an eye?"

"I can. Homicide said they're going to try and find someone, but they won't be trying very hard. I wouldn't worry about it. Even homicide doesn't give two shits for dirty little fuckers like that. But if they tie Xen to it, I gotta go through procedure. Sorry." O'Neil paused thoughtfully. "Xen did that?"

"Yeah," I said proudly. I was also grateful O'Neil didn't have a problem keeping Xen out of it … at least for now. I'd have to find a way to make it up to him.

"I'm impressed," he added, sounding like he meant it.

"So was I," I agreed. "Look, about T-Rex, I had an idea."

"Me too, and I wasn't going to give you a choice on this one."

"You're going to track the tankers and mark the dry-cleaners, right?" I deduced.

"You got it. We can get set up while you work your end. Easy peasy."

"Great minds think alike. Thanks, O'Neil."

"It's my job, remember? Now about these other two—the shooters who managed to snap off three headshots in the dead of night in downtown L.A … I'm kind of interested in them."

"So am I. The truth is I mostly don't know who they are."

"What do you mean, *mostly*?" He sounded exasperated.

"Well, I have an idea of who one of them is, but the other is a wild card."

"Can you at least give me a name?" O'Neil didn't sound hopeful.

"I'd rather not."

"That's obstruction, you know," *Captain* O'Neil pointed out in his official voice.

"No it's not, neither of us has any proof, so it's circumstantial."

"That's bullshit and you know it."

"Yeah, but look, O'Neil," I implored, "I've got a good feeling on this one, okay?"

"Your call. I have my hands full with everything else. I can look the other way for a while, but if you end up with a round through that shaved head of yours in the middle of the night in downtown L.A., don't come crying to me."

"I won't, I promise. And it's not shaved. I came into the world this way."

O'Neil clearly didn't want to get into hairstyles. He was too grumpy. "Are you close to moving on DiMarco?"

"Getting there. I'm putting the pieces together, but I need a week or two. Can you wait that long?"

"It'll probably take that long to wrap my hands around the dry cleaners, so it should work out. You've got your two weeks if you need them. But now that this is in motion with the department, I won't be able to hold things up. Internal Affairs would be all over my ass. I love you, man, but I'm not going to jail for you."

"Wouldn't want you to. I'll be ready when you are. Keep me posted if anything comes up, and I'll do the same from my end."

"Case?"

"You hate me, right?"

"I do, but that's not what I was going to say. Guess you're not so smart after all." I could hear O'Neil smiling through the phone.

"What then?"

"You're forgetting something," O'Neil prompted.

"I am?" I couldn't figure out what, but I did have a pretty good buzz off of sugar-spiked OJ and a half-dozen beer chasers.

"The *data*," he said, over-articulating each syllable.

I slapped my head. "Shit! I forgot. Sorry. I'll have that to you this afternoon. We're heading back to my place in a while."

"You better. I promised the lab I'd have it to them today. Is there any way I could treat it as admissible?"

"Not a chance," I admitted. "It's as stolen as stolen gets. But have your warrants ready on go-day and just raid the place. It'll be in a computer in Jackie's un-connected PC in the lab area. The password is gold fever zero nine, all caps one word, or at least it was last night. If it changes, I can get into it for you then, okay?"

"Deal. I have to get back to things here. I'll catch you later."

"See ya." I hung up. "So, Xen … you were saying?"

O O O

Xen shook his head to try and wake up, blinking his eyes several times as he made every effort to focus on the dashboard. His head still felt like a helium balloon, and every spot where a needle had gone in ached with dull pain. *This plan had better work*, he thought, *or all the suffering would be in vain.*

His next order of business, considering how he felt and where he planned to go, required that he eat something immediately. The clock on the dash showed nine p.m. He'd slept for six hours, and it occurred to him that the excitement of the previous night, a short night's sleep, and spending the afternoon literally sucking the life out of himself might have been a tad bit overtaxing. His stomach growled like a rabid dog. Scratching his head and yawning, he started the car, pulled out of the lot, and headed to his favorite Chinese buffet restaurant.

Halfway across town, paranoia gripped him by the short-and-curlies. What if whoever wanted him dead knew him well enough to know where he liked to eat? He couldn't risk it. He pulled into the next Chinese buffet he saw, parked, and went inside. It turned into a feeding frenzy. Xen ate like there was no tomorrow, which, it occurred to him, there sort of wouldn't be. He'd be dead tomorrow. A nervous smile crossed his face as he shoveled in another load of lo mein. The manager shook his head in disbelief as Xen got up for another trip to the buffet. Five heaping plates of nearly everything they had disappeared down his neck. He was rather impressed with himself, and in spite of a distended abdomen, he felt much better.

He pulled out his phone and realized it was eleven p.m. *Time for a motel and as much sleep as he can get*, he thought. He paid his tab, smiling at the manager, who gave him a polite bow of thanks. The look on the manager's face said, *Please don't come here again.*

Xen got in his car and headed down the road, looking for the first motel he could find. Ten minutes later he spotted a Motel 6 and pulled in. He went in, requested a room, paid cash, and went next door to a liquor store to get a small bottle of brandy and a bag of ice. He went to his car, dumped the ice on top of the blood bags and then went to his room. One hot shower later, he sat on the bed and taking swigs from the brandy. It burned a little going down, but what little drinking he'd done in the past usually involved brandy or cognac. It didn't take long for the alcohol to hit his system, even with a belly full of Chinese food. Crawling under the covers, he fell asleep before he could turn off the light.

o o o

A car crash in front of the motel woke him at nine a.m. Checkout was in an hour, so he had to move quickly. He got up, threw on his clothes, went out to the car, and brought in everything he would need for the day's exercise. He'd bought an oversized backpack large enough to hold everything but not large enough to draw too much attention when he went to SolCon.

On a Sunday he probably wouldn't run into anyone, but he didn't want to take any chances. He had the pack stuffed and bulging by 9:45. He went out to the car, put everything away, and checked out of his room. Back at the car, he stuffed his remaining belongings into a large rolling suitcase he'd picked up.

Forty-five minutes later he parked his car on the ground level of the parking garage at SolCon. He thought about the green Riviera on the top level … and its grisly contents. The thought made him shudder and forced him to focus on the task at hand. The ground level lay empty, with only three vehicles in the corner of the lot nearest the building. He parked at the opposite corner, closest to the street.

Grabbing the backpack, he looked into the rearview mirror. "You ready for this?" His worried eyes told him that he wasn't, but he didn't have a choice. He took a deep breath, stepped out of the car and headed into SolCon. He only had to slide his card-key twice on the long walk to his work area, and he didn't see a soul the entire way in. A few security guards patrolled the facility, but they were focused around the areas where more restricted products were researched or produced, like explosives. What he worked on didn't even rate as risky, let alone dangerous.

He looked around his cubicle one last time to see if he wanted to take anything with him. He kept his work area tidy, so nothing seemed worth grabbing. He walked out of his area and down a little further into the facility to another project lab. He'd talked with the chemist a few times over the past few months. The guy was also a contractor, an anti-social sort, but proud of his work. He was working on mass-producing a tetrachloroethylene variant being designed for abatement services. The guy claimed that it worked wonders with biological material.

It met Xen's needs perfectly.

Xen walked into the guy's much larger lab. It had room for his work-area, a cleanup station, a bank of computers, and three large storage tanks along the wall. Two of the tanks were open with two-foot-wide ports swung outwards. Xen laid his backpack on a table and checked the closed tank, finding it full. "Perfect," he said out loud. He went back to the table and pulled everything out.

The backpack empty, he stripped down to skin and threw his clothes into one of the open tanks. His glasses followed. He went back to the table, put on a pair of bikini underwear and grabbed the two blood bags. He emptied the bags into the vat next, first the blood then the cellulite, making a sickening splattering sound as the fluids and fat hit the stainless steel bottom of the tank. The two empty blood bags went into a gallon ziplock that he sealed up carefully. He then grabbed the green tin from the table and dumped his teeth into the vat.

He went back to the table and pulled out electric clippers and a black trash bag. He found an outlet and proceeded to shave his head, spilling the long black hair directly into the waiting bag. With his head completely bald except for low, coarse stubble, he turned his attention to his arms and legs, removing all of the sparse hair he had on his limbs.

Using a washbasin in the corner of the lab, he pulled his razor off the table and proceeded to carefully shave every surface of his exposed skin save his eyebrows, rinsing the razor as he went. Once finished, he put the razor back in the pack and emptied the bag of hair into the vat. Xen paused for a moment, taking in what he'd done. A nervous laughter bubbled out of him as he stared down at the scattered mess in the bottom of the vat.

"That's just nasty," he said and tried to get hold of his laughing.

He closed the swinging door and twisted down the sealing lever. It was time to put together his disguise. Panty hose went on first. He'd never worn them before and had no idea what to expect. They tingled as they went on, and he stood there looking at his legs for a minute. He realized that he actually had nice legs.

Pushing the rather bizarre thought away, he grabbed the padded bra he'd picked up and spent the next five minutes trying to put the thing on, straining his arms behind his back.

"How the hell do women do this?" he asked the bra.

Finally, he pulled it back off, hooked the clasps and pulled it over his head, adjusting it into place with a frustrated sigh of accomplishment. The dress went over his head next—a blue, high-collared affair with short sleeves and a skirt that went down to his knees. He buttoned up the collar and adjusted it in a few places.

He grabbed a tube of light red lipstick and a small mirror. Working clumsily, he put it on and pinched his lips together the way he'd seen so many women do. Even to his untrained eye, it looked pretty bad. He went to the sink again, grabbed some paper towel and rubbed it off, carefully avoiding spreading it around. He put some more on, using less this time, and went through the lip motion again. This time it didn't make him look like a bald, hooker, so he gave it a rest.

He pulled out a long, curly black wig and slipped that over his head, adjusting it carefully in the mirror. Shoes went on next, blue pumps with the lowest, widest heels he could find. He folded and compressed the first backpack then slipped it into a smaller one. The trash, razor, clippers, and everything else went inside, and he spent the next ten minutes walking around the area making sure that he hadn't left anything.

Grabbing more paper towels and using bleach, he thoroughly wiped down every surface he'd touched and every other surface even remotely nearby. When the area was as spotless as he could make it, he went over to the tank control panel and, using more paper towel to touch the controls, flipped the pump power switch.

When the light above it went green, he selected the tank with the mess inside as the receiver and the full tank as the sender. He pressed the transfer button and heard the satisfying sound of fluid pouring into the vat.

The finishing touch on his outfit was a pair of the biggest black sunglasses he could find. They covered almost half of his face. He grabbed his backpack and walked out, his ankles wobbling only a little, and his ass wiggling a lot more than he would have thought possible.

The walk through the labyrinth unnerved him, but he didn't see a soul as he made it to the last, long hallway that led to the main lobby. Turning the last corner, he saw two rent-a-cops walking his way. He almost froze, but common sense kept him walking straight at them. As the distance closed, his heart beat faster and faster, and he felt his cheeks flush. He stared straight ahead at the two men and realized something. Neither of them looked at his face. One was obviously a leg man, and the other couldn't keep his eyes off Xen's padded tits.

So this is what it's like, Xen thought ironically. It was no accident that Xen spent the rest of his life looking women in the eyes when he talked to them.

"Hey, how ya doing, miss?" the leg man said provocatively. They partially blocked the hallway, so Xen had to stop. He looked down slightly, trying to act shy. His mind raced as he tried to figure a way out of this.

"Are you new around here," the tit man asked. "I don't recall seeing you before."

An idea popped into Xen's head. He put on his best Chinese woman's accent and hoped it did the job. "Me … new … how you say …" and he made a typing motion with his hands.

"Receptionist?" the leg man offered.

Xen smiled broadly and nodded his head vigorously. "That it!" he added. "Me … new … rec-cept-shun-ist," he finished slowly. "Work late to catch up. Must go now.…" he added quickly and pushed between them.

"Have a nice day, miss," the tit man added.

Xen beamed as he walked away. He'd actually pulled it off. As he walked down the hall, he put a little more swing in his stride.

The two men stared at his shapely, swaying ass.

Xen owned it, walking like every hooker he'd ever seen in a movie … right up until his ankle gave way and he stumbled. He recovered quickly and heard some chuckling behind him. He started walking a little more stiffly to avoid tripping again, raised his right hand, and gave them both the finger.

Both men guffawed at the sight and applauded.

Xen walked through the lobby, waving at a maintenance guy talking to one of the office cleaners, pressed the door-lever with his palms, and walked out into open air. He'd made it. He breathed a deep sigh of relief, stopped, and set the backpack down. He pulled out a pay-as-you-go cell phone he'd bought at the mall. He'd spoken broken English then, too, telling the clerk that he'd lost his wallet and job and needed a phone to call friends and get everything squared away. It wasn't standard policy, but the kid caved in when Xen tucked a hundred dollar bill in his pocket.

Using his woman's voice and maintaining the broken English, Xen dialed the number for a major cab company to come pick him up out on the main road. He told them his car had broken down and he would be walking away from the plant. They said they'd have a man out in about thirty minutes.

Xen went back to his car, opened the trunk, pulled out his suitcase, and hit the sidewalk with fast, steady strides. About twenty minutes later a cab came up behind him. The guy helped Xen with the suitcase, trying to make small talk, but Xen laid it on thick with the accent so he wouldn't have to say much.

"Where to, miss?" the guy asked as they both got in the cab.

"Bus station," he said quietly. *I'm almost home free,* he thought as he stared at the cab driver in the rearview mirror.

"You got it." The cabbie flipped the meter and off they went.

Twenty minutes later Xen paid the man, adding a sizeable tip, and headed into the bus station. He paid cash for a ticket to the Grand Canyon and sat comfortably in his seat two hours later as it pulled out of the station. He'd always wanted to see the Grand Canyon, and on the possibility that he might actually get killed in the near future, he considered it a good place to lie low.

o o o

"I spent the week in a motel near the Grand Canyon," Xen said, "whiling away the hours walking around and enjoying the scenery." He pulled on a cigar and blew the smoke out proudly.

"Xen," I said, my voice filling with admiration, "you can have my job. That was a hell of a piece of work."

"Thank you."

"So, out of curiosity …" I stared at Xen with a great big smile on my face. "How'd you like the pantyhose?"

He looked unsure for a minute, glancing at both of us, struggling with some internal conflict.

"Come on, be honest. I just told you I was a fucking alien."

"Honestly?" he asked shyly.

"Yeah," Rachel prompted.

A subtle smile spread over his face, turning to a clowning one. "I kind of liked it."

We all laughed.

"So did I when I had to wear them," I said between laughs. "Glad I'm not the only one … Kilts are pretty cool too, especially commando," I added.

"I'll have to try that." He shook his head.

"You should, you have better legs than I do."

"That's true," he added proudly.

Rachel looked at both of us, grinning. "You guys want some help? I know a few clubs I could take you to. You could dress up real pretty. I'll even help you do your makeup … We'll get Marsha and have a girls' night out."

We laughed at that, and the laughing lasted for a while.

I finally caught my breath. "Shit, that's funny. I'm tempted to take you up on that just to see what it's like."

"Okay," Xen said, breathing heavily through the laughs. "This is getting a little weird."

"Prude!" Rachel shot at him, which renewed the laughter.

"Look," I interrupted, "I hate to break this up, but we really do have to get that data to O'Neil."

"Oh yeah, right," he said. "Do you have wireless here?"

"Nope, and there's too much data to use the dialup, even with the compression I have set up. And this far from my loft, the planet gets in the way of my primary signal."

"Oh." Xen looked disappointed.

"If it's wireless in your loft, why don't we just open the front door," Rachel offered, chiming in.

I was about to say something smart and then paused, thinking about it. "I never thought of that. Sweetie, you're a genius."

"Can we finish these, first?" Xen held up his cigar

"It *would* be criminal to waste them." I blew out a large cloud of Cuban delight.

A few minutes later, I sat in the living room with the front door open to my loft and the laptop in front of me. I stuck in the thumb drive, spent a few minutes zipping up data into sizes that would get through O'Neil's email gateway and then shipped them off.

I grabbed my cell phone and dialed O'Neil. "Hey. Yeah, it's me. I just sent that data over. It's in your email. A couple dozen zip files. Let me know if any didn't come through," I paused. "See ya." I closed my phone and turned to my friends. "Cigars and dinner at the casino?"

"Yes!" they said in unison.

I shot a thumb at Xen. "Dinner is on moneybags over here with his three hundred grand."

"My pleasure." He bowed his head, and we went over to the casino.

Just Like Normal People

After dinner at the casino, Rachel and I went to the loft for some private time and we fell asleep in each other's arms. In the morning, I opened my eyes to see Rachel sitting up on one elbow and scratching Mag between the ears. Mag, rasping quietly, had taken up residence between us. I suddenly realized that Mag and I had been a team, just the two of us, for over a hundred years. It never occurred to me that Magdelain might reject Rachel. I reached out and scratched Mag under the chin. The rasping picked up in volume.

"I take it you two are sorting things out?" I asked hopefully.

"I believe we already have." Rachel rubbed the top of Mag's head vigorously, and Mag returned the affection by licking Rachel's hand. "We've become fast friends."

"Can't tell you how happy that makes me. You're my two favorite people."

"She *is* people, isn't she?" Rachel's voice held a tinge of awe.

"Yeah. Treat her like a teenage daughter … well, more like sister," I corrected thoughtfully. "An incredibly deadly one. She understands English … and my native tongue, of course. And I'm teaching her Spanish. She just can't speak any of it, no vocal chords. There have been times when I wish they'd given her vocal chords and me claws."

"You two really were made for each other?"

"Yep. We share a lot of DNA, and we were designed to complement each other when we work … well, play is a better word for it, as sick as that sounds, even to me. The people who created us really did know what they were doing in that regard. We're the most dangerous brother and sister you ever met."

"So, I'm in bed with you and your sister?" Rachel raised an eyebrow. "*Kinky*," she added a bit seductively, putting her hand on my arm and Mag's back.

"Pervert!" I cried, feigning moral outrage.

Mag smiled and licked my face. Both females looked at me suggestively, and up until that moment, I wouldn't have thought Mag was capable of the feat.

"You're both perverts!" I repeated, but with considerably less feigning this time.

Rachel started laughed, and Mag gave me one of her *I-got-you* smiles.

My face shifted to the realization of a sobering truth. "I've just been outnumbered, haven't I?" A strange sort of fear struck at my insides.

"Yep." Rachel and Mag smiled even more.

Mag took her paw and put it on my mouth.

"I think she's trying to say, *Shut-up and accept your fate*," Rachel added.

Mag nodded to her and then looked back at me with a smile.

"This is going to take some getting used to," I said mostly to myself and then rolled out of bed. "How about a shower and some breakfast while I try and figure out how to get the upper hand on the two of you?"

"Only if you let me join you." Rachel stood up and walked towards the back of the loft.

I looked at Mag. "You want to come?" I asked a bit sarcastically.

She shook her head, gave me an *I'll-pass-on-this-one-ace* look and rolled over on her side, closing her eyes.

I followed Rachel through the back door of the loft, into the bathroom on the right. We spent the next forty-five minutes scrubbing, which turned into exploring, which turned into … well … none of your damn business. I dried myself off quickly, got dressed and went to prepare breakfast.

Rachel came out fully dressed fifteen minutes later, and we sat down to bacon, eggs, and orange juice. Mag still slept, curled up on the bed. Rachel walked over to the living area and fiddled with the remote when my phone rang.

I grabbed it and, seeing the caller, answered. "Hi Marsha! How's the job coming?"

"Really well," she said enthusiastically. "You did say carte blanche, right?" The hesitation in her voice told me she planned on doing the place to the nines.

"That I did," I replied warily. "If you haven't added in some video poker and live baccarat, consider it. Turns out Xen is a wiz at baccarat. Did Stanley hook you up with that designer?"

My TV came on to the news, and Rachel had to quickly turn down the volume.

"Yes! And she's really good … *at a number of things*," she added seductively. It sounded to me as if Marsha had found a new playmate.

"I'm glad to hear it," my voice carried an understanding smile. "You two an item?"

"Naw … this is just playtime. We both have our work, you know? But that's not the reason I called."

"Really? What can I do you for then?"

"The doctor gave me a clean bill of health yesterday. I can start training again, and I really want to. I've been going stir crazy from not being able to work out. Can we?"

"Hell yes! We'll start tomorrow tonight if you like. I think … hang on." I pulled the phone away from my ear and focused on Rachel who was engrossed in something on the television. "You want to start training with Marsha tomorrow?"

Rachel peeled her eyes away from the T.V. and looked at me, confusion turned to excitement. "You bet!" she replied enthusiastically. "I can't wait!" I saw a flicker of the predator show itself on her face and then disappear back into whatever had caught her attention on the TV.

I put the phone back to my ear. "It's a date. Come on over to the house around five and bring your gear. Oh, and if you want to stay at the house tonight and start working out on your own, you're more than welcome. We won't be there till tomorrow."

"I think I'll take you up on that … Oh, and Justin?"

"Yeah?"

"I'm glad you and Rachel finally got together. I really like her."

The comment made me feel warm. "Thanks, Marsha. Me too. I'll see you then."

"Ciao!" She hung up.

Rachel looked at me with an astonished face. "Justin Case?"

"Uhh … yeah … that's me." I looked around in confusion, wondering if it was a trick question.

"No …" She pointed to the TV. "You have a movie called *Justin Case*."

Realization flooded through me. "Oh shit! I forgot that was in there … yeah, I watch it every now and again."

"They made a movie about you?" she asked incredulously as she pressed pause.

I laughed. "No. That's the first movie I saw after arriving on Earth. I liked the character and the name, so I used it."

"Justin isn't your real name?"

"Sure it is. It says so on one of my driver's licenses." I reached for my wallet to prove it to her.

"You know what I mean," she accused. She shook her head.

"Yeah, I do," I said smiling a bit evasively.

"So, are you going to tell me your real name, or do I have to beat it out of you?" she challenged.

"Jalin," I said a bit somberly. "No last name. They used to call me Jalin, but he's dead … well, at least mostly. He crops up when the killing starts, though." A sad look flickered across my face at the memory, partly because of what I used to be, but more because of what I used to do. Jalin is the mean, heartless son-of-a-bitch who enjoys killing. When he takes over, there's just the sheer delight of ending people. It took me a long time to put reins on him, and I have him under control, but I feel a little dirty every time I let him creep out from under his rock and do what he does.

But now he does what *I* tell him.

"I didn't mean to dredge up painful memories…."

"No, it's okay. No secrets …" I smiled, walked over, leaned down and kissed her. "Not with you, anyway." She smiled up at me and put her hand warmly against my cheek. I'm sure she wouldn't press me on it, but I figured she wanted to know more about Jalin and why I hated him so much.

"Can I watch it?" she asked.

"Go right ahead. I'm going to get caught up on email while you do that. Want some popcorn?"

She shook her head and pressed play.

o o o

"How's Xen doing on the data?" Rachel asked as I handed her a beer. She lounged on the patio of the Costa Rica house, the afternoon sun tanning every inch of skin not covered by a skimpy, pink bikini. We'd come through shortly after the movie. When it ended, Rachel had said it was cute. I knew she was being generous.

"He's engrossed," I replied as I got ready to hit the beach. "I've never seen him work before, and he's tackling it with a passion. He did say that what Shao came up with is absolutely brilliant. Xen's words not mine, which is saying something. Basically, the bulk of the process takes place at DiMarco's plant, but the last phase happens on-site at the dry-cleaners with some sort of converter or extractor. He's digging into that now."

"Tell me something," she said, looking up through squinted eyes.

I moved to block the sunlight, reached over to the table and grabbed her sunglasses. I delicately put them on her face.

"Thanks," she said as I sat down. I wore a pair of Hawaiian print swim-trunks that I know Rachel had to force herself not to comment on.

"Anything," I said, meaning it.

"Why do you do it? Work as a detective, I mean. You obviously don't need money … and come to think of it, most of the people you work for almost never pay you. You might as well be a cop."

I smiled. "You know damn well that I'm not cop material. Like O'Neil is always telling me, cops have to play by the rules … or are at least they're supposed to."

"Clearly. But as you like to say, that doesn't answer the question. Why do you do it? Why risk your life and work so hard to go after guys like DiMarco?"

"The moment he came after Xen, he was a dead man. But that's not what you're asking." I looked at her closely. "You ever read Andrew Jackson?"

Her face told me she thought I was changing the subject. "A little … in college. Not much, why?"

"Well, when I first got here, I read a lot about your history … Earth history and American history … getting a better grasp of my new home. You know?"

"And?"

"Well, there's something he wrote that I think is applicable anywhere and everywhere sentient beings live. And people are people on every planet where there's a hut, town or stack of skyscrapers."

"What did he write?"

"*All tyranny needs to gain a foothold is for people of good conscience to remain silent.*" I took a long swig of beer, and my eyes were looking at something far off, something that troubled me deeply. "That's how I came to be, you know. Men of good conscience were silent as men without a conscience created me … and used me … me and Magdelain."

"Justin? Are you okay?" she asked.

"I hate what I was before, you know." I could feel tears forming in my eyes, and I took another swig of beer. "I'm ashamed of it."

Rachel reached out and touched my hand.

"Back then, I *was* DiMarco and Pyotr. Or at least the tool of such men … and I enjoyed it." My voice overflowed with self-loathing. "Right up until my father showed me what I was doing. He found out what these men were using his creation to do. My father was the first man of good conscience in my life who spoke up."

"I've never seen you like this," she said gently. "Are you okay?"

I sniffed and wiped a tear from my cheek. I looked at her and smiled, laughing slightly. "I am now … I have been since I got to Earth. And I do more than not remain silent with creatures like DiMarco because I *can*."

"You're a good man, Justin."

"I'm not a man at all," I reminded her with a wry grin.

She looked at my caringly. "Yes you are. The best I've ever known."

"You need to get out more." I winked, and we laughed together.

My swim forgotten, we spent the next few hours talking about life and the universe … nothing specific, the small talk of two people who, out of the darkness and chaos, found comfort in each other.

Tea Time

Alisa gave the man his change and watched a young couple walk out the front door of her Grandfather's teahouse. Looking at the clock, she saw it was twelve-thirty a.m. She walked over to the curtain, pulled it aside, and peered into the dining area, finding Galina all alone. "Is that the last of them?" she asked as her cousin wiped down a table.

"Mmm-hmm." Galina nodded. "It's empty back here. Go lock up the front. We'll finish cleaning and count out the drawers."

Alisa nodded her head and walked to the front. She turned off the Open sign in the front corner window and walked towards the front door. Three men wearing long black coats appeared in the window from that side of the building and kept pace with her as she approached the door. She saw a man running across the street and realized she was in trouble. She dove the last few feet, grabbed the lock and gave it a quick turn just as a big man pushed on the door. It didn't budge. Alisa looked out at four dark-haired men wearing black coats, a smile of victory on her face. She saw two more men coming across the street now. The second, smaller man at the door reached into his jacket and pulled out a pistol with a silencer, pointing it directly at her head.

"Open the fucking door," he ordered. "Unless you think this glass is bullet proof." The smile drifted from her face to his.

"Now," he added, tapping the glass with the gun barrel three times to emphasize the point.

She reached out and slowly unlocked the door. The moment it clicked, the big man hammered the doorframe, flinging the door hard into her face. She yelped and flew back a few steps, landing on her butt and holding her bloody nose. A red line ran from her jaw up to her forehead, and tears rolled down her cheeks.

Six men poured into the room. Two of them produced shotguns out of their coats and ran to the back of the room, standing on each side of the curtain. One raised the butt of his shotgun while the other leveled the barrel at the curtain. Antonio and Tommy stood over Alisa on either side, looking down at her as she bled.

"Awwww … look at that, Tommy," Antonio said, smiling. "You made her cry." Tommy remained silent, content to stand there looking dangerous. Intimidation and abuse was his favorite part of the job. Antonio pulled out a roll of duct tape just as Galina stepped through the curtain.

"Alisa, are you …" the butt of a shotgun crashing into the side of her face cut her off. She dropped in a heap, barely moving. The men at the curtain walked through it with the business ends of their shotguns leading the way.

"Tape them up in back," Bennie DiMarco walked in with an evil grin on his face.

It didn't take long to have both girls taped to chairs in the middle of the dining area.

Galina regained consciousness just as her legs were secured. She glared at Bennie. "You shouldn't have done this, mister. Do you have any idea who our grandfather is?"

Bennie laughed wickedly. "Yeah I do, as a matter of fact. You're grandfather … *is old*," he pointed out confidently. "And we're not. He should be more careful who he gives help to."

"My grandfather is going to rip your arms off."

"Tommy, show her what I think of that."

Tommy backhanded her across the face.

"Galina!" Alisa yelled as Galina's head snapped around, her eyes rolled back in her head and she slumped, unconscious again.

"Now, little girl," Bennie said, looking at Alisa with an evil gleam in his eyes. "Listen to me very carefully, and you two may live through this."

o o o

Yvgenny's cell phone woke him. He rolled over in bed, grabbed it off the nightstand, and looked at the number. He didn't recognize it. He set it back down, rolled back over, and closed his eyes. A minute later it rang again. Wrong numbers called once. People who needed something called twice. Rolling towards the nightstand again, he turned on the light and grabbed his phone.

"Da?"

"It's Alisa, *grandfather*," she said, slowing slightly on the last word. Yvgenny picked up a slight waver in her voice, and she never called him grandfather. She always used the Russian term dedushka. "Did you make it to your place up in the hills?" He didn't have a house in the hills.

He paused for a moment, thinking quickly. Something was very wrong. "Da, Alisa. What can I do for you?"

"Well, Galina and I were closing up, but we can't open the register. It's jammed. Can you come open it for us?"

"Of course, but it will be taking me a while to get there."

"How long, grandfather?"

He thought furiously, doing some fast calculations in his head. "About forty-five minutes, maybe an hour. Can you waiting that long?" There was a pause, and he thought he overheard some whispering.

"Yes, grandfather. But please hurry."

"Everything will be alright, Alisa. Don't worry. I'll take care of the problem. *I promise*."

"Yes, grandfather. I know you will."

He hung up, sat on the edge of the bed and thought for a moment. Standing, he walked over to his computer, moved the mouse and logged on. Double clicking an icon, a set of four video images sprung to life. One showed the patio above the teahouse, one displayed the kitchen, the next showed the cash register, and the last revealed six armed men spread around the dining area. One of them was Bennie DiMarco.

Yvgenny grabbed his cell phone, selected a number, and hit dial. While it rang, he walked over to the closet and calmly pulled out a KS-K Russian military shotgun. When no one answered, he dialed the second number down the list for the same person.

O O O

Rachel, Xen, and I decided to enjoy a casual night of gambling at the Costa Rican hotel. Xen continued to prove himself at the baccarat tables, but he'd taken it easy, so he wouldn't get kicked out again. I'd played poker, ruining several people, and Rachel broke even at blackjack. We'd gone back to the house, enjoyed another round of cigars and some of the scotch. When the last embers of daylight were gone and the snifters empty, Mag and Xen went down to the beach for some night-fishing while Rachel and I retired to the bedroom.

We excitedly helped each other out of our clothes, kissing passionately. I slid my hands up her sides and caressed her breasts, drawing a lusty moan out of her. She pulled me back towards the bed, leaning back as I stood there and parted her legs. She grinned wickedly and raised an eyebrow expectantly. I got the hint, kneeled on the floor in front of her and kissed my way up her knees to where she was already wet. I helped things along with my tongue, causing her to pant and moan. For minutes, I worked at it, almost bringing her to a climax.

She placed her hand on my forehead and pushed me away. "Not yet," she said seductively. "Come here."

I stood up, kneeled on the bed between her legs and kissed her breasts. She moaned again, more so now. She grabbed me by the ass and pulled me down into her. We both moaned as I crossed the threshold, and I thrust in and out of her, slowly at first and then with more force. She wrapped her legs around me and squeezed, forcing my rhythm to keep pace with her ecstasy. I heartily obliged her, increasing my tempo and pumping even harder. Our groans filled the house, and we finally erupted together. We lay together like that for long minutes, kissing each other tenderly.

I finally rolled off, our legs tangled together, and smiled. "That wasn't so bad, was it?" I looked at her, and she raised an eyebrow.

"Well, it was okay. But once isn't much of a sampling. If I'm going to make an honest evaluation, I'll need more data." She untangled her legs from mine, got up on her hands and knees with her head pointing away from me. She swayed her ass at me. "Think you have another one in you?"

"I believe I do," I said rising to the request, "which means you're about to."

"Then come over here and show me what you're made of." It was one order I had every intention of obeying.

We spent the next couple of hours slowly … well, sometimes not so slowly … exploring one another. Rachel stood, bent over with her hands on the bed and me behind her. Just as she approached another orgasm, my cell phone rang.

"You answer that and I'll kill you!" she gasped between moans.

The phone stopped ringing just as she climaxed, her legs shuddering slightly. We stood there for a dozen heartbeats, and then she lay down on the bed, exhausted. "Oh, my god," she sighed.

"Is that enough data?" I asked, walking over to the nightstand and picking up my phone. I recognized the number when my house phone rang. I grabbed it quickly.

"Yvgenny, is that you?"

"Da," the old man said. "I need your help, Justin. *Right now.*" He sounded worried, even scared, and I knew he was in a heap of trouble.

"Name it and it's done," I replied with steel in my voice.

"Can you be at the teahouse in forty minutes?"

"I'll be there in thirty. What's up?"

"Bennie and five friends have my granddaughters in the dining room," he said quickly.

I felt the old me rise out of the dark pit where I keep him locked up, and he was hungry for Bennie DiMarco.

Yvgenny sounded calm, but I could tell he had to work to keep it together. "Two have shotguns, the rest pistols," he continued. "Is it doable?"

"Of course. I'll work out the details on the way. You armed?"

"Da. KS-K with slugs and laser."

"Good, that's perfect," I replied, my voice full of loathing for Bennie. "Are you in your apartment?"

"Yes. The bedroom."

"Okay. Stay put. I'll call you when I get there … It'll be okay, Yvgenny. Trust me."

"I do, Justin. That's why I called you and not anyone else. You've never let me down."

"And I never will, old man. I'll see you in thirty."

"Thank you, Justin."

I set the phone down and looked at Rachel with a look in my eyes that clearly disturbed her.

"What's wrong, baby?" she asked, worried.

I took a deep breath, balancing myself between the old and the new me. "Bennie DiMarco and five other assholes are holding Yvgenny's granddaughters in the dining room of the teahouse. I'm going to go kill the fuckers."

"*We* are," she corrected. "We're a team, aren't we?" she asked, sounding more hopeful then she meant to.

The old me faded slightly, and I looked at her, kissing her deeply as I gave her arm a squeeze. "It's going to take some getting used to, but yeah, we sure are." I patted her on the butt. "Now go get cleaned up. Can you be ready in ten minutes?"

"Less," she said as she rolled out of bed and headed for the bathroom. "Do you have any chopsticks?"

"What?"

"Do you have any chopsticks?" she repeated, closing the bathroom door.

"Yes," I said, sounding a bit confused. *Must be a girl thing*, I thought.

"Good. I'll need one." The shower came on.

"You realize we're going to kill Italians, not get Chinese takeout, right?" I asked.

"Mmmmm-hmmmmm," she replied over the sound of the shower.

I walked out of the bedroom into the hallway and onto the patio.

"Mag! I need you," I hollered into the jungle. Xen came up beside me, rubbing tired eyes. He'd apparently been sleeping on the patio.

"What's all the fuss?"

"A friend is in trouble back home. Rachel and I are going back to take care of it."

Mag snaked her way out of the jungle and looked up at me.

"Want me to go with you?" Xen asked and scratched Mag behind the ears. "I'm starting to get a taste for this shit, damn it."

"I thought you might, but not on this one. The equation is full without you. I don't want to add any variables I don't absolutely need."

"Fair enough," he said, resigned to sitting on the sidelines.

"Go get dressed. You're heading back to the L.A. house, okay? And grab your money, if you haven't already. If this goes south, you can at least be back in town with some jingle in your pocket. Go see O'Neil if you don't hear from me by morning. Give him the whole story …" I paused and smiled at him. "Except the alien part," I added with a chuckle. "And let Marsha know what's up if you see her before I do."

"Okay. Is this really that bad?"

"Probably not, but I like to cover my bases. Go on … the clock's ticking."

Xen walked back into the house as I bent down and looked at Mag with my hands on her head.

"Playtime tonight, Mag. They've got shotguns, so be careful, okay?" She nodded. "And we'll be at Yvgenny's. Cougar suit only. Nobody sees the real you." Magdelain's coat shifted in the darkness to a solid tan across her whole body except for a white underbelly. I ruffled the fur on her head and went back into the house.

I grabbed two chopsticks out of a kitchen drawer, headed back to the bedroom, and got dressed. Rachel walked out of the shower just as I slipped my coat on. She wore jeans and one of my t-shits as she dried her still-damp hair, an expectant look on her face.

"One or two?" I asked.

"Just one."

I grabbed one of the chopsticks I'd thrown on the bed and tossed it at her. She caught it mid-air, threw the towel on the toilet behind her, put the chopstick in her teeth and then quickly braided her long hair. She coiled up the braid, grabbed the chopstick and jammed it through the knot of hair. She made a "voila" motion with her hands and winked at me. I smiled at her.

God you have a great neck, I thought, taking in the exposed flesh. "Sexy," I said out loud, looking her up and down like I wanted another taste.

She raised her eyebrow provocatively.

"Xen, you ready?" I yelled across the hallway.

Rachel gave me a disappointed look and then smiled.

"Sorry, gorgeous. We have to get to work," I added sadly.

We met in the hallway and walked out to the front door. I ran through the combination to the L.A. house and pushed open the door. "There you go, Xen." He stepped through and turned around. He had his bag of money slung over his shoulder. "Remember what I said. If you don't hear from me by morning, call O'Neil and spill your guts."

"Got it."

"Easy peasy," I said, closing the door.

"See ya … and good luck, you two."

I nodded and closed the door. I stepped over to a closet in the hallway, opened it, and pulled out one of my shimmering black coats.

"Planning on sneaking them?" Rachel asked.

I looked at her and smiled almost lovingly. "No. You are."

"Me?"

"Yep. Kills two birds with one stone. Try it on." I handed the jacket over. She slipped it on and mostly disappeared in front of me except for her head. It was way too big on her, but it would work for what I had in mind. I bent down and clasped the straps at her ankles. The fabric still sagged behind her and touched the ground, but not enough to trip her up. "Pull the hood up."

Rachel reached behind her, grabbed the hood and pulled it over her head. I grabbed the small face cover and pulled it down over her face.

"Hey! I can still see," she said surprised.

"Of course. Now go over to that mirror." She walked over as I dimmed the lights with a dial on the wall behind me, making the illumination roughly what it would be in the dining room.

"That's amazing," she said. She stared into the mirror, looking as hard as she could to make out an outline. There were little lines and creases that faintly appeared and disappeared as she moved but, for the most part, she was invisible.

"Take your shoes off," I instructed. "You'll be more quiet." She kicked them off and faced me. "Now you know they won't see you, okay?"

"I got it. I still can't believe this thing," she said, still astounded.

"Oh … wait. I want to show you something. Stick your hand into an inside pocket." She cocked her head to the side quizzically but moved her hand inside. "Once you feel the lip you'll have to pry it open to get your hand in." She did as instructed, and after a couple of attempts, slid her hand in. "What the hell?" she asked. I smiled. "I can feel a banana, some small balls, and a few other things I can't identify. "This coat should weigh a ton."

"Careful in that pocket. There's something sharp in there," I cautioned.

"The meat cleaver," she said, nodding. Her eyes got wide as the physics of the thing danced away from her imagination. There couldn't be that much stuff in the pocket.

"Now don't move." I slipped my hand it into the same inside pocket of my own jacket.

I brushed my hand up against hers inside the pocket.

She squealed in shock and yanked her hand out.

Laughing, I said, "Go ahead. Put it back in. Trust me."

She slowly moved her hand back, pried open the pocket and slid her hand in. I grasped her hand and we interlocked fingers.

"It's impossible," she said, completely dumbfounded.

"It works just like the doors, only smaller." We pulled out our hands. "The pockets in each jacket match up to one another, and every pocket in a jacket has distinct contents. Pretty cool, hunh?" I smiled like a big kid. "I still get a kick out of it, and it's been a long time."

"Pretty cool doesn't even come close," she said with amazement on her face.

"Oh, one more thing. Yvgenny's seen the coat. I told him it was something I stole from the government. And Mag is a cougar when we're around other people who know about her, okay?"

"Okay," she said and nodded her head abruptly.

"So, you ready for this?"

"Yes," she said, amazement still in her voice. "Aren't we going to be late, though? You said less than thirty, and the drive will take a while on a Friday night."

I smiled confidently. "Trust me." I placed my hand on the panel behind me and, without looking, ran through a combination I hadn't used in a while. I twisted the knob and kicked backward. The door swung open onto Yvgenny's patio.

Rachel cocked her head to the side as she stepped up to the doorway. She could see the door to the stairs that went down into the dining area and the patio table where we'd had lunch only a few days before.

"Mag, let's go."

Magdelain slid silently past us.

I motioned with my head for Rachel to go through. She did, and I stepped through, closing the door behind me. The sounds and smells of L.A. washed over us.

"I'm never going to get used to that," she said as she turned to me, lifted the facemask slightly and kissed me gently on the lips. "Thanks for trusting me enough to share this," she whispered in my ear.

I smiled, hugged her, turned and knocked on Yvgenny's door. Rachel faded back into the shadows. Thirty seconds later the door opened.

Yvgenny stood in the doorway and looked at me. He had a peculiar look on his face, sizing me up in a way he never had before. He wore black sweatpants, a big, baggy, black sweatshirt and a black turtleneck underneath. He had a toothpick in the side of his mouth, and he held a combat shotgun in his hands with a laser sight under the barrel.

"We made good time through town," I said and smiled. Yvgenny kept staring at me for a few seconds. I'd expected him to ask how we got on the roof, and I was prepared with a story about Xen driving my van, but he just looked at me.

"Of course you did," he finally said and clapped me on the shoulder. "It's good to seeing you, my friend. Again, I am in your debt."

"This doesn't even come close to evening the score, and you know you never need to worry about that."

"You know I always will, Justin." The old man grabbed me in a massive bear hug. "You're one of a kind, young ... *man*." Yvgenny let me go, and we looked at each other. I gave him a look of curiosity, but he didn't offer anything.

"So what's the layout downstairs?" I finally asked.

"I'll show you. Rachel, could you stay out here please?"

I stepped inside, raising an eyebrow at how he knew she was there.

"Sure," she said automatically. A few seconds later it occurred to her that he couldn't have seen her. "Hey!" she whispered. "How'd you know I was here?"

Yvgenny smiled out into the night, scanning the darkness for her, and closed the door.

"I was wondering that, too," I said as I walked into the living room.

"Come with me." The old man walked past me up a flight of dark wooden stairs. I followed, and we went into Yvgenny's bedroom. Yvgenny stepped up to his computer and pointed at the screen showing the displays of his security cameras. Cameras I didn't know he had. The first image showed the dining room, but the fourth image displayed the patio. Yvgenny had seen us arrive. He looked at me with a knowing smile. "We will talking later about patio, yes?"

"Yes," I assured him quietly.

He nodded. "As I said before, there are being six men. The big one is being back near kitchen and appears to be eating something. Cretin. The only two having shotguns keep those pretty much pointed at my granddaughters. With proper motivation, however, I believe we can convincing them to point them elsewhere. The one beneath top of stairs presumably has pistol, and he just sits there looking bored. That man sitting near bottom of steps has not moved, and Bennie is across on far side also eating something, the fat pig. He was doing something with his cell phone when I last looked."

"Okay." I examined the layout and quickly. Letting the old killer in me loose a bit, I worked out the final touches to my plan.

"You got a pistol in here?"

Yvgenny reached under the pillow, pulled out a Beretta and handed it to me.

I pushed the slide back enough to see a chambered round. "Let's go."

"Da."

We walked downstairs, out the door to the patio, and looked around. Rachel stepped out of a dark corner with Mag behind her. I nodded at her and motioned for her to come over. "Okay, here's what we're going to do."

The Lion and the Bull

So, has everyone got it?" I asked. "When I say 'I guess that's it, then' you both hit it hard, and the rest will take care of itself."

There were two nods, and I assumed the third.

I held the Beretta out and Rachel grabbed it. Stepping to the side of patio open to the parking lot, I hopped up onto the wall and jumped over the flowerbed. Looking below, I didn't see anyone close by, so I dropped the twenty-five feet to the ground. I landed lightly without making much sound and walked up to the corner of the building. The streets were clear, so I stepped around the corner of the building, walked up to the door, and used the key Yvgenny had given me to unlock it.

Whistling the theme to *Jeopardy*, I opened the door noisily, stepped in, and let it slowly close on its own behind me. I kept whistling as I walked up the middle of the room with my hands in my pockets. I heard some movement behind the curtain and kept going. Pulling the curtain aside, I stepped into the room and took it all in with a glance. Everything looked like it had looked on the camera, except Bennie had moved to the far side of the table to my left, and the man behind the two with shotguns had shifted a little bit farther away from the stairs. A dirty plate, empty glass, and a cell phone sat on the table where Bennie had been sitting.

"Don't fucking move, and put your hands where I can see them," Bennie said excitedly. Out of the corner of my eye, I saw the door at the top of the stairs open slowly.

I cleared my throat loudly and looked at Bennie with a condescending smile. I spoke a little more loudly than normal to cover any sounds from the top of the stairs. "Bennie, that's kind of a catch-22, isn't it?" I didn't move.

"A what?" Bennie asked, confused. "And I said put your hands up!"

"But you told me to not fucking move," I corrected, pointing out the obvious.

"That's true, boss," Tommy spoke up from the back corner, his mouth full of baklava. "You did say don't fucking move."

The other goombahs all nodded their heads. It was all I could do not crack up.

"Everybody shut the fuck up! I know what I said," Bennie shouted.

I got an even bigger smile on my face as I watched the two goombahs pointing shotguns at the girls heads look at each other and try not to laugh.

"Put your hands where I can see them and *then* don't fucking move," Bennie ordered.

I looked thoughtful as I pondered if there were any flaws with the directive. I nodded to myself. "Okay, Bennie. That makes more sense." I pulled my hands out.

"Real slow," Bennie said, aiming his gold .45 at me. I kept smiling and slowed the motion of my hands skyward to a crawl.

Benny's face went beet red, and the goombahs were grinning openly now, one of them shuddering slightly as he forced himself not to laugh out loud. Even Antonio smiled, albeit barely. He picked up his teacup and covered his face so as to not piss off Bennie any more than he already had.

"Faster, God damn it!" Bennie yelled.

I shot my hands into the air so they were straight up.

"That's better!" Bennie looked victorious, although for the life of me, I couldn't figure out why. What a dumb fuck. He stepped around the table and got in my face. "So, look what the good Lord brought me … It's not Christmas, is it?"

"No, boss," Tommy said with another mouthful. "That ain't till December," he added seriously.

Bennie looked back at Tommy and shook his head.

"Shut up, Tommy," Antonio yelled across the room.

I spotted Yvgenny in the shadows at the top of the stairs with the shotgun pointed at the ceiling. Mag crouched in front of him, her nose barely visible behind the railing, her tail twitching violently. I'd have to trust that Rachel was in position.

"Thanks, Antonio," Bennie said. "So, Case, here we were planning on using Yvgenny to get you down here, and you come all by yourself."

I was a picture of friendliness. "Yeah, well, he called me," I replied, grinning. "Probably not long after you called him. He said you guys were being impolite and asked if I would come down here to talk to you. See if we could work things out."

"Oh, he did, did he?"

I nodded with a friendly smile.

"I think you'll find you're gonna be disappointed," Bennie said evilly.

"Really?" I asked, acting confused.

Bennie nodded.

"Well, I guess that's it then."

I watched Yvgenny's shotgun barrel lower. His finger touched the trigger, and the laser sight came on. The red dot traced its way down the wall behind Bennie and then appeared on the ear of the left-hand goombah. All someone had to do now was see it, and the room would get very noisy very quickly. Yvgenny drifted the dot across the corner of the guy's eye to catch his attention just as the right-hand goombah noticed it.

"Hey!" the two goombahs shouted together and reflexively, swiveling their guns towards the top of the stairs.

The moment the barrels were no longer pointed at the girls, a massive shotgun blast filled the room. Yvgenny's double-loaded slug literally took the top of the guy's head off. The corpse reflexively squeezed the trigger, but the blast went off into the wood paneling of the stairs.

I slapped Bennie's .45 so it wasn't pointed at me, causing it to go off, and the round buried itself in the wood behind me.

Then everything happened at once.

Yvgenny's shotgun went off again, killing the other goombah holding a shotgun. Rachel opened fire on the guy at the bottom of the stairs who was yanking a pistol from inside his coat and turning towards the new threat.

POP! POP! POP! Rachel's Beretta barked, and three rounds made their way into the man's chest.

Yvgenny's granddaughters both screamed, and in a flash, Mag slithered down three steps and leapt over the railing, dropping on the man below her as he took aim at me. The pistol fired wide as eighty pounds of dratar landed on his back, and long canines sank into the back of his neck. He screamed, dropping to the floor as his pistol sailed across the room.

I dropped and rolled once towards Antonio.

Antonio opened fire, aiming where I had been, while Bennie swung his gun back towards where the shotgun blast had come from at the top of the stairs. Bullets hit the wall behind me as I rolled under the table and came up holding the edge of it.

Bennie's gun went off three times. I heard a grunt from the top of the stairs and the sound of a shotgun bouncing off the wall. Bennie ran towards the curtain.

Using the table to block Antonio's vision, I came up with all my strength as a round came through the table, barely missing me. Rachel fired at Bennie's retreating back.

I shoved the table towards the wall, pinning Antonio to it. The gun in Antonio's hand clattered to the floor, and then a shot went off behind me hitting the table under my arm and passing through it, followed by another round above my head. Bennie ran out of the room behind me. I let go of the table and let it drop, surprised to see Antonio fall with it. There was a neat, red splotch in the center of his chest where Bennie's round had passed first through the table and then Antonio.

Tommy stood at the back of the room, a dumbfounded look on his face as he took in the carnage that had taken all of about four seconds from start to finish.

"Rachel, cover Tommy! Mag! Track Bennie, but don't touch him!"

Mag leapt off of the dead man under her, his throat torn out, and raced through the curtain, hot on Bennie's trail.

"Yvgenny, you okay up there?"

There was an irritated groan from the old man, not unlike a perturbed bear. "Da. I'm fine. I'm being down in second." I heard him starting to get up, albeit slowly.

Tommy took a few steps away from the kitchen when Rachel took off the hood and opened the coat. His eyes got wide as he saw her appear out of thin air, still holding a gun on him and walking toward the bottom of the stairs.

"Hey, Tommy," I said in as cocky a tone as I could. "No gun?" Tommy turned his gaze to Antonio's dead body and then to me, glaring with a face that slowly contorted into fury. "So, um … out of curiosity, were you the one who messed up the girls?"

Tommy nodded deliberately, and a satisfied smile crossed his face.

"Am I late for party?" Yvgenny said walking down the stairs. The toothpick was still in his mouth, and it shifted back and forth like a tiger's tail as he spoke. When he got to the bottom, he finally got a look at his granddaughters. The camera hadn't been too clear. Their mouths were taped closed, and both of them had bruises on their faces. Alisa's right eye was swollen closed, and a long bruise and laceration marred the left side of her face. Both of their blouses were spotted with blood. Yvgenny turned to Tommy with death in his eyes.

"Not at all, Yvgenny," I said as he stared at the big Italian. "Tommy and I were just getting reacquainted."

"Are you the one who hurting my granddaughters?" Yvgenny asked as he stepped around Rachel and strode forward.

"That would indeed be Tommy," I confirmed.

"Mister Tommy. I am hearing of you. They say you are liking to break things. Apparently, this includes little girls." Yvgenny pulled off his sweatshirt and turtleneck. I noticed a bullet hole in them as he revealed a bulletproof vest. He dropped the garments on the floor. "They also say I was *unbreakable*." He released the velcro at shoulder and waist and pulled off the vest, dropping that on the floor as well. "An interesting coincidence, yes?"

Yvgenny stood in the middle of the room in his sweats and a dingy gray tank top, cracking the knuckles first of his left hand and then the right. "Come, Tommy. Let's see if you can break poor, old

Russian violin player." He turned to me. "Go Justin. I am handling this."

Tommy took off his jacket and loosened his tie.

"You sure you can take him?" I asked. "I could help. Or Rachel could just shoot him."

"It would be my pleasure," she offered enthusiastically. "I don't have too much compassion for men who hit girls." Rachel had released the straps at her ankles and taken the coat off, draping it over a chair.

"I am having boots older than him, Justin," Yvgenny pointed out.

Tommy unbuttoned his dress shirt and pulled it off, revealing a clean, white t-shirt. He had a tattoo of a bull on each forearm.

"That's what worries me," I said quietly.

"You insult me. No one touches my family and lives. *You* know this. I will make example of him. The world needs a reminder. Go. You have other things to attend to."

"Okay," I said, scratching my cheek a tad bit doubtfully but respecting the old lion's wishes. "Good luck … and watch the left."

"Luck is not factor. Rachel, will you please take my granddaughters out of here?" Yvgenny pulled a lock-blade out of his pocket and threw it on a table.

As Rachel grabbed the knife, I took off the tan coat, put on the black one and stepped out through the curtain, sealing up the coat as I went. Approaching the front door, I reached into an inner pocket and pulled out a small device that looked very much like an ultra-thin cell phone.

o o o

Yvgenny looked at the girls as I left the room. "Girls, take the guns with you when you go." He turned back to Tommy, and the two big men stood there eyeing each other as Rachel cut the girls out of the tape. Yvgenny and Tommy were loosening their shoulders and necks as they waited.

The girls were free in a minute, and Alisa grabbed the shotguns while Galina went for a nearby pistol. Galina picked up the pistol, looking at it closely. She turned, pointed it at Tommy and pulled the hammer back.

"Galina, no," Yvgenny said quietly.

She froze but kept the gun pointed at Tommy who stared back at her without fear. She looked at her grandfather.

"You are too young and do not needing blood on your hands. *Please*," he said fondly. "Go. Go with Miss Rachel. And lock door on way out."

Galina looked back at Tommy for a few more seconds and then, using both hands, gently let the hammer go down quietly.

"You should have begged them to let me shoot you, you son of a bitch," Galina said with pure venom in her voice. "My grandfather is going to fuck you up."

Tommy snorted confidently but said nothing.

"Go on, Galina," Yvgenny said. "I'll see you shortly. Rachel, can you please drive them to their mother's? Use my car. The keys are under counter up front."

"Of course," Rachel said quietly. They finished picking up the guns, and the three of them walked towards the curtain.

"Tell your mother to calling that weirdo Stanley for the cleanup." Yvgenny looked Tommy dead in the eye. "These men deserve to be eaten by pigs."

"Yes, *dedushka*," Alisa said, as the three walked out.

"What is it you dagos are always saying?" Yvgenny said derisively. "No women, no kids?"

"Yeah, well, I just do what I'm told." Tommy said. "Besides, who gives a shit about you uppity Ruskies, anyway?"

In answer, Yvgenny stepped up to Tommy and spat the toothpick in his face.

Tommy's eyes lit up with rage, and he swung a fast left-right combo at Yvgenny's face.

Good, Yvgenny thought as he leaned back to avoid the left. *The man can be baited and is young enough to let passion rule him.* He stepped back for the right. Yvgenny saw a brief opening for a boot into the mid-section, but it disappeared quickly, and he was still sizing the Italian up.

He threw a fast right jab to see how well Tommy responded, but didn't follow up. Tommy blocked the jab and came in low with a body blow to the mid-section that landed partially as Yvgenny stepped back again. Tommy smiled. The Russian drifted to his left, shortening up Tommy's right hand swing and opening up the left. Heeding the warning about the left, Yvgenny wanted to know exactly what he was dealing with.

As Yvgenny opened up, he raised his right elbow slightly, giving Tommy a clear path to exposed ribs. He saw Tommy tense, and the left came in hard, but Tommy opened up with his right just enough, so the wily Russian sacrificed his side for a headshot. Yvgenny twisted with Tommy's left to the ribs, but it still hit hard enough to hurt. However, the Russian's left was already in flight and connected just behind Tommy's upraised arm, landing squarely on the side of his face. Yvgenny pivoted and followed with a right hook that Tommy danced away from.

They faced one another again, and Yvgenny ran his left hand over where Tommy had connected. He nodded his head thoughtfully.

"Justin warned me about your left," Yvgenny said calmly. Tommy smiled wickedly as he wiped blood off the corner of his mouth with the back of his hand. "However, I have to wondering what he was worried about." The smile evaporated off Tommy's face, replaced with an angry grimace. Yvgenny smiled at Tommy as he would a disobedient child.

"I'm gonna wipe that smile off your face, you old bastard," Tommy snarled.

"Then what are you waiting for? Perhaps panties are being too tight?"

Tommy closed with Yvgenny quickly, winding up with his right, telegraphing the beginning of the combo the Russian already knew was coming. He braced himself and tensed to block as much of Tommy's assault as he could. Again, he was willing to take a little punishment. He wanted to wear the Italian down in preparation for the endgame. He'd fought men like this many times, and it always ended the same.

The right sailed straight at Yvgenny's face, so he leaned in towards Tommy's left to shorten that distance and reduce the impact, his forearm deflecting it. Tommy's left rose quickly in an uppercut, which Yvgenny leaned back to avoid. Tommy brought his knee up, but Yvgenny expected it and drifted his thigh in to block it. The left came around in a hook that was easily blocked, and then the right came in again, grazing Yvgenny's already turning face.

Yvgenny jabbed with his right, forcing Tommy to block and terminating the combination. He followed with his left, and Tommy blocked that, too.

The Russian stepped back and took a look at Tommy who breathed a little heavier now. Yvgenny's breathing came slowly and calmly. *It is working*, the old man thought to himself.

He came at the Italian, not wanting to give any time to rest, and threw up a series of left jabs, baiting Tommy. Tommy blocked each one casually … one … two … three … four jabs went out.

Yvgenny set the rhythm up and then, on the fifth, he flinched with his left. As Tommy's hand went up automatically, it found nothing but air. Yvgenny's right came in like a freight train as he planted his back foot and hammered into Tommy's jaw as hard as he could. Tommy's block came entirely too late, followed by an ugly sound of bone on bone that twisted his head around and back. He spilled over a table, tumbling to the other side, but came up fast. He shook his head to clear his vision. He stood there for a few seconds, sizing up the Russian and breathing even heavier.

Yvgenny smirked at him and walked around the table. His hands came up, and he led with a right this time that Tommy easily blocked. He sent in a left-right-left combo, and one of them landed just as Tommy caught him with a jab to the face. Tommy pounced on the opportunity and sent a flurry of left-right hooks, pressing Yvgenny back, fists impacting solidly on the old man's burly, tattooed forearms. Yvgenny kept backing up, drawing Tommy into another trap.

The blows hammered home. On the fifth step backwards, Yvgenny suddenly reversed his motion and stepped into the Italian, raising his arms in a fast arc and closing around both of Tommy's arms as the Italian wound up for another punch. Tommy's face was at a perfect level, and Yvgenny didn't hesitate. He smashed his forehead once, twice, a third. Then he released Tommy, stepped back, and planted a boot in Tommy's gut, pushing off and sending the big Italian backwards over another table.

Tommy got to his hands and knees slowly as blood poured out of his shattered nose and bloody mouth. He spat out two front teeth. Yvgenny felt a trickle running down the middle of his forehead then down between his nose and cheek. He ran a hand over his forehead and discovered where Tommy's teeth had gashed his skin.

Tommy scooted out of view behind the table, and then Yvgenny watched it lift up and come straight at him. He put his hands out to block it, but Tommy put everything he had into the charge.

Yvgenny flew back and slammed into the wall. The back of his head hit a shelf, and the table smashed into his face hard with a massive crash. It was Yvgenny's turn to see stars. Through a fog the old Russian saw the table fly as Tommy tossed it aside. It bounced off a wall, landing near Antonio's corpse.

A right fist came out of the fog and hammered into Yvgenny's face, spinning his head around. A powerful left came in low and caught him in the belly, and he grunted with the impact, bending over slightly but keeping his breath. Before Tommy's next punch was in flight, fury took hold of the old man. He shook his head, and the fog melted away just as a right came down at his cheek. He twisted his head, turning it into a glancing blow. The left came in hard and fast, and he blocked it, *barely*. Tommy pulled back with his right again and let fly, but Yvgenny was ready, set up for the finale. In flew the right, directly on target.

Yvgenny's left hand went up and grabbed the fist, stopping it cold. He lowered his right hand nearly to his knees and closed it into a hammer-fist. He brought the right up fast, lifting with his arm, shoulders and legs all at once. His fist caught Tommy directly below the chin. Teeth exploded in Tommie's mouth, and his head snapped back like the lid of a Jack-in-the-box as his body lifted off the ground several feet. He flew back limply and came down hard on the floor, his arms and legs flopping like rubber.

Yvgenny leapt atop his prey, straddling Tommy's chest and pinning his arms. The lion raised his right fist—a thing someone should have warned Tommy about—and brought it down like a pile driver. Tommy's nose and cheeks collapsed with the impact. The left went up and came down, rupturing his eyes and crushing his upper jaw. The right came down and caved in the whole of Tommy's face. Yvgenny's fist sunk in almost to the wrist in what was left of Tommy's features.

The battered Russian raised his fist again to send another blow hammering down into his opponent, but stopped as he drew it back and stared at his fist and the mess that covered it. He was breathing heavily now, and his body ached. He stood up and looked down at what he had done.

"*Unbreakable*," he said to the ruined husk lying on the floor. Yvgenny walked slowly over to the sink at the wait station and washed off his hands. He could still feel blood running down his face.

Reaching into a cupboard, he grabbed a kettle and filled it up. He entered the kitchen, set the kettle on, ignited the burner, and then headed back to the office for the first-aid kit. He set the kit on one of the dining tables and waited for the kettle to boil. It would be a while before Justin got back.

Alley Cat

I stood in the tea room and scanned the street. Seeing no one, I glanced at the slim tracker in my hand. It sent out pulses and read the reflected data, translating it into a blocky but useable outline of the surrounding area. It worked off matter density at the atomic level and was a key component in the work I used to do. Its range was limited to about a half-mile in metropolitan areas but could track at five miles out in the open.

It picked up Magdelain's implant about eight blocks away. She moved slowly south. I checked the street one last time and stepped out into the night, invisible. I darted across the street and turned down the alley, following Mag and Bennie as they traveled through the city. They appeared to be moving in a straight line. What a vile moron, I thought as I jogged through the darkness. I loosened the reins on the old me, feeling a mixture of guilt and delight about what I intended. It was time for Bennie to pony up for all the shit he'd done in his life.

I slid into an easy, silent jog, closing in on Mag's position. She'd slowed to almost a crawl for a short distance and then stopped moving completely. I was back in my old life. Justin Case disappeared and Jalin took over.

Much of what I had done for my old masters involved exactly what I was doing now—hunting … and killing. Mag would get on the trail of our prey, I would move in, and we would close the deal … except, now it was righteous. Bennie had it coming. I smiled wickedly. I'd been programmed—designed—to enjoy the hunt and the kill. Damn those bastards who'd made me, I thought as I jogged.

I reached another cross street and stepped back into the shadows. Mag hid in the next alley, motionless against a wall. Peeking around the corner, I waited for a car to pass by. When it turned down the next street, I ran across the pavement, found a shadow to disappear into, and peeked down the alley. I found a spot just inside the alley where I could crouch and get a feel for the area. I memorized every shadow, every outline of box and dumpster, all of it.

Only three pools of light shone between the far end of the alley and me, highlighting doors along the way. Office buildings towered above me. I peeked around the corner and saw a flicker of Mag's coat as she briefly shifted to a visible pattern. She stared at me from atop one of two dumpsters along the wall, and her tail twitched in anticipation. She motioned with her head for me to come over. Then she disappeared again. Bennie is here, I thought, and Mag is right on top of him.

I crept down the alley as silently as Mag had, and as I approached the dumpster, I picked up Bennie's heavy breathing. I snuck up and could finally make out Mag's faint outline. She hadn't moved from the dumpster, but now appeared to be looking down at something on the far side. I heard quiet gasping, so I stepped up to the edge of the dumpster and peered around the corner. Bennie sat on the pavement, his back against the wall with his gold .45 resting in his lap.

The idiot had both hands on the ground and was doing a poor job of being quiet while he tried to regain his breath. I stepped back a pace, reached out, and touched Mag on her haunches, motioning for her to come to the edge of the dumpster.

"Take the gun," I whispered in her ear, as quiet as a ghost. A few seconds later Bennie yelped, and I saw Mag's faint blur as she shot out from between the dumpsters. She had the gun gripped in her mouth. She snaked around the far side of dumpster in a flash and stood in the middle of the alley.

"What the fuck was that?" Bennie whispered in horror. His gasped fast and heavy now, his eyes filled with terror.

I whispered into the air over the dumpster, "I'm coming for you, Bennie," and then I kicked the far dumpster as hard as I could. The *BOOM* echoed through the alley, and Bennie screamed as the dumpster shot away from us, rolling to a stop fifteen feet away.

Still invisible, I came around the corner, grabbed Bennie's jacket lapels, heaved him into the air, and chucked him towards the dumpster. He screamed in terror, landed with a thud, and groaned with the impact. Quickly regaining his senses, he scrambled to his feet much faster than I thought the fast bastard was capable of. The mobster scanned the darkness, his head spinning left and right. He jammed his hand into a pocket and pulled out a switchblade.

"Where the fuck are you?" he yelled into the shadows.

"That's a fair question, Bennie," I said quietly, "one that deserves an answer." I pulled the hood back. My head was visible now, silhouetted in the streetlight behind me. Bennie's eyes got wide. "It's okay Mag, you can show yourself. There's no need to hide from this piece of shit." Mag came up beside me, the gun still in her mouth. I reached down, took the gun, and scratched her behind the ears.

"Jesus Christ! What the fuck are you?"

"Well, aren't you full of intelligent questions tonight." I said, my voice full of venom. "Not that the answers are going to do you much good." I held up the .45, pressed the clip release and let the full clip clatter to the pavement. Then I opened the breach and locked the slide in place. I looked down at the gun with a thoughtful look on my face. "You know, you really should keep one chambered. It's faster, and with a semi-auto, you don't have to worry about it going off till you cock it. At least you reloaded it," I added with disgust. "You're really not a very good gangster, are you? And another thing, do you have any idea how ridiculous this gun is? You're a joke, Bennie … a soft, frightened, incompetent joke."

I threw the gun into a pile of trash beside him. "And I could forgive all that, even with a slug like you. But tonight you crossed a line I don't let people cross." I glared. "Those were little girls, Bennie … and friends of mine."

I strode towards him like a juggernaut. Unstoppable. He slashed at me with the switchblade as I approached. I leaned away from the first slash, blocked the second, and then slapped Bennie hard across the face. He went down to a knee and glared up at me. I stepped away, giving him room to stand back up. He got to his feet and looked behind him. It might as well be miles to the end of the alley.

"That's an interesting idea," I observed, "but if you run for it, I'll have the cat chase you down and rip your belly open. Right, Mag?"

Mag took a step towards him and growled, low and steady.

"Keep that fucking thing away from me!" Bennie shouted.

"I'm considering it, Bennie," I said in a friendly tone. "I'll have to get back to you on that one, though, while I figure out how bad I want to kill you myself. I keep coming back to the thought of you and your boys burying those two girls in a shallow grave somewhere. And, frankly, it pisses me off."

"We were just using them as bait, Case. I swear! We were after you. We were gonna let 'em go! Honest!"

"You're not the kind of guy who leaves witnesses, are you? I mean, you're stupid, but even I know you're not that stupid. And I'm pretty sure Gino didn't send you after a well-connected Russian mobster by way of his granddaughters. He knows better. If Nikolov found out about this, what do you think would happen? You assholes would have to send a whole family of goombahs to his slaughterhouse as compensation, wouldn't you?"

Bennie looked at me wide-eyed, probably trying to figure out how I knew about that.

"The only thing that figures is that you came up with this gargantuan piece of idiocy all by yourself, you fat little turd."

Bennie glared at me and tightened his grip on the knife. The old me cut lose, and I didn't do a thing to hold him back. I let Bennie slash and stab at me a few times, avoiding it easily, and then let fly with another slap across the other side of his face, putting him down on his knees again.

Bennie screamed as he came up fast with the knife, a lot faster than I would ever have given him credit for. I could have blocked it, but I wanted to make a point. The blade hit home below my rib cage, dead center. I winced as it went in, grunting with the impact. Bennie followed with a pretty good left that glanced off my cheek as I turned with it.

I shoved Bennie back hard with both hands, bouncing him off the dumpster. I stood there, a condescending look on my face. Bennie stared back in terror, breathing deeply and waiting for me to drop to the ground.

"Not bad. Not bad at all. But I'm going to let you in on a little secret…." I placed my hand on the hilt of the blade and slowly pulled it out. I wiped the blood off on my pants and slowly closed the knife. I stared at him with dead eyes … a shark's eyes. Cold. Merciless. Hungry. "I'm a fucking alien, Bennie. That's why you couldn't kill me with that cheesy pistol, couldn't kill me with the airplane, and couldn't kill me with this toy."

I slipped it into a pocket and took one step forward. Bennie backed up, his eyes wide with horror. Mag moved in behind me, knowing this was the end and savoring it as much as I did.

I closed the space between us, and Bennie took a desperate swing at my head. I leaned out of it, stepped to the left and kicked Bennie's shoulder, knocking him face first into the brick wall. Bennie bounced off and staggered back towards me, twisting as he moved. I shot out a fast sidekick into his mid-section. He stopped dead in his tracks, gasping for air. I followed up with a knee to his face, sending him back into the wall again. The tricky part was that I didn't want to kill him or knock him out yet. I had to pull my punches and kicks just enough to hurt him, and the old me wanted to hurt him a lot.

Bennie slid down the wall, but I grabbed him and pulled him back up to his feet. I got nose to nose with him. I wanted to see the pain there, but his eyes rolled back in his head. I guess I hadn't pulled it enough. Not my lucky day, I thought.

"Time to pay the tab." I said with cold finality, and I have to admit, I was hungry for it.

I grabbed Bennie's tie tightly in my hand, and then, with a fast shove, spun him around to face the wall, holding him there. I turned quickly away from the wall.

We were back-to-back. I crouched quickly, pressed my back into Bennie's shoulders and stood up, pinning the fat son-of-a-bitch to the wall. I pulled as hard as I could on the tie and held it.

Bennie flailed his arms and legs, making pathetic gurgling and gasping noises. His face swelled, turned blue. He gripped at the tie digging into his neck and tried to pry it away from his collapsed windpipe. He struggled for a while and then finally went limp. I held him there for a couple of minutes, waiting for his foot to stop twitching, then I released the tie and stepped away from the wall.

Bennie DiMarco's corpse hit the pavement in a heap of limp arms and legs.

I stepped away from the body, turned, and looked at him. His tongue lolled out of a purple face like a dead dog's. I spat once. "Good riddance, you piece of shit," I said quietly. I put my hood back on and headed back to the teahouse to make sure Yvgenny hadn't underestimated the big Italian.

Insurance Policy

"You look like shit, old man," I smiled as I walked through the curtain with Mag behind me. She looked like a cougar again. I took off the black coat.

Yvgenny was taping a bandage to his forehead. He raised a condescending eyebrow at me and sized me up. "At least I having to work for mine. I could have sending Galina after that *tëlka*," which I knew meant fat girl in Russian, "and I'm sure Bennie still gave you hard time. I am thinking you barely escaped with life."

"Just like old times, eh, Yvgenny?" I smiled.

"Da." Yvgenny nodded his head and looked around the room, "Only there are fewer dirty cops."

I looked down at the remains of Tommy's face. "Jesus, I guess I should have warned him about *your* right."

Yvgenny chuckled. "Da. This thought occurred to me, too."

"You got a cleaner on the way?" I asked, looking around the room at the bodies. "Or were you thinking of calling the cops?"

"My daughter will be calling Stanley. However, I'm having idea about what to do before he gets here."

"What's that?" I sat down.

Yvgenny slipped a cell phone out of his pocket and handed it to me. "It belonged to DiMarco. Is Bennie's body someplace where you can taking picture with that?"

"It better be where I left it," I said with a mildly confused look on my face.

"Good. Go photograph the *tëlka* and then come back and photograph these fellows. I will call Nikolov."

I pondered the request for a few seconds and then got a huge grin on my face. "Oh, that's perfect! Ready-made protection. You think Pyotr will go for it? Technically, you don't work for him."

"He'll go for it. It gives him leverage for nothing, which is being best price in world."

"Gino will have to leave you alone or risk his deal … and a war … with Nikolov …" I gave him an impressed look. "You clever bastard."

Yvgenny smiled at me. "I'm having my moments. Now, toddle off child. Do your chores while I call Nikolov, and I might just give you your allowance."

"I'll be back before you can say 'soiled diaper.' And don't tell him I'm the one who helped you, okay?"

"Don't worry. I have story all ready. Meet me upstairs when you are done here." I slipped my coat back on as I walked through the curtain.

o o o

I got two pictures of every corpse and headed up into Yvgenny's bedroom. I listened in as he spoke Russian into his phone for a few minutes.

"So?" I asked when he hung up.

"I told him that he might finding situation useful, and he graciously offered protection. I expressed humble gratitude for his involvement, but he is being more than smart enough to know that I use him."

"He is a smart son-of-a-bitch. I'm going to have to be careful."

"It is rumored he is smartest and most dangerous in Solntsevskaya, and that he will lead the organization eventually. I do not doubt it … You have pictures?" I nodded. "And Gino's number is on phone?"

"Yeah, I checked." I held up the phone.

"Is Gino's email?"

"Sure is," I said wickedly.

"Then we are having what we need. Show me number," Yvgenny said and handed me a piece of paper with Pyotr's cell number on it. I memorized it for future reference. "I'll compose email while you send pictures to both numbers at same time." I worked on Bennie's phone while Yvgenny opened an email client and put in both Gino and Pyotr's emails. Then he typed while I sent. I planned on sending Bennie's picture last. Bennie's phone rang about halfway through the process. 'Gino' came up on the caller ID, but I ignored it and kept sending.

"Here, how does this look?" Yvgenny asked, leaning away from the computer for me to read. I sent the last picture and then leaned over. I read through it. "Perfect. It should be fine. You write English as bad as you speak it." I selected Gino and Pyotr as recipients for one last text message and then typed out "check email."

"Gino's going to have a heart attack." I said, and Yvgenny's chuckle dripped malice. "Alright, send it." We both hit send together and waited.

The email addressed to Gino DiMarco and Pyotr Nikolov read as follows:

Gentlemen,

It seems that members of the DiMarco organization took it upon themselves this evening to harming myself and my family. They invaded my place of business and taped my granddaughters to chairs, beat them, and threatened their lives. I will sending photos in morning of what was done to them. I have sent them someplace safe as precaution.

I am believing that Bennie DiMarco and his associates acted on their own, without the knowledge of his superiors, and will continue with this assumption so long as I have reason not to believing otherwise. I considering the matter closed, but I am communicating with both of you to ensure that everyone is aware of particulars. I have already spoken with Mister Nikolov, and he has graciously agreeing to offer his protection.

Should anything happen to me or anyone else in my family, he will be taking matters into his own hands. We will cleaning up mess ourselves.

We waited about ten minutes, and then two email responses came in, one from Pyotr and one from Gino. Both said the same thing: AGREED.

"Well, that should keep Gino off your back for a while, and once I finish up with what I'm working on, it won't matter."

"How close are you?"

"A week, maybe two. Most of the pieces are coming together, but there are a couple more I need to fit in before I move."

"Don't dawdle. This sort of thing will only work for a while. Eventually Gino will either get a chip to play, will get impatient, or both. The only reason this worked at all is because of the business deal. If that goes away, so does the protection."

"I understand, old friend. Look, if you ever get nervous, call me, and I'll set up anyone and everyone in a safe place till it's all over."

"As I said, we should being fine for a while."

"Okay. I'm getting out of here. I'll leave the way I came." I turned and walked toward the door.

Yvgenny paused and then finally said, "About that, Justin …"

I stopped in my tracks.

"We will talk about who you really are when this is all over, yes?" he asked.

"You got it." I said and walked out without turning around. "Don't tell anyone about this, will you?"

"You're secrets are mine, *old man*," Yvgenny said sincerely. "I would die to keep them."

I paused at the top of the stairs and tilted my head back, turning halfway. "Thank you, Yvgenny," I said somberly. "I'll tell you everything and more once I've buried DiMarco."

I walked down the stairs, out the front door and onto the patio. Closing the door behind me, I walked over to the garden and dug away some of the dirt along the same wall as the door. I exposed the palm reader I had installed below the surface of the soil several years before, placed my hand on it and ran through the combination for my loft. I covered the spot up with dirt again, walked over to Yvgenny's front door, pushed the door jam and stepped through it into my loft, with Mag close behind, and waited for Rachel to come home.

I had no doubt Yvgenny watched the whole thing on his security camera feed. I guess I really do trust him.

Where the Magic Happens

When we got back to the house, Xen was passed out in one of the lawn chairs by the pool. Rachel put a blanket over him and joined me in my room. We explored each other the way only lovers can and fell asleep.

I had set my internal alarm to five a.m. and woke up automatically. I went to the kitchen, not wanting to wake up Rachel, and fixed a pot of coffee while I waited for Marsha. At five-thirty she came out of the bedroom in a Grady's t-shirt and jeans.

I held out a cup of coffee to her. "Good morning. Work?"

She smiled as she walked into the kitchen and accepted the cup of Kona. "Good morning, and yes. Kenny and Jennifer should have already opened up by now, but I want to help them get through the rush at seven."

"Do you still go shooting regularly?" I asked bluntly.

"Every couple of weeks." She looked a bit surprised at the subject change … and curious. "I joined the club at the LAX Shooting Range last year. I even made some money on the side betting against the other club members, but they stopped. No one was willing to cover the odds anymore." She smiled. Her father had been a Seal sniper and taught her everything he knew about the use of firearms. She'd even proven it back in Vegas when I first met her.

"I have a favor to ask, but this one you have to feel completely free to turn down. It's dangerous and could get you killed. I'm asking because I know you could do the job, but I can work any number of things out if you don't want to do it."

"Justin, you know I'd do anything for you. I'm still alive because of you."

"I know, but that's not what I'm talking about here. There's really no reason for you to get involved in this…."

"What do you need?"

"I need a sniper … one who can kill at least four men in cold blood … and quickly."

"Friends of yours?" she asked, raising an eyebrow.

"Gino DiMarco tried to have Xen killed, so I'm going to bring the world down around the bastard's ears."

"I'm in," she said.

"Are you sure…?" I started.

"I said I'm in. I like Xen. Guys like him are rare. Almost as rare as you. He and I were talking last night while you and Rachel were cooking dinner. He told me a lot about what happened to him the past few weeks. No one should have to go through that, especially the bit about Natalia. DiMarco did that, too, right?"

"Yes."

"Then count me in. That's why you set me and Rachel up to train so hard this week, isn't it? To prep us for this hit on DiMarco."

"You're a smart lady." I said, smiling at her.

"I've been hanging out with you too long," she said.

"By the way, there's a bit of a bonus for you."

"Oh yeah? What's that?"

"DiMarco is the one who sent those guys after me. Essentially, DiMarco is responsible for trashing the gambling parlor."

As thanks, she grabbed me, pulled me down, and kissed me on the lips quickly but firmly. Then she let me go and said, "I have to get going. You can tell me more when I get back tonight. Is it okay if I spend the week here?"

"I hoped you'd be willing. Bring over whatever you need. *Mi casa es tu casa.*"

"Thanks, babe. I'll see you tonight." She went out the front door and closed it quietly behind her.

I stared at the door for a long while, thinking back to how the two of us had met. Marsha was one of the toughest people I'd ever known. Her father would have been proud of her. Thinking of Las Vegas reminded me of something. I'd have to call Papa Balducci in Vegas before I dropped the hammer on DiMarco. Balducci ran the Vegas operation for the Five Families, and Balducci had a soft spot for me. I had, after all, found the psychopath that killed Balducci's niece. The same psychopath that had almost gotten Marsha, which is how we'd met.

Balducci hated DiMarco, and it wouldn't surprise me if Papa would be happy to take DiMarco's little corner of America under his esteemed care.

With Marsha brought into the fold, most of the players were in place. We simply needed to get ready for DiMarco. I headed outside, sat in my favorite spot by the fountain, and worked through the plan again to see if there were any gaps in it.

Eavesdropper

Albert Zajac opened the front door of the condo and walked in. "It's just me," he said. His subordinate lay under a blanket on the couch. A bed, the couch, and some office furniture were all that adorned the small, otherwise empty rental. Albert had won the coin-toss, so he got the day shift to listen in on the subject's house.

He saw the form under the blanket move and heard the quiet snick of a hammer being carefully lowered. He had just gone to the café around the corner to get a large cup of coffee and some breakfast. He'd slept all night, gotten up around four, and greeted his partner on the way out.

"Did you hear anything?" he asked. An arm pointed out of the blanket at a notepad and pen on the table. He walked up to the console, sat down, and read through it.

It detailed the highlights of a conversation between Case and the woman from Grady's. Albert was surprised to learn that the woman was a sniper of some skill. He was even more surprised to learn that Case intended to use her in his assault on the plant. He finished reading the whole conversation, drinking his coffee as he went along. When he finished, he pulled out one of the two breakfast sandwiches he'd bought and chewed thoughtfully.

As he ate, he heard Justin say something through the speakers. The receiver automatically started recording. Albert grabbed the jack, slid it into the port and put the headphones over his ears to listen in on the house a quarter-mile away from the condo.

"Xen? How's the research coming?" Justin's voice came in clear.

Grateful his partner had had the forethought to place the bug when the opportunity presented itself Albert listened in and took notes.

o o o

"Well, I have to admit," Xen said, peeling his eyes away from the computer, "What Shao came up with is truly revolutionary. I had no idea he was this good. It's a shame, really."

"That you ratted him out?" I offered, smiling.

"No," Xen said chuckling. "That he had such an appetite for illegal drugs. He probably could have ended up naming his price at any of the major pharmaceuticals, if he'd stayed the course anyway. He took a shortcut, and it cost him."

"Shortcuts usually do," I said, remembering one of my early teachers. "So what have you found?"

"How it works," Xen said simply.

"Tell me," I said enthusiastically, stepping into the kitchen and starting another pot of coffee.

Xen set the laptop on the coffee table, took his glasses off, rubbed his eyes and stood up. He walked over to the kitchen, took a coffee cup off the small hanging rack and set it on the counter. "You have creamer?"

"In the fridge," I replied.

Xen grabbed the cream and sat back down with it in front of him. "Okay … as I said before, it's a five-step process, but only four of them take place at the plant."

"Really?"

"Yeah. It's really clever, too. What leaves the plant, if someone tried to ingest it somehow, would almost certainly kill them, or at least put them in a hospital for a long time." He put his glasses back on and continued. "In stage one they take the meth and coke and heat them separately to almost two hundred degrees Celsius, which is just past the melting point of both. In stage two, the two liquids are mixed together carefully, because both components are extremely flammable. Stage three requires heating the mixture further to two-hundred-twenty degrees and then gradually adding it to dichloroethylene that has been heated to the same temperature. The dichloro acts as a stabilizing agent to the coke and meth blend, reducing its volatility considerably. It's still dangerous, but not nearly as much as the original drugs at that temperature. Essentially, if you heated the drug mix by itself to around two-hundred-fifty degrees, it would simply ignite. With the dichloro, it can take more heat. Stage four is where the magic happens. The whole mix is heated to three-ninety-five and allowed to cook for a few hours under pressure and with a low electrical current running through it. This is essentially a distillation process, and everything they want joins together into a clever combination of loosely bonded but separate molecules. They distill this off, and that's what goes into the tankers."

"So, is that the T-Rex?" I set out coffee cups for us.

"No. That's what's really clever about all this. What they're shipping isn't drugs."

"So where do the drugs happen." I put in several heaping tablespoons of sugar as Xen smiled knowingly at the excess.

"At the dry cleaners."

"No shit?"

"Yeah. These guys have to have some kind of specially built cooling unit. Basically, you pour this mix into one end, cool the liquid to about negative ten degrees Celsius, and *voila*!" Xen snapped his fingers, "T-Rex crystallizes out of the liquid. The liquid is siphoned off and can be used as regular dry cleaning fluid. It's a little different, but probably just as effective. What's left over goes into west coast party-hounds as T-Rex."

"And soon the world, with Pyotr's help," I said filling Xen's cup with fresh coffee.

"Yep." Xen added cream, a little sugar and took a sip. "Like I said, it's brilliant. I couldn't have come up with it. It's given me some ideas, though. I think I understand why they wanted me dead, though."

I smiled. I'd already pieced that together, but I wanted to hear Xen's version. "Why's that?"

"Well, your stuff, the silicon-based molecule ..."

"Yeah?"

"Well it's cheaper to make, totally non-flammable, more effective, easier to dispose of and, if my calculations are correct, non-damaging to the environment. Silicon is basically sand, and your stuff would simply return to Mother Earth."

"Yeah. So?" I asked.

"Well, it would revolutionize the dry cleaning industry. Every state in the country would legislate requiring it, since your stuff probably isn't cancer causing either. It most certainly wouldn't contaminate ground water and soil the way the tetrachloroethylene does. DiMarco would be out of business."

"Exactly," I said, smiling.

"But what about Nikolov at SolCon? If he is who you say he is, then he'd have even more to lose with the silicon-based version."

"He's a very cool customer, that one. And he used it exactly the way he always intended. Leverage. He's all about leverage. With the threat of the new cleaning liquid, he could force DiMarco into a business deal whether the Italian wanted to or not. You ever read Sun Tzu?"

"Back in college," Xen said, "but I don't really remember any of it. Not my bag."

"Yeah? Well I've read *The Art of War*, and I like it. I'm absolutely certain Nikolov not only read it, he memorized it. Probably could have written something like it. That son-of-a-bitch doesn't make a move against someone until he's certain he's got his victim by the balls with a gun to his head. Then he lets the guy choose between having dinner or getting his testicles cut off. It's an easy choice every time, and Nikolov always wins."

"I bet he'd kill to get his hands on this data," Xen said ominously.

"I'm certain of it." I looked thoughtful for a while as I calculated the implications of Nikolov in the picture. I suspected that Nikolov had orchestrated most of what was going on from way behind the scenes. He also funneled the information about Natalia's project to DiMarco. If I was right, Nikolov was even more dangerous than anyone suspected. "Look, I've got to go do some thinking. Can you start digging into that data and see if you can pull out anything related to where they were shipping to and any other logistics?"

"Yeah. I was just getting into that stuff. I focused on the chemical data first 'cause I figured it was more important."

"You figured right. Now find out anything you can about the operation. I'll be up in a few hours."

I went downstairs and stripped down. I grabbed a blindfold off of the wall and placed it over my eyes. I stepped to the center of the mat and proceeded to go through my forms. There were fifteen of them, and I completed the first cycle at a very slow speed, the motions resembling Tai Chi. I repeated the cycle, increasing the pace. I rotated through them, getting ever faster until my body became a blur of motion.

I let the old me, the predator, take hold and kept the pace for another thirty minutes until my skin turned dark gray and hot to the touch. My skin would turn pitch black if I went long enough. Breathing deeply, I stopped and stood motionless for a few minutes, not feeling anything other than my own heartbeat. My thoughts were crystal clear, and the rational, sensible Justin burned away, leaving Jalin burning like a hot spike within me.

I removed the blindfold, stepped over to the nearest kick-bag and worked it with blurring speed. Elbows, fists, knees, shins, and feet flew into the bag from every direction. I hammered away at it in a hailstorm of blows. The sound became a mantra for me, a rhythm that cleared my mind and allowed the gears to flow freely. I stopped thinking about my body after the second or third rotation of the forms, and motions took on a life of their own, my body doing what it had been designed to do—inflict injury.

Finally, the blows came in slower and weaker. My body ached from the exertion, and I slowly became aware of my surroundings once again. Jalin faded, and Justin drifted back into phase. It's always a strange sensation shifting between the killer and what I've come to realize is the real me. There was a time when those roles were reversed—Jalin had been the real me, and Justin nothing more than a veneer. But the past couple of decades had allowed me to shift them, and that shift is what allowed me to have a relationship with Rachel.

I stepped away from the bag and lowered my arms, my breath coming in hard, fast pants that blew off the excess heat.

"Good lord!" Xen said from the stairs.

Jalin leapt into my consciousness. My fists came up fast, and my head snapped like lightning towards the intrusion. My face contorted into a mask of rage, my eyes wide, bloodshot, almost crazed. I stared at Xen for second upon second, my face slowly drifting from rage to one of calm as I forced Jalin back down and Justin came completely to the forefront. My body paled slowly as well, my breathing expending the excess heat.

"What are you?" he asked, a touch of fear and awe carried in his voice. He stepped up to me slowly.

I relaxed my shoulders and lowered my fists finally, stepping away from the bag and facing Xen. "I am what they made me, Xen." A deep, troubled sadness clutched at my insides. It's what Rachel had seen on the patio and what Xen saw now. It was that part of me that had been harnessed by tyrants and used to inflict agony and death upon any who got in their way. "There's something I wanted to ask you."

"What's that?"

"Do you think those Russians we killed deserved it?" I asked.

Xen looked surprised.

"Especially the last one …" I added, "and what I did to him?"

Xen thought about it for a while and then he nodded his head. "Yeah, I guess they did. He certainly did."

"You want to hear something funny?" I looked into his eyes, and he could tell there wasn't any humor there. "The funny thing is that the part of me that killed him … is just like him." I stole my gaze away and looked down, ashamed. "I used to be that guy, Xen. A long time ago, but it was me just the same." I took a deep breath and let it out slowly. "You wanna know why I do what I do? Why I keep going after guys like DiMarco and Nikolov and the people that work for them?" He looked at me expectantly. "It's because of a word not used that often where I come from."

I looked at him again, and I'm sure he could see the guilt in my face. "*Repentance*." He still didn't say anything as he tried to understand. "Xen, please don't be afraid when you see me do what I do. This is as much a part of me as my arm or heart. I could no more change this than you could your gift for chemistry. I've just learned to control it. Does that make sense?"

"Yeah. It does," Xen said, putting his hand on my shoulder in an attempt to comfort me. He pulled it back immediately, astonished at the heat coming off my body. "You're cooking!" he exclaimed and then put his hand back. He peered closely at my face and skin. "You're not sweating."

"Nope. They wrote out sweat glands. Unnecessary with my metabolism."

"Amazing," he said in disbelief. "Remind me to never piss you off."

"I will," I said, running up the stairs. "Come on, let's go for a swim. I need to cool off."

"Excellent idea," he said, jogging after me and pulling off his shirt. "Although I do want to get back at that data."

"Deal."

The First Domino

I swam a hundred slow laps to cool off while Xen continued his research on the laptop from a lounge chair on the patio. My skin turned back to normal, so I got out of the pool, walked past the engrossed chemist, and stepped into my bedroom through the sliding glass door.

"Can you do me a favor?" I whispered in her ear as I kissed her neck.

"Name it," she said, kissing me firmly.

"Do you trust Marsha?"

"Completely."

"Then can you find a way to bring her into the fold about all this? She's going to have to know about the doors, at least. If you can find a way to keep it at that, great, but she'll probably want to know more. Tell her what you have to, but don't offer much."

"Sure. I think I can do that. Why me?"

"Practice. You have to get used to tap dancing around this topic, and I trust her completely. There's little that can go wrong, no matter what you say, and you'll know what it's like to avoid certain subjects."

"I'll do my best."

"I believe that will always be more than enough, Rachel." I smiled and kissed her again. "Marsha will be back in a few hours, and Xen and I have to go take care of some business back at the loft." She nodded as I stepped towards the door. "Oh, one more thing."

"Yes?"

"When you talk to her, do it any place but the kitchen … preferably outside."

"Why?"

I winked at her without answering and went back outside.

As I closed the door, I turned to look at her. My insides ached for her in a way I'd never experienced before, suddenly taken again with the dread of losing her. I also feared her ever seeing what Xen had just witnessed. I couldn't change my nature, even if I wanted to, and the fact is I am very different from humans in many respects. I'm very different from j'Tarians as well, and it pleased me that I would finally have someone to share my life with, beyond Magdelain anyway. I could only hope that Rachel wouldn't ever be too scared to be with me.

I went back out on the patio, and Xen looked up from the laptop, setting it aside on the table next to him. "I have what you wanted."

"Logistics?" I asked.

"Schedules, volumes, and destinations. They're a month old, but the previous month's report isn't all that different, so there doesn't seem to be that much flux. It's simply gotten bigger. Do you think Jackie spent most of his time at the plant or at the downtown office?"

"I looked that up. He generally goes to the plant. I'm guessing because there's a smaller chance of running into anyone. "

"That sounds like Jackie. Life of the party … if he's the only one there, anyway."

"You're not that much different, you know," I said, smiling.

Xen gave me a hurt, *I'm-completely-offended* look and then chuckled. "Yeah, well, I'm much better looking."

"Not with that haircut!" I chortled. His rounded skull had grown a dark layer of stubble. I grabbed the laptop. "Come on."

I headed into the house, and Xen followed.

"Where are we going?"

"The loft. I want to check on Mag, and I need to use one of my terminals." I looked thoughtful for a moment.

"Sounds to me like you're already getting domesticated, mister," he said and chuckled some more.

I rolled my eyes at him.

"*Anyway*," he continued, "I asked about where Jackie spent most of his time, because wherever that is will most likely have the most recent data."

"I was thinking the same thing," I agreed. "That's where you'll be going when we hit the place Sunday night."

"Me?"

"Yep. And you'll be in their office building alone."

"Great," he said dejectedly.

"Don't worry. I've got it all worked out … well, mostly. There shouldn't be anyone in there."

"I thought you said Jackie liked to work nights … what if he shows up?"

"He'll be otherwise occupied. Trust me. And here," I handed Xen the laptop as we stepped up to the front door. I put my hand out on the panel, ran through the combination and pushed the door open into the loft. We stepped through.

"Mag!" I shouted. "Set up with the laptop over there," I said to Xen, pointing to the desk. "And use the chair. I'll stand. Send that logistics stuff to O'Neil, and let him know what's in it. If his guys haven't found it yet, that'll speed things up for him." I headed for the fridge, pulled out some orange juice, prepped it with sugar and guzzled it. "You want something?"

"I'm good," he said, shaking his head.

I pulled out my phone and composed a text as I walked back over to the desk. Mag came bounding in from the closet. "Hey, Mag. You want to spend a few days at the house?"

She shrugged and gave me an *Okay, sure* look.

"Alright, go eat something big, okay? And you'll have to stay cougar while you're there. Marsha's staying with us." Mag nodded and went back out the way she came. I finished the message and hit SEND.

"What are you sending?" Xen asked, looking up.

"Telling O'Neil to look for the data. You send it yet?"

"Going out now."

"Okay, compose a second one to him and give him a detailed description of how it all works."

"You got it." Xen started typing.

I stepped up to my computer, put on the circlet, tilted the monitors so I could see them from a standing position, and powered them up. "Search: VeniCorp systems," I said.

"What are you doing?"

"I'm going to create a user account for you and set up a card. It should give you maintenance and admin access, and then tonight we start setting off alarms at the office."

"What for?"

"Simple. If I disable the system from here any time between now and Sunday, someone could notice and turn it back on. You and I are going to make it look like the system is sending false positives. They'll turn the system off until they can get it fixed, which should buy us the time we need."

"What if they fix it before we go?"

"I'm going to fix that, too. They use ConSek as their vendor. I looked that up while I was researching the VeniCorp hit. Their trouble ticket is going to mysteriously end up at the bottom of the pile. It'll be next week before they complain about it, and by then … well, it won't matter." I turned back to my screens and raced through data, finally pulling up a list of users for the building's door and network access. I scanned it quickly. "Perfect."

"What?"

"Take a look. They've got an Ops guy with fat fingers who is also lazy, apparently."

"How can you tell?"

"Dupe logins with transposed characters. He even did one for Jackie … god, how I love Ops guys. It's guys like that who make my life *so* much easier."

Xen watched as one of the user boxes centered and grew on the screen. I pulled up the keyboard, rapidly typed characters into two boxes for the user SHOAJ and closed out of the box. I opened a drawer and pulled out a pen and sticky, quickly scrawling something on it.

"Here," I said, pulling off the sticky and handing it to Xen. "Memorize this."

USER: SHOAJ
PASS: B@ND1T
DOOR: 1234

"There, see … the *O* and *A* are transposed. Their guy should have eliminated the account. Instead, he gave me a Christmas present."

"Why the funky password?" Xen asked.

"They require strong encryption … needs a special character and a numeral. That 'I' is the number one. Someone on their team knows what he's doing, at least."

I grabbed one of the Prox II cards sitting on the desk and slid it into the imprinter. Navigating to the door system, I pulled up the SHOAJ account and activated it. The light turned green on the imprinter after a few seconds.

"Here," I said, pulling the card out and handing it to Xen. "Don't lose this either." Xen stuck the note to the card, folded it around, and then slid the whole thing in his pocket.

Mag walked into the room, her muzzle and claws stained with blood.

I looked up and nodded. "At around midnight we'll use the door to enter their building, walk around the inside of the office, set off the alarm, and then leave … and do it again at three a.m. Twice tonight, once Tuesday, none on Wednesday and two or three times on Thursday. By then they should disable the system until they can get it repaired."

"Are you sure?"

"I've done this more times than you've had cheeseburgers … and on dozens of worlds. Like I said, Ops guys are the same all over." I smiled and winked at him. "Let's head back. Marsha's probably back from Grady's, and we have to do our workout." I stood up and headed for the door. "We're changing things up a bit tonight."

Xen shot me a questioning look, but I didn't offer more. I hit the palm reader and pushed the door open onto the foyer in my house. "Come on, Mag. The bedroom patio door should be open."

Mag nodded and darted through the door. I watched her tail disappear out onto the patio, heading for my bedroom. Xen and I followed her out to find Rachel and Marsha sitting in lounge chairs, their backs towards the house as they talked and laughed.

"Evening, ladies," I called out.

"Well, if it isn't the man of mystery himself," Marsha said, turning to me and smiling a bit wickedly.

I raised an eyebrow at Rachel, and Rachel nodded back almost imperceptibly as a small smile hooked the corner of her mouth. Marsha didn't pursue the subject, so I would have to find out later how much she'd told Marsha.

"Okay, you all ready for another session?" I asked. They both nodded. "Head on down, ladies. We'll be there shortly."

Xen and I changed quickly and went down to find the two women sparring lightly but with impressive speed.

"Alright, alright," I said, interrupting them. "Stretching! I don't want you cramping up before the fun begins."

They spent fifteen minutes stretching out, and then I walked to the head of the mat. "We're going to pick up the pace tonight, okay. So keep up."

They took their positions, and I ran through all of the forms twice, but at about double speed. They were all breathing heavily when I finished. "Okay, tonight is all about defense in the face of greater numbers. To start, all three of you are coming after me. Observe how I position my body, where I look, and what I do and don't turn my back to … This is about staying alive and buying time, nothing else. The one thing to remember is to use your *ears*. We'll go for a while, and then the three of you will work with each other, two attacking one and rotating through a few times.

The three circled me, and I put my back to Xen, facing the two women. I relaxed my body and held my hands limply in front of me, slouching slightly in a wide stance.

"Full contact, if you please … BEGIN!"

I heard Xen's *gi* rustle behind me, and I stepped forward fluidly. Both ladies shot kicks at my mid-section, and I leapt over in a tumble, coming up behind them as they turned to face me. Marsha came in fast at my head. I blocked to her inside and stepped away, putting Marsha between Rachel and me. Xen came in again with a kick that I sidestepped, stepped back away from as I twisted. All three of them were now in front of me.

They looked at me, clearly impressed.

"Do you see? It's all about movement."

They nodded and came in again.

We worked like that for thirty minutes. Each of them got in a few body blows, and Rachel even clocked me across the jaw, but everything else missed or was blocked by hand, forearm, shin, or foot. As the fight progressed, I developed an even keener appreciation for my students. The three of them wordlessly began working together, becoming a single unit that anticipated what the other was doing. They started to predict where my avenues of escape were and closed them off. It was damn impressive.

My heart swelled with the pride of any teacher whose students start to become masters themselves.

"Enough!" I called out, and they all froze. "Okay, head gear, everyone," I ordered, running my hand over my jaw where Rachel had tagged me.

"Sorry," she said abashedly.

"Don't be," I said earnestly. "It was a solid hit. The three of you were really working well together. You should be proud of yourselves." They all smiled. "Okay, five minutes each. Rachel, you defend first, then Xen then Marsha. Rotate through for an hour. *Light* contact. I'm heading upstairs for a while."

"You're not training anymore tonight?" Rachel asked.

"No … I have to cook dinner for you all.…" I paused and looked at Xen with a sardonic smile. "Besides, I got my workout this afternoon … right, Xen?"

"Yeah." Xen nodded his head and put an understanding hand out on my shoulder.

"Get cracking, you three. Remember, light contact only, but don't go easy on anybody. And watch out for Rachel's right. It comes out like a rail gun."

I left them to their training, headed upstairs and prepared chicken basil pesto over penne. They'd need the carbs and protein after the past two nights.

o o o

"Xen, wake up," I said gently. Xen opened his eyes and saw me silhouetted in the doorway. "It's time to take a visit to VeniCorp."

He rolled quickly out of bed and realized that I wasn't wearing anything. "You're going like that?" he blurted, looking down at his boxers. "I figured we'd need to change into black outfits or something."

I tossed him a pair of the vision goggles. Xen caught them and slipped them over his head, resting them around his neck. "VeniCorp is in the next room, and there's nobody there. I checked the access logs. You can put something on if you like, but I figured you'd want to get back to bed as soon as possible."

"I do." Xen shrugged and followed me out.

We walked to the front door, I ran through the combo, and pushed the door open onto a short hallway and dark office space beyond. We both put on our goggles.

"Hey, these are cool!" Xen said as he looked around, everything looking as if it were in daylight.

"Leave the door open and let's go."

We walked down the short hall and looked around.

"That's the stairwell you'll use to go upstairs where Shao's cubical is."

Xen looked down the hall and nodded his head. When he looked out the window, the goggles magnified whatever his eyes were focusing on. "This feels really weird, you know?"

"What? The goggles?" I asked.

"No. Walking around an office in my underwear … and you! What is it with you and being naked all the time?"

I walked along the cube farm to the right. "I'm not naked all the time." I said defensively.

"You're naked quite a bit."

We strolled around the cube farm to the area under Shao's desk.

"I just like to be naked. Besides, where I come from we don't have the same notion of morality as you Americans. You know, Americans are just about the most uptight people on the planet when it comes to sex and the body." I had reached the far corner of the cube farm and pointed at the ceiling. "He sits straight up there. It's only a two-story building. In an emergency, you should be able to get up on the roof. It wasn't locked last time, and they had patio furniture up there, so I'm betting they keep it unlocked. There's a dumpster on the back side of the building that you could jump down onto if you need a fast getaway."

I made the turn towards the exit and spotted the glimmer of headlights shining from the direction of the sentry building. "Get down!"

We both dropped and crawled the rest of the way out. We came up in my doorway, and I closed it behind me.

"See? Easy peasy." I grinned like a kid.

"You really enjoy this stuff, don't you?"

"I really do," I answered simply. "And you're starting to, aren't you?" I accused.

"Yep." Xen's face cracked into a big, childish grin.

"Go get some sleep. Repeat performance in three hours."

He nodded. "Goodnight," he added and walked to his room.

We did everything again at three a.m. without incident, and the guards at the front gate responded more slowly. I checked the logs when I woke up in the morning and saw that a guard had come into the building shortly after we left, then locked the place up twenty minutes later. He seemed to have taken enough time to search both floors. Satisfied, I went back to my room and lay down next to Rachel. She was still fast asleep.

I lay down, closed my eyes for about thirty minutes, and then felt her move beside me. I opened my eyes, to see her up on one elbow looking at me.

She kissed me. "There's something I've been wondering," she said with a concerned look on her face.

"What's that?"

"Are you completely invulnerable to guns? You don't seem to worry about them at all."

"No, I'm not. Want a lesson in constructed j'Tari assassin anatomy?" I didn't need to tell her this, but I didn't want any secrets between us, and she had asked.

"Sure," she said with a look of curiosity on her face.

"I have three major parts to my brain, whereas you, and most j'Tari, only have the two hemispheres. The third is about the size of a racket ball, sits above the spine, and is incased in a sphere of incredibly tough … well, you'd have to call it bone. If a bullet, or anything else for that matter, goes through it … it's pretty much *adios muchacho* for me. Everything else seals and heals quickly. My skeleton is made of much tougher stuff, too. The swimming pool you know about, but I've been hit by cars and trucks, fallen off a building or three, and even been trampled by a stampede of kaypars." I rubbed the back of my neck, remembering the stampede.

"Kaypars?" she asked, confused.

"They're kind of like a cross between a buffalo and a rhino … only meaner. Delicious, though." I looked into her eyes. "I'm more worried about you, actually. There's something you have to promise me."

"What's that?"

"Always leave me behind."

"WHAT?" She looked horrified.

"Always leave me behind," I repeated slowly. I took a very practical tone, the way other people talked about their job cutting hair or tightening bolts. "Look, Mag and I have been doing this for a *very* long time. We've been in jams you couldn't possibly imagine. If I go down, you tuck tail and run. You understand me? I need you to swear to me."

"But …"

"No buts on this one. When it comes right down to it, working with people like this … like you and Marsha and Xen … I haven't done much of it. It's easier to work my way out of a situation when I only have to worry about myself. You'll be helping me by getting out of there. Now swear it."

She looked at me, searching my face for a long time. "I swear," she finally said quietly.

"That's my girl. You have to trust me."

"I do," she added sincerely. She kissed me hard and hugged me.

Emotional sex is often the best kind, and the two of us proved that before getting up for the day.

Fly on the Wall

I sat cross-legged by the water fountain, looking out at a most pleasant sight. Xen stood out in the middle of the lawn, going through the Tai Chi he'd learned as a teenager and taken up again in recent months. The mid-morning sun reflected off a bright yellow satin uniform as he moved. It had been a gift from one of his teachers back in China. Rachel sat with Marsha, who had taken the day off. They were on the far side of the pool talking about whatever women talk about, and Mag lay behind me in the shade of a tree looking very much like an average mountain lion … for Marsha's sake. I hadn't had time to talk to Marsha about what she knew, so I'd told Mag to maintain the façade.

All was right with the world as near as I could tell, and I was getting used to having people this close to my life. I never had before, and it felt sublime.

I guess I'm getting sentimental as I get older, I chided myself. I reached down and picked up the phone. It was time to set another duck in the row. I stood up, headed into the kitchen, grabbed a carton of orange juice, and sat down at the counter. I hit a speed dial and waited for an answer as I drank directly from the carton.

"Captain O'Neil," he answered.

"O'Neil, it's Case."

"Hey! Thanks for those emails. We've zeroed on the trucking, and we're setting up a sting on most of the dry cleaners."

"That's great. Will you be ready to go by this weekend?"

"Are you close?" He sounded surprised.

"Yeah. In fact, that's why I called. I have a request and a gift all in one."

"Request?" O'Neil was immediately suspicious.

"How'd you like to make your first arrest?" I sounded like I was offering steak to a starving man … which I sort of was.

"I got a hard on for it."

"Okay … That's too much information, but how about you get a warrant for Jackie Shao and bag him sometime late Saturday night?"

"He's the chemist that put all this together?"

"He's your boy."

"Done. I'll square it away with a Magistrate today and handle it personally." O'Neil sounded hungry.

"Can you keep him incommunicado till Monday morning?"

"It'll be part of the warrant, no sweat. We do it all the time."

"Good. Then prep your teams to drop the hammer on Sunday night. Plan on rounding up these guys around ten o'clock?"

"I'll make it happen."

"Thanks, O'Neil." A mountain of unsaid thanks went with it. I had known all along I was stretching O'Neil's generosity—and ability to stay out of something—to its utter limit.

"Hey, we're a team, remember?" he said, meaning it.

"You got that right." I got another jolt of that warm feeling of family that had been surrounding me so much of late.

"Any word on the Audi?" O'Neil asked, changing the subject.

"Nothing yet. Still a wild card, but I'm going with my guts on this one." I looked at the counter where Natalia had been sitting and raised my voice a little as I said, "In fact, I'm doing it this second."

I thought about telling O'Neil more, but we both knew that in police departments there are always guys who talk to people who give them money to share what they know. What O'Neil didn't know couldn't possibly get anyplace it shouldn't. I wasn't worried about O'Neil talking to someone. People like Pyotr have a government office bugged for fun.

"Okay. I just hope I don't have to ID you at the morgue," he added. "Imagine how embarrassed you'll be."

"I guess I'll have to cope," I said and hung up.

o o o

Albert took the headphones off his ears and finished writing down what he'd heard. He read through it again.

"Wake up," he called to the sleeping form under the blanket. "They're going Sunday. We have some phone calls to make, and we need to start getting ready. We're going to be there."

The form under the blanket moved slowly and then sat up.

Albert lifted some papers up off the desk and exposed a vlain. He pulled it out of the sheath and held it to his ear as the whine spun up out of the audible range. He tore off a piece of paper, held the blade of the vlain out, pointing up and slowly lowered the paper down on the edge. With no pressure at all, it passed through the paper, cutting as neatly as scissors.

"Who are you?" he asked, staring at the blade.

Fish in a Barrel

I was waiting in the kitchen again when Marsha walked out of the bedroom. I'd already poured a cup of coffee for her, black the way she liked it, and in a travel cup.

"How's Abby doing these days?" I handed her the coffee.

"So-so, I guess. She told me she almost lost her other job last week because she had been late twice. Her boss sounds like a real asshole, but she says she's kind of stuck there. She never has time to go look for work, and he won't budge on her schedule. Her Bronco is on its last legs, too. Kenny's been late a few times, but I'm not sweating it."

"I figure that thing is about ready for the scrap heap if it doesn't get some love and attention," I said.

"She says they'll just have to start taking the bus when it dies, but I know that will mean she gets even less sleep than she does now. Frankly, I don't know how she does it. She works harder than I ever did."

"Is Kenny scheduled for Saturday morning?" I asked.

"Yeah, why?"

"Because he's going to be late," I predicted.

Marsha raised her eyebrow and gave me a *What-have-you-got-planned* look.

"Someone is going to steal her Bronco early Saturday morning … around two a.m." Marsha got a very confused look on her face. "Do they live in an apartment or house?" I asked.

Looking concerned, she finally answered me. "It's a condo. It's the only thing that her mother left her before she died, and with a hefty mortgage, apparently."

"Does it have a garage?"

"Yeah."

"Are you sure?"

"Definitely. I've dropped Kenny off a few times. Look, whatever you're planning, those kids have it hard enough already. They don't need any more challenges."

"I know. That's part of what this is all about. I'm not stealing the truck. I'm actually buying it. There's going to be a surprise for Abby waiting for her in the garage. It'll be a stack larger than the one you found on your desk."

Marsha smiled and got a little teary eyed. She came around the kitchen counter, grabbed me and hugged me hard, holding it for a long time. She released me finally and looked at me with damp cheeks. "You're a rare breed, Justin Case. I wish there were more men like you. And I wish you were a *woman*. I'd steal you away from Rachel in a heartbeat."

I gasped, feigning shock and surprise. "Oh my god? You're a lesbian? But what about that night we had in Vegas all those years ago?" I sounded hurt.

"You know damn well that I bat for both teams … and that's not what I'm talking about. Stop changing the subject, or I'll kick you in the balls." She was suddenly both serious and sentimental. "You're like Santa Claus, Justin … just tougher and better looking … and *this* world would be a worse place without you in it." She kissed me and headed for the front door. "Don't ever change, Mister *Claus*. Don't you dare."

I smiled, added another tablespoon of sugar to my coffee, a little more cream, and then went to the patio. I sat down in a lounge chair and enjoyed the sunrise, a gentle smile stuck on my face brought about by the absence of secrets.

o o o

"Hi there," Rachel said as she bent over and kissed me. Xen was still at the laptop in the living room while I sat on the porch with a large piece of paper and a hand-drawn and fairly detailed map of an industrial plant.

"VeniCorp?" she asked.

"Yes," I said, squeezing her. "Laying everything out. It's like a chessboard. It lets me work through all the permutations."

"You're the man with the plan, aren't you?"

"Always."

"Did I hear you talking with Marsha this morning?"

"Yes. I had to let her know that Abby would be having vehicle problems Saturday morning, and that Kenny would be late." Rachel gave me a questioning look, so I told her all the details about what I intended to do. Her reaction was identical to Marsha's, except for the embarrassing correlation to old Saint Nick.

When she released me, she looked at me with a serious face. "There's something I've been meaning to ask you … for a long time now. I never did before, because I figured it wasn't my business and my paychecks always cleared." I gave her a sly look as she sat down next to me, having a pretty good idea of what she wanted to ask. "Justin, where the hell do you get all your money?"

"I'll answer this one because it's you, and I won't be holding anything back. But, like everything else, you have to keep this one under your hat. I'll bribe you to silence with a shopping spree. How does that sound?"

"Okay," her grin indicated I was in for another big bill.

I looked her square in the eye and spoke very clearly. "I make it," I said simply.

"Uhh … come again?" She gave me a blank stare.

"I make it," I repeated slowly.

"You're a … counterfeiter?" She looked shocked, almost appalled.

"They're not counterfeit," I said, easily. "They're as real as … well, as real as the real thing. And counterfeiting is such an *ugly* word." Her jaw dropped as she stared at me. "I do have to launder it, though," I added, as if I was talking about business suits. "It helps knowing the people I know … Yvgenny being one of them. Casinos help, too. But I'm quite diversified … well, not me actually, a bunch of people. I have seven different identities I use for banking, houses, insurance, vehicles, that sort of stuff. I'll show you all that later. We're going to have to get you some new IDs as well."

"But how?"

"It's a small e-mat translator. Takes non-living matter and duplicates it exactly. Doesn't work so well with live things, though."

"That's incredible! Does everyone have those where you come from?"

"Oh, hell no. They take incredible amounts of energy."

"Where do you get the power?"

I smiled and winked at her. "I'll show you that, too … but later. Let's take care of DiMarco first."

"You know I hate to wait."

"Yes, I do." I gave her a wink. "One day at a time, gorgeous," I added, chuckling.

"Hey!" she blurted and slapped my arm. "I think you enjoy making me wait just a bit too much." She stood up and glared down at me with a half-angry, half-joking face.

"I'll work on it."

o o o

"Justin?" Marsha called.

Engrossed in my planning, I sort of heard her, but not really.

"Justin!" she repeated more loudly as she stepped up behind me.

Jolted from my thoughts, I turned around. "Oh, hey." I checked my internal clock. "You're early."

"I decided to take the rest of the afternoon off. Light day, and they've got everything covered at the diner."

"That works out perfectly. Have a seat." She did. I'd been meaning to talk to her about something. "There was stuff your dad never told you about, right?" I asked.

"Of course. As a girl, I used to press him on his work, but he'd always brush me off. He finally explained something that I'll never forget. He'd just returned from a mission overseas, and he'd taken a bullet. He had his arm in a sling, and a pretty severe limp. I desperately wanted to know what happened."

"So, what did he say?"

"He said, 'When people need to know, they *need* to know. And when they don't, they *don't*.' He hugged me for a while with his good arm. Then he told me I didn't *need* to know. I never asked him about his work with the Seals again."

"Eloquent as always, your father. I miss him," I said.

"Me too," she replied with a distant, long-healed sadness.

"Well, it's time I show you some things, because you *need* to know. But like your father, this is stuff you can't ever talk about to anyone. If certain people ever got wind of who and what I am, they'd make it … difficult for me."

"I'd never put you in danger, Justin. I hope you believe that."

"I do. It's why you're here and why we're talking. Come on," I said and stood up, heading for the front door. "Mag! We're going home for a while. Come on, girl!" Marsha followed me, and I felt Mag come quietly up behind us from the bushes someplace. "So, what did Rachel tell you about me," I asked.

"She said that we would be using some special technology with the doors to get into VeniCorp and that it came—along with you and that cat of yours—from another world."

"You handled it well, I must say. And you didn't press me for more."

"I spent ten years in Vegas. I've seen it all … well, almost. And I figured you would show me when you were ready. Hell, I always suspected there was something *very* different about you."

I placed my hand on the panel, ran through the combination and looked at her as I pushed on the door. It swung wide, opening on my loft rather than the front yard, and Mag darted between us and ran for the closet.

Marsha stood there shell shocked. Hearing about it and seeing it were two entirely different things. I put my arm behind her and pushed her through. She stepped in and stared around the loft. She'd been there a few times before, but we'd always gone in through the garage.

"Want something to drink," I offered casually. She shook her head with her mouth still open. "Okay … now comes the fun part. Turn around."

She did. I put my hand on the panel, ran through a different combination and pushed it open. She expected to see the house again, but instead, she saw an entirely different living room.

"Go on," I suggested, encouraging her to move on her own.

She stepped through into a room she didn't recognize and, turning around, noticed windows on either side of the door. The windows looked out on a lush, green yard surrounded by a tall hedge covered with orange blossoms. She looked back through the door as I stepped in, still not believing the loft was … and *wasn't* … there.

The door closed, and I led her out back onto the patio where Mag sat in the shade, waiting for us in her green and gray stripes.

"Welcome to Costa Rica," I said and spent the next hour telling a still stunned Marsha most of what I'd already told the other two.

o o o

Tuesday night was almost identical to Monday. We went through the forms, some three-on-one training, and a long session of two-on-one amongst the three students. After that I checked in with O'Neil to make sure that the cops were on track with bagging the dry cleaners and shutting down that part of DiMarco's operation. So far, the bugs they had on DiMarco's people, including DiMarco himself, were quiet. No one in DiMarco's organization seemed to know that anything was coming down the pike.

At two-thirty a.m. I checked the logs at VeniCorp and woke up Xen. We went on our nightly sneak, but this time we waited on the first level for fifteen minutes to see if the guards from the post came. No one left the building.

"Come on," I said. "Let's go upstairs." I strolled over to the stairwell, opened the door and went up to the second floor door with Xen close behind.

"Wait here," I told him and then ran up the last flight. I checked the door to the roof, and as I hoped, no one had locked it. I went back down, opened the second floor door, and we walked in. I showed him Xen's workstation.

"Why don't we dig through the data now?" Xen asked.

"Not part of the plan," I said, smiling. Xen gave me a bored look, not believing it for a second. "Okay, okay. Because we don't need to, I'll still need you here on Sunday, and because you never know when someone might get tired of the alarm."

Xen spotted something outside. "Here comes one of them." He pointed at a man stepping out of the guard post and heading towards the truck parked outside.

"See?" I said, grinning. "Run!"

We bolted down the aisle, slammed through the door to the stairwell, blasted out through the first floor door and ran through my front door as the truck pulled away from the guard post.

"Can I go back to bed, now," Xen said breathing heavily and laughing as he spoke.

"Yeah. And we're taking tomorrow night off."

"Good. All this REM deprivation is going to give me a psychotic episode."

"We can't have that," I reassured him.

"No, we can't," he agreed.

o o o

We all slept in Wednesday morning, except Marsha who left extra early for reasons of her own. It turned into a lazy day for Xen and me. We simply enjoyed the sunshine.

Later, Rachel and I were in the kitchen, putting the finishing touches on homemade lasagna, when Marsha walked through the front door with her backpack and a long gun case. Rachel slipped the foil covered pan into the oven as Marsha set the case down on the kitchen counter and dropped her pack on the floor. She flipped open the three latches of the case, and Rachel and I stepped around to take a look. Xen came in from the patio to see what was going on.

"I'd like you all to meet Whisper." An immaculate XM 110 sniper rifle with bi-pod attachment and night-vision scope lay inside, the whole unit set perfectly into a declivity in the foam. Also set into the foam rested a Beretta pistol with a military insignia on the grip. Marsha lifted up a corner of the foam and exposed not one, but two silencers. The first was more slender than the other, and it looked as if the foam had been hand cut to fit the much bigger cylinder.

"Is that the 93R?" I asked, referring to the pistol.

"Yep. My father's ... a gift from an appreciative general. The extended clip holds thirty-nine plus one in chamber. It has single-shot, triple-burst, and full-auto. It weighs a ton, but the triple hits like a freight train. The full auto is really just for scaring people and wasting ammo, though."

"Do you need to sight in the rifle?" I asked, running my finger across the larger silencer.

"No. I went down to the range this morning and dialed it in … I did it in the dark, too."

"They let you on the range with those silencers?" I knew damn well the silencers were uber-illegal, and most shops would call the cops the moment they saw one.

"I worked out something with the owner's daughter when I joined the shooting club. She's my age. She's a … *friend* of mine," Marsha added with a naughty grin. "She let me in early this morning before they opened so I could sight it in with the big cylinder."

"How much range do you loose with the big one?" I asked.

"Conservatively, abut thirty percent. Will I be dealing with anything longer than 450 meters?"

"About half of that, max … most of it inside a hundred meters, and all of it down-angle."

She turned to us with a wicked grin and deadly confidence. "Fish in a barrel." She closed the case, set the case on the sofa, and looked around the remains of the cooking preparations. "Lasagna?" she said hungrily.

"That's right," Rachel replied with a nod.

"What's the occasion?" Marsha asked.

Of Bait and Traps

It's show-time for you two," I said, putting my hand on Rachel's shoulder and winking at Marsha. "Everyone go get ready. We're starting early tonight."

We all left the kitchen and met downstairs with our gear on. We went through a lengthy stretching session—I wanted to reduce the likelihood of injury—and then the forms. All through the session I caught Rachel and Marsha eyeing each other. They were hungry to see which one came out on top.

"Go get headgear, ladies," I called out at the end of the forms, "and mouth guards." They went over to the cabinet, pulled out the padded headgear, and buckled them on. "Three rules, ladies. One, no bone or joint breakers. I need you both to be able to dance Sunday night. Two, the first one to three points wins. Three, if you make your opponent say *maté*, stop immediately and enjoy your victory. Am I understood?"

"Yes!" they shouted together, facing me. Xen stood off to the side, watching closely. The two women bowed to me then to each other. They quickly moved into their stances, legs wide, hands up, eyes focused. Marsha used closed fists while Rachel held her hands loosely. Both of their faces were stoic, chiseled out of stone.

"BEGIN!" I shouted.

Marsha came in fast and hard with a series of punches at Rachel's face, driving Rachel back. Rachel slapped each blow to the side, shifting her head left and right out of the way, drawing Marsha in. On the fourth punch, Rachel quickly sidestepped and shot out a sweeping kick under Marsha. Marsha jumped … too late. Rachel clipped her heel, and Marsha went down on her side as Rachel lifted her other leg to bring it down on Marsha's mid-section. Marsha rolled out of the way and up into a squat. She moved into a ready stance before Rachel could move in closer.

Rachel leapt forward with a front kick to Marsha's chest, which Marsha stepped out of then came around with a back-fist at Rachel's head. Rachel ducked out of the swing and came up right into Marsha's other elbow. She managed to get a partial block up, but the elbow crashed into the side of her head and sent her sprawling.

"Point, Marsha!" I yelled.

Rachel rose slowly, shook her head to clear the stars, and moved back into her stance un-phased, the way she'd been taught.

They faced each other again. Marsha came at Rachel again with a flurry of punches. Rachel backed up exactly as before. On the third punch, she blocked hard with a punch at the incoming arm, knocking it wide. She moved in like a cobra, driving a series of blows into Marsha's mid-section and coming up hard with an uppercut.

Marsha staggered back, stunned.

"Point, Rachel!" I yelled. "Get to the center of the mat!"

The women shifted and took up their stances.

"BEGIN!" I shouted.

Rachel came in low with a fast front kick, forcing Marsha to drop a hand to block. Marsha punched with the other hand, but Rachel ducked out, stepping to the side, blocking Marsha's punch and pushing it away. She came in hard with an elbow aimed at Marsha's head, but Marsha stepped away from it. As she moved back, Rachel stepped into her with a back fist that Marsha had to get both arms up to block. She blocked her own vision, and Rachel came in with a roundhouse kick that caught Marsha in the mid-section. It knocked the wind out of her and sent her backwards, but she didn't lose her footing. She took her stance quickly, even as she struggled to recover her breath. I nodded, impressed with them both.

"Point, Rachel!" I shouted.

Rachel charged in, sensing weakness, but Marsha was ready for her. As Rachel kicked, Marsha caught it in both hands and twisted hard, forcing Rachel to drop to her side and yank her foot back out of Marsha's grasp. The moment Rachel hit the ground, Marsha jumped and landed on Rachel's back, driving a fist into the back of Rachel's head and bouncing her forehead off the mat. Marsha automatically cocked her fist but stopped before I had to say anything.

"Point, Marsha!"

Marsha stood up and helped Rachel up off the mat. Rachel nodded to her, acknowledging the solid move.

"Back to the center ladies. This next one is for the money."

The women took their positions at the center of the mat. Marsha went straight into her hard stance with fists raised. Rachel, her nose red with the impact with the floor, set up in a wide, horse stance, her open palms resting gently on her thighs.

I raised an eyebrow. I'd used the technique but never shown it to any of them. Essentially, I leave myself wide open, inviting my opponent into a trap. It requires lightning reflexes and quick thinking. I intended to show all of them how do to it, part of the reason I'd gotten them working on the pure defense technique on the first night.

Marsha sent in a low roundhouse at Rachel's leg. Rachel lifted the leg easily, avoiding the kick, but did not move otherwise. Marsha came in with a front kick that Rachel blocked and stepped away from. A jumping front kick came in at Rachel's face that she leaned out of, and then a flurry of punches that she blocked with open palms. She stepped back only when she had to and made no attempt to counter attack.

Marsha came in again, harder and faster this time, starting with a front snap kick and then a series of punches and elbows at Rachel's head and chest. All of them encountered forearm and hand blocks or empty air.

Marsha edged in closer, an inch at a time with her feet, arms tense and fists clenched. She shifted her weight forward and sent a blazing front kick at Rachel's hip, hoping to knock her off balance. Rachel saw the shift and twisted as the foot came. Before it had gone past her waist, she stepped into Marsha and brought up a fast inside back-fist that caught Marsha square in the face. Rachel brought her knee up into Marsha's belly hard and raised her arms up beside her face to block any counter attack, but none came. Marsha flew back and went down on one knee, coughing.

"Point, Rachel! And match!"

Rachel rushed over to Marsha. "Baby, are you okay?" Marsha gasped for breath but nodded her head and smiled. She held up her hand as she regained her breath. Xen and I stepped up, and Rachel had her arm around Marsha's shoulders.

"Nice knee," Marsha finally said when she'd gotten her breath back. "I took the bait, didn't I?"

Rachel nodded her head. "I'm sorry…."

"Don't ever apologize in here," Marsha said finally. "This is about being the best … always. I'll get you next time, now that I know about the baiting."

"You'll have to show me that, too, Rachel," Xen said. "But not now, I've had about enough for this evening. I'm gonna go for a swim until we eat dinner. You kids have fun." He gave me a funny sort of smile that I didn't understand.

"Xen, can you pull the lasagna out of the oven? It should be ready." Rachel asked as the ladies took their headgear off.

"You got it," he said, halfway up the stairs. I heard him close the door at the top of the stairs. We normally left the door open during the training sessions.

Both women looked at each other the second the door closed. In a flash they grabbed me by my arms, each wrapping a leg behind one of mine, and pushed, holding on tight as I went down.

"Hey!" I hollered, but they were all over me. They used every grappling move I'd ever taught them to subdue me, and it quickly turned into a tangle of arms and legs, with both women on top and pinning me.

"What are you two doing?" I asked, struggling, but not really trying to get away.

They both kissed me on the mouth, everyone's lips touching, and the women's tongues sliding into my mouth. Nothing could have taken me more by surprise than that. The women pulled their faces back and looked down at me. My face froze in shock, my eyes wide, a bewildered smile on my face. I blinked a few times.

"Uhhh …" I said, not knowing what to do or say next. "Umm …"

Marsha and Rachel looked at each other and grinned wickedly. "Did we just make him speechless?" Rachel asked, clearly delighted.

"I think we did," Marsha said with seductive hunger in her voice.

"Oh, that's perfect," Rachel beamed. She leaned over and kissed Marsha, pressing their lips together for long seconds.

"Oh my god!" I said, blushing as I looked at both of them, still not comprehending what the hell they had in mind.

"I've never seen him blush before," Marsha said and laughed. Rachel joined in the laughter as they peeled my bodysuit off.

"Hey! Wha-what … what are you doing?" I asked as they helped me up and led me to the steam room.

Rachel turned the steam on, and both women peeled out of their clothes as I stood there in awe, a wide, idiot grin spreading across my face.

They grabbed me by the arms and pulled me into the steam room. Their giggles turned to something else, and for the next hour, I thanked the universe for all things female as Marsha and Rachel devoured me. I did my best to give as good as I got, but in the end, I'm pretty sure I lost the game, set, and match.

Lucky me.

The Last Duck

Friday afternoon I set Marsha and Rachel up with the door combo the same way I had Xen, and then I took everyone to the house in Costa Rica. I treated them to a magnificent dinner and fine wine at the hotel. Laughter and talking and friends being friends filled the evening. No one had a care in the world, which was the point of the exercise. As the waiter set down dessert and poured coffee, Rachel got a serious look on her face.

"Justin, I don't mean to sound morbid, but this feels like a last meal." Everyone got very quiet very quickly and stared at me with questioning looks.

I looked at each of them confidently and then nodded. "This is tradition. My father taught this to me, and now I'm passing it on to you. What we're planning is loaded with risk. You never know what's going to happen, no matter how much you plan. So, rule number one is to always do something like this before doing something like that."

"You seem to have a lot of rule number ones," Xen observed.

I smiled but carried on unperturbed. "It's called being alive, and have any of you ever felt this alive?" Slowly, a smile appeared on the face of each of them, and as they looked at each other, the smiles grew, feeding off one another.

"No," they said together.

"I wouldn't go back for anything," Rachel added, winking at me.

"Good. Now finish your dessert. I have one last surprise for you all."

They finished dinner slowly, sharing laughs and pleasant conversation. I paid the considerable tab and then led them into the casino. I reached into a pocket and handed each of them two stacks of hundreds.

"Go enjoy yourselves, and don't worry about losing. When you don't care about the outcome, things usually go your way, right, Xen?"

"Absolutely," Xen replied, quietly.

"I'll be out on the patio till you're done."

They each headed off in a different direction. Xen made a beeline for the baccarat room, Marsha angled over to the crap tables, and Rachel went to try her hand at poker. I paid a visit to my friend Julio, bought a half-dozen Esplendido's and ambled out to the patio where a Latin jazz band played. They'd just finished a set and were drinking beers and smoking cigarettes. I walked up to the guitarist and whispered a request in his ear, slipping a hundred in the guy's shirt to accentuate the request. The guitarist smiled, nodded his head, and said it would be a few minutes.

I sat down at a corner table close to the jungle and away from the crowd. I clipped one of the cigars, lit it up, and leaned back, soaking in the beauty of a Costa Rican night. The band picked up their instruments, and the guitarist said something to the band. They smiled and nodded in my direction. The guitarist strummed his guitar and they went into a flawless rendition of "Blues for Salvador" by Santana.

I let the music wash over me and thought about my friends … about my life. I'd never been truly happy before. I mean sure, I'd been happy … like folks at a barbeque are happy, but not really, deeply, truly, soul-felt happy. Ultimately, the friends I'd had up until now, the times I'd enjoyed, it could all be categorized as merely contentment. I enjoyed my work, too, but the sensation of happiness was something I hadn't expected to enjoy as much as I did. The band wrapped up the song and went back into the normal set for the tourists. They played a solid set, and I was lighting up a third cigar when Rachel peeked out onto the patio. She spotted me and walked over with a sullen look on her face.

"Lose all your money?" I asked, smiling.

She straightened and flashed a gigantic smile. "NO! I won! You and Xen were right. I didn't worry about losing and played the way you taught me. I brought four guys down … cleaned them out!" She opened her purse at me, revealing several stacks of hundreds. "Forty-eight thousand," she whispered. She reached in and pulled out one of the stacks to hand to me.

"Keep it, silly. It's all yours. Consider it a bonus for putting up with me all this time."

"It was worth it," she said and kissed me. She sat down next to me, grabbed the last cigar, and accepted the clipper I offered. She cut it, and I lit it for her, watching her draw hard until the tip burned bright red. "We really could get killed Sunday night, couldn't we?"

"Yes," I replied seriously. "There are going to be lots of guys with guns, including DiMarco. And I'm pretty sure they won't be happy to see us. Under those circumstances, there's usually gunfire. But don't worry. The three of you should be mostly out of harm's way."

"I know, but you'll be neck deep in it."

"It's what I do," I said flippantly. I sobered a bit. "The truth is, I enjoy it. It's when I feel … I don't even know … It's like living my purpose, fulfilling it. And it's *righteous* now. I don't know if it's me … or what they programmed into me, but god, how I love it." I'm sure I had a strange look on my face, almost possessed, and I could see that at first it frightened her. But I think she quickly realized that this is who I am and probably always would be. She put her hand on mine, and we relaxed for a while as the music flowed over us.

Two hours later Xen and Marsha came back, both moderate winners, and we headed back to L.A. I put Rachel to bed and said I had to go take care of something. She looked as if she was about to ask something, but then I think she remembered Abby's car.

o o o

"I thought I heard someone pull in last night," Xen said to my backside.

I was waist deep under the open hood of a beat up '73 Bronco, hunched over the fender and twisting on something with a wrench.

"Yeah, I barely got it home. It'll be right as rain in a few hours, though. Wanna help?"

"I don't know a thing about cars," Xen said sheepishly.

"Well, come learn. And bring me those spark plugs on the bench … in the packages, not the dirty ones."

Three hours later, I got into the driver's seat, turned the ignition, and grinned satisfactorily as the motor hummed to life. No cloud of smoke, no sputtering, just the smooth rumble of eight tuned cylinders working perfectly.

o o o

I closed the bedroom door and lay down on the bed next to Rachel. I pulled out my cell phone and smiled at her as I dialed Information and put the phone to my ear.

"Las Vegas, Nevada," I said and paused.

She moved over and put her head in my lap.

"The Maltese Hotel and Casino," then another pause.

Rachel looked at me with a questioning look.

"The business office, please." I put my hand on her waist and waited.

"Yes, good morning. Could I please speak with Papa Balducci?" A pause later, "I know he doesn't usually take calls. Please tell him that Sam Spade is calling … Yes, from the movie. He'll know who it is … Thank you." I listened to some forties big band music and heard switches clicking in the background.

"Justin, is that you?" an older man asked in a thick Brooklyn accent.

"Hey, Papa. How the hell are you?" I asked with genuine friendliness in my voice.

"Old, but not tired. My doctor says I gotta lose weight and stop smoking cigars. I told him to go fuck himself, that pansy, piece-of-shit-bastard. What does he know?"

I chuckled. "You haven't changed a bit, Papa. It's nice to know there is still order in the universe."

"I told the family to bury me with a fucking cigar in my mouth. But enough bullshit, Justin. You didn't call me after all this time just to trade how-do-ya-dos, did you?"

"Direct as always," I said, "and no, I didn't"

"So what's up?"

"What are your feelings towards Gino DiMarco?"

"That MOTHERLESS NO GOOD PIECE OF SHIT!" I yanked the phone away from my ear as Balducci went on a rant. "If I could stab that son-of-a-bitch in the fucking throat with a pencil for lunch it wouldn't be too soon. I swear to Christ, that arrogant bastard is *ruining* the L.A. operation … and giving the family a bad name on top of it all!" Balducci calmed down in a heartbeat. "Why do you ask?" he asked in a tea-cozy sort of way. I always suspected Papa was a bit bi-polar.

"So there's no love lost between you two? I remember you weren't fond of him back when … well, you know." I didn't want to bring up bad memories of Balducci's niece.

"Love? I'm gonna piss on his grave when he finally goes. I'd help him along myself, but the Five Families won't let me."

"And what about the Five Families?"

"They pretty much hate his guts, too. He's into some new shit and starting business with people he shouldn't. But a made man is a made man."

"The Russians, right?"

Balducci paused. "I see you still got it, kiddo. Always into shit you shouldn't be and knowing things you shouldn't know. So what's this all about?"

"It's about *permission*, Papa."

"Are you asking me for permission?"

It was my turn to hesitate. Balducci and I shared a bond that went back seven years, and it ran deep. But unlike Yvgenny, Balducci was still neck-deep in the mob. He was as much a dangerous gangster as DiMarco. "Yes," I finally said. If it wasn't granted, I'd have two choices. Either give up the assault on the plant or have the Five Families after me, including Balducci.

"Is this business or personal?"

"A bit of both. Two friends killed, and he put a contract out on me. He's getting in bed with Pyotr Nikolov to go international with T-Rex. I've already had to deal with a Russian hit squad he sent along with his love." I didn't let on that Xen was still alive. "If I don't do something, he's going to bury me out in the desert along with a few more of my friends."

Balducci paused for few seconds. "Let me get back to you, okay? I'll call you on this number in fifteen minutes."

"I'll be here." We hung up.

"So, who's Balducci?" Rachel asked as I put down the phone.

"Oh, he's just a guy who owns a casino in Vegas." I said innocently.

"Don't you dare pull that tap dance crap on me! How the hell do you know so many gangsters?"

I smiled. "My business is what it is. However, I don't know Balducci because he's a gangster. I know him because he's an uncle."

"What does that mean?"

"Did you ever read about the Arroyo Grave Digger about seven years ago?"

"Yeah. I remember that. Something about serial murders in Vegas. They went on for a year or so. Then they just stopped. Nobody ever found the killer."

"That's not entirely true." I looked at her sideways, not really wanting to go into any details but also not willing to keep secrets from her.

"What do you mean?"

"I mean, Balducci's niece was one of the first women killed, and Marsha was almost the last one killed. That's where I met both Marsha and Balducci. And someone *did* find the killer." I gave her an evil grin.

Rachel got an astonished look on her face.

"You? You're the one who ended the killings?"

I smiled at her. "You should talk to Marsha about it one of these days. She'll tell you the whole story."

The phone rang, and I picked it up. "Hello?"

"You've got your permission," Balducci said with a satisfied chill in his voice.

"Thank you, Papa. I really appreciate it."

"I'll be the one thanking you. You get this done, and you've got a penthouse in the hotel any time you want it … for life. Just tell the front desk that Sam Spade is there for his room, and they'll hook you up."

"Thanks again, Papa." I smiled. "I don't know how to thank you."

"Cut that shit out, boy-o, or I'll kick your ass. Now go take care of business. You'll be doing me a favor. The last thing we want is to be in bed with those crazy fucking Russians. And stop in to see me the next time you're in town."

"You got it." I put down the phone. "One more duck in the row," I said to Rachel and kissed her. "Come on … let's go out on the patio and go over everything again."

o o o

At ten o'clock on Saturday night I went over the finishing touches of the plan with my team, and we *were* a team, now. Looking around, I was truly impressed with what these people were prepared to do and convinced they were more than capable of doing it. We all sat around the patio table, Mag lying under it looking up at us through the glass. I kept looking at my watch as I went over each step and what the alternate options were in situations where things didn't go as planned.

"Hey, Justin," Xen interrupted as I was talking about some of the firefight possibilities.

"What's up?"

"Well, you keep talking about firefights in exactly the same way we talk about getting fast food.… None of *us* are bulletproof." There was genuine concern in his voice.

I thought about what he was getting at. "Shit. You're right. I got so wrapped up in this…." I said, more than a little embarrassed.

"I understand, really I do. We all know you've got about a thousand things to figure out, but is there anything we can do?"

My phone rang.

"Don't worry, I'll take care of it. Thanks, Xen. Good thinking." I answered the phone. "O'Neil. We got our package?"

"Under wraps. They're taking him downtown now. We won't arraign him until Monday at the earliest, and since I was the arresting officer, I'm going to probably not show up until Tuesday. No one will hear from him before that. You're still a go, right?"

"Yep. You?"

"It's all staged. We'll start dropping them at ten tomorrow night if that's still the plan."

"It is."

"Whatever you're doing, Justin. Good luck."

"Not a factor, O'Neil. I'll call you when I'm in the clear. You'll probably already know where to go by then, though."

"Will you tell me what you're doing?"

"No. You need plausible deniability."

"Good point," he agreed. "What I don't know now, I won't have to arrest you for later."

"See you on the other side, O'Neil."

"Yep."

"And O'Neil?"

"Yeah?"

"Let's be careful out there." I hung up the phone and looked around the table. "Would you all excuse me for a bit? I have to go dangle the bait in front of DiMarco."

I got up and went back to my bedroom. Facing the monitors, I slipped the circlet over my head and navigated to Ricky Petri's workstation. However, rather than logging on as PETRIS, I logged in as SHAOJ. The desktop appeared, and I fired up the mail client. I spent a few minutes reviewing Shao's email to see if anything interesting had come in and to also pick up the right style I would need to make the email sound genuine.

When I was ready, I composed an email to Gino DiMarco.

Gino,

Meet me tomorrow night at the plant around ten. I've been looking over the expansions and have concerns about future output capacity. I'm working over the numbers and will have a full report ready when you arrive. Meet me at the cookers.

Shao

I sent the email, logged off of Shao's account, logged back into Ricky's account to reset the username, and then logged out again. I pulled out my cell phone and hit the speed dial for Yvgenny.

"Da?"

"Hi, Yvgenny. How are the repairs?"

"Everything is back to normal. The guy I hired did wonderful work. And the girls wanted me to thank you for them."

"Tell them they're welcome. I mean, technically, I'm the one who got them into it, so I should have been the one to get them out."

"Never thinking of it that way. This is the business we are in, and sometimes bad people pulling our loved ones into it. Now, what's up?"

"Easy one. Can you have three vests ready for pickup tomorrow around one? Mediums."

"I think I have them here. I'll go downstairs and look, but either way, yes. I'll have them when you arrive."

"What are they running these days?"

"Fifteen hundred."

"Fair enough. I'll see you then. Thanks, Yvgenny."

"No problem." I put the phone back in my pocket and walked out to the patio where everyone sat and talked quietly, smiles on every face. *It's all about the smiles*, I thought as I walked up.

"Well, that's the last duck. Shao is going to the lock up and will be on ice till Monday or Tuesday. DiMarco has an invitation to the party, and I'll be picking up vests for each of you tomorrow."

"I especially like that last part," Xen said a bit nervously.

"Don't worry," I reassured him. "Everything's in place. All we have to do is drop an anvil on top of DiMarco, and we can all get back to our lives … especially you, Xen."

"This stuff *is* your life," Marsha reminded me.

"True, but not everything is about me, is it?" They laughed and shook their heads vigorously as I sat down. We finished out the evening over drinks and conversation. I had Rachel go through the relevant door combos she'd need as we talked. When she had them down pat, we broke up and everyone went to bed.

Sirens

I had left around eleven a.m., gone to my loft, and taken the Chrysler to Yvgenny's. I said hello to Yvgenny's granddaughters, graciously accepted their thanks, and told them it was my pleasure. The repairs were, as Yvgenny had said, simply lovely. I could hardly tell where the shotgun blasts hit. Yvgenny had the vests, and I asked about Glocks. We went into the basement where he kept his inventory, and the old Russian let me pick out what I wanted. It was a fast drive back to the loft where I gathered what I needed out of the van and grabbed my black coat and boots. I also had to go into my ship's cargo hold to get two extra pairs of goggles for the ladies. Tucking everything away, I returned to the house via the front door.

I handed out the vests to each of them when I walked into the living room. Mag trotted along with me. I tossed two Glock .40s with silencers onto the sofa as well, each in a shoulder holster, and followed those up with two extra clips apiece.

"Compliments of Yvgenny," I said. "I thought you might feel more comfortable with those, and you never know when you might need one. Only handle those with gloves, please, and make sure you're wearing them tonight."

Wearing rubber gloves, Marsha had Whisper out and several boxes of 7.62 Match rounds lying in front of her. She examined each one and buffed the tips with ultra-fine sandpaper, taking off any burs and scratches exactly as her father had shown her. As she finished each one, she'd slip it into a waiting clip. There were two completed clips on her left and three waiting on the right.

"Here, you'll need these as well," I said. I reached into the backpack and pulled out the goggles for Rachel and Marsha. Xen still had the pair he'd used for our night visits to VeniCorp. "Xen, here's the detonator. You remember what to do, right?"

"Yep," he said with certainty. He slipped it into the black pants he would be wearing.

"One last thing." I handed out earbuds identical to the ones I'd used when Natalia and I had spied on Pyotr. "Commlinks. Nobody talks unless they have to. Xen, you're our eyes on the ground, Rachel, you're eyes in the air. Call out when you see anyone but me, and tell me how many and which direction they're going. I'll take care of the rest. If you hear me say get out, that's the drill. No matter what, you all understand me?"

"Yes," they said in unison. Rachel gave me a comforting look. "I promise," she added stoically.

"Okay, let's go over it one more time. As soon as the sun goes down, I'm heading out. Turn the music up loud on the patio and party your asses off, okay? In the unlikely event that the neighbors peek over the fence, tell them I'm out getting beer or something."

The moment the sun went down, I checked the building log to make sure the alarm was still off and that no one had gone in. Satisfied it was clear, Mag and I headed out the door. I could tell everyone was nervous as I walked out to the garage, but it didn't worry me. In fact, I'd have been surprised if any of them wasn't nervous.

I fired up Abby's Bronco—I'd rigged it so the ignition didn't need a key—pulled out and drove exactly the speed limit all the way to the plant. I used the same dirt road as before, killing the lights as soon as I left the highway. My goggles let me see what I needed. I parked the Bronco, lining up roughly where I thought the back door of the office building would be, and got out.

Putting on my black jacket, I cinched up the ankle straps and made sure I had all of my gear. A quick jog across the desert showed me that I was dead on. The back door of the office building lay directly in front of me as I came over the rise. Mag paced me, and we made an invisible approach through the desert night.

The compound had changed somewhat since my last visit. The double row of tanks in the southeast corner was still there, but they'd extended it another six columns towards the office building, taking up both the dirt field and parking lot that used to be there. The parking lot was now on the north side of the building and wrapped around the front. As I watched, I noted that they'd doubled the patrol around the perimeter from two pair to four. I had to assume that there were more armed men inside as well.

Drug dealers are so touchy about protecting their product, I thought. There were still only two men in the guard building by the front gate, though. That was something, at least.

I spent an hour circling the entire facility at a fast jog to see if there had been any more changes. I spotted a new pumping station up against the row of storage tanks that had pipes running between itself, the tanks, and the main lab. Beyond those, towards the office building, someone had parked a white van, and two fork trucks. As I continued around, I noted a similar pumping station on the west side of the lab that connected pipes between the lab and the main facility. I could blow the whole thing right now if I wanted, but that wouldn't give O'Neil what he needed. I would have to do it the hard way.

It was nine-fifteen when I got back to my original position. Mag and I jogged down the hill towards the building as a pair of guards passed by the back door of the office. I would have to work quickly. The next set of guards turned the far corner of the storage tanks as I slipped the pack off and pulled out a spool of what looked like sticky fishing line.

Grabbing the end stuck in the notch of the spool, I pulled out a few feet and dangled the end of the line near a link at the bottom of the fence. It drifted up against the link and stuck to it like a spider's web, invisible in the darkness. Pulling more off the spool, I stood up and traced an arc with the line over the surface of the fence as high as I could reach and then down again about ten feet to my right. The line adhered to the chain linking of the fence as soon as it touched the steel. When I got to the ground on the other end of the arc, I pulled the line firmly, snapping it with about three inches extra that lay in the sand.

I looked to my left and saw the guards about halfway down the line of tanks. With time to spare, I opened the pack and pulled out a small gray case that snapped open, revealing what looked like large white grains of rice or small capsules. I carefully removed one and closed the case, slipping it back into the pack. Getting down on all fours, I peered at the bottom of the fence where the three inches of line were hanging off and stuck the capsule firmly on the end of the line.

I grabbed the pack and stepped away from the fence, silently moving across the desert towards the two guards coming at me. I stopped and crouched down about twenty feet from the fence as they walked by. Pulling out the gray coil of zipper, I waited for them to get near the corner of the building and stepped up to the fence. I uncoiled the zipper, laid it on the fence silently and pulled the fob up, opening a gap in the fence. I stepped through, and Mag darted past me across the open space between the storage tanks. I pulled the fob down, closing the fence behind me. I grabbed the end and pulled it off of the fence, the material of the splitter seeming to ooze through the chain linking.

I followed Mag into the shadows of the towers as the next set of guards came into view around the corner.

I pulled out my phone, typed in "NOW" and sent it to Rachel's phone. Mag and I worked our way south between the storage towers and came out behind the pumping facility, well hidden in its shadow.

"I'm in," Xen's voice came in over the commlink.

"Get in position and start working on the computer. Copy everything you can. Keep an eye out for the limo. It should be here soon." I couldn't see Xen from my position, but I'd be able to see the arrival of the ladies. I stood up in the shadows, peered over the top of the pumping station, and focused in on the top of the tower. This was the risky part. A small light over the door illuminated the area. The rest of the platform that went around the top was dark. However, if one of the snipers happened to look for those few critical seconds, it could get hairy. From my position I could only see the top of the door. I saw the door open outward and then close.

"We're through," Rachel's voice came in crystal clear.

I scanned the entire compound as quickly as I could, starting with the snipers on top of the lab. Nobody moved. In the darkness above, I could see Marsha step up to the railing, take her bearings, scope in the four men on the roof below her, and then step back up against the superstructure. Rachel needed to stand on the other side of the tower, watch Marsha's back, and be the eyes in the sky if something went wrong on the ground.

"Marsha, call out when those two on the south perimeter turn the corner," I said as I watched the two men coming towards me along the fence line. "When you call it out, drop your four."

"I can't see the very end," she replied with a slightly worried tone. The two men had cleared the end of the restricted building and were at the halfway point towards the corner of the perimeter.

"Guestimate," I offered. "Xen, is the yard clear?"

There was a pause. Finally, he said, "Yes. You're clear."

"Get ready, Mag," I whispered as we moved around the pumping station and stepped into the clear. The men passed my position, slowly walking towards the corner. I waited about fifteen seconds.

"Go now," Marsha said calmly. The rifle whispered.

I darted out, pumping my legs as fast as I could. I hadn't taken ten steps when I saw a camouflage military cap come over the edge of the lab roof and fall to the ground on the other side of the high wall that enclosed the building.

"You lost a hat," I said as I ran.

"Sorry. Nothing I could do. It's around the corner from the entrance. There's no one walking the inner perimeter, so we should be fine. Targets are down."

"Nice shooting," I said as I dashed between the two fork-trucks and crouched down. "Xen, all quiet?"

"Clear …" There was a ten second pause. "Wait … Car coming in."

"Places, everyone. Here we go," I said. "Walk me through it, Xen."

"Car is approaching the gate … a limo … guards out … one in front of the limo, one at the back window … the one at the window is talking … nods his head … more talking … shrugs … nods … hands over walkie-talkie to someone in the limo … more talking …

nods … both guards head to booth … gate up … limo through and heading your way … *quickly*. The guards are back in the booth, talking. One is talking into walkie-talkie, and the other is picking up the phone."

"Shit, I think we've been made," I said.

"How?" Xen asked, perplexed.

Seconds ticked by.

"Shit!" Xen yelled. "Four guys just came out of the main facility and got into a car by the gate!" I could hear Xen's breathing get rapid. "They're hauling ass straight for me!"

"Stay calm, everyone. I factored this in as a possibility. Marsha, you see a head on the perimeter or in the compound, put a bullet through it. Work from the outside in and try to drop them out of view from the others. Make sure DiMarco can't see anything till he's out of the limo."

"Roger that," she said.

"Rachel, spot for her and listen for anyone coming up after you."

I watched the limo come down the pavement at me as I crouched behind the fork truck. Marsha's rifled *whispered* again.

"The car is coming right for the building!" Xen blurted. "Holy shit!" he shouted as he saw one of the windows of the guard building erupt inward. The guard with the phone dropped straight down, and the other dropped practically on top of him behind the desks.

"Guards at front gate down," Marsha said calmly. "Rachel, we've got company coming up … six flights down."

"Xen, get the data and get out. Can you make the door?"

"I'm copying the data now, and no. They've got machine guns … they'd probably hose me before I got through it …" A few more seconds passed. "Copy complete."

More whispers.

"Two guards in the northeast corner down," Marsha said.

As the limo passed by, Mag and I crouched and stepped in behind, pacing it as it approached the gate. Both the steel gate and the garage door began opening.

Xen's voice came in over the comm. "… Oh Jesus … the back door … I hear voices … Marsha, do all four in front have rifles?"

Another *whisper.* Someone hit an alarm somewhere, and a harsh siren blared through the entire facility.

"Yes … and I nicked one in the shoulder as they went in. He dropped the rifle, and it's lying by the car."

"I have an idea," Xen said suddenly very calm.

"Don't do anything stupid, Xen. Get out of there." I looked inside the lab for the first time and saw four men in cammies standing on top of an inner building.

"Trust me…." Xen said mimicking my own tone, which didn't make me feel any better.

"Mag, go help Xen!" I hissed as I paced the limo into the inner compound.

Mag bolted.

"Xen, when they come upstairs, go out the back window and make a break for the Bronco. Mag is on the way."

The limousine pulled into the restricted building and came to a stop. The garage door began rolling down. I looked around for what I could use as cover, but there wasn't much.

Whisper. "Two down, south east perimeter," Marsha said.

I winced as the sound of a machine gun going off in a small space blasted through my earpiece. Then all sound cut off for a few seconds.

o o o

Xen, his back to the wall, waited outside the elevators. The doors opened and a barrel slid into view. In a flash, Xen grabbed the barrel and spun into the elevator, using it as a shield and smashing into two men. The gun cooked off, the burst splashing bullets through the wall and ceiling. Sparks flew everywhere, and Xen felt several shards of metal nick his face. The man against the wall bled from the face as shards of metal tore through him. Xen's ears were ringing, and he couldn't hear a thing, but training kept him focused.

The third man in the elevator raised his own barrel, but the blade of the letter opener Xen had picked up off Shao's desk disappeared quickly into the surprised guy's left eye socket. An instant later Xen sent a hard knee up into the groin of the man holding the other end of the M-16 gripped tightly in Xen's hand. The gun came free as the guy doubled over with a harsh grunt. The one with the letter opener stuck in his eye slid down the wall and collapsed in a heap, his M-16 clattering on the floor.

The other man, his face covered in blood and still stunned by the hail of bullets that had entered the wall right by his ear, never saw the butt of the rifle crash into his temple. His body hit the floor. Xen stepped back and looked at the man still doubled over in the elevator. Then he looked at the M-16 in his hands, suddenly aware that he held it. The burst he fired caught the guard directly in the chest.

Ears still ringing and completely deafened, Xen turned and ran for the opposite corner of the second floor.

"I'm okay," Xen said, breathing heavily. "Three down in the elevator."

O O O

I breathed a sigh of relief when I heard Xen's voice. "Marsha, open an upper window for Mag," I said calmly, but dread gripped my insides. A machine gun burst from somewhere below the two women sent ricochets bouncing throughout the upper structure. Then the garage door blocked my view, sealing me in. A standard-sized steel door stood to the right of the garage door, but I still had to get my evidence, kill DiMarco, and set the fuse.

"I'm hit," Marsha said calmly but in a strained voice. "Rachel, you got that guy?"

O O O

Rachel had already moved down the stairs and made her way around the corner two flights below Marsha. She spotted the man with the M-16 and fired her Glock twice into his back.

She heard a sound behind her and ducked, spinning reflexively as a two foot crowbar crashed into the steel wall of the tower beside her. A big man crashed into her, slamming her into a thick steel support column holding up the outer walkways of the tower. Her Glock clattered down onto the steel grate flooring.

She gasped for air, but before she knew it, her elbow came down onto the man's collarbone with a resounding *CRACK!* He howled in agony. Her hands dropped down to his hair, grabbing tight. She lifted his head and then brought his face down hard into an upcoming knee that crushed his face. She lifted his head again and brought it down into her other upcoming knee with a sick, wet crunch. She twisted hard, planting her feet, and heaved his limp body into the railing. His body slithered over the side, followed a few seconds later by dull thumps against steel piping.

o o o

I heard a body boom as it fell from the tower and hit the piping outside. I was terrified it might be one of the ladies. "Everyone check in," I hissed.

"I'm good," Xen whispered.

"Mostly good here," Marsha said calmly, but I could tell she was in pain.

"Fine here," Rachel said, gasping somewhat.

"Hey, there's something behind the limo!" one of the guards yelled from atop the inner building in front of the limo.

"Everyone out. NOW." I whispered urgently.

o o o

Xen triggered the detonator. A ten-foot arc of light flashed across the fence, accompanied by a loud bang that echoed throughout the facility. The detonation filament cut a hole in the fence, and the severed circle of chain linking collapsed to the ground.

An M-16 burst came over the radio when Xen shot out the back window directly above the dumpsters at the back of the office building. The rifle clicked, empty, so he threw it aside.

He pulled the Glock and dropped onto the steel lid of the dumpster with a massive *BOOM!* Jumping down, he hit the ground running and sprinted through the cut section of fence. He raced across the sand at full speed. The back door of the building slammed open behind him, and two men shouted for him to stop.

o o o

Rachel turned around to look at the man who had first swung at her. He'd exchanged the crowbar for Rachel's Glock, and pointed it at the center of her chest. Fear clutched at her guts, and she tasted copper.

"That vest ain't gonna help you much when I shoot you in the face," he said as his arm rose.

The first triple-burst from Marsha's Beretta hit him just forward of the elbow, slamming his arm downward and forcing the Glock to go off into Rachel's side. The next triple-burst caught him in the lungs, heart and head as Marsha let the recoil lift the barrel.

Rachel bounced off the railing and hit the steel deck, clutching at her side and gasping for air. It felt like someone had hit her with a sledgehammer, and she couldn't catch her breath.

Marsha came down the last few steps, limping as she stepped over the man she'd shot. Both women heard footsteps running up the stairs behind Marsha. She turned and fired another burst from the Beretta, and the rounds ricocheted off the steel railing. She heard a yelp from below, and a man screamed. She quickly stepped up to Rachel and did her best to help her up.

"Come on, baby, we have to go back up," Marsha said. Rachel nodded and slowly got to her feet. Her breath slowly came back to her, but her whole side hurt. The two of them scrambled up the stairs. Marsha flipped the selector of her Beretta to full auto and emptied a clip down the stairs below. She heard men scrambling as she changed out the empty clip for a full one. They got to the top, and Marsha picked up Whisper. She set the barrel on the railing and scoped out the compound.

"Marsha," Rachel said, pulling at her arm. "You heard him. We have to go."

"But I can bag a few more," Marsha said confidently, despite a bullet in her leg.

"We have to go," Rachel said in a calm but commanding tone.

Marsha's face went from stern to one of defeat. Her shoulders slumped slightly, and she hefted Whisper off of the railing.

"That's it, Rachel," I whispered over the comm. "Call Yvgenny as soon as you get back. He can get a doctor for Marsha. Don't worry, I got this. *Trust me.*"

"I do," Rachel said, sounding more confident than she probably felt. The two women stepped up to the door. Rachel lifted the sign covering the palm reader, ran through the combination, pushed the door open, and lowered the sign again. She helped Marsha through and then closed the door behind her.

o o o

Xen saw the shadow of his body in front of him as one of the men trained a flashlight on his back. He ran harder, pushing himself to the limit, trying to at least make the cover of the ridgeline. The scream of a bullet zipped by his waist, the crack of the gun shot coming right on top of it. Another scream-crack of a bullet went by him. He was almost there, another thirty feet to the ridge. Xen's left leg lifted up from underneath him, breaking his stride, and the crack of the gunshot that brought him down filled his ears. The Glock went flying out of his hand into the darkness, and hot pain screamed through his thigh as he spun and dropped into the sand.

Xen rolled on his back and scooted backwards up the hill away from the men now walking towards him, wincing with each move as his leg bled. The two guards approached slowly. One guard held a flashlight that blazed in Xen's eyes. The other held an M-16 casually across his belly.

Crap in a Hand Basket

I quickly scanned what little of the lab I could see from behind the limo, which wasn't much, and I heard the four men on the roof of the lab, fanning out. No Smoking and Flammable signs were set on almost everything, and I flashed back to what Xen had told me about the volatility of damn near every container in the building. I briefly considered charging the four guys with the machine guns, but the odds were one of two things would happen.

Option one was that one of about a hundred bullets would hit that sweet spot in the middle of my skull, and I wouldn't get to kiss Rachel again. The other option was that one of the bullets would ricochet into something flammable and we'd all go up together, in which case I wouldn't get to kiss Rachel again.

I rejected both options as unacceptable. If I absolutely, positively had to pick one of the two, I'd go for the second option, because I *really, really* wanted to kill DiMarco, but I wasn't close to making that kind of decision … yet.

Looking down, I noticed that everything sat on heavy-duty steel grates, with a concrete sub-floor about six inches beneath my feet. A panel of light switches lay to my right just this side of the standard door. One length of conduit ran up from the panel, over the garage door and straight into an electrical panel on the far wall behind about thirty more drums marked flammable. A series of other conduits shot straight up the wall and spread out to all of the lights in the ceiling on this side of the building. There was also a panel to open the garage door next to the light switches. I heard a car door open behind me and peeked quickly around the driver's side of the limo. Four more men with machine guns walked out of the inner lab building. I saw a giant bank vault to the left of the lab and concluded that's where they keep the raw coke and meth. A plan popped into my head, and I had to move now.

I opened myself to the darkness and let Jalin take hold. Putting my hand around the vlain, I smiled as it spun up. I reached into a pocket and grabbed a flash-bang just as the driver figured out that the engine was still running. The driver put it in gear with a *CLUNK* of the transmission ... *presumably reverse*, I thought. I pressed the buttons on either side of the ball and tossed it over the car.

Three things happened at once: the flash-bang went off, blinding the shooters; I darted to the right, raising the vlain; and the engine revved crashing the limo into the reinforced garage door and stalling it out. Three machine guns opened fire at the area near the back of the limo where I had been, the bullets bouncing easily off of the heavily armored car.

Men shouted to cease fire and something about explosions and stupid fuckers. That's when I slashed the vlain through each of the conduits above the light panel. The front half of the building went into darkness, and I dashed behind the blue, plastic 55-gallon drums stacked in the corner. The driver tried to fire up the limo, but it wouldn't start. I heard a window open on the limo.

"Stop shooting and use your fucking tasers, you morons!" Gino screamed from inside the car. "You want to kill us all?" The driver tried to start the limo again and failed. They all slung their rifles and pulled tasers from their belts.

I took the stiletto blade of the vlain and slowly pressed it into the side of one of the drums about two inches above the steel grate flooring. It slid in slowly, the hyper-vibrating blade easily working its way through the plastic. I wiggled it around to create a bigger opening. The semi-sweet fumes filled my nostrils. I worked faster, punching holes in seven more drums. I heard men moving in the darkness. I peered through a gap in the barrels. Three of the four men on top of the building moved towards the stairs near the vault, and the four from the lab spread out around the drums where I hid.

"Hey, do you guys smell that?" one of the men asked, but it was exactly too late for all of them.

I moved, nothing more than another shadowy blur in the darkness, stepping up to the first guard. I grabbed the hand with the taser and slashed up with the vlain from crotch to throat, opening him up. I stepped to the left, putting the disemboweled guard between me and my next victim. He gurgled as his mouth filled with blood, and the next man in line pivoted and fired the taser. I let go as the taser shot into the gurgling man's back. His body stiffened, blood spurting in a fountain from his gaping chest and coating me in slick crimson.

Fast as a cobra, I reversed direction, stepping around the upright corpse and bringing the vlain down across the second man's wrist. The hand came free, and I hit him in the chest with a hard palm strike, shoving him backwards into the next man in line. They tumbled down together in a heap, and the handless man screamed. I leapt to the right towards the drums as the fourth man's taser went off. The prongs shot by me and ricocheted harmlessly off the curved side of a drum.

I placed my foot on the side of a barrel and pushed up hard, lifting off the ground and coming down with a diagonal swipe across the fourth guard's chest from shoulder to abdomen. I saw the third man untangling himself from the handless one, so I spun to my left, bent down and punched him hard three times in the forehead. The spikes tore through his skull into his brain, pressing deeper with each blow, and then the untangling stopped.

I looked up and took stock of the situation. Three of the remaining four men were on the steps, one at the top, one in the middle and one on the bottom, and all of them scanning the shadowy corner of the building blindly for a target. The fourth man stood by himself on top of the lab, highlighted by lights at the back of the building.

I pulled another flash-bang out of my pocket. I'd be safe from a fire as long as it didn't bounce back down near the floor. Priming it, I closed my eyes and tossed. With a *BANG!* it blinded the man on top of the building and the one at the top of the stairs. I dashed across the floor towards the stairs.

The imbecile had turned to see what had exploded, and the stiletto of my vlain entered silently into the back of his head, protruding out through his mouth. I wrenched it out with a gruesome twist, grabbed his lifeless body, pivoted, and pushed away from him as a taser barked. The man on the middle of the stairs stepped back in fear, but I was already moving up the far steps towards the blinded man on top. For a brief moment the lights at the back of the warehouse outlined my camouflaged body.

A taser I hadn't accounted for sounded off behind me as I reached the top of the stairs, the vlain raised to kill the man in front of me. I felt the prongs sink into my back, and my body went rigid as electricity coursed across my hypersensitive nervous system. My momentum carried me past the man I'd intended to kill.

Reaching the end of the taser cables, the prongs ripped out of my back as I fell over the side of the building, losing consciousness.

"I GOT HIM! I GOT THE SON-OF-A-BITCH!" Gino's driver shouted from the open car door.

The man on top of the lab looked down at my shadowy, motionless form. "What the fuck is that?" he said, looking down at a mottled, nearly transparent outline.

o o o

Xen stared at the men before him, standing a short distance from the crest of the hill. The flashlight shone at his feet, so he could almost make out their faces. His heart pounded, his head spun, and his leg below his right butt cheek throbbed with pain. The thought occurred to him that people always say their lives flash before their eyes when they're about to die. All he could think about was how much his ass hurt.

"Thought you were gonna make it, didn't you?" the guy with the flashlight said in a whiny voice. "Too bad my buddy here is a crack shot."

The man with the rifle smiled wickedly as the barrel of the M-16 drifted towards Xen.

Xen stared at the gunman, eye-to-eye, not willing to show any fear. His stoic face turned to one of surprise as the man's eyes exploded outward, and the left side of his skull came apart, splattering his friends head and shoulder with blood and brains. The guy with the flashlight turned his face directly into the round that blew out the back of his skull. A figure with night vision goggles and a desert Ghillie suit came out of the darkness and stood above Xen, staring down at him for a few seconds.

"Here, put this on it," the woman said with a familiar accent, dropping a combat bandage into his lap. Her voice was muffled, but Xen swore he recognized it.

A low growling rumble rose out of the darkness behind the shooter who spun quickly. She raised the rifle, her head swiveling to find what had made the sound.

Xen recognized it immediately. "Don't shoot! Please!" he shouted. The rifle lowered, and the shooter turned to him. "She's with us, I swear … Mag, come on over here."

Mag, looking like a cougar, came slinking out of the darkness and took a position between Xen and the shooter, growling.

"It's okay," the shooter said. A gloved hand reached up and lifted the night-goggles and Ghillie suit so Xen could see her face.

Xen could only stare.

Chemical Burn

When I came to, four burly men in tactical gear held me suspended head down over the rotating blades of an industrial sized grinder. White dust coated the blades, and the smell of cocaine blew up in my face. I tried to move but only managed to wiggle a little. Under normal circumstances, I might have been able to break free, but I was still wonky from the taser.

"Oh shit," I said.

"Oh shit is right," DiMarco growled. He pulled out a cigar and bit off the end. "I'm glad you're awake. I finally got you, Case. Now you're going to pay for what you did to Bennie."

I tore my eyes away from the grinder and looked upside-down at DiMarco. We were inside the vault. There were a dozen crates on either side of the entryway piled high with plastic bags full of white powder on one side and semi-clear crystals on the other. Two large hoppers, one on each side of the grinder, were full of drugs. Augers underneath pushed the narcotics into the grinder. There were three other guards with M-16's standing between me and the door, and Gino's driver stood next to the mobster, my vlain in his hand.

That could be a problem....

"You sure you want to do this?" I asked. I needed to buy some time.

"Case," DiMarco said, "I've never been so sure of anything in my fucking life." He lit the cigar, eying me thoughtfully. "Flip him over. I want him to go in feet first."

"If you drop me in there, every person in the lab is gonna hear me go. You can't tell me all of those people are willing to be accomplices to murder." I tried to move a bit, but the guys holding me still had a firm grip and my muscles felt like noodles.

"Everyone's gone, Case. The fire hazard was reason enough to get them to haul ass out of here without an argument. And there isn't a man in here—" he motioned with the cigar at the guards around the vault, "—who hasn't lost a friend or three to your meddling."

Every head in the room nodded.

"Hell, I could sell tickets to this little show. Right boys?" DiMarco added with a chuckle.

The men nodded again, chuckling in a most unsympathetic manner.

"Now turn him over … nice and slow. We don't want the bastard getting lose, do we?"

I took a deep breath and let it out slowly. The four men tightened their grips and then slowly turned me over. I'd been in some bad fixes before, and Mag usually was there to save my ass, but I had no idea where she was. There wasn't much she could do in this scenario anyway. She'd get shot to pieces before they dropped me into the grinder, anyway. At least Rachel and Marsha had gotten out. I could only hope Xen made it, too. It occurred to me that I needed to work on my planning a little better. Things were so much easier when I worked by myself. And I *was* a little out of practice.

The sliver of a shadow moved in the doorway, a mottled form, but it looked like the head of someone wearing a Ghillie suit. *A wild card*, I thought. If it was who I thought, I had a chance. An idea took shape in my head.

I faced the wall, my feet held together over the grinder. I could survive some pretty severe injuries, but once that little sweet spot at the base of my skull hit those gnashing metal teeth, I was a goner. I looked over my shoulder at DiMarco.

I raised my voice as I spoke, "You know, if the lights were out in here we would be having a very different sort of conversation."

Gino thought about that for a second. "You might be right. It's too bad for you they're not." Gino looked at the men holding me. "Lower him in … slowly. Let him savor those last few seconds like they were a lifetime."

"It's gonna make a hell of a mess in there. What about all your drugs?"

"I'll have someone hose what's left of you out of there in the morning. I might even pay them triple overtime. It'll be worth it knowing there's nothing left of you but a puddle of blood and shit."

They lowered me towards the grinders, I struggled, but only weakly. Three feet … two feet … *Come on,* I thought. *Hit the god damn switch!*

"Goodbye, Case. It's been a real pain in the ass knowing you." The smile on DiMarco's face made me want to tear his arms off and watch him bleed out.

The lights went out and the scream of the grinder cut off, the rotors slowing rapidly.

"*What the!—*" men shouted in the darkness.

Jalin took over, and I let him flow through me like liquid fire. I twisted with every ounce of strength I had. My four captors shifted to the left as I twisted, moving my body away from the grinding blades below. I felt an arm break free. The men around me discovered they had a tiger by the tail. They were nearly blind, but I could still see well enough to jab my fingers into the eyes of the man holding my leg. He screamed and let go. I brought a knee up into the belly of the man holding my leg as the others tried to grab at me in the dark. With a *WHOOF* of air forced from his lungs the man let go of my leg.

"Shoot the platform!" DiMarco shouted.

I dropped to the steel grate and rolled sideways, knocking one of the guards over as I went. Then the room filled with gunfire. The strobe of multiple muzzle flashes turned the room a flickering orange. The three guards still standing on the platform screamed as bullets ripped into them and I rolled down the steel steps.

I came up beneath the barrel of one of the guards, grabbed the muzzle-grip, and dick-punched him as hard as I could. He squealed like a piglet and dropped to the ground, wrapping his entire body around the agony flaring between his legs. The shooters on the sides figured out that where the trouble was and tracked their aim towards the screaming. The beauty of human eyes is that when they go from bright to dark to flickering muzzle flashes, they're pretty much as useful as cauliflower in a gun fight. Rifle in hand, I dropped to the ground and tumbled towards the nearest gunman. As I came up, I spotted the shadows of DiMarco and his driver darting out through the vault door. I heard someone slap a panel outside, then a buzzer sounded, and the door started closing.

"Dammit!" I growled. I punched the nearest guard in the throat, heard him gurgle, and then hurled the rifle as hard as I could towards the last guard. The stock caught him in the temple and he went down hard.

The door was nearly closed.

I leapt, turning sideways in mid-air, and sailed through rapidly shrinking space. My body brushed against the door and jam as I passed through, nearly pinned in the gap.

With a massive *BOOM!* the door slammed shut behind me. Something yanked me up short.

I turned to see my coat caught in the door. I yanked on it once just as something hit me hard in the mid-section. I *WHOOFED* with an impact as pain lanced through my insides. I looked down and realized someone had stabbed me in the belly.

I looked up to see DiMarco's driver holding the weapon just as a hammering fist crashed into my temple, smashing me back into the door. I slid to the floor, and pressed a hand against my seeping belly wound. Shaking my head, I tried to focus on the driver, but all I could see was a big blurry shadow.

"Cut his head off!" DiMarco shouted. I spotted his blur standing in the doorway of the limo, using the door as a shield.

DiMarco's driver raised the vlain, ready to slash down at me.

Where the hell is the guy in the Ghillie suit?

Still dazed, my reflexes kicked in as the driver approached. I swung my leg hard into his ankles and brought him down. The guy was good. He'd already rolled out of the way as my heel slammed down where his head had been. Blood poured from my belly, but the driver didn't give me time to worry about it.

He rose in the semi-darkness, moving in slowly with the vlain held in front of him. He was obviously a knife fighter, and the thing looked far too comfortable in his hands. I tried to stand, but got caught up in my coat. If I kicked out or swung at him, all he'd have to do is block with the vlain. I'd end up dicing myself into little pieces. That thing would cut through me as easily as it did everything else.

"Fuck," I grumbled, looking around for an easy way out. I quickly realized I'd have to do it the hard way, and it was going to hurt. In one motion I pulled my knees to my chest and punched downwards with both fists. My knuckles hammered into the grate, cutting the flesh to the bone, but the force propelled me up a foot. I twisted my legs underneath and stood against the wall.

Blood poured down the deep gashes across my knuckles as I waited for the bastard to come at me. Pinned as I was, at least he'd be overconfident. I couldn't dodge worth a damn, which meant only one thing. I put my back against the vault door and waited. I thought about trying to slip out of the coat and rush him, but to do that my arms would be pinned behind me long enough for him to open me up like a side of beef.

"Double or nothing," I said, goading him on. I came up in a rather stiff fighting stance, the best I could manage pinned against the door like that. Now all I had to do was stay conscious and not lose anything important.

DiMarco's driver smiled as he approached. "I'm gonna fuck you up," he said. "I'm the one who trained Tommy. He was a punk compared to me." He raised the vlain and slashed at my head. I ducked beneath it and threw a punch at his face, but he stepped back, looking for an opening. He slid in slowly, keeping his feet on the ground. As he came within reach, I feinted a kick at his mid-section and pulled it up short to keep his down-swing with the vlain from taking my leg off.

I had only one way to end this. I took a deep breath, lowered my hands, and gave him an opening a mile wide. I focused first on the vlain and then beyond it. His attack would start with his eyes. Life may be about the smiles, but violence begins with the portals to our souls.

A flicker, his eyes narrowing, shifting left then right. A microscopic twitch.

The vlain moved in towards my shoulder. I threw out a weak block, enough to make contact with his forearm, which I knew he would pull back. He spun, arm extending as the vlain came around to take what he thought would be an exposed side.

I stepped out, my coat coming taut ten inches from the door. I reached up and grabbed his wrist as it came around. I placed my palm at the back of his neck and twisted, using my coat as leverage. With every ounce of strength, I smashed his face into the armored steel door with a wet smack and crunch of nose and cheek bones. With one hand still gripped around his wrist, I grabbed a handful of his hair and smashed his face into the door a few more times as his body went slack. I let him slide down the wall as I pried my vlain out of his hand.

Gripping it, I slashed down and cut myself loose from the door. As I turned I heard the receiver of a pistol slide back and snap click into place. DiMarco stood in the door of the limo with a .45 pointed at me.

"You motherfucker," he growled. "Now I've got you."

I held still. "DiMarco, if you miss me, you could blow the whole place up."

"I'm a pretty good shot, Case. I won't miss, and this thing has soft nose hollow points. They'll make a mess of your insides, but they ain't coming out the other side."

"I would not do that if I were you," a deep voice said from the far side of the limo. The words echoed through the facility as a shadow moved towards the door. It was the sweetest sound I'd ever heard—next to Rachel's voice, of course.

DiMarco and I turned to see a man in a Ghillie suit moving towards the doorway. He had his Kalashnikov pointed at DiMarco.

"Now drop the weapon!" he ordered. The way he said it had law enforcement written all over it.

"Empty threat pal," DiMarco said. "Like Case said, one spark will blow the place sky high."

"It would, but I too am a very good shot, Mister DiMarco." He sighted down the rifle. "From where I'm standing, the bullet will go through your head, pass through the glass of those labs behind you, and settle somewhere safely inside." His finger moved to the trigger. "Besides, I am in the door and you are not. By the smell of things, you would not want to run across here if there was a fire, yes?" He paused and let that sink in. "I will not ask again."

DiMarco slowly set the weapon on the grating at his feet. His face was so red I thought he might explode.

"Please come here, Mister Case."

Who was I to argue?

"Perfect timing, Albert," I said, stepping away from the vault door and into the open. My rescuer's head tilted to the side. I slipped out of my now ruined coat, wincing at the still bleeding belly wound, and draped it over my shoulder. With my free hand I pulled my goggles down to dangle around my neck. My head ached a bit, and I felt a little dizzy … but it's a lot better than being dead. Jalin slowly receded into the background. "Hey, Gino, maybe you should get back into the car and relax."

"Mister Case …" Albert said, concern filling his voice.

"Trust me."

"Case! This isn't over, you motherfucker!" Gino screamed as he got into the car. He slammed the door as I stepped up to Albert.

I scolded the fat Italian. "Temper, temper, Gino. You'll give yourself an aneurism."

"What if he has a weapon in there?"

"Gino's not stupid," I said quietly. "He'll wait for his lawyers at this point."

Albert nodded. "How did you know it was me?" he asked, keeping the Kalashnikov aimed at the limo.

"That's a long story," I replied.

"We should not talk here, then." Albert said. "Come outside while we wait for the police." He backed up to the door, his rifle never wavering.

"Police? I came here to kill that piece of shit," I said indicating DiMarco.

"I am aware of this. Please. Come outside and we can discuss it."

"Alright," I muttered. I walked with him towards the door.

Albert opened the door and motioned for me to go through.

I stepped halfway through and then stopped dead. "Oh, wait, I want to do one more thing before they take him off to jail."

Albert sighed and shook his head. I walked over to the massive black vault door and stared at the electronic keypad set into it near the edge. I reached into an inner pocket and pulled out a small, gray device that looked like a calculator but with fewer buttons. I placed it over the door keypad and hit a button. An amber light flickered on, and some characters appeared in a small screen. I hit a few more buttons, and the amber light went purple. I stepped back and watched characters flicker by quickly on the readout. A few seconds later something buzzed and clanked inside the door. I grabbed the device and put it in my pocket as the door slowly swung open. I stepped around the door and walked inside, slipping my goggles up over my eyes.

I already had what I needed, but I wanted to scan the area one more time, and record clear images of the interior with my goggles. With the evidence in hand, I walked out the door, hitting the close button on the panel. The hydraulics spun up again, and the massive door slammed behind me as I approached the limo.

"Gino?" I smiled and used an excessively friendly tone to talk to the doomed gangster.

"Fuck you, Case!"

"I wanted to say goodbye. It's unlikely I'll see you again except on TV, okay?" He didn't say anything. "Okay. Goodbye then," I said cheerfully and waved like a child. "One last thing … you *really* should stay in the limo until the police come."

I turned around and walked back to the doorway as Albert stepped out into the night. I brushed my left hand against the concrete wall as I stepped through the door.

Albert closed the door behind us and pulled off the headgear of the Ghillie suit. I casually drifted away from the door.

"Come on over here, Albert," I said, continuing to drift towards the steel gate. "It is Albert, right?"

"Those are the credentials I am using, yes."

"By the way, you didn't happen to cut your way through the fence near here, did you?"

"As a matter of fact, I did. Straight towards the fence, over near the gate. Why? What's wrong?"

I quickly stepped out through the open gate and looked. "Ahh, I see," I said, spotting the opening.

"What's going on, Mister Case?" Albert was clearly curious about the need for haste.

"Oh, nothing," I said, trying to sound innocent. "What did you use to cut the fence?" I had a funny feeling I knew the answer.

Albert reached into the Ghillie suit and pulled out a vlain identical to the one now in my belt.

I smiled. "From the truck, right?" I held out my hand, motioning with my fingers and drawing Albert closer to me and away from the warehouse. "Can I have it back?"

Albert walked up to me, placed the vlain back in the sheath and handed it over.

"Thank you." I smiled and peered back at the lab door. "By the way," I said casually, "how fast can you run?"

"Very. Why do you ask?"

We heard the metallic hiss as the burner I'd placed inside the warehouse door cooked off, and we both heard Gino scream. Albert shot me an accusatory look, and I'm sure I looked as guilty as senator in a whorehouse.

"Because ... well ... we should run ... *NOW*!" I shouted as the roar of a bigger fire *WHOOFED* to life inside the building.

I bolted for the hole in the fence-line just as one of the drums inside the lab exploded. Albert was hot on my tail. We leapt over the piping connecting the main facility to the restricted building and dashed through the gash in the fence. The single explosion turned into a string of them.

o o o

A stack of 55-gallon drums ruptured, bounced and sprayed liquid fire throughout the front area of the bay. A flaming drum, propelled by the explosions, flew over DiMarco's burning body, bounced off the limo, and ricocheted across the steel grate flooring into the stack of drums, landing directly below the electrical panel. The flame coating the drum heated the contents to the ignition point. The drum ruptured, dousing the double stack of drums around it with flame. The concentrated fire heated them quickly, and they exploded almost simultaneously.

o o o

"*Justin, we're coming around in the Bronco!*" Xen shouted over the comm.

A massive explosion shot a chunk of the lab's roof into the sky with a bright orange plume of flame shooting into the darkness above.

"From the North side!"

"Where the hell have you been?" I screamed.

"Sorry … batteries got knocked loose," he replied, and I heard the roar of a motor in the background.

"You better *hurry*!" I yelled over the eruptions, laughing as I ran. Albert and I cut right to meet the oncoming four wheeler bouncing across the desert.

O O O

An inferno blazed inside the building, and the liquid that hadn't burned off in the initial explosion poured under the large row of heating columns along the south wall in a flaming torrent, spreading across the floor. It took only seconds to raise the strictly controlled temperatures of the columns the few degrees necessary to ignite them. Another detonation tore out a chunk of the lab's wall, and then the pipelines began to blow like giant, bursting fuses.

The twenty-foot section of pipe connecting the building to the pumping station ruptured, and then the pumping house went, setting the piping on fire in both directions. One length led towards the main facility and the other around the back of the lab towards the long, double row of storage tanks on the north side of the compound. Another twenty-foot section cooked off, jetting higher concentrations of the fluid, and then, when the air to fuel ratio hit critical, exploding and igniting the next section.

O O O

The Bronco, headlights off, came at us hard and fast in the rapidly shrinking darkness being chewed up by the fires and explosions filling the desert night. It bounced over the rocks and dunes, shaking the old frame to the point where I worried for its safety … and ours.

Another section of pipe exploded along the fence line between the lab and the main facility. There were only two left before the pipes disappeared into the interior of the main plant and reached the inner pumping housings. Once it got into the superstructure, things would deteriorate quickly.

The Bronco came straight at us, and Xen sat in the passenger seat. The driver wore the mask of a Ghillie suit and had on night vision goggles. I stepped away from Albert as the wheels locked up, and the Bronco skidded to a stop between us. Mag sat in the very back behind the seat. Albert and I yanked open the back doors as another section of pipe lit up the desert with a brilliant orange flash. Only one remained. Albert leapt into the seat and slammed his door closed. The driver revved up the engine, preparing to tear off into the desert and escape the inevitable explosion of the hundred-and-fifty-foot storage towers of the main plant.

Sounding all the world like a mildly enthused tourist, I said, "Wait … I want to take a picture."

Four heads, including Mag's, slowly turned and gave me an *Are-you-out-of-your-fucking-mind* look. They all held it for a few seconds as I stared back at them.

"What?" I asked innocently, pretending not to understand what the big deal was.

"Get in the fucking truck," Xen growled.

"Oh … alright!" I said, dejected.

The engine revved as I stepped into the Bronco. The driver dropped the clutch the moment my butt hit the seat, and the tires ripped giant gashes out of the sand beneath us. The force threw me back against the seat and slammed the door closed.

We tore through the desert, rocking and bouncing over stones and dunes. As I reached for my seatbelt, the Bronco lurched to the right and hit a big dune. Mag had dug her claws into the carpet glued to the floor, but I got tossed up and down like a doll in a dryer. I bounced off the ceiling, then floor then ceiling again, laughing like a maniac the entire time.

"You might want to take it easy on those, Natalia," I said between the laughing. "This thing is older than you are, and I think we need to get farther away."

Albert and Xen turned surprised faces at me, but the driver never took her eyes off the desert in front of us. Nobody said a word. I looked out the back window and saw the next section of pipe detonate. Seconds later the first section inside the superstructure went. I could see flaming shrapnel ricocheting around inside the piping and supports of the plant. A triple explosion inside the superstructure—*boom … Boom … BOOM!*—rocked the desert.

I watched in fascination as a bright, jagged, orange seam opened up in the side of the main tower, starting at the bottom and streaking up. As the tear widened, gouts of flaming liquid jetted out of the steel tower, pouring onto the spot where the Bronco had stopped for us. When the jetting flame reached the top of the column, the entire top opened up like a kernel of popcorn. It inverted itself and came apart in large pieces. A thick pillar of flame shot into the sky and spread out like a brilliant orange and yellow mushroom. I watched several large sheets of flaming steel separate from the main section and drop towards the row of storage tanks in the northeast corner. I could see the shock wave heading straight for us.

The storage tanks went off like a string of massive firecrackers, only moments between each burst, and those columns of fire joined the main one, burning their way towards the heavens. The remaining two towers of the facility, north of the main one, went off simultaneously, seams rupturing and the tops popping off in unison. The shockwave looked like a hazy, orange storm front racing towards the back of the Bronco.

"Cool," I said, enthralled.

Natalia looked into the rearview mirror and yelled "Hang on!"

I covered my face, and Mag dropped down as the shock-wave hit and the back window shattered. Shards of glass peppered everyone like confetti, and I felt a few cuts open and blood trickle down my face. Another bounce of the Bronco sent me ricocheting around inside the cabin, prompting another round of laughter from me like a kid on a roller coaster. With the major explosions behind us, Natalia slowed down to a more reasonable speed, and we rolled over a desert floor still brightly illuminated by the raging fires of VeniCorp.

"How long have you known it was me?" Natalia finally asked, her voice muffled slightly by the Ghillie mask.

"I was pretty sure that night in the alley behind VeniCorp."

Xen turned his head and gave me a truly hateful look. "How could you?"

"I had my reasons, Xen. I'm sorry," I said sincerely.

Xen turned towards the front and didn't move. His shoulders were as tense as Natalia's must have been. It was strangely quiet, considering what they'd gone through.

"You two can stop being mad at each other, you know," I offered. Both of them snapped their heads at me, Xen glaring and, although I couldn't see it in behind the goggles, Natalia must have been too.

"He had no choice but to fake his death, Natalia," I touched the nerve on purpose.

"Yeah," Xen accused.

"You could have told me! I could have helped!" she yelled at him.

"But he had no idea if you were using him or not, Natalia. Put yourself in his shoes. He's seen enough spy movies to know that beautiful women generally don't go for the underdogs … no offense, Xen … and I know for a fact he is still amazed that you fell for him. He had no choice."

Natalia's shoulders relaxed slightly.

"And you had to have seen me at VeniCorp!" Xen accused heatedly. "You could have let me know you were alive!"

"Xen," I said gently. "She did see you. No doubt. But put yourself in her shoes. She's got a job do to, and Albert here took them underground. If she's dead, then neither DiMarco nor Pyotr are looking for her. She had no choice … Right, Albert?" I asked, giving him a sidelong glance.

"That's correct," Albert said, staring at me, an impressed look on his face. "For what it's worth, Mister Li, she even asked. I could not permit it."

"You two did exactly the same thing to each other for exactly the same reason. You had no choice. Xen …" I prompted.

"What? I'm still pissed at you. *You* could have mentioned something to me. You knew all along! You said so. I was in *agony*!"

Natalia's head turned when he said that. I saw her hand start to reach out to Xen and then pull back.

"I'm always calculating, Xen. You know that. What if you'd gotten caught and been forced to roll her over? Besides, I figured we'd probably have this exact conversation at some point. I did it so that both of you would know that you each did what you had to, did it to each other and that neither of you had a choice. The score's even, if you think about it. You both *know* I'm right." I let that hang there between them for a minute, but the silence carried on.

"So ... when we pull up to the black Audi parked out here somewhere, I expect you to get out of this heap, kiss, and make up. You hear me?"

They stayed silent, but the tension that had filled the space between them grew softer as they pondered the circumstances.

"There is one question I have, Natalia."

"You mean you don't know everything?" she asked a bit curtly.

"Not by a long-shot ... although placing the bug under the kitchen counter was very smooth." Natalia and Albert both looked at me with astonished faces. "No. What I couldn't figure out was how you managed to pick up my trail at Grady's from the get-go. You and I had never been there, and I don't recall mentioning it. Xen, did you ever talk about Grady's?"

"Not that I recall."

"There were several Grady's t-shirts in Rachel's closet as well as the one I slept in. I took a chance."

I smiled. "Clever."

A black Audi came into view at the bottom of an abandoned rock quarry.

Santa Claus

Kenny stepped through the door, holding a tray of sicklys and some fritters.

"So what's going to happen with you and Natalia," Rachel asked from beside me as we reclined on one of the plush, new, burgundy sofas.

"She said she had some travelling to do," Xen replied. "She did say that when she got back we'd be together." Xen had a most appealing smile on his face as he sat across from us.

"Glad to hear it, Xen," I smiled at him. He'd forgiven me for my deception about Natalia almost immediately.

I leaned forward and looked around the room. The walls had been stripped and the carpet torn out. All of the functional gambling tables, TVs, and decorations were stacked up and covered with drop cloths in a far corner out of the way while the work continued. I couldn't smell any gasoline, and the bloodstains had been eradicated from the concrete floor. I faced the back of the parlor watching drywall workers come in and out with their equipment. Rachel sat next to me while Marsha and Xen reclined on the sofa opposite us.

"Looks like Stanley has things well in hand," I observed, taking the sickly Kenny handed me. I took a sip and placed it on the coffee table.

"He's been great," Marsha remarked, sipping a cup of tea and looking over her shoulder at the parlor. She scratched at the gray triage unit I had put on her thigh when I'd gotten home. Xen had one, too, but he sat on his. The triage units would have them stitched up and back in shape by the following morning.

Kenny added, "It's too bad those vandals broke in and trashed the place."

I smiled at Kenny's innocence. "Sure is, Kenny. It's terrible. I'm glad the insurance company is willing to pay for it all. It would have cost Marsha a fortune, especially with all the renovations and upgrades I keep hearing about." I looked at her with a pained smile.

Dryly, she said, "Yes, I have a very special insurance agent. Totally understanding. It's almost as if he feels responsible."

Kenny wiped a bead of sweat off his brow. "Do you need anything else, Marsha? It's pretty busy up front."

"No, thanks. You can go on back. I'll call you if we need anything else."

Kenny stepped up to the door and then stopped, turning quickly. "Hey, Justin! Did you hear? Abby bought a winning lottery ticket?" Marsha and Rachel looked at each other but didn't react otherwise. "And on the same day Abby's car got stolen … What luck!"

"No, I hadn't heard, Kenny," I said smiling. "Marsha!" I threw her a stern look. "Why didn't you tell me about that?" I added in a hurt tone.

With a sardonic grin, she said, "I'm sure I told you. You must not have been paying any attention. You know how distracted you can get."

"Of course," I said and snapped my fingers. "That must be it."

"Tell her congratulations for me, would you, Kenny?"

"Sure!" Kenny turned back to the door and saw Abbey standing there.

"You can tell me yourself, Mister …" she broke off and then corrected herself, "Justin." I stood up and faced her. She had the most wonderful smile. "Would you excuse us, Kenny?" she asked.

"Sure. I have to get up front anyway. See ya." He closed the door on the way out. Her eyes grew rosy, and I could see tears forming. She slowly walked up to me, wrapped her arms around me and gave me a gigantic hug. She put her lips to my ear, whispering, "You saved us. I was about at the end of my rope. I can't thank you enough."

I hugged her back and whispered, "Just don't tell anybody, okay? And make sure he keeps painting. Do that and I'll consider us even. It'll be our little secret." She nodded as we let go and stepped away, tears running down her cheeks. "I have to get to work, but it was good to see you, Justin. I wanted to stop in and say hi." She walked out, and as the door closed I sat back down.

Xen, Rachel, and Marsha stared at me, grinning like crazy.

"What?" I scowled at them, my cheeks turning red. "Nobody say a word."

"We wouldn't dream of it," Rachel said, placing her hand on my knee and squeezing.

Marsha tried to control herself, "Of course we wouldn't …" but she lost the battle … "Santa Claus!" Everyone laughed except me, and my cheeks got even redder.

Breakfast at the Rio

O'Neil sat across from me in the Rio Grande Café south of San Diego. He'd already polished off most of his pancakes, eggs, and bacon, with a second order of bacon on the way.

I'd picked him up in my T-Rex auto-cycle, a low-slung, two seat three wheeler with a roof and a sportbike engine. I had bought it two years prior as a perfect highway vehicle when I needed to go fast, corner hard, and avoid people chasing me. I'd chosen it that morning in celebration of the T-Rex case being blown sky high … literally. The auto-cycle didn't have doors, so it had been difficult for us to talk on the way down. This was also part of my master plan. I had already downed my own breakfast of huevos rancheros and a double order of bacon.

Over breakfast I'd related most of the significant facts to O'Neil so he'd have everything he needed to put together the case against Shao and all of the dry cleaner operators. Xen had already sent all of the data he'd copied from Shao's computer, and I provided the pictures from the whole facility by way of my goggles.

"I should still be pissed at you, by the way," O'Neil said around his last mouthful of pancakes.

I was genuinely confused. "Why's that? You're a hero." I poured six packets of sugar into a fresh cup of coffee and stirred it, staring at O'Neil.

"You never mentioned blowing up half of the California desert as part of your plan. I played hell covering that for you. We're blaming it all on Russian gangsters. The two tons of coke and meth in that giant safe made things easier, though. A lot of it had been melted and charred, but still identifiable."

"Me? There you go again always blaming everything on me." I gave him a hurt look, and he paid it back with an *I-can't-believe-you-just-said-that* look. Then he drank some coffee. "I'd never tell this inadmissible information to Captain O'Neil, but as your friend, I can assure you, Mister Smarty Pants, that I know with absolute certainty that Gino DiMarco is the one who set off that explosion."

O'Neil's disbelief was palpable. "Yeah … sure he did."

"No, really. I wasn't even in the building…." I took another sip of coffee and added three more packets of sugar. "It's not my fault he opened the door of his limousine. I mean, sure … I did cover the floor with flammable liquids, and I also put the motion sensing explosive by the door, but he's the one who filled the building with all that stuff in the first place. He was reckless … and irresponsible. And I'd warned him to stay in the car. Had he done like I asked, he'd be fine … maybe." I took another sip of now perfect coffee.

"So, how'd you find out about this place?" he asked, changing the subject as his second order of bacon arrived. "Come here often? It seems a little out of the way."

I got a knowing smile on my face. I loved it when my plans worked out exactly the way I wanted them to. "Funny you should ask. An abatement guy told me about this place. Weird guy. He's into all sorts of stuff. He's a clown, you know."

"Real crack-up, hunh?" He took a healthy bite of bacon.

"No. He's an actual clown … make-up, funny nose, the works."

O'Neil's face looked confused around the bacon. "I thought you said he was an abatement guy."

"He is … Stanley Fast Abatement Services." I waited.

O'Neil paused, his fork hovering between mouth and plate. "Wait … Stanley Fast? As in Stanley Fast Catering and Clowning?"

"That's him," I confirmed, nodding.

Recognition spread across O'Neil's face. "I know that guy … he did a birthday party for a friend of my youngest. Good food."

"He does both … and more," I added subtly. "Well, apparently he comes down here every now and again … part of one of his side jobs. He knows this pig farmer. They work together sometimes. Stanley said this place had the best bacon he'd ever eaten." O'Neil took a big bite of bacon, clearly enjoying it. "So … how do you like it?" I asked, preparing to drop my bomb.

"You know, Stanley's right. This is the best damn bacon I ever had. So, you said you were gonna tell me what happened to Bennie DiMarco."

"Oh yeah, that's right," I said snapping my fingers and grinning wickedly.

I proceeded to tell O'Neil of Bennie's demise. And then I told him how Bennie could very well have ended up on O'Neil's plate. O'Neil stared at me with bland disdain, but he didn't stop chewing, partially out of pride. I knew he'd be damned if he was going to let me get the best of him. I waited for what I knew was coming next.

"I hate you Case," he said around a mouthful of the best bacon he'd ever had.

"I know," I said, sipping my sickly sweet coffee.

Malice on the Rocks

A gust of wind sends ice crystals hissing across the canopy. Watching my killer's hand descend towards the actuator, I think about that cup of coffee with O'Neil … about that bacon. I think about Rachel and Xen and Mexico.

It's funny. The next part of this whole story started in a town not far from that diner, only a handful of miles past the Mexican border. It was even O'Neil who sent me there. Then something pops into my head that I didn't expect. There was only one question about home I ever really wanted answered. And this guy is the only one who might be able to answer it for me.

"Wait," I say. I look at him, one killer to another.

His hand pauses, and he smiles. He's enjoying the game.

"What now?" he asks.

"What happened to Hallex?" We both know I'm trying to buy time. "What did they do to my father?"

He laughs, and it's a wicked thing. I dread the answer, but I need to know. "He's still alive," he says, and his smile is a grim line of malice. "In a pain station."

An agony of emotions tears at my insides—regret, guilt, a litany of helpless rage.

I sure as hell didn't want to go out this way.

About the Author

Quincy J. Allen, a cross-genre author, has been published in multiple anthologies, magazines, and one omnibus. *Chemical Burn*, a finalist in the RMFW Colorado Gold Contest, is his first full novel. He made his first pro-sale in 2014 with the story "Jimmy Krinklepot and the White Rebs of Hayberry," included in WordFire's *A Fantastic Holiday Season: The Gift of Stories*. He's written for the Internet show *RadioSteam*, and his first short story collection *Out Through the Attic*, came out in 2014 from 7DS Books. His military sci-fi novel *Rise of the Thermopylae* is due out in 2015 from Twisted Core Press, and *Jake Lasater: Blood Ties,* a steampunk western fantasy novel, is also due out in 2015.

He works part-time as a tech-writer by day, does book design and eBook conversions for WordFire Press by night, and lives in a cozy house in Colorado that he considers his very own sanctuary—think Batcave, but with fewer flying mammals and more sunlight.

You can follow his travails at:

quincyallen.com
facebook.com/Quincy.Allen.Author
twitter.com/Quincy_J_Allen

Other WordFire Press Titles

Our list of other WordFire Press authors and titles is always growing.
To find out more and to see our selection of titles, visit us at:

wordfirepress.com

30509140R00266

Made in the USA
Middletown, DE
27 March 2016